Praise for Jason Bellipanni

"Jason is a dazzling writer. Sh[...] interesting, and wholly original. T[...] [...]cepts behind his work are formidable and impressive, but they are woven into thematically rich but accessible narratives. He has enormous talent…"

Dean Bakopoulos, author of *Please Don't Come Back from the Moon and My American Unhappiness*

"Jason is one of the most talented writers I have worked with; his facility with language and his ability to maintain tension within an intergenerational narrative betray his intelligence, diligence, and artistic vision."

Lewis Robinson, author of *Officer Friendly: Stories* and the novel *Water Dogs*

"I found Jason Bellipanni's protagonist in 'Skin and Rain' to be one of the most compelling characters I've come across recently."

Wanda Wade Mukherjee, Editor, *Paper Journey Press.*

"*The Last Elf-Mite* most definitely did surprise me, like some skewed but ordinary Harold Pinter domestic episode eccentrically reworked by Isaac Asimov. I found it courageous and fastidious and unflinching in its courage. A writer well worth watching, I feel."

Patrick McCabe, author of the Booker nominated novels *The Dead School, and The Butcher Boy.*

"As Editor-in-Chief of *The Cream City Review*, I read hundreds of submissions by emerging and established fiction writers each year and I can tell you with absolute certainty that Jason's work is not only refreshing and cutting edge, it's topnotch and represents some of the best new writing I've seen. He's a writer to watch."

Professor Karen Auvinen, poet, University of Colorado

"(Jason) is a brilliant and dedicated writer. His work has an unusual emotional depth and technical breadth"

Lucia Berlin, author of *Homesick: New and Selected Stories, Where I Live Now, Safe and Sound.*

"Like few other writers, Jason has the ability to write from the point of view of a younger character, preserving realism that allows one to believe the character without forsaking the adult experience that renders the experience meaningful in a larger context."

Philip Baruth, author of *X-President, The Dream of the White Village,* and *The Millennium Shows*

"I deeply admire the completely fresh approach which Jason uses in his short fiction. I am an avid reader of many fine literary journals in current press, but I seldom encounter short fiction which appeals to me as much as Jason's work Each sentence contains an extreme musicality; each word is a volt. His work has the patina of metaphor without too-loose lyricism.

Alexandria Peary, author of *Lid to the Shadows and Fall Foliage Called Bathers and Dancers*

About <u>*50 Stories: How to Read and Write Experimental Fiction:*</u>

"*Fifty Stories* is a rich and eclectic collection of short stories, separated into five categories: Realist, Science Fiction, Absurdist, Surrealist, and Meta-fiction. Written and edited by the award-winning writer Jason Bellipanni, this book serves as a literature text for colleges and universities across the country.

"The book investigates the purpose and intention behind some of postmodernism's most experimental genres. He writes,

> Despite the vast differences that exist among the various types of extreme or experimental fiction, each type seeks to explore the less accessible, but no less true, areas of human experience. All of these techniques operate on the principle that the limits imposed on realistic fiction make it ill-suited to the discovery and investigation of the deeper human truths.

"The stories that serve as examples were written over a period of fifteen years. Many of the stories or excerpts thereof have appeared in literary journals, university composition texts, and international anthologies. With a strong voice and a masterful manipulation of language, Bellipanni has created utterly original stories that evoke thought and emotion with equal skill. The focus on the reader's role in interpreting non-traditional fiction could serve a template for art appreciation across all disciplines.

> 'Possibly the most enduring consequence of experimental fiction is that the work forces the reader to shift in their approach to fiction. The reader is blocked from traditional interpretation and forced to look for the meaning of the story in a different place. Successful interpretation of an experimental story is not unlike a viewer's successful engagement with a painting by Miro; the connection is dependent on the ability to shift focus and expectations. In literature, this means the reader must locate those elements in the story which reveal the vitality of the creation or at least,

the author's intention. The reader's approach to a story, like the viewer's approach to Miro, Matisse or Kandinsky, will determine whether or not the art succeeds.'

"As his success with first-year university students establishes, *Fifty Stories* is an artistic as well as an academic triumph. The volume introduces concepts and ideas about perception and reception to the reader that continue to inform their interactions with art long after they've read the final story."

--The Story Review, February 15, 2013

Fifty Stories

How to Read and Write Experimental Fiction

Jason Bellipanni

Published by Story Review Press, Northeast: MA, NH, VT, ME
4 Grand Hill Rd, #504, Mont Vernon, NH 03057 USA
Story Review Press, NH, Registered Offices: 107 N. Main Street, Concord, NH 03301-4989

The Last Elf-Mite was first published in Feathers and Cigarettes: An Anthology, Fish Publishing, Ireland, 2003. Dust was first published in The Berkeley Fiction Review, University of California, Berkeley, 2000. Skin and Rain was published in BLINK: Flash Fiction Anthology, The Paper Journey Press, 2006

First Story Press Review PRINT edition: January 2013
TRADE PAPERBACK ISBN-13: 978-1-939644-01-5

Library of Congress Cataloging-in-Publication Data

Bellipanni, Jason (1971-)
50 Stories: How to Read and Write Experimental Fiction / by Jason Bellipanni
450 pages BISAC: Fiction / Short Stories
ISBN 1-939644-01-1
1.50 Stories: How to Read and Write Experimental Fiction

Contents

Description

When seeking any sort of meaning or information from life experience, there are two places in which to look: content and process. This simply means that when you attempt to interpret an episode, when you seek to learn something, or at least figure out what's going on, you need to look in both of these places. This is a function that we are very good at when it comes to human relations.

When the boyfriend, about to break-up with his girlfriend, turns his head away from her to check out a young woman walking by, yawns, and then says, "It's not you, it's me—I'm just not ready for this relationship," his actions are as powerful as the content of his statement. Meaning, how he delivers this will communicate at least as much, if not much more, than his words convey. Body language, tone of voice, gestures or lack of gestures, all of these contributes to the entire meaning of a human interaction.

In writing, of course, your tools are much more limited. You need to translate complete meaning using only these tiny black symbols on paper. Therefore, it is necessary to learn how to make-up for this lack, by paying attention to how information is delivered in written form. This means that the ultimate meaning goes beyond the simple content, and relies heavily on the way the content is delivered. Nowhere is this skill more important than in descriptive writing. For example, take a look at the following statement:

The man fell down the stairs and broke his leg.

This is a statement that successfully delivers content; it is informative. But without making use of the process, that is, giving some attention to HOW this information is delivered, a reader does not know what to do with this statement, beyond, `So what' or for those inclined toward empathy, `Sucks to be him.' The process in this case, is to provide the context of the action; description is all about delivering two elements at once: the information and the context for that information. The context is what helps a reader understand the information in a certain way. In descriptive writing, the goal is almost always to convey an emotion or a tone along with the information. Now imagine the same statement placed in the following contexts.

    A. The 18 year-old young man stood on his skateboard at the top of the stairs.

    B. The 40 year-old man had not been out of his bedroom in 23 years. Squinting, he shuffled toward the top of the stairs, ready to face the world.

    C. At seventy-nine, Harold valued his independence above everything else. On this spring day he walked to the top of the stairs, pausing to check the button down the front of his sweater.

    Each one of these descriptions gives a certain meaning to the event of a man falling down the stairs. In this case, the simple fact of the matter, the bare information of the event, does not provide the entire meaning. Whether description is used in a story to make the reader feel as if they are present, or whether description is used in a news report, the goal is always to provide a deeper understanding, a more comprehensive meaning of something that fact alone is never able to achieve.

How to Describe

Descriptive writing is based on 4 basic principles:

    1. Awareness—make yourself be aware, make yourself notice (without judging) the world around you. This mental activity is very close to the desire to 'remain present' discussed earlier. You are a sponge, taking in details of the world, using a sort of hypersensitivity and all of your senses.

    2. The six senses—yes, yes, I know that there are only 5 senses, officially, and while this sixth sense does not refer to seeing dead people or mind reading, it does have to do with the mind. This sense is the attention we pay to the thoughts that occur while the other senses are gathering sensory data.

    Living in a visually dominant society often means that we all rely on our sight far more than any other sense. So descriptive writing gives us the chance to hone our other senses: sound, smell, touch, taste and thought. Of course, thought is the sixth sense that I refer to, which means, that while you are observing the outer world, attempting to experience the present moment in all of its power, you are also observing your own mind and noticing the thoughts that flow through.

It is EXTREMELY important that you let thoughts pass through, and that you do not connect to or focus on one particular thought. Let your mind go, and if you feel yourself being pulled into future speculation or past memories, return your attention to the details of the outer world.

3. Take note of as many details as possible.

So this is not simply a visual exercise, you must actively engage the present moment. Touch things, smell thing, taste things—it's up to you to seek out details to perceive and not expect them to come flowing into you without effort. You should write down the sensory experiences you have, so that you will have a large quantity to draw from when you sit down to write descriptively.

4. Use similes and metaphors.

By now, you know that similes and metaphors are devices used to compare one thing to another. Similes use the words `like' or `as', while metaphors do not. If I say, "He was an Arnold Schwarzenegger," I am attempting to help you better understand my own perception. "The headache was like feeling a nail driving through the top of my skull"; again, this is an attempt to convey a detail to another person. Similes and metaphors are the written substitutes for tone of voice and facial or hand gestures.

Adding similes or metaphors to your work may be easier for you to do after you're done gathering the raw material. Occasionally a comparison will occur to us as we are having a sensory experience, but more often than not, the comparison comes to us as we try to explain ourselves to another person. So there is no need, in the detail-collecting stage, for you to try and formulate similes—only after you've decided what the detail is to `mean' will the similes and metaphors come in handy.

Why Describe?

If all writing must have a purpose, what is the goal of descriptive writing? There are three goals: to inform the reader, to communicate a certain tone, and to convey emotion. If you describe your dorm room or your room at home to me, you will be providing information: big or small, windows or not, the furniture, the location, etc. All descriptive writing provides information—this is the basic goal and it must be met EVERY TIME. Instructions, directions, and recipes are examples of descriptive writing; they are located, as we've seen, on the far side of the literal continuum. But this is a very narrow segment of descriptive writing; the majority of description must be doing something else while it informs.

Tone is what I refer to as the emotion of a place or a situation. It is the way a place or a situation feels, and it is created to give the reader clues as to how to interpret the story. The creation of tone depends entirely on the words you use to describe something. A drop of rain can be described in a way that conveys sorrow, a sense of freedom, or an atmosphere of joy. You, as the writer, control what the details mean. In order to do this, you must have a fairly good idea of the effect you want to achieve. Descriptive writing is much less about factual accuracy, and much more about emotional impact.

Conveying emotion is one of the unique and valuable abilities of descriptive writing. Valuable because, as you may know from your conversations with other people, human beings often desire to communicate or express their emotions. Again, this is much easier to do in a face-to-face conversation, using tone and facial expressions. On paper, you are very limited, and so good descriptive writing can be the key to any successful communication.

Again, you could describe your dorm room, and while you provided me with information, you could also communicate a feeling. I would know, just from your description, whether you were depressed or scared or overjoyed, and this would not happen by simply telling me, "I'm depressed." The whole point of descriptive writing is to engage the reader, to try and make the reader feel the emotion, and not just understand it in a cold and intellectual way. It's a difficult thing to do, especially in writing, but when it works, descriptive writing can impact a person as much as an actual experience.

Narration

Telling Stories

Narration is the act of telling stories, and if there is one thing that we are all very familiar with, it is the story. We are told stories as little kids; we learn to read stories. We spend most of our days relating stories of one sort or another to each other. Whether you realize it or not, when you describe a class that you've just been in, or repeat a conversation you had last night, you are telling a story. All of history is a story; in fact, most disciplines relay at least some of their information through stories. It is the way we learn to read the world, interpret our experience, and derive meaning from what happens to each of us. Since the way we view the world and the meaning or value of our own lives depend on storytelling, it might be useful to study this particular writing strategy.

Unlike description, which has a limited purpose and very specific goal, narration is a little broader tool. (In fact, narration uses description as one of its main tools). As we have seen in our own lives, telling stories can be used in a variety of ways. I can tell you a story of a poor family in Haiti in order to help you glimpse an alternative perspective on human life. I can tell you a story about the new technology of criminals in order to scare you. Or I can tell you a story about my own life, in order to give you some sense of who I am. But this is an important point, so pay attention, you'll learn as much about me by the way I tell my story as you will by the content of my story. Again, just like all of life, narration breaks down into content and process; there is the story you tell, the event or episode, but the way in which you tell that story, will determine what that story means.

This is major: the way you tell a story determines what the story is going to mean. And this is a choice, an active choice on your part. You decide the meaning of events and when you tell a story, you do it in a way to convey that meaning. I can repeat a conversation I had with one of my friends and tell it in a way that tries to convey how inconsiderate and mean the friend is, or I can tell it in a way that will make you feel badly for that friend. Our intention comes out in the WAY we tell the story. We may think that events happen and that we are simply interpreting them, as if we are passive observers simply relaying information, but in fact, we are MAKING the meaning. We assign meaning to events and then convey them in order to communicate that meaning. Being aware of this mental activity is the first step toward controlling it.

The Story

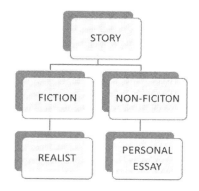

Learning to tell stories, that is, learning to identify and shape the elements in a story is not only essential for human communication, but it is even more crucial if we hope to understand ourselves and the meaning of our lives. Already, most of us view our lives through the scope of a story; we can narrate our existence on earth from our birth to this moment. We would proceed chronologically and pause to describe those experiences that have affected us one way or another. This means that one of the main ways that we see the world is as an unfolding story. This perspective has its strengths and weaknesses, but without the thought tools that storytelling sharpens, we might forever remain in the dark about our purpose in this sphere of life.

The basic story is made up of elements that many of us first learned in grade school: plot, character, and setting. And while the core of storytelling remains the same, our more mature perspectives, enhance, complicate, and use these elements in much more focused and intentional ways. The Intention of the storyteller is the component that has changed the most since we were in 4ᵗʰ grade. Now, you must firmly grasp and attempt to focus in on the reason or goal for your story. This is especially true in writing, when you don't have the luxury of using your tone of voice or physical expression to convey elements of the story.

What is the Goal?

All (good and worthwhile) stories have the same goal: to describe change. Good storytellers always strive to focus on the change that takes place as the story proceeds. Think of your friends and acquaintances. Can you think of anyone who has the power to instantly bore you with their stories versus someone who keeps your attention? This is the difference between good and bad storytelling: the ability to describe and portray the change that takes place in a person. More often than not this is the narrator of the story; telling you about an experience, and even if they do not explicitly state how their perspective or life was changed by the event, it is usually implied.

It is essential, then, that you know exactly why you are writing your story, meaning that you know what type of change your story is attempting to convey. But check it out—you do not have to know the goal when you begin writing the story. In fact the reason or meaning will make itself clearer to you as you begin to sketch out the story and remember the details.

Show, Don't Tell

This is a mantra in the creative writing world and it ought to be the mantra of anyone telling a story for any reason. The idea is that the writer uses description and detail so well that the reader feels as though they are transported to the event itself; this even extends to emotion. Your goal in narration is to make the reader feel as much as possible, the emotion of the moment. Therefore simply saying, "I was angry," does not translate into emotion for the reader. Whereas, "I gripped the hammer and threw it as hard as I could at her retreating car," gets a little closer.

Memory

The personal essay is based on something that you've experienced in the past. The theory is that by concentrating on one episode and attempting to capture as many details as possible, you will be able to interpret the meaning. It is very rare for the 8 year-old who has just broken their leg to pause and reflect on the situation, or to consider the significance of this episode in their life. We experience life events; but the meaning of those events usually cannot be seen/created until many years afterward.

The main idea to keep in mind regarding memory and the personal essay is that this essay is not an exercise in pinpoint accuracy. Whether you wore a red or blue shirt on the day your dog ran away is not the focus; the accuracy you're trying to capture is not factual, it is emotional. You want to develop the significance of an event; and I use the term develop to indicate that it requires your active involvement. The significance of some past event is NOT just sitting there, waiting for you to discover it: in fact, you are creating and assigning the significance to an event.

It is a type of detective exercise. You comb through the memory, sift through details and circumstances, and slowly, you develop the significance of the event. You must look to the details and the life that surrounds your episode in order to find the clues that will help you develop the significance.

Plot, Character, Setting

The plot of your story is basically the sequence of events. In order to write a successful personal memory essay, something must have happened to you in the past. You need to go through some episode; you need to be an active player in the event. Plot is a series of cause and effect, usually told in a chronological order. It is the skeleton of any story and it keeps the reader involved and wanting to know what will happen next.

Characters can be introduced into the story in three different ways: physical description, action, and dialogue. When a writer physically describes a character they are doing it in a way to communicate something about the character's personality. If a detail does not help reveal who a person is, then it does not need to be in the story: description is probably the least effective way to communicate the personality of a character.

Characters can be introduced into the story in three different ways: physical description, action, and dialogue. When a writer physically describes a character they are doing it in a way to communicate something about the character's personality. If a detail does not help reveal who a person is, then it does not need to be in the story: description is probably the least effective way to communicate the personality of a character.

Showing physical action of any sort always helps to shed light on a character's personality. The whole goal as far as characters go is to try and reveal who they are as quickly and efficiently as possible. When you think about the real people in your life, you are basically thinking about a group of characteristics that you have learned about them through one of these three ways. It is the same with characters in the story: you must reveal the characteristics that will best help your story. Any attempt to completely reveal who a person is would probably take thousands of pages. You are only concerned with the part of the character's personality that matters to the story you are telling.

Dialogue in story is the single most effective tool to reveal a character's personality. When a person speaks, they have the ability to show how their mind works, what their priorities are, and what their motivation is. Unlike life, only the most revealing dialogue must be used in fiction. . If you were to write down an actual exchange between two people, you might find that there are plenty of useless words. In story, you must condense and only use dialogue that works to illuminate a character's personality AND to move the story forward.

Significance

The significance or meaning of your story will come from the change that happens by the end of the story. Your perspective must change from the beginning of the story to the end. This means that you see life in a certain way before the episode and then your view shifts, due to the event, and you view some aspect of life differently. So here it is: You must identify, precisely, what your perspective is before the event, and what it is after the event, and tell the story to reveal this process. You must establish pre-event perspective so that the change is obvious when you present the post event perspective.

Traditional Story: Purpose & Intention

Purpose: to narrate an event or series of events that provides information to the reader

Intention: to connect with the audience in a way that allows the audience to comprehend the information being communicated

Traditional Story: Main Components
-Setting-Place
-Character-People
-Plot-action, conflict, climax
-Language- *Figurative and Literal*
-*Point of view*-1st person "I" 3rd person 'he/she'
-Structure-the order in which the story is told
-Setting

Traditional Story Outline

Introduction—Describe setting & main character. While setting the scene, YOU MUST MAKE VERY CLEAR THE PERSPECTIVE OF THE MAIN CHARACTER. This is their particular view on life that will change by the end of the story. Achieve this by using description and detail to make the character's view of the world very clear.

<u>Tension Begins</u>—This is when the main character's perspective comes up against some obstacle. Something has begun to go wrong, or is not quite right. A problem or potential conflict must begin in this section. This 1st obstacle will inevitably lead to the climax and the change in perspective.

<u>Dialogue</u>—While it is suggested that you include a conversation of some sort at this point in the essay, dialogue can be used in all sections of the essay as long as it does the following: 1. Reveal the personality of the speaker 2. Help promote the tension/conflict 3. Move the story along. A conversation at this point in a personal essay is often very effective at all three.

<u>Climax</u>—This is the moment that the story has been building to. It is what the reader has been wondering about. Also, it is in this moment, when the perspective of the main character shifts. (You do not explain the shift in this section, but the action happens in a way that makes the change possible.)

<u>Resolution</u>—This is where you make the new perspective clear. Remember whatever was set-up at the beginning must have shifted.

Interpreting traditional fiction:

When a reader interprets traditional fiction, they will look for information and meaning (sometimes called the theme) in certain places within the story. Readers expect stories to contain certain elements (setting, character, and plot) and they expect these elements to provide certain information. Sections of the story *"Dust" by Jason Bellipanni* have been broken into these three main components. As you read each section, note the specific information that each component contributes to the story as a whole.

FOCUS ON SETTING—

A pair of yellow eyes through the dust. An animal for sure. The eyes vanish. Breathing from somewhere behind the car. The wind swirls sand

A glowing green puddle the size of a Frisbee. The animal's legs pass behind a rear tire.

Swirling funnels of dust. The miniature tornadoes dancing the hip dance. A broken window, a wooden sign with flaking blue paint, a rusted car frame with its nose to the ground. .

Like falling on a frozen pond, smacking against the ice.   A single cloud hangs like a smoke ring in the sky.   Nothing to pass through it, no airplane thread, no imaginary boat.   Just a cloud ring floating along
    The shock like cold water, the animal smell.
    Dirt has changed into mud smears.

FOCUS ON CHARACTER—(THE WHO)

I can barely see an elk? A deer? I hear the breathing from somewhere behind my car. I pop the hood. The wind stings my bare legs, my arms.

It probably just needs oil, or it needed oil. I'm afraid it is beyond needing anything. On my hands and knees I see a glowing green puddle the size of a Frisbee. I can barely see the animal's legs pass behind a rear tire.

When I stand I see the outline of an old gas station down the road,

Steps follow me and I hear snorting. I can see the yellow eyes in my mind and I trot toward the station. I stop and turn and it stands three feet away. It gallops toward me. I face him and raise my arms to make myself look bigger. I tense my body to deflect the hit, but the bone colored horns pound flat against my chest.

A chill runs through me when my back hits the road. Losing my breath, waiting in silence for air with the thought that I may be dying. Maybe this is what it's like to die. Until my body remembers what to do. Breathe. I stand, head bowed to acknowledge defeat. To plead mercy while I walk backwards in the direction of the gas station. The ram lowers its head, nodding to me. The sandy pavement gritting against my head. I never make it to the gas station. I spend my time bruising my ribs and coughing up dusty spit. A few times I'm sure my shirt is heavy with blood, but when I look down it is soaked clear.

Each time I stand, I wait for the ram to be satisfied or bored, and finally someone stops to help. A teenage girl in a pickup helps me to the passenger's side. She tells the ram to scat.

FOCUS ON PLOT—(THE HOW)

I pop the hood. Steps follow me and I hear snorting. I trot toward the station.

I stop and turn and it stands three feet away, curled horns lowered. It gallops toward me. I face him and raise my arms to make myself look bigger. I tense my body to deflect the hit, but the bone colored horns pound flat against my chest. I never make it to the gas station

Finally someone stops to help. A teenage girl in a pickup helps me to the passenger's side. She tells the ram to scat. I fall in love.

Days have passed

"Will you marry me?" I hear myself ask.
She says, "Yes."

Narrative Outline—All About Change

Introduction—Describe setting & main character. While setting the scene, YOU MUST MAKE VERY CLEAR THE PERSPECTIVE OF THE MAIN CHARACTER. This is their particular view on life that will change by the end of the story. Achieve this by using description and detail to make the character's view of the world very clear.

Tension Begins—this is when the main character's perspective comes up against some obstacle. Something has begun to go wrong, or is not quite right. A problem or potential conflict must begin in this section. This 1st obstacle will inevitably lead to the climax and the change in perspective.

Dialogue—while it is suggested that you include a conversation of some sort at this point in the essay, dialogue can be used in all sections of the essay as long as it does the following:
1. Reveal the personality of the speaker
2. Help promote the tension/conflict
3. Move the story along.

Climax—this is the moment that the story has been building to. It is what the reader has been wondering about. Also, it is in this moment, when the perspective of the main character shifts. (You do not explain the shift in this section, but the action happens in a way that makes the change possible.

Resolution—this is where you make the new perspective clear. Remember whatever was set-up at the beginning must have shifted. This does not need to be a "lesson-I-Learned" since most of those are bull. It should be a new thought or new idea that has come about because of the event that has taken place.

Narrative: Story Structure: Each section has a purpose & intention

Introduction

Purpose: to describe main characters and setting. To lead into the next section (tension begins)

Intention: to clearly convey the main character's belief or view that will change by the end

Tension Begins

Purpose: to start the action of a story

Intention: to introduce the conflict, problem, discomfort or obstacle into the story

Conversation

Purpose: to increase the tension/danger/suspense of the story-to cause the climactic event

Intention: to reveal someone's personality, to show the relationship between people (how and what words are spoken often show the nature of a relationship)

Climax

Purpose: to describe the action that is the high point of the drama. To answer the question 'what is going to happen'

Intention: to describe the event that causes the main character's change in belief or perspective

Resolution

Purpose: to describe what happens as a result of the climax. The consequences or results of the climactic moment.

Intention: to clearly reveal the change that occurs in the main character-a perspective shift, change in belief or view of a person, change in a belief or view of the self.

Creative Non-Fiction

While many readers may interpret the term 'non-fiction' to mean real or true or factual, a more accurate understanding of the meaning requires a shift of attention from the material being presented to the person presenting the material: namely, the writer.

In general the term 'non-fiction' better describes the intention of the writer rather than the material itself. Since much fiction is created out of the same 'real' that we perceive around us, it too could be described as non-fiction if we used the content of any piece of writing as the sole measurement.

Fiction is often packed with many provable facts or situations copied directly from our reality, but it is the intention, and therefore the presentation of the material that can best determine whether or not a piece of writing is fiction of not.

In a broad sense, and writing that intends to accurately communicate actuality while also making use of certain literary techniques could be called 'creative non-fiction.' Any subject matter that is structured and relayed using the elements of storytelling is creative non-fiction.

While a writer who uses story to help explain the process of assembling a nuclear bomb would be practicing creative non-fiction, it's fair to say that this is not a common practice among this sort of technical non-fiction. For the most part creative non-fiction usually refers to the writing about one's own experiences and lifestyle in a literary way: which is to say, by using the conventions of story.

Memoirs, personal essays, auto-biographies are all types of creative non-fiction. The biographies and histories that use suspense or tension while revealing their content would also be examples. In "Devil in the White City" by Erik Larson, he tells the story of the 1893 World's Fair in Chicago while also describing the activity of a serial killer in the area. His writing uses the same techniques as a suspense novel to keep the reader engaged and wondering what will happen next and why.

The goal of creative non-fiction is different from news reporting, for example, because it seeks to deliver emotional content along with the facts. The focus in creative non-fiction is always on the main character and events are described so as to help the reader forge an emotional connection with the people involved.

It is this alteration in the intention, the shift from the strict adherence to factual accuracy in order to accommodate some expression of the emotions and the people who cause or who are affected by the factual events being described.

Purpose: to narrate an event or series of *actual* events to provide information to the reader.

Intention: to display 'real-life' episodes in a way that allows the reader to acquire knowledge about a specific subject, and to learn the causes and consequences of the action and reaction to the circumstances being presented.

SETTING
- The place where the actual events took place
The time period in which the events took place
- Factual Accuracy of detail is VERY important-must be as true to physical detail as possible
- No invented detail may be included
- While a detail may be described in different ways to achieve a certain effect, no object may be added that was not present in the actual occurrence.

Example: --to reinforce the sense of Einstein's status as an outcast or to represent his frustration at the beginning of his career, the writer might chose to include a description of the tree that actually existed outside of his childhood home--

"The leafless oak tree stood in the frigid air, its bare limbs black against the gray Vienna sky, hundreds of branches straining upward, like the thin and gnarled fingers of the damned, frozen in the act of grasping at the emptiness, the nothing that only Einstein could see."

Taking Shots

For the first two years of my son Lucas' life, I was a stay at home dad (which has, in my case, a very telling acronym: SAHD). As I drove him to the doctor's office and his four year old check-up, I couldn't remember much about how we'd spent the time. If I didn't start to pay attention, or make myself focus on him when we were together, I'd turn around one day, and he'd be driving or going to college or getting married.

It could be argued that I was the worst SAHD of all time. I did not sign up for the 'Yoga, and Your Baby' classes which would have put me in the community aerobics room with a group of mothers and their babies exchanging nap time tips and joking about how difficult it was to lose the weight. I'd gained 25 pounds during the pregnancy.

I enrolled in nothing, joined no groups, and barely made it to the park a few times. Where had the two years gone? I know we went to the Laundromat. We seldom shopped and only for food. Two years of eating, sleeping, peeing and practicing strangleholds on the cat.

During the rare social occasion, I loved and hated drawing attention to my status as a SAHD. I enjoyed spreading the misconception that I was more enlightened than other males. A languorous shake of the head, a pained smiled and the words, "You have no idea, man," were enough to prod compliments from the other men.

They would proclaim that they didn't know how I could do it, but their faces conveyed the truth. As if I was bragging about being able to gargle for 5 minutes straight, like 'Wow, that's probably quite an accomplishment in some alternate universe.'

A hint of insincerity was tolerable, better than being asked, "How's the writing going?"

The events that stand out were the trips to the doctor. My mother had repeatedly warned me that vaccinations could have side effects such as blindness and death. The doctor would take the usual measurements, talk about development, and then the bargaining would begin.

Me: Alright Doc, I'm thinking Mumps, Measles and Rubella, today.

Doctor: Looks like he needs Mumps, Measles, Rubella, polio, diphtheria, whooping cough and chicken pox.

Me: Chicken pox? You're making that up.

Doctor: One shot now and a booster when he's twelve.

Me: Not happening. Haven't we cured polio, like fifty years ago?

Doctor: Used to be called infantile paralysis. Babies had to live inside iron lungs.

Me: Jesus Christ, okay, okay. Mumps, Measles, Rubella and polio. That's it.

Doctor: Diphtheria causes the brain to dissolve and leak out of the child's ear.

Then I'd cave.

The parent who does not immunize their child falls into one of two categories: the negligent stupid-head or the hippie-freak stupid-head. The negligent parent wants their child to die while the hippie-freak distrusts whatever 'The Man' recommends.

Luckily, my mother was one of those anti-establishment free range hippie tofu lovers, and she had happily filled me in on the potential dangers that immunization posed. She's a somewhat loose-lipped, flighty woman who lets comments flow out of her mouth without necessarily knowing or caring about truth. She's in it for effect. Whenever I mentioned an upcoming immunization she'd end our discussion in her chirpiest upbeat voice: "Well, the brain damage may not be too bad, and if he's blind, he might get some sort of scholarship to college."

Even if there is some evidence that not all immunizations are necessary and that some may have mildly harmful side-effects, it's easy to know where the majority of American come down on the issue. Tell any new parent that a shot will protect their baby from any disease, no matter how rare or how slim the chance, most will gladly agree.

Which is why I'd sit there, pinning my son to my chest and waiting to hear the type of cry that signaled real pain. Sliced finger, head-cracking-coffee-table pain. And I'd restrain my son, for his own good, soothing myself with the belief that he would never remember the scene.

On the morning of the four year old checkup, the possibility of shots had not once crossed my mind. Four year-olds were full-fledged little kids, they remembered. I walked into the waiting room, holding my son's tiny hand, calm and totally unprepared for the needle.

We walked in and sat down after the receptionist gave me a developmental checklist to go over with my son. I was ready for this. The four year old check-up was all about proving my son's genius.

Children from two to four took this test, so it wasn't very difficult to begin with. I drew a straight line and asked my son to copy it. His was slanted and short. The question read, "Did the child draw the line correctly?" I reviewed the example answers and my son's line fell under the NO category. This was a kid who could already write his name. One quick pencil flick and the line fell under YES, which I circled and moved on.

My son was supposed to jump over the clipboard, lengthwise, and land without stepping on the paper. On the sixth attempt, he nailed it.

When we talked with the doctor he commented on various aspects of my son's advanced development. He was exactly in the middle as far as height and weight, and this absence of physical prowess convinced me of his inner brilliance.

The visit went well and my son talked and talked. He narrated parts of movies and imagined the doctor's pocket instruments as animals. When the doctor brought up vaccinations, my son was laughing as he climbed up and down from my lap.

The doctor stared down at his clipboard. "We've still got a Mumps, Measles and Rubella, a Polio, and let's see…looks like a whooping cough and a chicken pox as well."

Impossible. All vaccinations should have been done by now. He'd already had hundreds, maybe thousands of shots back when I was a SAHD. It felt like I'd been set up.

The doctor restated the situation. I put on my concerned parental face and nodded. I promised that I'd definitely set up the appointment today—on the way out.

The doctor smiled.

"This is the appointment," he said. "I'll have Gary get them ready."

My son said, in a casual way, that he didn't want any shots.

I was unable to move. Then I remembered that kids could sense fear. Or maybe that was only dogs. Just in case, I pushed myself into a playful mood while we sat and waited in the office.

The male nurse came into the room and right away I hated him. I held my son in my lap and I promised that we'd get doughnuts afterwards. He shrugged and descended with the mood in the room into silence. My son looked up at me, blue eyes and blond hair. He asked me if it would hurt.

"The first one's a killer," the male nurse said, proving why men should not be nurses

"It'll sting a little," I said.

The idiot nurse sanitized the top of my son's arm. My son had started to sing, 'Daylight come and me want to go home.' The nurse paused to relate an anecdote about hearing that same song when he was a boy. As he told the story, I shot bullets from my eyes. Take your time, I thought, let's drag this out as long as possible.

The first shot stabbed into my son's pale arm and officially, the world ended. My son let loose a piercing shriek that froze my blood.

The nurse withdrew the needle and dabbed at blood with cotton. I didn't remember seeing blood before; I was certain that the nurse had screwed up.

"First one's a killer," the nurse repeated. "That'll bruise. Okay champ, two more to go."

I wanted to drown this man.

My son's chest convulsed and he hiccupped his pleas. "No. more. Shots. I. doesn't. Like. Shots. No. more. Shots. Please."

The nurse prepped and my son squirmed and turned up the volume. I squeezed him and told him not to look. He strained against my arm clamps. I felt an iron bar lodged in my chest.

The last two shots were quick and relatively painless.

"All done," I said, over and over again.

My son had stopped crying by the time we walked to the car.

I felt like a betrayer.

My son sniffled and shuddered with sighs as I gingerly lifted him into the car-seat.

Once buckled, I saw that his nose had started running.

"Here," I said, pulling a tissue from my pocket.

My son's eyes were red and he held his stickers in one of his small hands. He looked up and straight into my eyes.

"Thank you," he said, tentatively reaching out for the tissue.

These two words split me in half and I started to cry.

"I'm so sorry," I said. I pressed my lips to the top of his head and said, "God, I hate doing this."

Skin and Rain

There is a moment, a flicker, when you suddenly recognize that someone, a person, is an animal—their naked chest, warm and collapsible and so much like clay. You worry that raindrops will leave scars.

I help lower my mother-in-law step by step down the narrow staircase into my basement; the one I'm finishing with a playroom and a workout room and closets that won't click closed. The one I build each day, by myself—the one I will never use because two weeks after my mother-in-law dies this house will go up for sale and we'll move in with her husband of forty years.

The walls brush against my shoulders as we descend; I'm behind her, with my hands secured under her arms, supporting her weight. "That's the best," she says and I'm glad that I'm doing it right.

Her husband crouches in front of her, helping to lift each leg and place it on the next step down; he makes sounds of encouragement. We pause on each step so she can conjure or re-group or hold herself together—like she'd spill out of her skin if she didn't want to see the basement. Then after a moment, she makes herself solid and stiff and says "Okay."

I lift, glad that I am strong enough to do something about this situation. At last she arrives at the bottom. The standing lamp illuminates an unpainted room, two rooms, which are more solid in my imagination than in physical reality. The white walls are bumpy and peeling with drywall tape that won't stick; the ceiling is low, an inch taller than the top of my head, and made from pieces of stiff white foam with ragged edges that do not meet. The air smells like cut wood and wintergreen tobacco.

The walker unfolds easily and my mother-in-law shuffles in her blue slippers across the cement floor from one room to the other, complimenting my efforts. She says that she's glad to see this, that she needed to see this—but I doubt that.

Her naked baby's back, my hands under her arms, and I raise her up until her head almost touches the ceiling. She smiles down at me.

And in one instant, one flicker of a breath, I recognize her frail animal body, too tender, and too smooth to ward off anything. I blink, and I know that one day, raindrops will melt this baby away.

Success

"Perhaps it will turn out that you are called to be an artist. Then take that destiny upon yourself and bear it, its burden and its greatness, without ever asking what recompense might come from the outside." Rainer Maria Rilke, Letters to a Young Poet.

I sat in my seat on the plane to Ireland and tried to settle on a perspective for my upcoming reading. Fortunately, five years earlier, my wife and I had traveled the same route—to Ireland and then down to Sicily to meet up with my parents. At least there was a type of precedent. But even so, it would be hard to argue that Ireland was 'on the way' to Sicily.

I could have adopted the 'I'm such a nut, I'm up for anything' posture as a way to make the trip as casual as possible—as if I was indulging some zany artistic whim. I didn't feel zany. It was important for me to figure this out because at that moment, I was a father of a four year-old boy and currently making about $17,000 a year as an easily expendable adjunct English professor. I'd been steadily writing fiction and sending out for almost a decade.

As a rule, I truly wanted to obey Rilke's sage advice. I tried not to focus outward or expect too much compensation from the world as far as success went, but all the while my secret mind quietly whirred with speculations about fame and success and stability. And money.

But I didn't think about that. But I did.

On the airplane aimed toward Ireland and the 'book launch,' I became acutely aware of my current situation. From one perspective, which I referred to as the 'Nobel Prize version,' I was flying off to Ireland because I'd been asked to read from a story that had been selected for Fish Publishing's 7th annual international anthology.

The more distasteful view suggested that I was forcing my wife and child to fly eight hours and then drive five more so that I could attend a reception that was equivalent to the launch of a small university literary journal.

I sat on the plane and considered both possibilities. I had almost convinced myself that success was not the issue. We pulled back from the gate, and I was ready to accept the journey as a type of personal tribute to literature, a conceptual toast to the struggling artist. Then, as my back was sucked against my chair, I spotted a book in the hands of an older woman across the aisle. She held the brand new Harry Potter novel.

Harry Potter reminded me of what else I never thought about—the success of other people. I was totally disinterested in other writer's wildly impossible success. No way. Not me.

I loathed Harry Potter with a fiery and irrational passion. Jealousy? Perhaps, but a mature writer, as Rilke himself might have said, did not expend energy on distractions such as stupid, stupid, stupid Harry Potter.

My wife's family had read each Potter book, and they never failed to point out the spiritual contributions that the books had made to our world—bringing generations together, encouraging children to read, and on and on until it seemed that this boy, Harry Potter, was worthy of his own Nobel Prize.

My wife had read them as well, but she was not a fanatic. She had not been one of those people waiting in line at midnight to buy the new book. I had the distinct feeling that her current disinterest in the most recent book was actually a well-intentioned (and well-received) gift to me as we headed to Ireland and toward my murky future as a great writer.

The plane ride to Ireland from Boston is not long enough. The simulated night only lasts a couple of hours so it's impossible to trick your body into believing that an entire night has passed. We slept for an hour on the way to Ireland and we arrived to pick up our rental car at 3:00 am non-local time.

Before my wife became ill because of her jet lag and lack of sleep, I drove on the left-hand side of the road, shifted gears with my left hand, and considered the qualities of success. Was it simply a matter of personal perspective? No.

"Are they paying your way?" my father had asked me over the phone.

Money. If others (non-relatives) recognized the value of your work enough to pay your way, then you had succeeded. Flights and car rentals and hotels were 'taken care of' as a way to honor your achievement. I had not bought our plane tickets. They were 'taken care of' by my parents because they wanted to see their grandson in Sicily. Hardly the proof of accomplishment that I sought.

The car's passenger seat was fully reclined, and my wife's eyes were closed, her red cheeks had turned gray. My pale, dazed, but stable four-year-old son sat in his rented car seat with his Walkman headphones over his ears. The exhaustion and impending vomit prevented me from using the concept of 'brief Irish vacation' to sidestep the issue of success.

We stopped after three hours in the car so that my wife could lay in a bed with a cold wet washcloth on her forehead and a plastic bag by her mouth. While she tried not to die, my son and I fell onto a nearby bed and fluctuated in and out of consciousness.

We arrived in Bantry the next day and checked into the Bed and Breakfast.

"I'm here for the book launch," I casually told the older woman. I stood in the hall and attempted to project myself as an international author.

She asked forgiveness because she had no idea what I was talking about.

So I said, "The literary festival," and still no recognition. I considered the possibility that we had arrived in the wrong town.

And so I clarified, "The literary festival—it's happening with a music festival."

"Oh yes," she said. "The West Cork Chamber Music Festival—delightful, just delightful. I heard them last year, quite lovely. What instrument do you play?"

If there hadn't been any winners in the anthology that might have been a little better. If someone hadn't won $1500 and another person won a week at a writer's retreat in Ireland. If it had simply been an actual anthology rather than the results of a contest. It might have been better because then I wouldn't have had to deal with the growing suspicion that I had completely overreacted to the publication of a single story. A good story, but even still.\

Connections. Supportive writer friends in the US had urged me to go to Ireland because of the potential for connections. It was at these events, especially in Europe they assured me, where international publishers and editors created their first impressions of you and your work. My friends and I tried to remember the names of the writers who had first been discovered and published in Europe. We ended up with a list that included James Joyce, Virginia Woolf, and yes, J.K Rowling.

"Is it a real anthology?" my father had asked over the phone.

Following the launch there was to be a week of workshops and readings and literary get-togethers featuring Roddy Doyle, David Means, and possibly Pat McCabe (all of whom I'd read in preparation for the post-book-launch mingle.) If a connection moment presented itself, I wanted to be able to make reference to their work. None of them came to the book launch however, and I was not staying for the conference.

People were incredulous. They could not believe that I would leave so soon. Hadn't I traveled all the way from America? Certainly I hadn't flown all that way to read for five minutes and eat cheese and crackers?

"We just stopped by," I said, "On the way to Sicily."

Without the crutch of conference attendance to legitimize my presence, my last hope was still to make a 'connection' or two. With over 300 rejection slips in my career, I had become quite adept at believing in impossible events. Not just hoping, understand, but truly believing. Just as I expected to swallow my reception cracker after I chewed it, I fully expected fate to provide me with one hell of a connection.

I would later learn that the middle-aged woman with gray hair and glasses who shook my hand and complimented my reading was a famous English publisher. She could tell that I'd read before, and that I'd had practice speaking in front of groups. The first place winner, a twenty one year old Brit, wearing a suit jacket over a tee shirt and jeans, came up and joined our conversation. He had probably known who she was.

"What are you working on?" the woman asked me.

Wrongly assuming that she was a struggling writer and a kindred spirit as far as failure went, I described the novel that I'd been trying to force together for years and the disaster it had become and how I'd always had so many ideas that I'd also started a screenplay, a stage play, two other novels, dozens of stories, and I loved poetry—intimidated by it but loved it, and I'd finished a bunch of stories, some prose poems-what are they called? Short shorts? And my one story collection had fallen completely apart which drove me crazy especially when they mixed with ideas for essays, even though I'm not a huge believer in reality, and sometimes I went back to fix the old stories, but I was so overwhelmed with ideas and thoughts that it was usually a complete mess—my writing career was basically a natural disaster.

Oddly enough, the publisher did not whip out a contract and sign me on the spot. Instead, she smiled without parting her lips, raised her eyebrows, and turned her attention to the Brit winner.

"Quite right," the Brit said. He continued to speak without looking at me. After all, he'd only been able to sell his first novel after two months of grueling revisions. He shaped his conversation like he was blowing glass, creating delicate and precise figurines that he then offered to the publisher for approval (which she gave in a series of I know what you mean nods).

We left the next morning for our two-day drive back to the Dublin airport.

No money. No literary connections. I sat in my chair at the Dublin airport and took out one of the prize books to read. My wife had taken my son to tour the airport shops.

As I read the introduction to the collection I saw that Pat McCabe, author of Butcher Boy, had compared my story to a Harold Pinter episode re-worked by Isaac Asimov. He'd said that the story was courageous and fastidious and unflinching in its courage. According to him, I was a writer to watch.

I was stunned. I re-read the three sentences to make sure that he was referring to my story. I couldn't wait to show my wife. I felt like these few words would somehow, at the last minute, save the entire trip. Look dear, your vomit has launched my career.

I was giddy by the time my wife returned, but I hesitated. I felt a twinge of guilt about my excitement—a sudden Rilke reminder that I shouldn't have cared. She pulled out a book that she'd bought and sat down to read. If I cared too much about these few complimentary words I'd be doomed to certain failure. I kept the good news to myself.

My wife looked up at me and shrugged. The title of her book? Harry Potter and the Order of the Phoenix.

I returned my attention to the collection, and my secret mind began comparing the other stories to my own.

Realist Fiction

Traditional or realistic fiction tries to reveal truths about human beings by duplicating reality. By creating a copy, we have an accurate representation of reality that can be objectively studied and interpreted. Unlike reality, finished art remains fixed and unchanging so that our ability to interpret it is not altered by the passage of time.

In science, we take samples to study, believing that a sample is representative of the whole, so the information we learn from a single skin sample, will give us information about the entire body.

Art is a sample, not of the body, but of the perceptions and emotions of the culture in which the art was created.

Realistic stories and paintings offered the individual the chance to better observe and grasp the qualities and characteristics of human beings and human relationships.

The main benefit of realistic fiction is that it can be easily accessed by most readers because of its familiarity. We readily recognize the relationships described and we are allowed to hold onto all of our assumptions and expectations. In a realistic story, no one will suddenly begin to fly or morph into a lion. The world in the realistic story resembles our own world and this allows us to focus on the relationships, emotions, and actions of the people in the story.

But the ease with which we access realistic fiction has drawbacks as well. Because of the familiarity, the quality and quantity of the meaning we derive is necessarily shallow. After all, just as our reality is limited, any copy of reality must necessarily be limited. What this means is that while we might experience any number of emotional reactions or learn substantive information about other cultures or events in history, we are forever limited the intra-human world by the same restraints that limit our real life, namely, our perceptions and perceptual apparatus (the five senses).

Instead of breaking into a new cave and exploring, realistic fiction allows us to enter a well-explored cave and travel through, walking on wooden planks and passing electric lights that have been strung along the cave wall for our safety. This is not meant to be a disparaging judgment against realistic fiction, but an attempt to describe the limits of the style. After all, not everyone would choose to try and break through a mountain side to find a new cave, especially if there was no guarantee of a finding a cave, but only a guarantee of many hours of hard work ahead.

Realistic fiction represent, literally re-presents, reality to us in the same way as a mirror. We look into the mirror and see the familiar, but of course, what we see id not a precise replica. And why not? Because what we see is a reverse image of everything, and it is perhaps this slight alteration that gives realistic writing enough difference to make it interesting for most of us.

Purpose: to narrate an event or series of invented events to provide information to the reader

Intention: to portray a 'life-like' representation of actual life in a way that allows a reader to discover deeper truths (emotional, psychological) about the human experience

Realistic fiction relies on the following assumptions in order to convey meaning:
1. -a knowable, objective reality
2. -access to this reality by application of consistent and accurate sensory perception
3. -a universal human connection with this reality.
4. -undiminished control of human beings over other creatures and all technology.
5. -the stability of language and concrete nature of language
6. -immutable physical laws of nature

SETTING
Since the only rule regarding setting in realist fiction is that it be familiar, recognizable and most importantly, BELIEVABLE, the fiction writer can use the setting to reinforce the story in several ways

1) Setting can be the central and most dominant characteristic of an entire story--it could be the characters primary goal and the element that creates the cause and effect chain of the plot

    a) Example: a story about a group of kids going to a giant maze, becoming lost & disoriented and struggling to survive.

    b) Example: a prisoner chained in a cell--the setting is the main cause of the characters immediate distress

2) Setting can be used to create a certain tone or mood-the feel of a certain place becomes the feel or tone of the story--while remaining 'life-like' details of a setting are portrayed using language that works to create a specific feel (creepy, frightening, celebratory)

3) Setting can be used in a way to demonstrate the mindset of a particular character. The way a character interacts with their setting can reveal parts of a character's personality and how they feel at the moment.

    a) Example: Setting: the interior of a car being driven 130 mph through a small town

    b) Setting: an ice fishing hole into which a character dives

    c) Setting: wilderness, character uses parts of the wilderness to survive. *Castaway*

4) Settings don't need to be actual or real in a fictional story. They can be used not only as the place for the current action, but as symbols in dreams (a flooding town), or as part of a character's imagined future or past (to reveal the character's personality).

"**Realism,** term applied to literary composition that aims at an interpretation of the actualities of any aspect of life, free from subjective prejudice, idealism, or romantic color. It is opposed to the concern with the unusual which forms the basis of romance, but it does not proceed, as does naturalism, to the philosophy of determinism and a completely amoral attitude. Although the novel has generally been considered the form best suited to the artistic treatment of reality, realism is not limited to any one form. As an attitude of the writer toward his materials, it is relative, and no chronological point may be indicated as the beginning of realism, but the 19th century is considered to mark its origin as a literary movement. The example of science, the influence of rational philosophy, the use of documentation in historical study, as well as the reaction against attenuated romanticism, all had their effect in creating the dominance of realism at this time." Literature, 1995, James D. Hart and Phillip W. Leininger:

<u>Characteristics of Realism</u> (from Richard Chase, *The American Novel and Its Tradition*)

    1.   Renders reality closely and in comprehensive detail. Selective presentation of reality with an emphasis on verisimilitude, even at the expense of a well-made plot

    2.   Character is more important than action and plot; complex ethical choices are often the subject.

    3.   Characters appear in their real complexity of temperament and motive; they are in explicable relation to nature, to each other, to their social class, to their own past.

    4.   Class is important; the novel has traditionally served the interests and aspirations of an insurgent middle class. (See Ian Watt, *The Rise of the Novel*)

    5.   Events will usually be plausible. Realistic novels avoid the sensational, dramatic elements of naturalistic novels and romances.

    6.   Diction is natural vernacular, not heightened or poetic; tone may be comic, satiric, or matter-of-fact.

    7.   Objectivity in presentation becomes increasingly important: overt authorial comments or intrusions diminish as the century progresses.

    8.   Interior or psychological realism a variant form.

Themes

    1.   Theme is the Significance or Meaning of a Story

    2.   The Theme is part of the Intention behind a story--It is the way in which a writer connects with a reader.

    3.   It is not an explicit message sent from writer to reader. More of a general idea or concept that emerges from the story which the reader connects with.

    4.   When a Reader connects with or relates to a story, this means that the Reader grasps some specific with the theme being presented.

    5.   Examples:

        - The theme of a fable is its moral.

        - The theme of a parable is its teaching.

        - The theme of a piece of traditional fiction is its view about life and how people behave.

    6.   In fiction, the theme is not intended to teach or preach or send a particular/specific message.

    7.   It is not presented directly. The Reader must extract the theme from the elements of story Locate the following moments in the story.

Bobbing For Mother

Terry's fishnet legs come into full view on the staircase, and then her seventeen year-old body. She pauses on a step, thrusts her chest forward and turns to wink at Melody on the downstairs couch. Melody sucks in a quick breath. Terry looks precisely like their mother, if their mother had ever been a call girl or a hooker in a mining town saloon. The similar structure of their faces however, captures Melody's attention.

A black feather sticks out of Terry's blond hair and her cheeks look bruised with rouge. She licks her lips. She wears one of their mother's old strapless black dresses and teases it up to her panty line, revealing her black fishnet stockings and a black garter. She kicks her shadowy leg like a call girl and tosses her head back to laugh. The black shoe lands at the bottom of the staircase and Melody shakes her head. Terry even wears a pair of their mother's shoes.

"What's the matter, cowboy," Terry asks. She tilts her head and smiles at Melody. Red lipstick has smeared on her front teeth.

"You'll freeze to death," Melody says.

"Not if Chad's around," Terry whispers. She smoothes the dress over her thigh and slips the high heeled shoe onto her foot, taps her toe into the floor. "So what are you going to be?" Terry asks and sits on the arm of the couch, crossing her legs. It seems to Melody that her sister's body perfumes the entire room. A five layered pearl necklace presses against her throat and a solitary pearl rests between her padded boobs. They were their mother's pearls.

Melody turns away. "I'm not sure I'm even going."

"Haven't we been through this?" Terry asks, and she exaggerates a quizzical face. "You can sit in the car all night for all I care, but in half an hour we are both walking out that door." She picks at the nylon around her calf and then stands. "You know it and I know it." Terry walks into the kitchen and down the hall. "You'll be lucky if I don't leave you in the middle of nowhere," she calls out.

Melody would much rather be left in the middle of nowhere. Away from the costumes and the sticky red punch that will smell like cough syrup. Even the idea of bobbing for apples makes Melody gag. Plunging your head into a vat of warm saliva and the view from the bottom of the barrel; painted faces plunking into the silence and horse-chomping teeth stretching out of their gums, gnashing for a grip on the waxy red skin.

A knock and Melody walks to the front door and stares out at a man wearing a black hat and mask. Even from her side of the door, she feels the Halloween chill. A cape flows around this man's shoulders and a black leather vest matches his pants. Melody opens the door and he swoops in, slides his hand around her waist. "Fear not my dear for I have come to save you," Chad says swinging Melody out of the way.

"And where is Ronald McDonald?"

Chad shakes his head. "I am Zorro," he says. "The king of beers." He gestures dramatically and smacks his hand against the closet door. He rubs his knuckles, instantly irritated. "Where is she?"

With the Lone Ranger. Chad stands with his chin raised like a prince. The eternally famous captain of the football team with the best fake license for buying beer.

"You coming with," he asks.

Their father insisted that Terry could not go unless Melody went with her. Even though he knows this Chad's tone begs Melody to decline anyway, to say that she won't be around to spy.

"I wouldn't miss it," she says cheerfully and flashes her best smile.

Chad lifts his hat and combs his fingers through his perfect brown hair.

"Is that my favorite hero, come to save me from my wretched life?" Terry asks. She walks up to Chad with her limp wrist pressed against her forehead. She tries not to stumble in her high-heeled shoes.

"Zero is here madam," Melody says with a slight bow. The couple kisses lightly and turns to Melody.

"Isn't she a riot," Terry says but Chad stands quiet, his x-ray eyes locked on Terry's chest. "And what, may I ask, are you to be, little Miss Priss?" Terry asks.

Melody walks to the couch and picks up a newspaper. Terry and Chad smooth and pull at their costumes. They whisper.

Terry announces that they are leaving in ten minutes and Melody walks upstairs to the hall closet. She pulls out a worn sheet printed with tiny football helmets, and cuts two holes. She slips under the sheet and opens her eyes, one cut lower than the other. She smells her mother in the fabric and flows down the stairs feeling the sheet ripple and sway against her body.

"And what the hell are you supposed to be," Chad asks loudly. He wipes lipstick from his mouth and Terry blushes through her make-up.

Melody raises her arms above her head. "I am the ghost of bad acid flashbacks. Beware, beware." She twirls around the room.

"You really are a freak," Chad says and Melody follows the couple out the door.

Two months after her mother's death Melody's father threw a Halloween costume party. The word had gotten around town, mostly through Diane the sexy therapist, that family suicides were best dealt with quickly, with a definitive step forward. It became common knowledge.

At the party Melody refused to dress up or even come out of the coat closet. She sat underneath a growing pile of coats, enjoying the weight. Her father gave up trying to coax her out and closed the door. Melody heard him tell Diane that it was not the way a fourteen year-old girl ought to act, and Melody sunk deeper into the smell of cigarette leather and perfumed scarves. She curved the arms of a fur coat around her neck and heard the two of them in the kitchen. Melody pictured Diane laughing in her shiny red bra and cape, and heard her father slurs his words.

When the door opened, the outline of a ghost appeared and motioned from beneath a red flannel sheet. "Do you think I could come in," the ghost asked. Melody nodded in the dark and the ghost stepped into the mass of coats and pulled the door shut. Melody helped the ghost sit.

"You didn't dress up," the ghost said. "You really should've dressed up."

"Halloween is stupid," Melody said. "What are you anyway? The ghost of old men's pajamas?"

"You should've dressed up anyway. It makes it easier to talk, and plus you can't see if my tongue is sticking out at you or not."

"Well you can see mine," Melody said, pushing her tongue between her lips.

Melody waited, listening to the red ghost inhale and exhale. "You're mom just died, huh?" the red ghost asked.

"So?"

"Well, you'll probably think I'm stupid but I think you're lucky."

"What?" Melody turned to face the ghost but she could only barely make out the shape.

"Sure. I knew you'd think I was stupid, but it's true anyway."

Melody pushed the fur coat away from her sweaty neck. "Do you even know?"

"That she killed herself? Sure I know that. My aunt Diane thinks it's good for me to be here, she thinks I'll see how lucky I am, but instead I see you're that you're the lucky one."

The ghost settled back into the closet until the mound of coats towered in front of them. Melody allowed the ghost's elbow to rest against her arm.

"So I guess that's why you're in here," the ghost said.

"Not really," Melody said. "Why are you in here?"

"Because I hate having to shake everyone's hand and tell them what grade I'm in. And because my aunt Diane introduces me like she's saying, 'This is the one I was talking about,' and everyone feels sorry for me. It gets so boring, I hate parties like this."

The red ghost rested a knee on Melody's thigh. "I don't mean to sound like a jerk, but my mom has been dying for almost two years, and the doctor says it could be another six months, but he's always said something like that."

"Why, you want her to die?" Melody leaned into the red ghost and smelled perfume.

"No, not really. But she sends me away when I don't want to go. I guess she thinks I need a break, or that my aunt can help me. But I just want to stay home, and they won't listen. I don't know, it all sounds so stupid."

The two leaned against the back wall of the closet. Their shoulders pressed together, and their hands connected. The red ghost's palm felt warm and sweaty and Melody tried not to squeeze too hard. She heard the ghost's breaths like the sounds of the ocean. Then the red ghost turned and Melody felt moist cloth lips press against her mouth. She pressed back.

Diane opened the door. "What are you girls doing in here? Are you back there sweetie?"

Melody felt the ghost's hand slip away.

"The party is out here ladies. Are you necking back there or what?" She laughed over her shoulder and the smell of cherry liquor seeped into the closet. Diane bent down and her boobs stretched the bikini toward the coats.

Melody saw this woman's blurry face, her dripping smile. "Now why don't you both come out and talk to me. I'm sure I could help." She moved her hand forward. "Come on now, that's right, let's get up. No more kissing for you two, no more girlie smoochie smooch." Diane's hand paused inches from Melody's face. In an instant Melody leaned forward and bit down as hard as she could on Diane's salty skin. When her teeth released she tasted blood run onto her tongue.

For a moment there was no sound, just Diane's dazed smile, Melody's warm mouth. Then Diane gasped and stepped back into Melody's father. "It's okay, it's okay," she said to him.

Her father's angry face peered into the closet, his head swayed side to side. The red ghost crawled out and disappeared. He slammed the door closed on Melody and eventually she fell asleep to the sound of the footsteps in the hall.

A three story wooden monster and Chad drops his first empty beer bottle into a bush by the mailbox. The first story windows shine like teeth and pumpkins line the path to the house. Cardboard bats and spiders bounce on strings from the gutters and a paper skeleton sticks to the front door. The inside swarms with costumed people and Chad's arm slips around Terry's waist, pulls her into the crowd.

Melody walks quietly, hoping no one can see her. She bumps into an older bear who'd been illustrating a diving catch. She recognizes one of her mother's co-workers without his glasses.

"Excuse me," says the bear. And then he asks, "Well what do we have here, the ghost of football past?" The circle of spectators shifts and a group of cheerleaders stare at her. Melody recognizes some of them from high school's football team and their muscles bulge under their leotards. They squeeze and adjusted their imitation breasts and nudge each other with pompoms. "Maybe you could tell us the scores of the football future," the bear says. "I bet we could make a bundle in Vegas."

"And I bet the ghost couldn't tell us the scores from football yesterday," Chad says. "How about it? The score of yesterday's game?" A slight hush falls over the group. Melody notices the hair on Chad's arm through his fluffy white Zorro shirt.

She shakes her head.

Terry sits on the edge of a couch talking with one of her beautiful friends. The friend wears a silver bikini and wolf ears stretched across her head. Dark whisker lines are drawn across her cheeks and a plastic nose covers her real one.

Melody turns to speak to the red flannel ghost. "They should be frozen by now," Melody says. Terry and her friend stop talking and look at Melody. Terry shakes her head, covers her face in exaggerated embarrassment, and the two girls giggle. The playboy girl snorts and as she walks onto the porch Melody wonders if a plastic nose would feel anything like regular make-up and make it hard to breathe.

Melody stands outside and shadows shift on the lawn. She sits on a wooden porch swing and laughs. "I'm not really a football ghost, you know? And you're probably not the ghost of old men's pajamas."

Melody stands and waves her arms in the air, careful not to lift the sheet above her ankles. "I am the ghost of bad acid flashbacks." She pauses and laughs, "And I'll bet you're the ghost of feverish nights." Melody dances and twirls and laughs until she stops and grabs onto the porch railing. Her stomach aches from laughing and air chills her throat. She tastes blood. Her eyes fill and she shuts them, shakes her head.

"Your mom is probably dead by now," she says to her invisible friend. "Probably sitting up in heaven talking to my mom. Watching us I bet, laughing at how we all dress up like freaks and walk around in the middle of the night. Did your mom used to wear a lot of make-up?"

A group emerges from the door and Melody sees Chad and Terry walking with a group of hairy cheerleaders. Melody says, "Finally, what we've all been waiting for."

Chad picks up a pumpkin and hurls it into the street, where it lands with an un-dramatic thud. A cheerleader shouts, "FORE!" and hits it with a baseball bat. Some cheerleaders have lost parts of their chest and a few swing bottles to their mouth.

"Bring out your dead," a girl shrieks.

Melody trails at a distance. "They are up in heaven probably saying what funny creatures we humans are. They must wonder what drives us to dress up in bikinis and walk through the winter streets smashing fruit."

Chad slides behind Terry like a night animal and hugs her, pinning her arms to her sides. They begin to spin and Terry's shoe flies onto a lawn. A bottle breaks. Terry shouts for him to stop.

Melody sees her sister's face appear and disappear. Her cheekbones and nose highlighted by the street lamp as she spins around in Chad's arms. She remembers seeing her mother's face in the mirror saying, "I think we have a winner."

Melody closes her eyes and spreads her arms. She twirls in the middle of the street and she remembers the red ghost's lips. She wishes Diane had not opened the door, had not spoiled everything. That mother would be dead by now just like her own mother, and the ghost probably did not feel very lucky at all. When Melody falls to the ground nothing hurts and a strange warmth floods her body. Like she could curl up and disappear into the road. She lies on the pavement until she hears Terry's scream crash into the street.

Melody jumps up and runs toward them. Chad struggles to stand and Terry lies beneath him with her face pressing into the pavement, with her arms twisted to her sides.

They turn her over and Chad trips backward. "Oh Jesus," he whispers. His breath stinks. "Accident," he mumbles. "Oh God."

Melody shouts for someone to get help, and two of Terry's friends carry their shoes and help each other run back to the house. Melody looks down at her beautiful sister.

Terry's nose sits loosely on her face, crushed to one side, and blood pours from her forehead. "It's okay, I'm okay, help me up," Terry says. Her words bubble out from somewhere beneath her lip and a few teeth have disappeared. Melody hears Chad getting sick in the gutter.

Eventually, the flashing lights come around the corner and two paramedics in white uniforms hop out of the ambulance to examine Terry. They pull a stretcher from the back and tell everyone to step back. Melody brushes her sister's hair away from her face. "I'm sorry," she says. "I'm so sorry."

Melody's throat tightens when she stands and she holds Terry's hand while they fasten her to the stretcher. "Don't worry," Melody says. "You'll be fine." Melody rubs her sister's arm and says, "I didn't like you with all that make-up anyway, and those horrible shoes."

Terry's green eyes flash. She offers a feeble smile. Then she closes her eyes and remains still except for the slow movement of her chest.

Before they shut the ambulance doors, Melody looks out at the group. Chad sits on the curb, his head between his knees, and a huge cheerleader nudges a pumpkin bit with his foot. A few girls cry with their arms around each other and sadness loosens in Melody's chest. She looks down at Terry, wearing her mother's bloody and disfigured face. Tears pour down her cheeks and Melody winces and smiles at once. As they drive away, sobs erupt from Melody's body, shocking her chest like ice water, and she kneels with her sister's hand in her lap. She stares at Terry's face, perfectly still, with drying blood around her nose and mouth. Someone touches her shoulder and Melody soaks the sheet around her face.

Make. Believe.

Our mother sits at the breakfast table in a brilliant yellow sundress and drinks chilled white wine from a frosted glass.

"She doesn't drink wine," my sister Sara says.

Of course she does, but Sara is 11 years old, too young to recognize the situation. She wears a straw hat with a yellow band and sunglasses.

"But she doesn't drink wine at eight in the morning," my sister says again. "You're an alcoholic."

My father moves through the house, as heavy and dark as an oil slick. He can't find his wallet.

"Who touches my wallet?" he demands to know. "Why would you touch my wallet?"

I'm hoping that Sara didn't leave the wallet in her bedroom again. He's never found it there, but of course it would only take one time.

Get your father's wallet, my mother says with a flick of her wrist.

I find it on the floor next to his dresser.

My dad closes the main gate and latches it when he drives off to work. Sara's pony, Blue Boy, stands in the backyard on my mom's overgrown garden and rips up clumps of weeds with his big yellow disgusting teeth.

I don't particularly like horses, and I don't think about Blue Boy much, except on the winter mornings before school when I stand in front of the corral and try to breathe into his nostrils. I read that it was a secret way to communicate, like one prisoner signaling another. I see the icicles from his mane along his neck like a row of crystal daggers and he fixes me in his dead black stare. His slow breath escapes from his rubbery nostrils and mixes with my own.

I am not to leave the house, and Sara has been sentenced to her bedroom for the day. We should be vacuuming, dusting, and suffering consequences.

I wait until I see my dad's blue car pause at the end of the half-mile dirt road and then turn onto the highway and head to town. I jump out of the living room window and pause on the front sidewalk. I glance up at Sara's darkened bedroom window. After a moment, a Candyland card appears—double green. I unhook the front gates, pull them apart, and set a rock in front of each one to hold them open.

Sara pulls away her bedroom's screen window and climbs down the rock wall and jumps onto the front porch.

I'm 14 years-old and I drive a Volvo station wagon born in the same year I was, 1971. I sit tall on my bedroom pillow in the driver's seat, and my eleven year old sister Sara rides in the backseat. It's strange to put a piece of the bedroom in the car, like the world now has a drowsy tang or an unusual sweatiness to it.

Seatbelts are years away from being taken seriously.

I drive down the dirt road like it's something I do every blasted day, an event that I'm pretty well sick of by now. I try a facial expression that I've lifted from my father, a look of supreme irritation mixed with a subtler sadness. I even sigh like I would give up if it weren't for the secret burden that I carry, like the President or Jesus.

Navigating the dirt road is not an issue; after all it's a dirt road. Sara could do it, if she weren't sitting quietly in the back seat. I'm after doughnuts, and maybe some soda— illegal junk food. Sara has come along to buy carrots for Blue Boy. I'm rolling over the giant puddle craters and passing the few houses along the way. I act for the camera that is always on me, the studio audience that constantly watches, ready to turn me in if I slip up.

"I can't believe I finally got my license," I say.

"Me either," Sara responds.

This is not some epic journey. We only need to turn right onto the highway, which is not a problem since I am practically an expert with the traffic signal wand, and then travel about a mile to the gas station where they sell mini-powdered doughnuts, cola, and all sorts of chocolate. I've seen people buy gas and then when they're in the store they're like yeah I could go for a chocolate candy bar, maybe two, and on a Tuesday afternoon in July, I watch them buy as much candy as I usually get for Easter.

But I don't know how it goes, in their head, I can't imagine how to get to a casual level of candy consumption, where I could treat chocolate bars like a glasses of water—like I could just ask myself, am I thirsty or not and then exercise restraint, instead of ramming fists of chocolate into my slobbering mouth like Jabba the Hut.

I stop the car to wait for the goddamn traffic that has only gotten worse since we've moved here—back when I was eight, before my mother disappeared, before I even knew how to drive—so long ago. God how it irritates me, to have to wait like this every blasted day. How many times, I wearily think (for the benefit of the studio audience that hears my thoughts like a voice-over), how many times have I found myself behind this wheel just waiting for a safe break in the constant stream of cars?

I ease onto the hot summer asphalt and accelerate.

"We've got to trade in this piece of junk," I say. "I'm tired of driving this heap."

"On to Disneyland!" Sara shouts.

I guess my dad could come home at any moment, it's certainly possible. He once arrived just as I pulled a coffee cake from the oven. I wore the green baking mittens and I ran into my room and hid the entire pan on the bookshelf. I told him that I'd made cinnamon toast to explain away the aroma, but he found the empty pan that night. I was stupid for making the cake and stupid for eating every last bite, but I was most worthless because I lied about something as stupid and worthless as cake.

The whole driving process only takes 15 minutes, which is what makes it so tempting. I'm in the far right lane and up to about 40 miles an hour. I drive with one hand on either side of the wheel, and the car pulls to the right.

"Did you bring the money?" I ask. I tilt the rearview, pretend to adjust it for the road, and capture her reflection. Sara has long stringy brown hair and a sickly body. She wears a red plaid jumper and clear plastic sandals, and she sits as if she's been punched in the stomach. Her skinny white limbs have a bluish hue and her wide brown eyes never seem to shut, even when she cries.

She holds up a twenty dollar bill. It's the most she's ever taken.

"You'll get us killed," I say, but I'm not angry. I'm recalculating the number of candy bars I'll buy.

"Are you sure they'll have carrots?" she asks. Sara still wets the bed. The car chugs up the incline and around the bend. Only a few drivers pass us on the way, and not one of them comes to a dead stop, gets out, pulls me from the car by my collar and calls my father. Not one.

Sara and I tour the store. It's like the donation bin of convenience stores, like the food has somehow been used and taped back into the wrinkled original package.

I have no idea if they sell anything remotely like carrots.

I put seven packages of doughnuts, ten candy bars, and a six-pack of soda on the counter. I'm feeling like a genius, driving at 14. In any event, I see a small bag of mini-carrots at the bottom of a cooler, and at that exact moment, I remember the front gate.

Once Blue Boy escapes, then the whole question of how he escaped must be addressed, which leads to an open gate, which leads to why an open gate, and my father insists that he closed it and maybe I lie and say he didn't and he hardens like concrete under his skin.

I wait at the traffic light at the top of the hill with my left signal clicking and with a growing fear that I'm attempting to convert into anger. Anger prevents the *really* bad from happening because it creates a type of shield. But you really have to be angry and not just pretending to be angry (the studio audience knows) in order for the shield to work properly. When I'm sick with a cold, for example, I'm sent to my room and my father's anger buries me and saves me from major disease. After Sara came down with pneumonia, my father left the house in a rage.

I turn left onto the highway and all goes well, but now I must remain in the left lane, since I have to turn left onto the dirt road. The left lane is the lane of doom and horror. I've learned this just by the way my father reacts to the idiots who regularly use the lane. These selfish idiots carry no burden. I am pushing 35 miles per hour as we cruise down the highway. My cold soda and seven packages of doughnuts sit in the passenger seat and my sister holds the bag of carrots in her lap.

"Fuck shit fuck!" I shout, casting a futile anger spell onto the approaching scene. I'm driving on the straightaway now, maybe a hundred yards away from turning, and all of the traffic in the opposite lane has stopped at my turnoff, next to the row of mailboxes. Blue Boy lies on the pavement, and his head keeps moving up and down like he wants to check out the rest of his body, but can't bear to look. A woman in a business suit gets out of her car and walks up to stand over Blue Boy.

I put on my clicker, but instead of pulling all the way onto the dirt road or stopping in my lane I misjudge. I am forced to stop in mid turn with my front bumper a few feet away from Blue Boy's hairy hind legs.

It probably looks like I hit him. I know that Sara sits in the backseat on the passenger's side, but I don't turn around.

"What?" Sara asks, straining her neck.

"It's okay," I say and I think, someone will probably have to shoot Blue Boy.

Then I see the car on the shoulder of the road, the car with the passenger's side caved in and a young girl driver standing with her head bent by the driver's door and crying. A jogger and a cyclist are near her and talking to her, trying to calm her down.

"It's my horse," I say when I step out of the car and the business woman does not glare at me or ask my age or call my father.

"I'm sorry," she says, "No one was hurt," and she means people, she means the crying girl. Blue Boy grunts and wheezes and I think I hear a death rattle, like a growl wrapped inside an asthma attack.

"I'll get my mom," I say in a last ditch effort. If I can make it home and park the car and then run down the road to the scene, I will camouflage my mistakes behind a story in which all of this happens, the escape, the dead horse—

I don't see Sara open her door. I haven't looked at her in the mirror because I don't want her to be here. I don't want her to see Blue Boy and I am particularly frightened by the possibility of seeing the bag of carrots—the bag of carrots at this moment seems unbearable.

I don't see the irritated driver either. The idiot who must be late. I hear his engine roar, but only barely, as if it were miles away and I don't see him pull out of the line of cars and accelerate into the center lane. I don't see anything except Sara's dying horse, and I work through potential lies like I'd work through chess strategy.

The idiot's car passes like a vision in my periphery and hits Sara. I don't see it, but I hear it, the gasp and thud, like someone slammed up against a wall.

I turn to look.

Like a knockout punch in my gut, as spilled carrots roll on the asphalt.

Catching and Fishing

One year ago, a few days after our high school graduation, Daniel died in this river and they never found his body or his inner tube. My feet move like stumps on the river bottom and Sandra stands next to me in cut-off jeans. A dawn mist brightens the sky above our shadowed valley. She doesn't mention the cold and her breath disappears like cigarette smoke in the dark.

She says, "You are the fish, Jake. You have to believe their hunger, cultivate it. Fish hunger is your hunger. The more you want to eat the fly, the more the fish wants to eat the fly. It's like voodoo Jake, like casting a spell." She dangles the hook in front of my face, "Otherwise tonight, you will be eating the fly."

While she talks I examine the hook in my own hand, hidden beneath the yellow fuzz. I press down and watch the metal sink quietly into my fingertip. I maneuver it out and suck on my finger wondering if the fish will be attracted to the blood.

Sandra wades downstream. "Good luck Mr. Fisherman," she calls over her shoulder. The stained canvas bag floats behind her already containing her first catch of the day. The eyes bled after she knocked it against the rock and then she held it close to my lips and made kissing sounds. I'm definitely glad that she will gut it. I work on my appetite and watch my yellow fuzz breakfast land on the water with a flick.

When the river flooded our town nearly 100 years ago, a reporter wrote that a three-story wall of water swallowed the town. He called it a ghost canyon because the only human evidence ever found was a woman's bra caught in the branches of an uprooted tree. No human bodies, no livestock. My friend Daniel hung the famous black and white bra photo in his room. He always said the tree roots look like Medusa's head.

On the night of my thirteenth birthday, Daniel climbed the tree outside my window and tapped on the glass.

"What the hell are you doing," I whispered. Daniel straddled the branch and his wet black hair fell past his face to his chest. A few strands stuck to the corner of his mouth.

"I was just taking a bath and I thought you might be dead." He bit his lower lip and blinked his eyes, as if still deciding what to do.

I pressed my fingers against my chest and pulled my hair. "So far so good," I said.

Daniel took my hand and examined my fingers. He even stuck his head through the window and looked at my feet.

"But you look like a skeleton, Jake," he said. "The color of bone."

I shrugged.

"Well happy birthday old man," he said and patted me on the shoulder before descending. I stood at the window and watched his bare legs balance on a log across the river to his house.

"You dead Jake?" Daniel would yell from his window across the river, his hands cupped around his mouth. He always thought I might be dead but just didn't know it.

"So far so good," was my line and Daniel always cracked up laughing. We spent the summers calling to each other from our windows and building rafts. I drafted graph paper with exact measurements and Daniel tore down trees and chopped them into pieces. We dreamt of building a boat with a kitchen and a bed so we could live on it while we rode to the end of the river. Eventually you come to the ocean, Daniel told me, and that was where the spirits lived.

The year Daniel rode to the end of the river we turned fifteen and we found a stack of magazines inside a storage closet in Daniel's house. Naked women sucked on men in the pictures and sometimes licked other women. A few wore lacy underwear or leather belts and they all seemed to gaze at us with half-closed eyes and parted wet lips.

The night we found them I slept over and we scanned each picture with the light from a candle. Daniel's hand passed over the glossy women and the flame moved across their bodies, pausing and reflecting their shine. In the middle of the night, Daniel pinched the candlewick and we lay down on the sleeping bags next to each other. A fever crept into my body and I tossed in a sweat that soaked my chest and stung the back of my neck. I couldn't seem to keep my eyes closed at all and I kept scissoring the sleeping bag between my legs and pushing it away.

In the dark, out of nowhere, I suddenly felt Daniel's hand on my stomach and I held absolutely still.

I knew that I should have wanted to say 'Don't.' My body was supposed to recoil, perhaps, as the word 'Don't,' left my lips. Instead, I turned my head to the side and stared hard at the electric outlet near my face, attempting to peer into the small black holes that would accommodate the prongs. The rest of my body remained perfectly still.

His palm patted me lightly on the stomach and then slid under my shorts. His fingers wrapped around me and his wrist moved. Images of skin patches, of wet fingers and hair flooded my mind. His hand gripped me until I was sure that I'd scream, and then the fever drained away. Daniel didn't wipe his hand on my stomach or drag it across the floor. He lifted it away and disappeared. I swallowed hard and pressed the pillow to my chest.

The next morning Daniel told me that he'd ridden to the end of the river, after I'd fallen asleep.

"It was like drifting down a river of oil," he said. "The trees looked bigger, the branches reached down like pythons. I held my knife and pushed off the rocks with my feet. It seemed like days passed and I was worried I wouldn't get back home, when I suddenly saw the enormous lake, the ocean, with the ghosts standing in the middle." Daniel leaned closer.

"Most of them were white and wrinkled and dancing with their arms linked, like a party. A few naked bodies sat on invisible chairs and drank from imaginary cups. They moved their jaws without any noise and I drifted closer. Suddenly they stopped and turned toward me.

"I shivered even though I wasn't cold at all. One of them, an old woman, nodded her head and waved. And when I reached out to her, just then, they all sunk beneath the surface. A warm gust blew over my face, but the water didn't move."

Daniel asked if I wanted to go with him next time and I shook my head. He laughed and said it was because I was already a ghost.

A week later Sandra the college girl moved into Daniel's house. She rented the upstairs bedroom and bathroom from his parents. After a few days Daniel had drilled a hole from the storage closet into her bathroom. We used the fish eye lens from a junkyard motel door, and when Sandra stood in the shower, we took turns. The lens bloated her stomach a little and her breasts seemed sort of pushed up toward her throat.

With her head tilted back she rubbed her body with soap,

shampooed her hair. A few times the water traced her body enough for Daniel to take me in his hand again. But the one time I touched him in the closet, he pushed me away and left the closet even before the steam had the chance to cloud our view.

Sandra followed Daniel up to the frozen lake during the winter of our senior year of high school. He told me that he'd just set up his tent, and begun a small fire on the lake when he saw Sandra stumbling through the trees.

"Her legs were turning blue and some snow had caught around the edges of her cutoff jeans. I swear I thought she was a ghost at first. She wore a windbreaker and a baseball hat. I yelled over to her and she lifted her arm to wave and face-planted onto the lake. The ice soaked in the blood, turning it brown, and I picked her up and carried her to my tent. I practically had to set her on fire to thaw her out.
"Eventually her lip stopped bleeding and I said that she didn't look like she was planning to camp overnight. She said that the cold never bothered her, that she wore shorts year round. She drank some of the tequila I brought while I set up the hole and baited the line. She looked up at me with those cat green eyes and said, 'So when do we eat,' and I pointed to the pole and said, 'When they're ready.'

"The first three fish were tiny as hell and I explained that they were just like children. Kids learning about life and shit so we threw them back. I caught one about the size of my hand and she was excited, but I unhooked it and threw it back. Man you should have seen her face. I told her that it was only a teenager, and that we always give them another chance.

"She's kind of pissed because I said we had to wait for the big ones, the old ones whose time is up. Anyway, we waited, and I swear, suddenly my pole almost jumped into the water. I'm standing and pulling my ass off, sliding on the ice, until I yanked it up and it landed with a crack.

"Jake, I'm not kidding, it was the biggest son of a bitch you ever saw. It must have been two feet long. So I knocked it out and gutted it right there.

"The next thing I know I still taste fish from the frying pan and we're at each other's throats and mouths, and I'm trying to pull my clothes off, slipping on the lake. She kept her shorts on and held my knife to her crotch and before I could speak, I saw this slice in her jeans. The whole time I only felt our breaths getting warmer, and she pulled

me into her and we did it, right there on the ice under the stars, smelling
the campfire smoke and the water all at once. I remember wondering if
our bodies would melt into the lake. But that wouldn't be such a bad
way to go, now would it?"

Sandra was there that day, last year, and so was I. She lay on the
shore sunbathing in a red bikini and listening to a baseball game
through headphones. It was the first time I saw her skin up close and I
pretended not to notice her slick body when she moved and her muscles
grooved and shone under the sun. She had bought us a case of beer and
Daniel stood on the shore in his blue tee shirt, surveying the water.

He knelt to place his beer on the ground while he gathered his hair
into a ponytail. "You going to the end," he called out to me.

"Not until you clear the way," I said. The river was the highest it
had been in years. It had rained for two weeks and the mountain snow
was melting in record sheets. Signs along the bank forbid fishing or
swimming.

Sandra said she was hot as hell and she smeared lotion all over her
body. Daniel had just finished rubbing the cream into her back when
he grabbed another beer and winked at me. Sandra lay on her back,
propped up on one elbow, watching us. A couple of guys from school
filled the tubes with bicycle pumps and drank. Daniel tapped the
bottom of his can, forcing out the last drops, and slid the safety rope
over his head, secured the loop around his waist. I watched Sandra lay
down, and stare for a moment at the blue sky before she closed her eyes.

The water raged. The muddy surface rushed and swirled like sour
chocolate milk, churning up the river's bottom and whisking along
broken bottles and soaked trash. Daniel called it the vomiting river and
pretended to retch. He turned toward Sandra who slept, and stared at
her bare legs for a moment before stepping into the river.

He fought his way through chest-high water, holding his tube and
tightening the rope around his waist. "This is what it's all about," he
shouted over the roar.

I nodded and grabbed the end of the rope with one hand, opened a
beer with the other. Watching Daniel stride through the water, I felt
immovable, solid. Daniel jumped back onto the tube.

"Don't forget to write," one of the guys yelled out and Daniel
waved. Coils of rope disappeared into the brown water and I looped my
end around my wrist. Daniel bounded down the rapids. I shouted for

him to say hello to the ghosts but the rush swallowed my words. I turned and saw Sandra's eyelids twitch, her chest rose and fell. Then I felt a tug.

"He's down," someone yelled and my fist gripped the rope. I dropped my beer and saw that the rope was snagged on a tree root sticking out of the water. The tube flipped and careened around the bend, and for an instant I was upset about losing it. Daniel struggled to stand, flailing his arms at the air. It seemed as if none of it was actually happening, as if it were only a brief moment of vibration when the pine trees and mountain rocks and water noise flashed in brilliant sync around my head.

I heard it like the cracking of a bat. Daniel's head snapped forward onto a rock. He floated face down and I yanked on the rope with both hands, sweating down my sides. One of the guys ran down the bank shouting Daniel's name and then the rope slipped from around his waist down to his ankle, and he was whisked away.

I stared at the disfigured root that tangled my rope and I heard someone sprint toward the houses.

Sandra lay motionless with her headphones covering her ears, and a smear of white lotion glittering on her chin. I jerked on the rope, over and over. At one point, mixed into the constant echo of water rushing down the canyon, I thought I heard Daniel call out to me.

So I shouted, "So far so good." I never heard his voice again.

Last night we walked along the river, holding hands. Sandra asked, "Do you believe in fate."

"Not really," I said.

"I mean about Daniel dying, and you and me together. You don't think that's anything?"

"We both miss Daniel, that's something."

She stopped and stared at me. She let go of my hand. "You don't think we were meant for each other, that we belong together?"

"A person doesn't drown just to bring two people together," I said. I turned away and tried to find pieces of logs with nails in them to show her. I pulled up a few pieces, but they weren't from our rafts. I said they must have been washed away last year. "We were building a giant raft with a kitchen," I said. "With a kitchen and a bedroom."

Sandra hadn't moved. "People die to save giant trees," she said. "They die to protect horned owls." She stood with her hand on her hips glaring at me. "Of course they die to bring people together, Jake. That is precisely why they die at all." She turned and walked away from me along the riverbank. Then she yelled something that I couldn't hear over her shoulder and began to run.

I tried to catch her, jogging as fast as I could, being careful not to stumble. The cold air froze the sweat in my shirt, and just as I almost had her, she fell down in front of a clump of raspberry bushes. I bent to help her up.

She yanked her hand back. "Fuck you," she said and slapped my face.

My mouth opened and I held her wrist as she stood. Her blond hair blurred white, like a halo against the dark. She drove her fist hard under my jaw with a crack that split in my ears. Blood rushed into my mouth and my entire body hummed.

She knelt down and pulled the bushes aside. I crawled on my hands and knees and followed her into a small cave, smelling her breath in the air. The darkness and humidity swallowed me and she moved like a shadow. She pulled off her shirt and lay back on the soft dirt. A white haze filtered through the rocks around her breasts and open mouth.

My shorts were down around my feet and thorns scratched my calves. Sandra dug her heels like hooks into my lower back and pulled me toward her. No underwear. She grabbed my chin with one hand and held me steady, her wet eyes fixed on me. I closed my eyes and sweat rolled past my eyelids, dropped onto my lips.

I heard the river outside our cave and the still pools of water appeared in my mind, quiet and clear enough to see sand on the bottom. I watched Daniel's body surface with his long black hair floating around his head like ink.

Sandra dug her fingernails into my chin. "You and me," she said.

I saw Daniel's eyes open, heard the water lap against his skin again and again. I felt his sweaty hand one more time, burning and squeezing until I ground my teeth and balled my fist into the dirt. I shouted from inside the cave.

"We're all right now," Sandra said, her own body settling. "We're all right." Her panting voice soothed me and I let myself fall further away from Daniel with each caress against the back of my sweaty neck.

The sun has almost disappeared and I guess it was bound to happen. Sandra stands next to me and coaches while my line zigzags across the river. My pole bends and the tip almost touches the water.

"Easy now, not too hard," Sandra says. "You don't want to lose the fly."

I reel and am eager to get it over with when my thumb knocks the latch and yards of fishing line spit into the river.

"Come on Jake, concentrate. You have to pull steady first— I said steady," she insists. "All right now, a little faster, okay— now really yank on the fucker."

The fish jumps out of the water and hangs in the air, its tail twitching. I wrap my hand around the small body and the paralyzed fish watches me with its peripheral eye while I pull the hook from the cheek. It is a little bigger than my hand with an orange belly and Sandra takes it from me.

"Not bad," she says and goes to knock its head against a rock on shore.

"It's a teenager," I blurt out and she stops. Stares at me, glares at me. My jaw aches and I glance down at the water. My body feels dead below the waist.

"Look," she says lifting the canvas flap. There is still only the single fish she caught earlier. "It's almost dark and I'm starved." Her eyes narrow and she shrugs. With a quick thud the fish is done and inside her bag.

I swallow and feel a tiny bone scratch its way down my throat.

Dust

I can barely see a pair of yellow eyes through the dust. An animal for sure, but an elk? A deer? The eyes vanish and I hear the breathing from somewhere behind my car. I pop the hood. The wind stings, swirling sand onto my bare legs, my arms.

It probably just needs oil, or it needed oil. I'm afraid it is beyond needing anything. On my hands and knees I see a glowing green puddle the size of a Frisbee. I can barely see the animal's legs pass behind a rear tire.

When I stand I see the outline of an old gas station down the road, through the swirling funnels of dust. The miniature tornadoes dancing the hip dance. A broken window, a wooden sign with flaking blue paint, a rusted car frame with its nose to the ground. Steps follow me and I hear snorting. I can see the yellow eyes in my mind and I trot toward the station.

I stop and turn and it stands three feet away, curled horns lowered. It gallops toward me. I face him and raise my arms to make myself look bigger. I tense my body to deflect the hit, but the bone colored horns pound flat against my chest.

A chill runs through me when my back hits the road. Like falling on a frozen pond, smacking against the ice and losing my breath. Waiting in silence for air with the thought that I may be dying. A single cloud hangs like a smoke ring in the sky. Nothing to pass through it, no airplane thread, no imaginary boat. Maybe this is what it's like to die. Just a cloud ring floating along until my body remembers what to do. Breathe.

I stand, head bowed to acknowledge defeat. To plead mercy while I walk backwards in the direction of the gas station. The ram lowers its head, nodding to me. Then the shock like cold water, the animal smell, and the sandy pavement gritting against my head.

I never make it to the gas station. I spend my time bruising my ribs and coughing up dusty spit. A few times I'm sure my shirt is heavy with blood, but when I look down it is soaked clear. Dirt has changed into mud smears. Each time I stand, I wait for the ram to be satisfied or bored, and finally someone stops to help. A teenage girl in a pickup helps me to the passenger's side. She tells the ram to scat. She wears no bra and spits tobacco juice onto the ground.

For a moment I see her like my nurse. I fall in love with the bruise on her knee. My nose is inches from it, my ear to her crotch, and as she drives I clutch my body in order to hold it together. Sandy is her name and she looks down at me without expression. I wonder if beaten men often curl like puppies on her lap, and she brushes my hair away from the side of my face.

She says I've got something on my cheek and she rubs a wet thumb to wipe it away. She watches the road and I think about her tobacco spit, swaying in a glass jar at the base of the long stick shift.

Her brothers used to beat her up when she was younger and she knows how I feel. Once they chained her into a metal trashcan and rolled her off the hayloft. Another time they roped her down and made the cat lick food off her. That wasn't so bad, it even tickled, but afterward they always called her tuna delight.

I suddenly believe in internal bleeding and I think a faucet roars inside my stomach. I can die on Sandy's lap. In fact I would rather it, and she raises her miniature spittoon past my head. Spit echoes in the glass jar.

She says the most important thing is to stay awake so that I don't slip into a coma. She pokes her finger inside my ear once in a while to make sure I'm listening. Daddy will be at home watching the Price Is Right and he'll know what to do. Could be nothing but a few bruises, maybe a sprain. Sandy hopes she'll be able to keep me. She is seventeen and her hand rests against my cheek.

It feels like a toilet flushes inside my chest cavity, pours into my stomach.

Daddy sleeps on the couch so Sandy helps me up the stairs into a room. She opens a closet door and gingerly guides me down onto the musty mattress. Sandy thinks it's funny that I lie on the same mattress her brothers used that time with the cat. She kneels and tells me it will be okay. She kisses me on the lips until I fall asleep.

While I curl in the dark, the kissing continues in my dreams. I open my eyes and stand, brush myself off before stepping into the room. My chest aches but whatever had been sloshing around inside my body has either hardened or evaporated and I try to stretch.

Sandy sits cross-legged on her bed staring out the window. The thunder in the dark sky rumbles alone, not a drop off rain has fallen. I clear my throat. Sandy doesn't move so I go and sit on the edge of her bed.

She says, "I love the sound of thunder."

"We could use the rain," I say. It doesn't even smell like rain.

Her profile against the window startles me and tears collect in my eyes. My ribs feel tender, and suddenly I speak out loud without recognizing my own voice.

Sandy turns to me and says, "Don't ask if you don't mean it, Randy. Don't be such a little boy."

I wonder when she learned my name and slowly I remember that days have passed. I have eaten chicken soup. I think about the gas station and the ram. I kneel near the bed and grope in the dark until I find her cool hand. I remember the bruise on her knee.

"Will you marry me?" I hear myself ask again.

Sandy turns to me and her cheeks shine, polished. She says, "I chew tobacco and wear the same underwear for days."

"I chew gum scraped off the sidewalks," I say. "You must be the most beautiful creature on earth."

Now I sit on the bed, holding her hand in my lap while she stares out the window. The thunder continues like a bowling alley and I kiss each of her knuckles, one by one.

She says, "Yes." She closes her eyes, tilts her chin up. "We love each other. Don't we Randy?"

I say we do. I say it's one of those crazy things that happen. Fate. I remember the fluorescent green puddle under my old car, and the dust turning to mud on my shirt. The rain taps against the windowpane and we lie down and fall asleep on Sandy's bed.

Adjustments

My ex-roommate Jeremy should've been well tuned. He'd studied in Ireland for the year while I stayed on campus. He called me a few times and talked mainly about the fried egg sandwiches he ate and the French girl he met. I believed the part about the fried eggs.

He wasn't a liar by any measure, but something about the way he'd said *Europe* and *fine tuning himself* unnerved me a little. Before he left he'd wanted to be a junior high school teacher and kept greasy car parts in a cardboard box under his bed. He was 19 and liked the way the moonlight reflected off them at night. I had no idea why he wanted to go to Europe except, I guessed, to drink.

Since he'd been away, the house was full and Jeremy rented an apartment a few miles away. I guess he thought I would save him a space, but I said I couldn't get in touch with him when the lease needed to be signed. Maybe I was still a little angry at him for going off to Ireland, like he betrayed me or something. But he wouldn't even notice, Jeremy told me, because he'd probably end up hanging out in our house anyway. We'd have all the parties and he'd probably end up sleeping on the couch anyway.

Jeremy came back looking European. He had a reddish brown beard that hadn't been trimmed and frizzy red hair. He'd gained a few pounds and smoked nonstop. Jeremy showed up on campus the first day of classes with the visiting French girl on his arm. They both smelled very European, and seemed to enjoy nuzzling into each other's armpits. She didn't shave anywhere on her body, Jeremy told me, and he absolutely loved it.

At our first party, Jeremy spent the night sitting on the stained easy chair we'd recently found behind the gas station and when some girl asked about Ireland, he said that it had been incredible. She didn't know what to say to that so Jeremy raised his beer cup and said he really learned how to drink over there. The girl laughed and Jeremy drained his beer in a couple of swallows before excusing himself to the kitchen for a refill. Then back to the chair.

I walked upstairs and the French girl yelped when she saw me and threw her arm around my neck. She was drunk and remembered meeting me. I smelled her again and she followed me into the kitchen. I pumped the keg and watched foam fill my cup. She was happy she came to America for a visit, she shouted in my ear, and really happy that she had finally met me. Even her laughter had an accent. She'd heard so many things about me. I raised my eyebrows and nodded.

I lifted the cup to my mouth and sucked foam, watching her. Suddenly, she laughed and her hand swatted at my face, knocking the cup into the sink. Beer suds slid off my chin and when I tried to smile she stepped forward, pressed her thigh into my crotch, and kissed me. But not in any normal way. Instead I felt her teeth on my lips, almost gnawing. I tasted her beer breath and when her thigh began to insist even harder than her mouth and I finally pulled away and excused myself. I left down the back stairwell and stood alone in the backyard.

There were no stars that night. Only the sounds of traffic from the highway nearby, and music and laughter from the third floor.

Jeremy sat on the chair in my apartment after everyone had fallen asleep or left. Plastic cups and potato chip crumbs announced my footsteps. When he saw me, he looked down at his feet. And when he started, it sounded so loud that I was sure it was a joke, like play-acting. A wail so loud that it sounded like sarcasm, like he was mocking his own words. I'm so alone, so horribly alone type shit and for an instant I was glad. As if he realized that his fine-tuning experiment and precious French girlfriend had been a terrible mistake.

It's difficult to tell the truth in college. Maneuvering through the verbal mazes of meaning, attempting to appear nonchalant and above all, confident. So when a guy starts crying like that in front of you, so raw and blatant, I guess you kind of expect it to be a joke. Face buried in cupped hands, the sounds of sobbing. You can only believe it's real after you gradually get used to the sound. You obviously missed me too much, I wanted to say at first, this is what you get for leaving. But then you shuddered and began to rock back and forth in the chair.

After the second or third wail, your body vibrated so hard that I knelt in front of you because I believed that you might actually shake apart. Your beard looked worse, and your forehead creased and flushed and glistened. I reached around and put my palms on your back, and the shudders were real, the tears and snot and sweat were real too. So was the sound. Sobs coming up like belches onto my shoulder, and it wasn't funny at all. Not in the least bit.

I said it was okay, over and over and I meant that you could keep crying. I meant that I was not going to stop you, and that you shouldn't feel bad or embarrassed because it was okay. I inhaled through my mouth and knew that I was crying, that I was coming apart. I couldn't believe I almost laughed at you and I said I was sorry, again and again.

I patted your sweaty back as we calmed, rubbing it up and down, and I said I was glad you were back. You trembled like a colt. I am sorry, I whispered, and suddenly, I was being honest.

Morning Crew

On the morning of their last row, the four college boys grip the boat with straight arms above their heads and walk out of the boathouse. Coxswain's voice whispers in the dark and her breath disappears like cigarette smoke. Their socked feet patter down the ramp to the floating wooden dock. Tiny clouds of fog hover above the water and spread out to conceal the lake. One of the boys, the first in line, spits. To her count they roll the boat to their sides, and then lower it down into the water. One by one, they step in and sit down.

Coxswain grips the dock with her fingers to steady the boat. The air smells of wet wood, an under-layer of egg. Stroke used to dip his thumb in the water and pull it out, half-missing, dissolved by the polluted water. To make her laugh, he'd lower one finger and then the next, one by one, until he'd lost them all to the cesspool. Back when he was taking steps toward her, when each practice was an opportunity for him to increase his value.

The shoes wait, bolted to the footboard, curled in on themselves, damp and cool. The boys pry at the heels with their fingertips, rocking their ankles back and forth and tilting the boat with each motion. Finally, they settle onto the wooden slides and lock their oars into place. The lake ripples and then becomes the smoothest dark mirror.

"Push away," Coxswain commands.

Stroke reaches out; his massive hand grasps the corner of the dock and when he straightens his arm and locks his elbow, the boat stills, and time pauses. For a moment, nothing happens. In this micro-instant, Stroke's bronze arm halts the earth's rotation and fixes all of them in this boathouse scene. A sensation of permanence surrounds them, as if they are frozen in a photograph, being viewed by hundreds of invisible eyes.

Before Two's skinny white arm fully extends to help shove the boat away, before he can even begin to claw at the dock with his skeletal fingers, Stroke grunts once and sends them away, drifting sideways; the two oars on the starboard side scrape on top of the wood planks until they plunk into the water.

Coxswain tries to yell and whisper at the same time. She says, "Bowman and Three, arms only," and "ready y'all row."

The oars cut into the steaming water and they glide away from land. The night's stillness hasn't loosened.

In the center of the lake the fog thickens and the boys can't see.

"Way enough," Coxswain says.

The boat slows, and blades lift into the air, rotate, and spank down on the water's surface. The crew drifts to a stop and sits slack, backs curved. Coxswain takes off her winter hat and combs her white-blond hair with a small pink comb.

"Aw, you don't have to look pretty for me," Stroke says.   She tosses her hair back and does not look at him. Her legs look painted with black spandex and she stretches them out, resting her feet on Stroke's shoes.

"He'll probably call it off," Coxswain says. "I couldn't see an ocean liner coming at us."

A wisp of fog hides her face. She reappears, rouged high cheeks and dull blue eyes set close together.

The fog drifts in between the boys, covering their heads and rolling along their backs. They sit still.

Bowman slouches forward and closes his eyes. They will need to row even if practice is canceled. The rowing ritual defends against the black mornings which sometimes pour into Bowman like cooling steel, making his head too heavy to lift from his pillow. The leg muscle burn, the sticky, thirsty mouth that tastes like blood and lung, the sudden nausea and quick vomit over the side of the boat—each stage purging the magnet inside him that attracts the darkness.

Bowman tugs his red Santa hat over his ears and sleeps while he waits.

Three sits in front of Bowman, chin to his chest, eyes also closed, but he does not sleep. He listens and tries to identify every sound: the drip from a raised blade onto the surface of the lake, a rustle of nylon, Coxswain clearing her throat. This distracts him from the turbulence in his stomach; this task helps him ignore the stomach acid that burbles at the base of his throat. His breath and his life taste like tequila gone sour.

"Well," Two says. Two sits erect, both hands on his oar-handle and still, he cannot see past the broad wall of Stroke's back. He leans to the side to speak. "Maybe we should warm up," Two says. The boat tips. "Head toward the bridge."

"Maybe you should shut up about it and sit still," Stroke says, turning his head and speaking to the air next to him. "Or you'll fucking dump us."

"He'll probably cancel," Coxswain says. She pulls her knees up to her chest. She unlaces her running shoes and slides one off. "I'd probably run us straight into someone's living room." She peels away her white sock and rubs the bottom of her foot. "Speaking of— try to keep your voices down." She holds up her hand and cocks her head. "Did you hear that?"

No sound except breathing from the bow.

Coxswain takes a small red jar from her coat pocket and shakes it. She wedges her heel in place, flexes her toes, and dabs red paint onto a toenail.

Stroke could cover her foot with one hand. Her feet make him think of skinned rabbits; they are as smooth and white as bone. So small and perfectly shaped and Stroke maneuvers an elbow to adjust his crotch.

Stroke worries that the bulge signals a lack of concentration, a failure of leadership. The coach is always saying, 'Keep your heads in the boat.' But with Coxswain facing him, sitting in full body spandex, knees bent and parted enough to glimpse the cleft in her crotch, Stroke thinks mainly about the head in between his legs, moving from under the waistband of his boxers and pointing like an arrow at his stomach. Coxswain flexes her bare feet, the tip of her tongue pressed between her lips.

"Give me a fuckin' break with this," Stroke says. "No curling iron?"

Two leans farther, the boat tilts more, but Stroke says nothing. After a while two says, "It must be excellent to paint your nails. To have that as something to look forward to. Especially bright red."

Coxswain finishes one foot and starts the other. The paint looks moist and fresh. It makes two hungry and he leans to get a better look.

"Jesus back there. Keep your pants on, she's not going anywhere." Stroke jerks his body to level the boat. He doesn't even turn his head to speak; he just says the words while glaring at the top of Coxswain's bent head. Like he's trying to drill a hole through her skull.

Coxswain does not look up from her task.

Stroke remembers peeling the clothes from her drunken body and spreading her out like a buffet, on a toilet. This is not the thinking that will get his pecker in line, so he tries to blur his mind, tries to drift away from his insistent erection. He wonders what he still wants from her. What else is there to get? But the thoughts are too wispy, too much like the fog moving past his face. Maybe getting isn't possible. What if there is nothing to get? But there is, there must be. He could start, he thinks, by biting her foot.

Three says, "Oh God," and no one responds. Head still bowed, eyes still shut, he tries to stretch his leg muscles. Not just practice, he thinks, someone should cancel the whole day.

Later, when his body is saturated with post-practice lethargy, when he's moving through the day with a dream-like detachment, he'll have to face the red-haired girl who left his room last night without even a kiss. He'll have to look into the eyes of this girl who refused to believe his sincerity, who denied his declaration of love because he was drunk.

He should insist on the truth of what he said, he should grasp her shoulders and explain that he is in love with her, but that he is afraid of being disillusioned, of learning the difference between the real her and the idea of her that he has constructed in his head. She will fail him, he'll explain, but she is not to blame—it is his fault for making up such an impossible and extravagant character in his own head. An ideal that no human could ever compete with.

And instead, Three will make some joke about being drunk, as if everything he said was part of a good natured, friendly, not-so-subtle plea to get laid. Is it possible to be drunk and sincere? Of course not, he will say, the context of any love declaration is more important than the actual words. Saying the words is easy, meaningless—it's when and where you say the words, the surrounding conditions that give the words their true meaning. Who doesn't know this? And the two of them, still very good friends, will laugh it off. Three will apologize again and again, and continue to develop the character of the red-haired girl that lives in his head.

Three's stomach sours and he hangs his head. The longing hurts him square behind the eyes and he prays for universal cancellation.

Two asks, "Why do we do this?"

Coxswain looks up to see Stroke elbowing his crotch. She remembers the taste of a party—a party flavored with too-sweet fruit punch and too-strong cherry vodka, where Stroke's saliva dried on her neck and something warm dried on her bare belly.

And throwing up, for the first time in her life, without experiencing any of the usual relief. Her stomach paused on 'purge' and no amount of retching could reset her body. She remembers the security guard, with his black leather belt and flashlight, crouching, warm hand on her bare shoulder, gently waking her to the smell of sick and the downstairs bathroom stall. Still naked.

"Because we need friends, we have no life," Stroke says and laughs. "What the hell kind of question is that?"

Two says, "We never win. We never will."   "I do it to stay in shape," Coxswain says and Stroke looks over her breasts for the millionth time. Restrained and outlined in black. She never sweats at practice on the water, but always at the gym with the guys in a sport's bra and naked shiny back.

Two continues, "We get up in the middle of the night to row back and forth, trying not to freeze and hoping to click on ten or fifteen solid strokes. Then we sleepwalk through the rest of our day. I don't know."

Coxswain lowers her voice to imitate the coach, "To pull our balls off."

Stroke says, "And if you're not into it there are at least three guys who'll take your place."

Coxswain twists the cap onto her jar and puts it into her pocket. She blows on her toes with a rounded mouth. Flecks of lipstick have fallen away like paint chips.

"I'm talking about when this is all over," Two states. "When we're sitting around somewhere, far away from each other. After this day has blurred into a hundred others, and we're wondering what the hell we were trying to do all that time on that lake. "

"In the fog," Three mumbles.

As if on cue, the fog seems to thicken and hides one person from the other. Each person sits alone, inside their own Styrofoam cooler, packed with dry ice.

"Sometimes it doesn't add up to much," Two says to himself.

Their legs feel weak and bruised. The boat drifts in the water and the lightest rain begins, misting down on the five, partially hidden, motionless figures. Coxswain stops them. They've drifted under the bridge. The relative quiet is broken by the sounds of a single car, as it moves across the asphalt far above their heads.

"It's a waste of time." Bowman's loud voice echoes.

"That's not what I mean," Two begins, but Bowman talks over him.

"Trying to add it up," he says. In a pinched and nerdy voice Bowman says, 'Let's see, the boat plus the water plus the fog, divided by the cold and night equals aerobic fitness plus thigh muscles....'"

"Plus vomit," Three says.

"Plus a raging hard-on," Stroke says and grunts at his own comment.

"I'm just saying," Two begins.

"I'll tell you why," Bowman says. "I'll explain the point of it all, the purpose of our self-inflicted toil."

As they wait, it's as if a plug has been pulled and the crew's collective sluggishness drains away. The hum of blood moves through ear canals. Sweat rises on upper lips, pumping hearts begins to jog. By the time Bowman speaks again, it feels as though hours have passed.

"We're in charge of the dawn," he says, barely jostling the boat as he ties his feet into the shoes. "We pull the sun into the sky and without us..." Bowman leaves the rest unspoken while the others set themselves in place.

Coxswain gives a command and three oars cut into the water, turn the boat and pause, holding the boat still.

After slipping on her shoes and tucking her legs back into her space, Coxswain turns to look into the fog bank they were about to enter.

The boys grip their oars and slide forward until their butts almost touch their heels.

Coxswain holds up her hand and cocks her head.

One by one, each boy turns his head and stares at the wall of white fog. Visibility matters very little to the boys; even on the clearest, sunniest day, they can't see the finish line. They might glimpse the land that streaks along the side of the boat, growing ever smaller as it moves toward the horizon's vanishing point. The boys do not steer; they do not aim themselves in any direction or know exactly how much longer they'll have to pull before it's over. They are the engine, and Coxswain controls the throttle while she drives. This morning, they know that she can't see any better than they can.

Everyone listens for the sound of the coach's launch or any noise from the direction of the parking, but they hear nothing.

When it comes, Coxswain's shout echoes like a gunshot under the bridge. She yells, "Ready y'all—"The last word stops, poised on the edge of a cliff, leaning toward the drop...

The boys wait, stretched forward, hands wrapped around their oars, muscles compressed like coiled springs.

"Row!" The volume and the sound of the single word booms like thunder.

For an instant, the power of the first pull lifts the front of the boat up and out of the water, and the stern pierces into the bank of fog. The sensation is of skimming above the water, gliding on a cushion of air.

Coxswain barks out commands and the boys rip their oars through the water, their muscles speeding toward burn, each boy trying to feel their way into a rhythm, into the groove that will transform their single pull into a force that changes night into day.

Legs slam down, backs hinge, arms pull and the boys send themselves backward, faster and faster, toward an end they cannot see.

Coxswain screams, "Come on you guys, I want ten right now, ten at full power—One!"

The pitch of her voice rises with the stroke count; each number demands more from the boys, forcing their taps deeper and deeper toward the glowing, burning, fire at their inner core.

The boys hear no words, only the insistent, urgent tone of Coxswain's shrieks. With fibers tearing deep in their muscles the boys rocket through the water, pulling sunlight into the fog around them and moving farther and farther away.

The last thread of caution, of hesitation, that separates each rower begins to disintegrate and one by one each boy vanishes into movement.

Clicked into the power of their synchronized rhythm, the crew flies away.

Morning.

The Babysitter

When Travis saw the girl sitting at one of the round two-person coffeehouse tables, she was bent over an open trail map with a green pen in one hand. Early twenties, blond curly hair down to the middle of her back, a mountain girl with bare arms and legs, all tan. Up until the accident, and even a little while after, Travis had often fantasized about having sex with the girl's mother, Ellen. But the brief memory of lying on Ellen's bed, his head sunk deep into her pillow, draping a pair of Ellen's lace-fringed panties across his face was too quickly pushed out of Travis' head by the name Christopher, the girl's younger brother.

The memory of the red silk on his bare stomach and thighs corkscrewed into the memory of a four year-old Christopher standing on the top step of the big kid's slide, maybe twenty feet high. His forehead covered by blond curls, eyes wide and empty. He looks at Travis, releases his grip on the thin metal banisters and falls backward.

During the moment without sound, Christopher's head bounces off a metal step; his legs flip over like a ventriloquist's dummy, and he lands on the asphalt below with the thud of a stuffed duffle bag.

Travis moved his tongue around his mouth and sucked air through rounded lips to judge the aroma of his breath. He started walking toward the girl before he'd remembered her name. It would come to him.

He wondered how to play this one; he continued his casual stride, moving toward the girl as if they were scheduled to meet.

This seat taken?" Travis asked before he looked to see that there was no chair on the opposite side of the small table.

The girl looked up; her face was as tan as the rest of her, blond curls tucked behind her ears. A little too thin, but rugged, with long bicep muscles, her calf was flexed above her one foot which was poised to run.

"Not much table space," she said without sarcasm, nodding to her map.

"Enough for me," Travis said and he pulled an empty chair from a nearby table and sat down.

She looked at him for a moment without any hint of a smile before returning her eyes and her green pen to the map.

Planning an escape?" Travis asked.

"I work for the park service," she said. She continued scanning the map, making a checkmark in one spot, an X in another.

"My name is Travis Adler," he said. He sat back, expecting her to look up, wide-eyed, maybe a quick intake of breath, a huge bright smile and perhaps even a laugh. She would say, 'I don't believe it,' or something like that.

"Laurie Shutter," the girl said without looking up.

Laurie. Travis wanted to suggest that she might remember him, might recognize his name if she thought about it. But maybe she wouldn't, and what about that? It all depended on how he should play it. Would it be in his best interest to keep quiet, maybe let her figure it out? That always made girls feel good.

"I'm a kitchen manager," Travis said. "A chef."

"Oh," she said.

"At La Roma, down the street," Travis said. Laurie looked up, but her eyes darted around the room, barely glancing at Travis. She had her mother's small nose and her bottom lip was fuller that the other. "Would you like to get coffee sometime?"

She stared at the limp brown teabag on her saucer. "I'd take a re-fill," she said.

Travis stood; he picked up her silver hot water pot and paused.

"Mandarin orange," she said, circling something on the map.

Travis went to the counter for a refill of hot water, a new tea bag, and a cup of coffee for himself. He would tell her. He would say, 'I guess you don't remember me, but it was so long ago. For two years, I babysat for you and your brother. You were five and your brother was two when I started. He wore cloth diapers.' He returned to the table.

"I've never been to the top of Bear Mountain," Travis said, setting down the hot-water pot and leaning to look at her map before sitting down. It was a tough call. She might like his care-giving qualities, but going out with her ex-babysitter might creep her out. Too soon to tell.

"You hike?" she asked. She glanced up at him.

"Of course," he said. "I'm pretty sure it's a crime if you live here and don't hike or ski or something."

She nodded, poured hot water into her cup, and lowered the teabag until it sunk below the surface. "Something," she said.

"I'll bet you know the best trails," Travis said. "The ones that no one else would be able to find."

Laurie looked up again and stared at him. Travis prepared himself for the moment; he scanned her face for a hint of the revelation, beginning with the spark in her eyes and flooding into the muscles in her face.

"Maybe one or two," she said. "The hard-core hikers have pretty much found them all. They're like animals." She smiled, cupping her tea mug in both hands and blowing on it through rounded lips.

"That's what gets me," Travis said, having located a vein. "It's supposed to be such a peaceful and serene experience. Hiking through the wilderness, getting away from humanity, but every time I go I run into dozens of people, jogging, walking their dogs, talking on their phones. Like it's becoming impossible to get away."

Laurie stared harder at Travis, and he saw the look of recognition. "It's true; I know exactly what you mean. Sometimes I feel like I'm waiting in line or walking through the mall."

Travis laughed and nodded. He raised the cup to his lips and sipped coffee. "You should take me," he said. "The next time you go on one of your secret hikes. I promise not to tell anyone."

She lowered her head, and looked at the trail map with renewed concentration. Her cheeks blushed. "Actually, I was thinking of going this Saturday, if the weather is any good."

"Is that an invitation?" Travis asked. He was sitting back in his chair with a good natured smile on his lips.

Laurie's body stiffened. She started to fold the map.

"I guess that would kind of defeat the whole solitude purpose," Travis said. "I didn't mean to invite myself, believe me, I can completely understand. Maybe some other time."

She slid the map and the pen into an army green backpack on the floor next to her chair. "I usually stop here for coffee first, around seven," she said, pushing the words out of her mouth.

"I'll see you then," Travis said.

She stood, giving him one brief shy glance, and walked toward the front of the coffeehouse and out the door.

A week after the accident, Ellen called Travis and asked him to come over. She said that she'd been worried about him and she wanted to see how he was doing. He shouldn't feel too badly about what had happened to Christopher. Accidents happened. Her nose was stuffed up.

"It'll do us both good," she said on the telephone. "I've got something you can help me with for a class I'm taking."

Travis was curious to see what Christopher looked like, and to ask how Laurie was. He couldn't remember seeing her that day, even though he was one hundred percent sure that she had been standing right next to him watching her brother climb to the top.

The slide from which Christopher had fallen was located behind the tennis courts at the far corner of the park, away from the main playground. It was the last piece of equipment left over from a school that had been torn down and because it stood on pavement or because it was old or because it was twenty feet high, the city had created a perimeter of sawhorses around the slide to indicate that the slide was off limits. A piece of yellow plastic police tape printed with DO NOT CROSS was wrapped around the slide itself. A parent had painted UNSAFE in red on a piece of plywood and nailed it to one of the sawhorses. Kids routinely ducked under or leapt over the barrier.

After the fall, Travis was sucked into a hurricane of parents running to call for help, a tennis player asking for his name, two policemen in dark blue uniforms, other children shouting, Ellen crying and patting Travis on the head while she told him not to worry, that everything was going to be okay, Ellen climbing into the back of an ambulance, sirens ripping the air apart.

Travis arrived at the Shutter's front door. He tightened his grip on the small brown bear; the animal wore a tiny white tee-shirt that said GET WELL. He raised his other fist and knocked on the door.

At first Travis thought that Ellen was sick. She answered the door wearing a stained white tank-top without a bra and a pair of torn gray sweatpants. Her feet were bare. The skin around her eyes and under her nose were red and the warm and humid smell of wet socks and illness enveloped Travis as he stepped into the house and closed the door behind him.

"How's Christopher?" Travis asked.

"Sorry for the mess," Ellen said and her voice sounded hoarse, her nose stuffed; she turned and walked up the small staircase and into the living room.

Travis stared at the wiry black hair growing out of the large red mole on the band of exposed flesh above the waistline of her sweatpants. Her hindquarters moved, the large muscles barely flexing as she took her last step.

Children's books were strewn on the green carpet like multi-colored tiles. Stuffed animals, and wooden blocks dotted the landscape, and Travis tried to casually brush them aside with his foot as he followed Ellen into the kitchen. When Travis sat down at the kitchen table he realized that Ellen had been crying. The sink was stuffed with plates featuring smears of dried ketchup, a bowl balanced in a ceramic crevice with milk and soggy cereal floating at the bottom. Nothing felt right, and Travis listened, but as far as he could tell, they were alone in the house.

"I brought him this," Travis said placing the bear on the table.

"He's back in the hospital," Ellen said. "There's some trouble with his circulation. I'm sure he'll be fine." She smiled and looked insane.

Ellen poured them each a glass of apple juice that turned out to be iced tea in an old apple juice glass container. She set the glasses down on the table and said, "I'll be right back." She touched his shoulder when she said this.

She returned carrying an old army green backpack. Travis could see her breasts when she bent over and unzipped the pack, retrieving a notebook and a pen. But the image, along with her sniffles and the strands of hair that stuck out like straw, caused him to suddenly think of Ellen as a wounded animal.

Ellen blew her nose and retrieved a purple cloth bag from her backpack. She flashed him a dead smile, an expressionless, mechanical twitch of her facial muscles and reached up to pull on an old fan in the center of the ceiling. Her forehead shone with sweat, and her armpits were shadowed with stubble.

Travis's attention shifted to the purple cloth bag; he'd seen it before, in the bottom drawer of Ellen's dresser, toward the back, next to several unopened plastic eggs filled with pantyhose.

Ellen opened up her notebook, uncapped her pen and asked Travis, "Where do you put your problems?"

"Excuse me?" Travis said.

"When something bad happens, or you feel angry, or hurt. Where does the pain go, where do you put it?"

"Nowhere," Travis said.

"I want you to think now Travis. It has to go somewhere; what happens to it?"

"It just goes away; I forget about it or start thinking about something else."

"What do you think about? Now be honest."

"Sex," Travis said. He didn't blush or look away.

"You mean that you fantasize about it?"

"It distracts me," Travis said. "After Christopher fell I spent two days in my room, going through all different scenarios?"

"Yes, well—so you never deal with the sadness or the guilt? Would you say that you keep them hidden inside?"

"I guess," Travis said.

Ellen shook her head and wrote in her notebook; then she looked at Travis with an expression that was probably trying to communicate understanding, but that looked much more like a wince. Ellen reached her free had into the purple bag and took out one of the smooth stones. Travis knew that all of them were smooth and gray and tinged with pink.

"That's very unhealthy," she said. "Very dangerous. If you continue to distract yourself with images of sex instead of dealing with the real issues, it could create problems for you later in life. You might subconsciously connect sex with guilt or anger or shame and it could ruin your sex life forever. I'm sure you wouldn't want that."

Travis shook his head.

"One trick I like to use is to take a stone, like this one, grip it tight in my hand and sit quietly in my room for a few minutes. Then I direct all of the negative energy into the stone, I command it to flow out from the surface of my skin and into the minerals of the earth."

Travis could smell the tang of her sweat.

"And when I'm done, after I've completed a few rocks, I gather them up and I take them into the mountains and bury them, so that the guilt and the anger can't harm me anymore; I've expelled them from my body. Do you understand what I'm saying?"

Travis nodded because he knew that it was the obvious answer.

But he also knew that Ellen truly believed in this rock therapy. While the condoms in the bottom drawer of her husband's bedside table and the spermicidal jelly in Ellen's top left drawer had remained virtually untouched over the past two years, Travis had noticed that the number of rocks in the bag would vary. At time, it was extremely full, and then probably after Ellen had buried them all, the bag would be empty again.

"Do you think you could try this technique for me, and tell me if it works for you?" Ellen asked. "Children often have a difficult time with complex emotions like guilt or shame. I think this really might work for people your age, and even younger. Laurie's just started and she's only seven."

Travis nodded like it made perfect sense, even raising his eyebrows to communicate that he was impressed.

"All I want you to do is try it, and then write down the experience in a notebook. Describe what your feeling before, during and after you've transferred the negative energy into the stone. And don't forget to write about burying the stone, how it affects the way you think about the guilt or the shame. Will you do this for me?"

Travis said that he would and Ellen gave him three 'fresh' stones to start with.

He would kiss Allie whenever they got to wherever they were going, and then he would probably press himself against her body, pull her toward him, and maybe they would proceed. Up against one of these pine trees or maybe she was taking him to some sort of clearing or cave; it was secluded, he knew that much.

'I used to give you and your brother baths,' Travis could have said. 'You used to make beards out of the bubbles.' Bubbles which were illegal. The Shutters did not approve of bubbles so Travis had to use squirts from the organic orange scented dishwashing liquid.

Allie broke off from the trail and bounded up the steep slope, grabbing at the trunks of pine trees to help propel her up. Her old fashioned hiking boots with red laces, left waffle patterns in the rich black dirt until she'd arrived at the trail above.

"You coming?" she asked. She wore a gray sports bra under her white tee-shirt and tan shorts. Her curly hair was pulled back from her sun-darkened face in a ponytail, and she pulled the water bottle from her waist-pack and squirted a stream into her mouth. Same lips, and her chest barely rose and fell from her detour; she was in good shape. A small trickle of blood had dried on one of her shins.

"There's a reason that they maintain these trails," Travis said. "You should know better." He continued to walk up the moderate incline of the switchback trail until it turned and he walked up behind Allie.

She yawned dramatically, bent to pick up a long stick and held it out to him. "Maybe this will help."

Travis took the stick and Allie started walking on the trail again. Travis was breathing heavily and he followed, using the walking stick.

"That causes erosion," Travis said, nodding to the place where Allie had scrambled up. He hadn't had enough time to catch his breath. He checked his watch. They'd been on the trail for forty-five minutes.

He trudged ahead, and that was definitely the right word, or marched, yes, he marched forward. Step after step, his thoughts conforming to the rhythm of his steps; it was impossible to think wide and blurry ideas while he walked up a dirt trail.

Allie broke off again and scrambled to the next level, even laughing while she went. Even saying, "Come on old man."

But instead his mind, attached to his physical movements went methodically, step by step. First a kiss, then his hand moving up her sweaty belly and onto her breast, squeezing it, fingering the nipple. And then another date, and a date after that, and a weekend at a bed and breakfast somewhere in the mountains. The time for revelation had passed. He didn't need to talk about the babysitting; he didn't need to bring up the baths he gave them, her naked body, her brother spitting water like a fountain.

"Are you coming?" she asked.

An irrational and masculine desire to prove something propelled Travis off of the path and onto the steep slope. His feet could not hold and instead, pushed the rich dirt as he slid back down onto the path. He re-doubled his walk and turned the corner and walked up behind Allie, who was not squirting water into her mouth.

"I guess I just don't have what it takes," he said.

"I guess not," she said and she started walking again.

"Are we far?" he asked.

"A little while longer," she said. The tone of her voice struck Travis as very solemn and even a little sad, as if she'd just remembered something she had to do later, something unpleasant.

The Shutters did not own a television so Travis used to make up games to play, like shark-attack. This involved the two kids trying to run from one end of the room and hop up onto the couch before the shark, Travis lying on the carpet, grabbed them and took them down in a fit of tickling and gobbling sounds. He had always let Christopher get to the couch until one day when Allie said, "It's not fair that he never gets caught." So on the next run Travis grabbed Christopher and pulled him to the ground and his head accidentally knocked on a wooden block and he began to cry.

Allie did not leave the trail for the next twenty minutes. Travis followed, feeling his lungs burning, and he was trying to decide how much damage to the potential relationship would occur if he told her that he had to turn back. Then Allie shouted, "Follow me," and she broke from the path up the side of the mountain, but she did not arrive at the trail above. Instead she was running on the slope, farther and farther into the trees until Travis lost sight of her.

So he did the same, struggling to keep his balance on the slope, his feet sliding in the dirt, soil spraying against his shin and falling into his sock. He saw her legs at last, her head pumping up and down. She was slowing down. They had left the trail far behind and Travis began to walk, breathing heavily, using the trees as handholds to pull himself forward.

There was no path and Travis had to stop a few times and listen in order to locate Allie. After about fifteen minutes of barging through the forest, Travis walked into a small clearing. Allie had stopped at the entrance to a small cave and was sitting down on a boulder under a tree.

Travis sat cross-legged on the dirt, and took a long drink from his water bottle. "It's beautiful here," Travis said. He wanted a cigarette.

"My mother used to bring me here; I think it was sort of like her special place," Allie said.

"Does your mother live near you?" Travis asked. He'd walled off the possibility of revealing himself to her. From now on, he would just be some guy that Allie met; they would get to know each other; maybe she would turn out to be the one.

"She died when I was little," Allie said. And then she added, in that false upbeat tone of someone who has practiced talking out loud about a tragic event, "She killed herself when I was eight."

Travis could not breathe. Steam rose from inside his neck and up into his head. He cleared his throat.

Allie took out a couple of stones from her waist-pack and held them in her hands. She sighed. "We should probably get moving if we want to get back for dinner. And that is an invitation," she said, smiling. Then she stood and walked around the side of the cave. Travis rose; his legs felt like pudding.

He walked around the cave and up to Allie who stood on the edge of an enormous pit, a crater that was easily twenty feet across. He wanted to put his hand on Allie's shoulder, but could not make himself do it. When she tossed the stones into the pit, Travis shifted his attention. That was when he saw that the pit was filled to the edge with small smooth stones.

"It's stupid," she said nodding at the pit, "Just something my mom taught me about."

"Are all of those yours?" Travis managed to ask. His voice startled him and made him realize how much noise was going on inside his head.

She looked at him with a strange expression and nodded, "Yes," she said slowly. "They're all mine." She did not move her eyes away, but stared even more intensely at Travis who could not move. His stomach ached and he almost fell onto his knees. The look of recognition finally arrived, but it was not followed by a laugh or an expression of surprise. Instead, anger burned in her gray eyes, her lips clenched shut.

Without saying a word, she turned around and ran through the trees until she disappeared. Travis did not follow.

Volley

You are a female honey, a hottie, and when you're pointed out to me I almost faint. I inadvertently grab my friend's arm, a reaction which he probably construes as a clear indication of my latent heterosexuality. I let go and he stands with his question hanging in the air, arms crossed across his chest, challenging me. We see you at the bus-stop, your skateboard in hand, tanning your face with your eyes closed. It's probably only an offhand comment, an investigation to see how I'll react, but I take it as a dare. A dare because I know you, and we've done this before.

So my friend points you out, not knowing that we have met (the beauty of it!), and asks something like, "So you'd enjoy kissing her body," or something like, "Would it excite you to touch her?" Testing me. And so now, you sweet thing, you've become part of a gay man's dare, how poetic, how delicious and I walk up behind you.

A hand covers your eyes, tilts your head back. Perhaps you see cracks of blue sky beyond the shadows of my fingers and your body freezes still. You can probably tell that it's a man's hand, a young hand. I gently squeeze the back of your head like a volleyball, and you allow yourself to be turned. You close your eyes and brush your eyelashes against my skin. My hand swivels to keep your eyes covered and when you stop turning you smile and your mind must rotate for guesses that never come. You say nothing. You seem to have no idea.

You part your lips to speak and something touches them. Fingers, you think for an instant. But no, lips press against yours, a warm mouth with wintergreen breath and a flittering tongue. The tongue slides one final time between your teeth and then you are released. You probably could've bitten down. You might wonder if I tasted your stomach acid, or the remnants of your lunch.

Instant brightness, like staring into the sun and my grinning face comes into focus. You smile and step back.

You turn bright red and say, "You scared me half to death." You look embarrassed, almost pained beyond articulation as your eyes size me up and down. A tall man, thin, with parted brown hair. Fortunately I am clean shaven with white teeth. My dark green windbreaker hangs over a red flannel shirt buttoned to the top. I lick my lips, swallow. Still you look confused.

I ask, "Don't you remember?" You smile harder now and nod. Perhaps the sound of my voice helps. Yes, yes, your face awakens, your eyes say of course and I say, "It's me Randy!"

You remember Saturday afternoon volleyball inside a new Catholic gym that smelled like rubber cement and echoed with streaking shoes. You sat against the wall, knees up, wearing short shorts and revealing your bare legs. Your friends sat next to you and leaned toward you because you were their center of gravity, their star. You smiled at me and pretended to stretch, arching your back and pushing your chest forward. Your breasts were large then, especially for a 16 year-old.

I was not the star of the volleyball team or any team. I have always thrown like a girl and the word around school was (Homo) that there was good reason for it. But in the Catholic Youth league everyone must play. Perhaps you were staring at me because of the way I ran around the court, the way I tossed my head, also like a girl.

You sat with your brown hair tied in a ponytail. I had played the last game next to you and decided that the sweat from behind your neck smelled like an onion. You had bent over to tie your shoe and I stood over you with my legs spread trying to be funny, trying to scare you when you looked up. But you stood up without looking and knocked your head into my crotch. My face broke a sweat and nausea grooved through my body.

You apologized and rubbed the back of your head like you'd bumped into a shelf. You giggled a little, and so did your girlfriends on the sidelines, and I stood bent at the waist, hands on knees, and then you pressed your face closer, kissed my cheek. That was when I thought you smelled like a sweet onion.

From the opposite court, your boyfriend smiled at me, at the situation. A boyfriend who moved like a golden retriever, with wavy blond hair and a tan face. A bona-fide superstar. Formidable biceps for being 16, and the star of every team in the city. I glanced at him and he smiled in a friendly way, a sympathetic way, his soft movie star face pausing on me in my wilted condition before he palmed the volleyball and re-focused on the game. It was the same look I'd gotten from him once before after someone had pissed on my locker and threw my combination lock in the toilet. But he was always above that, always moving through the school or across the playground with his own entourage surrounding him, a group that now included you as his queen.

Your breasts still seem much too large for your body, and you are tan with brown hair still pulled into a pony tail.

"God it's been forever," you say smiling. "How are you? Are you in school?" You look for the bus to come up the street.

"I'm a painter," I say

Your empty stare. "Wow, an artist. I can totally see that." You hug books to your chest with one hand and glance at your feet. "That's great."

You remember after that volleyball game, after I had caught my breath, you sat against the wall smiling at me and talking to your girlfriends. They giggled, looked at me, and giggled some more. Then your boyfriend came over and crouched down so you could whisper in his ear. He turned, looked at me and smiled. Then he took keys out of the pocket of his jacket on the floor and tossed them to you. The girlfriends scattered and re-grouped in another section of the gym, pretending not to watch the dare go down.

You stood and walked over to where I sat on the ground against the wall. You reached out your hand and pulled me up. I saw your boyfriend smile again as he shot a volleyball through a basketball hoop and we walked out the green doors underneath the four EXIT signs that were never lit.

You drove for ten minutes to a deserted elementary school and parked the car that smelled like your boyfriend. Bucket seats in the front with a stick shift between us. The knob on the stick-shift was expertly wrapped with black electrical tape. We sat quietly until you said, "This looks good." We still hadn't touched and we got out of the car.

The only place that made any sense was the side entrance to the school covered by a flat concrete roof across the playground. You brushed small pink pebbles and sand off the sidewalk with your foot and sat down. A tiny rock had made its way into my shoe so I took them off and stuffed them with my socks.

We sat cross-legged next to each other and then you asked, "Can I kiss you?"

"You have to ask?" It was all I could think to say. I must have decided that if this was going to be a game, then I would try and win.

For a moment I thought about the kissing games at playgrounds like this one. How the girls used to chase us and tag us and bring us back to the cave. We were given a choice then, either ten kisses on the cheek or one on the mouth. The one time I chose the mouth, the little girl refused and said that she already had a stomach ache from playing the game too long. Ten pecks and it was over.

We kissed ourselves onto the ground, squirming on our sides trying to get comfortable. We wore tee-shirts and shorts and our hips pressed into the concrete. When you moved your hands underneath my shirt and across my chest I guessed it was time to move on, and I peeled up your shirt and bra.

I licked and sucked and when I bit too hard you said, "They're not water balloons." You laughed and kissed me again and then started to slap your hand against my crotch. You would rub once and then slap your hand into me like you were killing a bug. I noticed a small hair around your nipple and nudged your head toward my crotch.

"Nope," you said. "I don't do that," which was fine by me since all I really needed was for you to stop smacking me. But once you said that, like it was some policy you had devised, something your vast experience had taught you, I knew at once I was somehow losing. You were on top of me and I would never have done any of this if it hadn't been for you. So I pushed my hand up your thigh and peeled away your underwear with two fingers.

You say that you're having a party this Friday and that I should stop by and we could catch up.

I'm trying (and failing) to get something from you, a reaction perhaps. Some indication that you remember what happened, how you once acted toward me, how everyone acted back then. But you just smile, mostly disinterested in me, mostly waiting for the bus.

I promise to go to the party, but do not ask for your address. I begin to feel foolish and to wish that I had never seen you standing here. I think it would be better if I never saw you again.

The bus arrives. "Good seeing you again," you say and you lean over and kiss my cheek before stepping through the door.

I have not moved.

My elbows and knees ached, pebbles grooved into my calves like glass shards. I knew your heavy breaths placed us at a certain level as far as health class was concerned. It meant that you'd reached the danger level. The electric level where, in an instant, we might somehow do the regrettable, the obvious, the normal human deed. Most of all, it meant I was winning.

I worked my fingers as fast and smooth as I could, feeling the raging discomfort of my position. Your body pressed my back to the ground and your kisses drove my head into the gritty cement. My legs felt like they might separate at the waist, but I would not give up first. I focused on the rhythm of your breaths while my hand worked and I smelled sweet onion from behind your neck. Finally, thankfully, you stopped and rolled away.

"I think we should take a break," you said, as if we might have been on the verge. I sat up and arched my back. Scratches burned my skin and bones ached. Our legs were covered with pock marks, and pebbles remained impressed into them. You pointed to my heel dripping blood onto the cement.

You said, "I hope it was worth that."

I said it was, but what else could I say?

In the bathroom, before the next volleyball game, I scrubbed my hands until they were bloated and red like blisters. Until they smelled like hot water. I wanted everyone to disappear, no one to see me.

You drank a soda from your seat on the floor. Your boyfriend sat next to you and your girlfriends leaned toward you like a huddle. You said a word, maybe a few, and they tossed their heads back and laughed, they slapped the palm of your hand as if you had made a great play. Your boyfriend didn't even look at me and you winked, smiling at me from behind your soda can.

Obviously I had lost.

After the bus motors away, I see that my friend has disappeared from across the street. It seems I have lost again. I have no idea where you live, but I can still taste your mouth as I begin to walk. Apparently I was mistaken: it's impossible to even the score of a game that has been finished for so long.

A Mother's Quiet

Her baby had to do with a clear day in October. Sandra stood on a football field in her thrift-store jersey with a red number 13 printed on the front. Bright yellow leaves with blood orange tips hung in the trees along the sideline, and she played touch football in jeans with two ripped knees. Back then, her brown hair was just long enough to chew on in the huddle, and she warmed her palms against her thighs.

The group of them laughed and ran and slapped hands, cracked smiles. She was drawn to a certain man's voice, attracted by the way he moved across the field, like a dancer. His blond hair tied back in a ponytail.

Sandra sensed her muscles that day, as she sprinted down the sidelines and cut across the field. She had absolute control over her moves. Like when she was a little girl playing after dinner, running through the woods by her house. Over logs, under tree branches and through bushes, always with the sense of someone gaining on her, someone on the verge of clutching her shoulder. But Sandra had always escaped with the best moves, tumbling and twisting away on her belly. She jumped and caught the football with two hands in the air and the blond wrapped his arms around her waist, held her high.

Then the hugging and the smell of grass stains, of sweat. Everyone's skin blushed as beautiful as she'd ever seen, all of them glowing healthy and raw. They were off to drink and toast to the highlights. The blond pressed his knee against hers under the table. As close to a beer commercial, she told the blond, as close as she'd ever been.

Later that night, she pulled the blonde's apartment door closed and stepped onto the sidewalk. She wrapped the fuzzy pink scarf around her neck and felt as though she fit into her skin. She walked home and stretched her body to smooth out the wrinkles, feeling herself settle all the way to her fingertips. She laughed and remembered when he said something like, "You were real fresh out there today kiddo, real fresh."

Eventually, Sandra sat on the toilet in her bathroom and cried into her fist. Careful not to be too loud because the sounds she made would probably scare her, but her extreme control made her entire body shudder and convulse. A coffee mug of urine with a pregnancy stick that showed baby sat in the sink. Another stick had already been thrown into the bathtub for showing the same thing. Too many tears and after a while she could not see. She was thirsty, but did not dare move. Maybe it would disappear and as she trembled on the toilet, Sandra was forced to breathe through her mouth.

The nurse began the process. The same nurse who visited two days after the hospital sent Sandra home, and who started by weighing the baby and asking about cigarettes and beer. Then she talked about breast feeding and eventually alluded to the man. The nurse referred to him as the donor and wrapped the black cuff tight around the mother's arm.

A foreign man," Sandra said, "not from this country." Small lies, she found, helped shape the situation in a certain way, helped make it less heavy when it sometimes felt like her chest would explode from the pressure. The nurse pumped the black rubber balloon until Sandra's veins felt like they swelled through her skin. "Very sexy," she told the nurse. "A tall, dark and delicious man," she said and the nurse released the air in a slow hiss.

The broker arrived wearing a gray suit and he understood her concerns, her situation. He wore a white tie with a bundle of red balloons printed at the tip and he touched the baby's cheek with one finger. He smiled at Sandra and said he couldn't imagine how difficult it must be to decide. If she wished though, he could definitely help her because many couples would die to have such a beautiful baby.

"This is not the way it goes," her friend April told her. "It never goes like this. It's supposed to happen at the hospital, so the baby can go straight home with the new mother. Something about the mother's scent. Meanwhile they sew you up and some do-gooder might tell you how you did the right thing or else not a person speaks to you. More likely this. Not a word is said except to ask if you're hungry, if you're comfortable.

"Then you begin to wonder if anything happened at all, or if it was made up, like you were there for some other surgery and you start feeling shitty and you go home and recover like a good survivor does. Or you don't. But this," April shook her head at the newborn in Sandra's arms. "Trust me, it never goes like this."

Sandra sat on the edge of her single bed and looked at herself in the mirror. She smiled. She liked herself, always had, but today that wouldn't matter, it wouldn't help at all. From the basket in the corner of the bedroom the baby cried, had been crying for at least five minutes. Sandra pulled on purple socks and new hiking boots with red laces.

She took the silver-backed brush from the dresser and saw her lips in the reflection. Perfect lips, the blond had said, sweet to look at and pluck like cherries. Blond streaks lightened Sandra's long brown hair that fell along either side of her face and she brushed it against her chest. The baby's crying shaped the morning into patterns of sound and Sandra leaned toward the mirror, turned her face from side to side. Not too red or pale or particularly dry or shiny. Her blue eyes, always dull on rainy days. She assumed the sprinkling continued outside with the gray clouds hiding the mountains, fog traveling on the ground. She stood and picked up the baby's escaped pacifier with one hand and the baby basket with the other.

In the kitchen she placed the basket on the ground and lifted the baby onto an old towel that was spread out on the card table. She set the last bottle of formula in a bowl of hot water to warm, opened the cupboard and put the remaining cans of formula into a paper sack.

"The way to get through it," her friend April had said, "was to get rid of the evidence. Anything connected with the baby must be put in a bag and left with the new parents. The house needed to look as if the baby had never been there at all, had never existed."

For the two weeks since she left the hospital, Sandra was careful to keep everything organized in or near the baby's basket. Most of the items in the hospital's care package sat unopened in a plastic bag by the kitchen door. Sandra peeked into the other cupboards to be sure. Everything was in place, ready to go.

The baby stared first at one hand and then the other. Sandra opened the refrigerator and looked for evidence. Then she poured herself some orange juice and leaned over the sink to look out the foggy window. Rain.

With the baby in her lap, she held the bottle steady and tried not to look, but she saw the baby's eyes look up at her. A blue color like her own, wide open eyes and alert. Sandra turned her head away and stared at the white paint peeling off the bottom of the kitchen door. Her car was probably 25 steps away and she visualized her path while the baby swallowed the formula.

When she returns home today Sandra will burst into the bathroom sobbing like a child, and turn the bathtub faucets on full blast. She'll want as much noise as possible to distract her. She'll want somehow to disappear. Gripping the baby's pacifier in one hand she'll dump green soap into the hot water until the tub overflows with bubbles thicker than steamed milk. Her clothes thrown into the hallway outside the bathroom door. Maybe she should burn the clothes, she'll think, because the baby's smell seemed to be everywhere. A pack of cigarettes and bottles of beer on bathroom floor next to the tub. Stepping into the scalding water and gritting her teeth against the burn. Maybe she deserves this pain, but Sandra will mix cold water into the bath with her foot.

In the tub, swallowing beer after beer, Sandra will smoke and wait to calm down. Nothing will sound from any room in the house except the words she shouts to fill the space. After she cannot stop crying, after she hits herself in the head with her hand, Sandra will sink lower in the tub until the suds rise around her head, close her off. Steam rises and water drips from the ceiling, rolls down the tiles. She'll stare at the pacifier looped around her finger like a ring, the nipple rising from the palm of her hand. Close her fingers and it disappears, then reappears again. What a ridiculous idiot she must be and she'll think, the poor baby, the lucky baby. But what an obviously wretched mother she would have been, right? And instead of oblivion, she'll cry until the water turns cold. When she stands with her nose plugged from sniffling, she'll shiver and bend down to drain the bath. The cool shower will not be able to dissolve the invisible film off soap that sticks to her skin. The rubber nipple will rub against her palm.

In her silk robe she'll walk around the barely furnished house with her arms folded across her chest. She'll force away thoughts about the furniture she plans to buy with the money, the two door refrigerator, the polished maple wood kitchen table. In front of a mirror the twinge inside her chest will bring her cries to the surface, and show her blubbering face. Who cares about stupid drapes, she'll think, who gives a goddamn about jewelry, and she'll touch the new gold necklace against her throat.

Maybe she will get the baby back. Maybe this will turn out to be the biggest mistake she ever made.

The baby was drowsy from feeding and Sandra set him on the table. She sat in a chair and pulled herself closer to the table. Her hands wrapped around the tiny bare feet and she examined the impossibly small toenails. "All those little piggies," she said. The baby's eyes searched for Sandra before the eyelids began to shut. Sandra brushed the feet across her lips, held them for a minute against her cheek.

Sandra crouched next to the table, re-folded the hospital blanket into the basket on the ground, and lifted it onto the table next to the baby. She changed the baby, holding both feet in one hand. She slipped the plastic diaper out from underneath the baby and rolled it up. She tried not to look, but could not help and see the small face, the wrinkled forehead.

"Some animal mommies," she said. "They just leave their children right after they're born, just pick up and take off and good luck." The baby turned his head to the side, clenched and unclenched the tiny hands, jerked his feet. "You're a lucky one, yes you are," she said and slid the last diaper underneath. "You'll be the best baby ever." She finished and wrapped the baby in a yellow blanket, placed him in the basket.

With the baby and the sack of formula in the basket Sandra opened the back door and paused in the doorway. She picked up the plastic bag of evidence and looked at the card table in the center of the kitchen with the four empty chairs, and the old gas stove next to the office-sized refrigerator against the wall. Rain misted in front of her face and onto the kitchen floor. She stepped outside and closed the door. The dead bolt clicked into place. She turned away from the window with the basket held in front of her, and her body disappeared into the fog toward the street. The sound of her steps faded.

Quiet.

A pacifier sat on the bare wooden floor for Sandra to find when she returned.

The nipple rested in a small pool of liquid.

Portholes and Train Tracks

John pulled his soon to be ex-wife alongside the railroad tracks. His hand gripped her wrist and she followed after him, casually, not willing to resist, but not wanting to give any signs of compliance either. She said things like, "John," and "Take it easy, John." Sometimes the arms of the trees extended to the tracks so John would have to crouch and pull and maneuver the two of them down the path.

"Why are you doing this John?" Emily asked.

They came into a clearing a few yards away from the train tracks.

"Okay," John said. "Let's just clear our heads and try to make this work."

"Make what work?"

"We must go through all of the gestures, say the words. It will be like acting."

"Why do we have to act, why don't we just walk around like adults, and look for it?"

"We pretty much started off this way, just move a couple feet back and to the side. I think I started."

John cleared his throat. "So this is our last talk, the big grandaddy of them all," he said. "Make or break time."

John nodded and winked at Emily, urged her to speak. "I don't know why we're doing this," she said.

"Good," John said and he nodded as he paced around in a circle, barely glancing at the ground. "Our last chance to call off the dogs, to keep it together."

"You mean to work it out?" Emily asked. "We've been trying to work it out for two years, John."

John walked over to Emily and turned her body so that it faced away from him. He pushed her head down as if he were directing a live model. "Go on," he whispered.

"We just weren't meant to be together," she said.

"It's because I'm fat, isn't it?"

"You're not listening. It's not like we've even grown apart, John. The fact is, we never grew together."

Emily walked and sat under the same tree as the night before. She pretended to fidget with her wedding ring and then raked her fingers through the dirt.

John took off his shirt and tried to suck in his stomach. "There," he said, his face straining. "Do I look any better now?"

After a brief pause, John fell to the ground and laid in the dirt, quivering. Emily bolted up and went to kneel by him. "John are you okay, was this in the script?"

His body kept quivering there in the dirt. "Stomach spasm," John managed to say.

She had seen it once before, during the summer when they drove to the beach together. He was not a fat man, but carried a few extra pounds around the middle. So whenever he got up the courage to take off his shirt he would spend all of his energy sucking in his gut as far as possible. The doctor said that it put incredible strain on his stomach muscles.

John's twitching eventually came to a halt and he stood. He put on his shirt and brushed off his pants. "Sorry about the break," he said. "I'll try to stay in character. Where were we again?"

Emily walked over and sat down under the tree, fidgeted with her bare ring finger.

"Why can't we grow together now, why can't we push through this?" John asked.

"We're not in love, John. Don't you see that, can't you feel that we're not in love?"

"And we never were, is that it? We were just two silly kids looking for a good time? I don't think you have any idea at all about what love is."

John started to walk out of the clearing toward the railroad tracks. Emily followed. At night the tracks had looked more romantic. Easing their way out of the tunnel in the distance, shining in the moonlight. But in the morning, with white sunlight reflecting off the polished silver rails they suddenly looked more dangerous. As if they might be electrified.

"If I threw myself in front of a train, you wouldn't care, is that right Emily?"

"Of course I'd care. It's not about caring John; it's about being willing to go on day after day, about building a family."

John laid down on the train tracks and spread out his arms and legs.

"John, this is definitely not part of the script. Turn over and try to see if my ring is in between the slats."

"You don't want to build a family with me."

"No, I don't John, and I've already told you that a hundred times. Now get off the tracks before you get yourself killed."

"Do you believe that there are such things as soul mates?" John asked.

"Maybe I do," Emily said.

"I don't," John said. "We all have points of entry, of access, and once in a while we latch onto another person through these portholes. But it probably can't ever really last." John sat up. "Wasn't there a part where you threw rocks at me?"

"It was mostly dirt, not rocks, but it's over here," Emily said. "Now come over here so I can do it again, just like you said. So we can find my ring."

John stood up and went over to Emily. He stood a few feet away and said, "You know what you are Emily? You're a bitch, an egocentric bitch."

Emily bent down and picked up a handful of gravel, sifting for a moment, looking to catch a glimpse of the diamond. She threw it at John. "I'm sick of this John, of fighting every goddamn day, of listening to you go on and on about your life, about how everything affects you. Life is too hard for you John, and living with a person like that is too hard for me."

"Did you say all that last night?"

"Most of it, some of it I just added in, right now."

The two of them walked around with their heads bent down, sweeping across the gravel with their feet. "I'm still in love with you," John said.

"I know you are."

"It makes me crazy to feel like this, like we're finished," John said.

"Good thing we didn't have kids," Emily said. "Less messy."

"Good thing," John said and he went to sit on one of the rails. "If I got hit, would you love me again?"

"Look John, I'd probably feel horrible. I'd probably cry my eyes out and even get the hiccups from my sobs. Yes, I'd definitely be a wreck."

"But you wouldn't love me again, all of the sudden? You wouldn't see my body all mangled up and think, "Goddamn I love that guy after all," you wouldn't think that?"

"Get off of there, you're making me nervous."

"You care about me."

"Of course I care about you, I'll always care about you."

"Even next year when you're in bed with some guy with a great strong back and huge biceps and he's going into you from behind and you're going crazy from the sensation of his hands on your waist. Even then?"

Emily looked away.

John lay back so that his body covered the tracks.

"Come on John let's get up and get on with it. This was not part of the scene. We still have to walk through the field and past that old barn."

"Can we have sex in the barn, one last time?"

"Like I told you last night, no."

"Then I'll stay right here and we'll never find your ring."

"I don't give a damn about the ring, just get up off the tracks I think I heard the train in the tunnel. You are being a baby about this."

"I just want something to go my way for a second. For one goddamn second I want to call the shots."

"Get up!"

They could both hear the whistle of the train and Emily stepped forward and grabbed John's wrist. She pulled on him, but he remained lying down.

"I could lose weight," he said dreamily.

"This is not in the scene John, you're screwing everything up. Now stand up!" Emily pulled as hard as she could but it was like trying to move a dead body. She eventually lost her grip and fell backward onto the gravel.

Only the Beginning

A young American woman recently named Emily McMaster begins her married life at the bottom of a deep well. Despite the remarkable depth, her fall could not have been easier, facilitated as it was by so many well-wishers and event coordinators. So many false bottoms had dropped out from under her, that her final impact had been entirely painless. Only now, as she traversed the streets of Paris, did she begin to feel the bruising that she's sustained during the fall. There seemed to be places inside herself that she hadn't known could experience pain; lazy and unused regions of herself which were only now relaying those danger messages to her brain.

The wedding day jitters and bridal anxiety had not, in fact, abated as promised, but instead had strengthened and grown more confident, seizing more territory inside her and tying it in knots. How deep the well into which she'd so casually let herself be thrown.

"And this is only the beginning," she says to herself, during the long and tedious walk that began hours ago at the Paris train station. And for fleeting moments, while the two newlyweds trek across the avenues looking for a place to stay, Emily the New Wife wishes herself dead in her hiking boots. *The streets of Paris*, she thinks, her boots pushing the sidewalk away like a treadmill, *big deal*. She wishes for death, though, in a vague and flighty way. In the same non-threatening, dreamy way that, at the moment, she also wishes for a strawberry smoothie or a quick divorce. But even as harmless as her thoughts are, Emily is careful not to wish any of this out loud because her husband, John McMaster, has recently accused Emily of silliness and morbidity.

"I wish I were in that blender," Emily had said the night before at a London airport bar, during an extensive and exhausting layover. "It must be excellent to have your fate so absolutely decided for you."

"Our honeymoon," John said, shaking his head. "Suddenly everything is death and blood to you." After a sip of beer he added, "This is precisely what the French are expecting, you know, another morbid and silly American."

The longest Wedding Day in history, going on 42 hours; rehearsal dinner, no sleep, early hair appointment, pictures, church, more dinner, dancing, more pictures, more no sleep on one airplane, and then another. At the reception, with friends saying goodbye to Emily, the married lady, and speculating on life without her it seemed more like Funeral Day. It became clear to Emily that even her memories wouldn't survive the marital leap, with everyone crushing the boxes she had assigned them to. Her 1st grade best friend with the red pigtails danced with the shark–tattoo-on-his-arm-cousin, and they too spun out of orbit away from Emily, as if she were, in fact, a dead sun.

But morbid was what John said and so it hangs in the air as she follows him, waiting to be verified or disproved with every word she says. With the traffic whizzing by, however, at least being dead seems possible, more possible than finding a hotel room in Paris at 9 o'clock at night. But Emily does not say this as she walks, the giant backpack weighing on her leg muscles. Instead, the evening shadows of the buildings stretch into dusk around them, and Emily wonders out loud at how light it is for being 9 o'clock at night.

Irritated John says, "Paris is much further north than America. The solar position is completely different here." Emily thinks the tediousness of it all must be killing him.

They stop walking and John holds open the guide book. He pivots his head up from the page to the address on the building. He'd taken French one year in college, but hadn't yet used it except to say thank you to an American stewardess.

He turns to Emily and speaks. "The book says it's a last resort. Are we at last resort yet?"

How could we be anywhere else, Emily thinks, and then says it to John.

John pays no attention. They will find a better place in the morning.

Had it happened the week before or even the day before the wedding, Emily could have followed Oprah's advice and called off the whole ceremony, no matter who it offended or how much money had been spent, since after all, this was love we were talking about on the

Oprah show six months earlier, when everything about Emily's marital plans and life goals still seemed to be in order, congealed. But instead, Emily's mental shift only barely begins during her walk down the aisle with her father, passed the well-dressed friends, passed a church jammed with expectations being fulfilled, maneuvering in her new shoes between the projections of idyllic love hurled at her like stones. Still she smiles at these people who, at the moment, believe; in her, in the two of them, in the sacrament of marriage and God and all that is true and good, and only then does she sense the change, like the trace beginnings of the flu. She knows that somehow, even suddenly, things have gone too far, gotten out of hand. To say the marriage vows Emily clears her throat again and again.

It's much worse by the time she cuts the cake at the reception with John and all his tall tuxedo handsomeness who pushes his large piece of cake gently into her mouth and the two of them pose, being very tasteful about the whole cake-eating thing and trying to do everything with tact in front of the families and then it's Emily's turn, though her cake hand pauses while she masticates, just enough to avoid the pictures that would have her look like a cake stuffed hog, and the piece of cake she holds in front of John's thin lips trembles, the outline of his smiling tan face illuminated on the periphery by flash bulbs capturing the special moment. "Come on," he may have said. And then of course, the seemingly involuntary spasm and Emily lunges like a professional boxer and ends up ramming the cake so far up John's nose, that he actually has to be taken into a back room by the hotel doctor and flushed out.

The Paris hotel is falling down and the sheets of rotted plywood and stacks of broken 2 x 4's lay in the entrance hall to prove it. Everything is dirty, as if this is not a hotel, but a child's imaginary projection of a hotel onto what is actually a giant abandoned chicken coop. The front desk man has dark skin, long yellow hair and missing front teeth. His office is no bigger than a utility closet, and he smells like the bottle of liquor that sits on his desk, next to the black and white television. Everything smells like plumbing, and alcohol.

"Welcome, welcome," the man says and holds out his hand. "I speak English and you've come to the best place. Need a room? How many nights?"

"Just tonight," John says.

"You are two beautiful kids; wish I was as beautiful as you. American? Of course, what am I saying? Boots. All these Americans and their mountain boots in the middle of the city. Beautiful. You pay first. Now, two nights you said?"

"One night, just tonight," John says.

"We give you the top-notch room, the number one best. Americans love the best. You want the best?"

"It's just one night—"

"Tonight, same price for the best room, okay?"

Emily senses the secret and subtle communication that is being attempted by her and her new husband as they stand in wedding form in front of this eager and generous man. Dozens of verbal and nonverbal cues zing past each other, and ricochet off the peeling walls, off the bare bulb hanging from the ceiling. Emily wants to leave, would rather sleep leaning against the Eiffel Tower, while John thinks it's not so bad for one night. Then they switch and so on, never gathering the combined force of will to turn around and leave. Instead, they somehow bully themselves into paying and Emily finds herself following the man to the foot of the stairs.

An older gentleman comes down the narrow staircase wearing a blue derby hat, a Hawaiian shirt and yellow pants.

"Gerome, we have guests tonight. Meet the Americans. I'm giving them the best."

Gerome stands in front of Emily and says, "Very nice." He has a large doughy head with a gigantic nose and eyeballs that move independent of one another. One eye regularly slides to the corner and twitches. He keeps shaking Emily's hand until she nods politely and pulls away.

Doors open on each floor as they climb, skeletal old people with cotton-white hair and dressed in thin nightgowns peer out of their dimly lit rooms. It seems to Emily as though everything is flaking paint, even the people.

The room is located on the very top floor of this building that seems to sway to the rhythm of the staircase. It happens also that this is their official wedding night. In their room they find a well-made bed, and a stained shower curtain hanging in one corner that Emily the Morbid suggests is evidence of a gruesome shower scene. Touching the shower area is out of the question.

It is not, she knows, so simple. With John being from a good family and money and posture. Insurance all over the place and so on. But it is not simply that Emily has become a communist or an eco-terrorist, it is not as easy as an ideological shift. As best she can tell she has fallen out of desire of John, and she worries that it will get worse until she eventually falls into repulsion and is forced to wait out the marriage contract until he dies in forty or fifty years.

There is a wadded up Navy-blue ski jacket stuffed between the top of the wardrobe and the ceiling. John says it's obviously a homeless person's jacket. John re-reads the guide book and cannot believe that they listed this dump. What year was the book published anyway, would the restaurant recommendations be as horrific? Emily imagines a drunk man coming back for his jacket, pounding down the door, or worse, not pounding it down and just hitting it all night, without rhythm. Opening the wardrobe is even further out of the question. An atmosphere of life in prison develops in the room, but they have already paid and since it is after ten o'clock, they decide not to go out. Instead they sit on the edge of the bed and eat the packages of saltine crackers Emily took from the plane, and drink from water bottles.

It's not like they haven't done it before. After all they lived together for a year before the wedding. John's parents pretended it wasn't so, and Emily's parents tried to play down their daughter's relative moral character. They would not pull back the blanket on the bed for fear of other stains. They would sleep in their clothes. And still John wants to consummate the marriage.

Emily says, "I want to have homosexual children, John." And though it is true, it comes off sounding more like an avoidance maneuver than a reproductive proposition. There is a fairly large hole in the crotch of her jeans that they both know about, loosely held together by a safety pin. It is a prejudice she has recently developed, sort of a bigoted way of seeing life, her belief that all gay people are generally more compassionate, more willing to be catchers, she calls them, catchers of the human spirit and not scientific analysts about everything.

John the Scientific Analyst says, "It's genetic, Emily, biological. You know choice has nothing to do with it."

"But maybe it does," she says.

"It doesn't."

"Maybe."

"Emily, do we have to do this now, here." John opens his arms, his jeans are unbuttoned, fly down.

"Do you have any gay genes in you, John?"

John ignores her by talking. He articulates their situation as newlyweds and the task set before them. He enumerates. First off, it would just be plain bad luck to start off like that, to have the first official wedding night go by without what he suddenly decides to call, the sacred union of flesh. And second, in fact, somewhere in the Catholic doctrine, and somewhere in God's eyes, they are not truly man and wife until the job is done for the first time after the marriage ceremony. Perhaps, he suggests, the ritual may even stem from a more ancient and indigenous tradition. Either way his tone is clear, it is undeniably standard policy.

Fully dressed, and with eyes closed, the consummation begins. While it happens Emily drifts and is grateful to find herself away, in the midst of a vision. *I am here on this rainy summer patio walking among these restaurant tables trying to find the person who drinks from my glass of milk. And in fact, the rain is making it difficult for me to see which glasses are full of milk and which have simply turned misty white and warm from the fizzy summer rain.*

It ends with John grimacing in real pain and neither of them ventures to use running water of any sort. They can wait this night out and John gingerly zips up his jeans, wincing all the while. It ends with Emily wanting to find the keeper of her glass of milk. There are traces of blood on both of them that will not be included in John's version of the story.

John's version of the story would go on to be told the next year at his family's Christmas dinner. He will not glance once at Emily as he tells, with an insistent rather than humorous tone, about how neither one of them could sleep in this disgusting Paris hotel, lying on that disgusting bed, staring at the disgusting coat, waiting for the mangy, disgusting owner to arrive, to smash the door down, and breathe hot liquor breath in their faces. Can you imagine a more miserable wedding night? And then how at 5 am, which was as long as they could endure, they heaved on their backpacks and waited by the door, breathing, loading oxygen into their tense leg muscles and more awake than they'd felt in weeks. Then bursting out the door and down the steps like athletes training, knees high enough, past the floors with the closed doors, trying not to see anything and still smelling the alcohol, the stopped up plumbing. Down to the front desk where no one sat, throwing their key into the office, most likely onto the floor, and bursting outside. And never had rainy Paris looked more glorious, more spectacularly beautiful even to any released POW than it did to those two newlyweds, jogging with backpacks down the street and shouting, laughing out loud. They had been freed, his story will go, and when asked by John's family to concur, Emily will avert her eyes and nod her head.

Emily stands at the hotel room door and glances at the stained shower curtain. This part is not any more real than the rest of it; she is not leaving her new husband. She is not escaping from these suddenly very heavy and very obvious, yet still metaphorical, handcuffs that bind her to this truly despicable man.

She touches her crotch and discovers that the safety pin has come undone. She pulls it out, tosses it up at the coat and watches it disappear. And now the time on her digital watch glows 5:00 am, their first official day as a married couple. Lying on top of the well-made bed, John sleeps in his clothes, his mouth open.

She is sending a message. Or is she making a point? She's definitely not taking a stand. She's taking a step, yes, that was it. She has found the first toehold, sunk the fingertips of one hand deep into the cold soil. She has lifted herself off the bottom of the deep well; she now clings to the side and looks up. She remembers the joke about a train engine's headlight being the light at the end of the tunnel.

She thinks, "This is only the beginning."

With her backpack on and boots re-tied Emily pauses at the door and stares at John. Not to give a farewell salute or blow a kiss, but simply to see that he still sleeps while she opens the door and descends to the street as quietly as possible.

Breathe In, Breathe In

After we marry, I fully expect to die from suffocation. One night on our honeymoon, my wife and I decide to skinny dip in the Mediterranean. This is after a couple bottles of wine at dinner and we stand naked for a while on the beach and kiss each other while we undress. The water rolls warm over our feet and after a few minutes, like some sort of drunken hero idiot, I turn and run straight into the water, flailing my arms like I once saw a Scotsman do in a movie. I splash, but I do not shout because I do not want to get caught before we have a chance to consummate the marriage, again.

I use that word all week.

When I stop and turn my head I see my new wife dive into the water without a single splash. In my mind I see images of bare-chested Mermaids, of shipwrecked women adrift in torn clothes, and when her head surfaces in the dark for air, I see an otter.

For some reason I want her to chase me and I swim further out, where the water becomes colder and I feel extremely naked. Cinematic images move through my mind as I kick my legs, color close-ups of human skin, shadows in a doorway. The movie angles hold still for a moment and then disperse when I blow water bubbles out my nose. Entire stories flash in sync with my muscles, stories which in Spanish are called quite beautifully, *Ficciones*.

When I finally stop swimming I cannot touch the ocean's bottom and I tread water, moving my arms and legs like a dog. I see my wife's silhouette above the water and she motions to me with her shadow arm. Dim moonlight glints off her wet skin and I know there is zero chance of us being able to consummate anything out here, where I find the water to be two or three feet above my head. But before I move toward her, I swear that something pulls me under. I check my naked body sensors for indications of torn flesh since my first unoriginal idea is of course, shark. But no animal devours me, only an underwater river sucking me along. Every so often I must have been pushed up to the surface because this went on much longer than my one breath would have held out.

Of course even as I drown I cannot escape the damn images. Drunken giant shadow monsters splash in confusion around me, licking me, roaring in my ear, and then tossing me from one to the other. I gulp, as if this will help stave off death, as if it will preserve the precious oxygen that I am sure I can feel dissipating in my blood. The color of my blood turns a darker blue, on its way to black. As I fight against dying I remember that mythology comes from people who live through moments like this. Therefore, it is possible to live.

Then all at once I float on my back and my wife pulls me to the beach. She says something about enjoying my performance. As if nothing really extraordinary has happened she slips on top of me, and we actually consummate on the wet sand. Saltwater washes over our legs and pulls sand out from under us, slowly sucking us into the ocean. Soon I don't notice. Her lips move to make sounds that are distorted by the waves of water applauding around us and for me everything is air. I breathe as much as I want.

It's not as if the wife had never exploded, or lost it completely with her new husband who would eventually ask her to pose naked with another woman in front of a video camera. Which by the way, she absolutely refused to do. He was a difficult man to live with, to get an angle on. Mostly he told lies even though he loved to call them, quite theatrically, his *Ficciones*. And all day she worked as a Kindergarten teacher and all day he stayed home with the baby, and still the wood floors hadn't once been vacuumed or mopped. Walking around was like crunching and sticking to a movie theater floor. He watched movies all the time, maybe five or six a day, because he said he was perfecting his craft, his profession. She had asked him more than once if he could please perfect it while he picked up the baby's toys or scrubbed out the bathtub. And he had replied each time that no, he most certainly could not.

What I will not do is drink before noon. I set my limits. But sometimes I need a serious distraction from around 9 in the morning until noon so I'll put the baby in a backpack and just walk from our backyard into the mountains as far as I can.

This day I'm walking with my head down and it is hot. So hot I can feel my tee-shirt soaking with sweat where the boy's legs press against my back. It's a dry and dusty trail without any shade until you hit the trees, and as usual I haven't brought any water.

Anyway I'm walking, looking at the ground and when I finally look up I see her, this mountain lion just crouching in the grass off to the side of the path. I try to remember what to do, and I slowly raise my arms to make myself look bigger even though I'm pretty sure this is the drill for seeing bears.

And even as I remember this, as I'm thinking that maybe I'm supposed to back away quietly, just then, the boy starts to yell. Not a regular sort of crying, but these little piercing shrieks around which he moves his lips. I think that it's probably autism or teething that makes him screech out these noises, but in any case, I know damn well that an explanation of any sort will not help matters at all. This is not a movie theater. The big cat rises up and sort of saunters in front of us, perhaps curious about me with my arms like I'm the Karate Kid, and my boy with his little autistic yelps. Though I would never do such a thing I think that if I left the boy, I could easily run for it. It's a terrible thought, I know, but it comes and goes just like hundreds of others. For example I also wish that I had taken that slab of steak with us on our hike. The one that's been rotting in the fridge for two weeks. Never would a piece of raw meat have come in so handy.

Most people do not know exactly how you die when you're eaten by wild animals like a pack of wolves or a mountain lion, but I do. Explained to me by two hunters in a movie scene as they headed into the woods to hunt one New Hampshire winter. I forget what the movie was about, but one man in his fluorescent orange hat explained that the mountain lion would first tear away the throat of the victim, which cut off oxygen and instantly smothered the prey. He said the throat was the way to the quickest kill because of air not just blood like everyone thought. Waiting for a prey to bleed to death could take hours.

Anyway I am pleased to find that I have been stepping backward at least and also to find that the big cat has seemingly lost interest. But like an idiot, I turn and run. And then I hear the animal alongside, behind me, trotting through the brush and probably running a preliminary check on all instinct, probably secreting hormones that will provoke the killing impulse and heighten the desire for the taste of blood.

The boy bounces like a ball in the backpack and now I honestly hope I don't eject him into what must be a horrible, though short lived, fate. Then I see a group of joggers. Greek goddess warriors is how I see them, the seven women joggers coming toward me. It is they who will save my life and they do. The cat disappears into the foothills and they all stop. One in particular, one with long red hair and a white sports bra, puts her hand on my shoulder as a kind of half embrace. I am crying at this point and while the rest of the fearless group runs on, she walks with me back to the house, taking care to talk to the boy who has ceased his noise and sits dumbfounded by this particular goddess. At the house I make a pitcher of lemonade and vodka.

The wife had even dipped into his precious vodka supply while the husband was at the movies one Saturday afternoon. Imbibing enough to propel her to carry the butcher knife into their bedroom and begin slashing through his things looking for evidence. Eventually, she was able to cut a nice sized filet out of the mattress. And she ended up cutting several more times into the mattress because it turned out to have the most satisfying result, with the sound of the puncture and the precise strip-like tears parting the fabric.

At first she had tried to slash into his sock drawer but only succeeded in pulling pairs of his socks onto the floor. She was looking for love letters perhaps, as those would prove to be the most fulfilling to find. At the time she thought they would give her the fuel it would take to finally deal with him in a significant way, to get rid of or leave him. Though unfortunately for her, she had found all the evidence that there was to be found in the car. Even as she dumped out his clothes, or tore into his pillow she had the feeling that it was a hollow search, and so eventually, basic destruction took over as her main objective and that was when she began on the mattress.

She had found a black pair of women's Jockey underwear on the floor of the backseat of his car. Underwear that had dried stiff from sweat and she knew what else. During her rampage the baby stood in his walker unable to push into the bedroom since the doorway was too narrow. He had discovered a piece of clothing and was chewing on it, even as she threw herself on the bed and cried as loud as she could into her undamaged pillow, pausing every once in a while to turn and smile and wave to the child who would look up and smile and sometimes wave back.

My wife does not allow me to smoke in the house so I've devised a system that works nicely, though it requires a good deal of effort. I remove the screen from the living room window and stand outside, in full view of the television. I smoke almost two packs a day, so I guess in the end it's worth the trouble. I set up a fan that blows inside air out, and of course I have bought plenty of fresh pine aerosol. The boy is usually the most difficult element to negotiate, except when he's napping, which is like a freedom beyond freedom. Other times I watch him through the window as he sits and plays on the floor or moves his walker to the plant where he strips off leaves and eats them. Still other times, when he's being especially difficult, I keep him in the backpack and stand outside, bouncing him up and down with my legs.

The runner woman visits me on Wednesdays and Fridays, usually around nap time though that varies. She shows up at the door after her run, all smiles and sports bra, and sometimes she even plays with the boy so I can take notes on a particular movie scene I'm watching.

I'm in the midst of writing a screenplay in which, by some bizarre twist of capitalist logic, dishwashers in the restaurants rise to the top of the service industry and are recruited by the top dining establishments worldwide, though my story will take place in Las Vegas. They require agents. I've already written the title, *Dishin'*, and I've sketched scenes in which people gather in an auditorium to watch two dishwashers wash piles of dishes on stage. They do acrobatic things around their respective machines, like rack silverware behind their backs or toss dishes to one another over their heads. People love it and these guys are pulling down NBA-like salaries. But I know the focus must be on one dishwasher in particular, his rise and fall. The money and women just aren't enough for him and his fame actually causes him to forget why he got into washing dishes in the first place. In fact the whole society has seemed to have forgotten what dishwashing is truly about, at its core. Of course it should all end quite tragically, probably with his suicide involving drowning and a dish machine. The runner woman says it's brilliant.

Sometimes the boy doesn't go down for a nap and the runner woman and I have to take a drive in the car to calm him down. Or sometimes we just have sex standing up in the hall, where I can, once in a while, peek around a corner and monitor the baby sitting on the couch in the living room. We've entitled that situation *The Peek-A-Boo.*

The Friday that the husband stopped breathing in the kitchen was the same day when the wife came home a half-day early. A risky proposition, she knew, and she even looked through the window first, not wanting to walk in on anything that might further cripple her emotional state. After all, she had come home to rest and maybe to have an important talk, but mainly to rest while the husband took care of the baby. Through the window she saw the husband on the couch with a drink in his hand and the bottles of vodka and tonic next to his feet. He watched a movie, alone in the room.

"Where is he," she asked when she stepped through the front door.

"He's hurt," he said without moving his eyes from the screen.

She dropped her bags and walked quickly down the hall into his room. The Jockey woman looked up. She knelt on the ground with the boy lying on his back in front of her, gnawing on a lime. The Jockey woman wrapped his small foot with medical tape.

"What happened," the wife asked and she crouched next to the boy who smiled up at her from behind the lime.

"A glass broke in the kitchen and all of a sudden he was there, in his walker. He stepped on a big one, but I think it's all out."

"My God," the wife said and stroked the boy's head. "Did you put any gauze?"

"All that I could find in the bathroom. I've changed it once already, but I don't think he needs stitches."

"You know this because you're a doctor," the wife said, trying to force out sarcasm.

"I'm a nurse," the woman said. "I visit newborns."

While the wife waited for the correct reaction to the situation, waited to become hysterical and feel that surge of emotion that would help her pick up this woman and toss her from the house, perhaps through the roof, she lay on the floor next to the baby and cried. The Jockey woman stood and held out her hand for a moment as if about to touch something, and then she turned and walked out of the room.

That evening the husband stopped breathing in the kitchen, or more accurately, he stopped breathing effectively. His mouth wide open, his shoulders thrown back (at that point he still stood) not unlike a hooked fish, arcing to no avail. But the wife could see that little if any air was getting through. Maybe a single drop as if through a tight mesh sieve, but the wife knew that air was not like water. Small bits were practically useless.

The Jockey woman had gone home long ago, and no one had spoken a word since. The husband sunk slowly to his knees, perhaps to conserve energy, and he grabbed his throat as if he was choking, which he was not. A couple of years ago when they were newlyweds without a baby, he told his wife in an offhand way that she might have three minutes to get him to a hospital in this scenario, maybe five tops. He couldn't quite remember since he hadn't had a severe attack since he was a baby. In five minutes he could be dead he had told her, but this scene contained some joy in it for the wife because at that moment she sort of wanted him dead.

The baby sat in his high chair with the barest amount of blood soaking through the bandage on his foot. His small face was covered with green smears of mashed peas and he waved his hands in solitary joy, his face working through various expressions. He would have to be cleaned off before she could put him into the car seat and then drive to the hospital. But first things first and she walked into the bathroom to retrieve the asthma inhaler buried deep inside an old shaving bag. When she returned the husband had sat himself down in a meditation pose, and was gulping. If he could not pull any air into his lungs, then he could not receive the asthma medicine that would open the airways. She dropped the inhaler in his lap anyway and he began squirting the mist into his mouth, tilting his head back. Perhaps, she thought, he has confused his stomach for his lungs.

The wife had thought about calling an ambulance, but they lived at the end of a dirt road off an obscure highway. At that moment she had confused the ambulance with the roofer, to whom she had recently given directions three times before he arrived, two hours late. No, an ambulance would never make it in time. If she sped it could be a ten minute drive to the hospital. Maybe as an adult he had fifteen minutes to live instead of five, and that is what she decided.

There must have been a human animal mothering instinct in her that propelled her to act in the interests of her husband, since she could not seem to allow him to suffocate while she cleaned up the dishes. He writhed a bit on his side and the inhaler went skidding across the wood floor. Eventually he was able to stagger to the car, leaning on her arm, and she considered that some air must be coming in through his nose perhaps, even though his face had gone white and not a sound came from his body. The car-seat belt needed to be adjusted because the baby wore a tiny puffy ski jacket. She could tell that things would be frozen later that night, but the car started right up.

There is not usually a whole lot of time for reflection at a time like that, and yet somehow, the wife was able to reflect. Sort of a fast forward contemplation process, enough to get flavor of this man's faults, a sense of why she was not completely hysterical with him dying in the passenger seat. His head had fallen back with his eyes closed. Perhaps it was some sort of animal preservation stage, some sort of shock. She pulled up to the hospital's emergency entrance, turned off the car, and yanked on the emergency brake. She took the boy out of the car seat and walked through the automatic sliding doors. One man, a large man, came out to the car a moment later. He picked up the husband and carried him into the hospital like a new bride.

He was unconscious, that much was for sure the doctor said, which might have been a blessing since his lungs had somehow begun to take air again. Still, he was not stable, not out of the woods yet, and they had hooked him up to a respirator and an I.V. because he was terribly dehydrated. And no, the doctor confirmed, the boy's foot would not need stitches because children healed much faster than adults. It was hardly a worry at all.

"Do people slip into comas," she asked the doctor, meaning, in this situation.

Of course they do, he explained, but that would be extreme in this case, it would be an unexpected long shot. He was simply out cold and under observation, but that was all. If she wanted she could stay the night at the hospital, but the doctor didn't believe it would be necessary or particularly comfortable, especially with a little one.

"Routine hospital procedure," he assured her.

The wife stopped in to see her husband on the way out. He laid on the hospital bed, his eyes still closed, and his face as smooth and white as the bed sheet.

The wife believes that there is a moment of extra sensory perception that occurs just before major life changes. As if the body senses what will happen and begins to tune itself, runs a check of all instruments that will soon be called into a long and serious battle.

When the hospital calls at 2:42 am, they will initiate the wife's new phase of life. The process of grief, of producing a funeral. Many sad interactions with relatives would follow the phone calls, and giant cards printed in cursive would arrive along with the wreaths made of pink and white roses. The wife would eventually have to work through a stack of Thank You notes. Then there would be decisions about moving out of the house, about daycare, and about living with her parents for a while. She'll employ language having to do with healing, with getting back on her feet. And of course money will play a star role in this production. But all the elements will orchestrate in a single effort aimed at weighing the wife down. Gravity will dominate each step across her parent's lawn, and tug her skin further away from her bones as she sits in the bathtub.

But not yet. Just before the call, in fact, it was quite the opposite. She lay awake in their bed with the baby sleeping beside her, and she felt a thrill exuding from her pores like light. As if she were at the core of a giant halo.

She swam in the Mediterranean then, naked and warm, but she did not aim in any direction or try to reach a certain spot. Her face broke the surface of the water again and again, and she tasted the salt, celebrated her freedom to breathe and swim at will. The night sky made it possible for her to believe that she swam in the air or breathed under the water, and her muscles answered her inclinations without hesitation. When she stopped, the water remained still and she stood waist deep with her palms resting on the surface, wanting nothing, looking for no one. She did not expect or desire a single thing. She was empty for a moment, perfect.

Then it faded to black. The baby kicked her in the leg when the phone rang. She reached over and her entire body took a deep breath, as if each pore were sucking in as much as possible, pulling and pulling and storing, packing it away. She gulped once and trapped everything inside her body. She held the receiver to her ear and listened for a moment. Then she said, "Yes, I am on my way."

Impressions

It seemed to David that only a few things in life could ever really hit him all at once. A truck, for example, speeding through an intersection. Or perhaps a flaming piece of hot air balloon falling from the sky. The impact of most events seeped into David, like inkblots through cloth, and what he felt at one moment often distorted and bled away into the next.

Two years earlier the doctor had explained fertility counseling to David and his wife Janet. The doctor had described the stress that infertility could cause, and all David could say was, "They're empty." His testicles, his frame of mind.

They weren't technically empty, the doctor said, but by then David could not concentrate. He only barely heard the doctor's voice explain to Janet the theories behind his virtually zero active sperm count. Sitting in his chair, David sensed the compassionate tone behind the doctor's words, encouraging the two of them to pull through this, to avoid blame, to expect their relationship to strain, to fade out, to murmur, to mumble. David closed his eyes and floated up, up, and away.

David began to play the same lottery numbers each week because he was not usually a haphazard chance taker. He chose the annuity each time, so that the prize money would be portioned out to him at an even pace, equal chunks over twenty years. Responsibility, his middle name.

A few months after the doctor's visit David stood partially naked with his good friend April beneath a clump of pine trees while it stormed above them. He stroked her wet black hair and kissed the rain droplets off her neck. At one point, the water rolled off April's lips and into David's mouth and the two of them slept together for the first time, standing up and using wet boulders and bare shoulders for support.

They walked home in soaking clothes and April said, "You should've married me David, I don't even want kids."

David began to play the lottery twice a week. A vague and empty hope stirred in his mind as he sat with his square piece of paper in front of the television set. The false security of being a long-shot took hold and he knelt on the floor, moved closer to his salvation. The hollow balls swarmed in chaos inside the machine and David longed to be chosen. His muscles tensed and he willed destiny to pluck him from existence, to make him a god. One by one the balls were sucked into the tube and delivered onto the woman's palm. The crushing despair, on the other hand, was neither vague nor empty.

His good friend April began to call David with various household problems. When he arrived one night to help fix her water pump, she sat naked in a bathtub filled with soapy bubbles and smiled. She said that the pumping problems must have corrected themselves on his way over.

Soon, everyone had cheated and gone back on their word. Janet needed the physical experience of giving birth. His good friend April extended her sudsy hand one night and said, "Leave her David. She is brilliant and beautiful and you can't love her now. Then everyone gets what they want. Everybody wins."

"Everybody can't win," David said. "Everybody never wins. And what about friends and lovers, oil and water?"

"I say burn us up. Set us on goddamn fire for all I care. Maybe we'll turn into some bizarre super material that is both rubber sealant and Italian gourmet chocolate syrup. Besides, I can taste your lips this very second. You want your own baby? Come here and I'll even give you your own baby and a brand new car!"

"Less than two percent of my guys even attempt the swim, April. I'm not sure if the lake matters all that much."

"The ocean, you mean. You mean my foamy fertile ocean." She splashed in the tub. "The rhythm of the salty warm-water-waves, David? No difference you say? Where do you think all life came from in the first place?"

And David moved head first into the ocean.

On Halloween David leaned back in the ten-dollar office chair his wife Janet bought at a garage sale. He wore a white pair of gloves and carried a lottery ticket for the night's eight million dollar drawing in his wallet. At that moment, the eight million dollars were central to his plan. He took out the small square of paper and reviewed the numbers like a code. What he wanted was a section of Italian sky, perhaps over

Florence, in which he would live as only a balloonist could, in an elaborate two or three room basket held aloft by two giant, low maintenance hot air balloons.

David would never have to walk on the ground again since a smaller balloon pod would transport him over the open-air markets where he would take up his ripe produce and fresh fish by the utility-basket-full. What he still saw when he made love to his good friend April was the circular mouth of the giant balloon receding into a clear night sky. One afternoon they had lain on their backs imagining the sensation in the basket, with the fire flaring above them and keeping them off the ground.

Janet had gone out to do Saturday chores and learn final results from the Pregnancy Doctor. Before she left she had leaned over David's shoulder to look at the lottery numbers he held in his hand. "Maybe today is our lucky day," she whispered and then she kissed him on the ear and left.

Again, the phone rang and David turned over the hand held unit on his desk. He leaned over and pressed his ear to the receiver.

His good friend April said, "David? I hear you breathing. Talk to me, I'm buying the plane tickets."

Part of the plan was not to get caught, and so David took precautions. He whispered, "Viva Italia," into the mouthpiece but did not pick it up. When he heard the click on the other end, goose bumps rose on his skin and he began to feel nervous, began to fidget. Airplane tickets. The process was gaining momentum. He switched off the telephone ringer and stood up. He sat down and turned the ringer on again. He crossed and then uncrossed his legs.

At least some of his agitation had to do with genetic codes and heredity, since after all, his mother lived precisely the same way. Her muscles always twitched like a terminally spooked horse and she was just about as thin and thirsty. With her pacing mind, her frenetic head movements and physical ticks of the elbow and wrist, she could barely swallow an ounce of anything before leaping up to say that she'd heard something, sensed bad weather, unnatural disasters and so on.

The phone rang again and David left it alone. He considered for a moment his mounting irrational fear, the irrational situation. So little rational anymore.

"Infertile," his mother had said to him. "It's nothing to get worked up over David, after all it's not like you're a praying mantis. I mean here you have history's holiest insect, and out of love or habit or nowhere, the female eats the male's head after he's ejaculated into her. Did you know that? Fertile or not David, you see that there's no counseling for him."

David returned the lottery ticket to his wallet and walked into the kitchen. He popped ice into a tall glass; cut a wedge of lime, and poured gin halfway, tonic the other half. He took his crisp fall drink into the bedroom and sat in front of the dresser mirror. He must make himself comfortable on this difficult Halloween day, and he took off his gloves and pulled out potential outfits. He searched for his best pair of flesh colored leggings.

At the bottom of his drawer he found the two wrinkled balloons, one blue and the other pink. Given to him at the beginning of all this by the Pregnancy doctor as a sign of good faith, she said, an omen of good luck. He blew up the pink one and let it go. After it smacked against the closet door and fell to the ground, he tossed the blue one into the corner and dressed.

David's black hair was slicked back against his head as the hair gel dried. Thick eyeliner framed his view and his cheeks were dusted with blush. His lips glistened red. He sat in the living room now, fabric shoulder pads stuffed in his black-lace bra, wearing a white blouse and a black leather skirt that crept up his thighs. He crossed his flesh colored legs and tasted the lipstick that left a red smear on his drink glass. The lottery numbers on the piece of paper in his lap did not sing to him, or glow, or otherwise signal to David how the night would turn out. He tucked them into the pocket of his leather skirt.

The gold-bordered mirror on the wall reflected the outside view behind him and the sky had dropped to hide the mountains behind a moving wall of rich gray clouds. Fog searched close to the ground.

David saw his tiny mother emerge from the fog in the mirror. She walked toward his house from the canyon with a giant white bag slung over her shoulder like Santa Claus. As usual, she had been filling the trash bag with aggressive and noxious weeds that threatened to exterminate the Columbine flower and other preferable mountain growth. With the mist around her ankles and the weeds puffing like veins inside the giant white bag, she could easily have been traveling through a fairy-tale.

Eventually she drifted out of his view and soon enough he heard the knock on the front door. He answered with one hand on his hip. When he cocked his head a long silver earring brushed his shoulder like tinsel, making him feel glamorous. She stood on the porch, a handsome woman, with long gray hair and a slim face.

"Welcome, weed lady," David said.

She placed her work gloves next to the giant white bag on the porch and her hazel eyes registered his outfit. "In this country one in twelve couples have infertility problems, did you know that David? Did you know that they link it to groundwater pollution and high voltage utility wires?"

David spun in his black leather pumps and led her into the kitchen. When she touched the phone it rang and she answered.

"Just a moment," she said into the mouthpiece. "It's for you."

David swallowed and gripped the phone. He smiled and licked his teeth—lipstick. "Happy Halloween," he said.

April said, "Now I'm waiting at the airport and maybe I've got your ticket in my hand."

"Is that so," David said, smiling his all-teeth smile. His mother checked under the kitchen sink for water-pipe leaks or radon gas.

"I know where there is a perfect piece of blue sky for sale over the hills of Florence, David. Overlooking carved marble columns, green grass, olive trees—"

"You don't say," he replied, smiling harder.

"At midnight I turn into a pumpkin, David, I'm serious. I disappear. You can do this. I love you."

"I'll keep that in mind."

His mother took the phone from his hand and hung up. "It's a simple root change to action, you know," she said, hanging up for him. "From infertility, I mean."

"What's a root change to action?"

"Infertility to Infidelity. Same prefix and suffix but fundamentally different roots. Sounding similar but contextually opposed. Infertile—barren, blank, and so on, mainly a static, passive absence. Infidelity also means absence, but an absence rooted in motion, rooted in action itself. An absence of faithfulness means an act of dishonesty complete with consequences and the whole bit. It's simply a four-letter-Latin-root-change, twisting meaning from passive to passion, static to ex or ecstatic. You see what I mean."

"Not really."

She dialed and listened to the phone. "Could I have a moment, please?" she asked, waving him away. "Can't you go re-stuff, or refresh something?"

David pivoted and walked with a hip-sway into the bathroom. He sat on the toilet and shook a jar of fingernail paint.

When a person sneezed, David's mother always encouraged, saying, "Good for you." She advocated the expulsion and eradication of contagions across the board, visible or not.

"Everything so sacred about the sneeze," she once told David. "Historically of course, the gateway to the spirit, Godblessyou and all that. Fact is, we breathe, we change, and we don't even realize it. I'm talking way beyond illness David, way beyond allergic reaction. All of life moves from one infection to the next. You catch the contagion lust, for example, or depression and they cycle through you, affect your mindset. But then you must expel David, you must go on to catch something else."

Even when David had allergies or a cold, she would be sure to "good-for-you" each one until he stopped or removed himself from the room. Sometimes she would shout after him as he left the room, "Purify your soul David, blow your nose."

"Good for you," his mother said again on the phone. David heard her pacing in the kitchen as she talked with the man she'd been dating, an astronomer who wore knickers and went through messy divorces.

After a brief conversation having to do with someone burning old love letters, his mother hung up and cleared her throat. David flushed the toilet and emerged. He touched his crusty but perfect hair with the palm of his hand, his fingers splayed, fingernails drying. He smiled and said, "You're not leaving so soon, are you?"

"Can you believe him? That's a scientist for you. I told him that humans always transfer their emotions to physical objects. I said, 'How do you think demolition crews get any work done, or terrorists?' I mean, why else would people kiss photos or sleep with a stranger's underwear? I said, 'I kill weeds for Christ's sake.' Anyway—it's not the best time for an affair, gorgeous," she said to David. "But I suppose you know all this by now."

"Come again," he said and she nodded from the other side of the screen door. She walked down the road, into waves of fog that had moved in from that direction. Perfect Halloween weather and David shivered in his skirt while her white humpback disappeared into the clouds.

The telephone.

David withdrew his lottery ticket and studied the light pink design of the paper itself. Then he tried to receive a signal from the numbers themselves, whether they felt confident, whether they had pre-cognitive knowledge about the results. In general they seemed darker in color than they had the last time David checked. Perhaps they had begun to prepare. They gave no other clues or predictions and David folded them away. After he won, he decided, he would hide the ticket in a box of cereal.

He couldn't leave the phone off the hook. He turned the ringer off and then back on. In the kitchen he cut another slice of lime, popped more ice, poured and poured more, stirred and sipped. David toasted the ringing phone and said, "Refreshing indeed." His face felt sealed with mud when he spoke and the corners of his mouth itched.

"I can help," David said the moment Janet walked through the door.

"Don't," she said, jerking her head once. She carried a hamper of soaking wet laundry and pulled two helium balloons through the door. One blue, one pink.

She walked past him and into the living room. He held his hand in front of his mouth and tried to smell alcohol on his breath, tried to gauge if his words would be credible.

She turned and stared at him, her cheeks red and cold. Long blond hair in a single ponytail down her back.

David batted his eyelashes, puckered his lips.

"Good news," she said. "It's official. I'm officially pregnant."

"Wow," he said. "Wow," he said again and opened his arms. They hugged while he tried not to smear her hair with flesh colored base. She smelled like she had tumbled through a dryer and the two balloons bumped against each other and rolled along the ceiling.

They stood outside in the fog and hung the sopping laundry on the clothesline. He pinned a shirt and watched the sleeves drop to the ground, the wrists bent on the dirt. He wondered how anything would ever dry in this weather.

After a while David asked, "Am I the father?"

"Of course you're the father, silly. Don't get started on this, please don't. You will definitely be the father David, understand that."

"Him and me," he said. "The King and I."

"We don't even know him David, remember? We are the parents, you and me." She grabbed his hand and pressed. "Please don't."

They walked inside and left the clothes sagging low in the Halloween fog.

The telephone.

"That's weird," Janet said from the bedroom. "They just hung up."

"Don't," he said.

David cooked. He poured wine for himself and a celebratory splash for Janet. He sautéed broccoli, onions, strips of marinated beef. He rolled them in tortillas with beans and cheese and set them to bake. The phone rang until the answering machine picked up and recorded the click. They sat down at the kitchen table and David removed his shoes and rubbed his feet under the table.

"It's kind of eerie," she said. "The phone I mean."

"Just a Saturday Halloween," he said, like it was one of those things he had come to expect by now. Everything was like spilled oil off a duck to him. And precisely what David was under at the moment, was extreme control. He checked the kitchen clock, and wondered if he was on schedule. He would soon have to tell Janet that he had to go to the grocery store.

"Just too many people with time on their hands, feeling ghoulish," David said. He winked and his eye stuck closed for a moment. He checked his reflection in a butter knife but could make out nothing except his huge red-veined eyeball embedded in gallons of painted porous flesh.

"Well it's still creepy," she said.

"Remember in college when we were dating and I called your house and said, 'You don't know me' and you hung up right away?"

"See? That stuff has always freaked me out."

"Well you didn't," he said.

She rolled her eyes. "You didn't know you, David."

The telephone rang.

"Why don't we turn the ringer off at least?"

"Just don't think of the calls that way," David said, pointing his fork at Janet. He admired his Corvette red fingernails. "It could be something entirely different, even beautiful. An unborn child, for example, calling to see if we are fit parents. Yes, that's perfect. Souls shopping for homes on Halloween."

"How sweet," she said. "Dead people calling customers on the phone, looking for a womb. Much better."

"What, no womb at the Inn?"

At this point everything seemed thicker and confused to David. His leg hair pressing through the pantyhose became the weeds inside his mother's bag. He sank into the couch with his after dinner liqueur while Janet crocheted and watched television. He took out his lottery ticket and placed it on his lap. David heard the balloons whispering against the ceiling and he closed his eyes.

David knew he would have to re-spray his hair and redo his lips before he went to any airport. He pulled his eyelids apart, smearing black and blue, and he heard Janet choking and gasping on the couch next to him. He jolted himself out of his sick tasting nap and saw that she held a hand in front of her mouth as tears poured down her cheeks. He sat up, grabbed her shoulders, and spun her around. He hit his palm against her back.

"You'll be okay, just take it easy," he said thinking that he was probably dislodging a crocheting needle from Janet's throat.

"Stop it," she stuttered. "S-T-O-P," she coughed out.

Janet cried and sniffled and shook. When she began to laugh David considered the possibility that she might combust right there on the couch. Perhaps she had answered the phone and spoken with his good friend April.

"Who was it," he asked, meaning the phone and thinking Florence.

"I don't know what happened," she said. "Just a commercial with the kids in their little shoes, going down the red plastic slide. We are going to have our own baby David, our own child."

He picked up a scrap of paper from the floor and his mind malfunctioned. Perhaps someone left a note, he thought, slipped it under the door. He stared at the perfectly square piece of pink paper and couldn't make sense of it. No human handwriting at all. Then the numbers became familiar and he remembered the plan. The drawing was less than a half hour away and David folded the ticket into his pocket and sat back on the couch.

On an airplane aimed for Rome, David and April would hold hands. David would drink tiny bottles of wine and April would read excerpts from the travel book she'd brought. David would look down at the receding lights of the airport and the view would make him uneasy, nauseous. He would remember that he had never even ridden in a hot air balloon. Arrival in Rome and then a train trip to Florence, and one morning David would wake up and April would be there in the bed with him and he would feel as though he'd been hollowed out. As if he were floating and April would touch his shoulder as he looked out the window of the small hotel. The air, his clothes, even April's lips would suddenly mean that it was too late. Something would definitely be too late by then.

Then David would ask, "So now what?"

April would say that the possibilities were endless.

David would hear that the possibility had ended.

"So now what?" Janet asked which seemed to be the first words that had made sense to David all night. Her face was flushed red and she wiped her eyes with the sleeve of her shirt. She smiled and David was relieved.

"For starters, you're the one who'll have to give birth," David said, not having any idea what to say. He crossed his legs and straightened his skirt, smoothed it out.

"I can't believe we're actually going to have a baby. Look at us; we don't even know how to react."

"Stunned," he said. "We're both stunned, especially with how we're reacting."

"Right." She sat back and crossed her legs.

"But all this can't be too good for your body. That's something. You should probably go lie down," David said.

"Are you kidding? I won't sleep one bit, not yet. Not until we can figure on something."

The phone rang once and stopped.

"I want to know what we are going to do, something actual," Janet said and she folded her hands on her stomach. She stared at him.

A windstorm calmed in David's head. He looked up at the clock and knew that the drawing would happen in a matter of minutes. He saw the corner of the lottery ticket peek out of his pocket and he pretended to be a father. David would make himself come up with something, some answer. He tried to focus. "Tomorrow," he said. "Tomorrow, we could go downtown and get ice cream." He found that he could breathe much better than he would have expected.

Janet paused and then smiled. Then genuine laughter. "Good," she said and she shook her head as if she couldn't believe it. "Actually, that is perfect."

She stood and gave him a kiss on the cheek. "I might borrow these sometime," she said and touched his earrings. The bedroom door closed.

He lit the witch candle that had melted into a pair of green hands holding a broom handle and the flame eventually rose from blue to yellow. He picked up the candle and walked into the kitchen. Shadows wavered on the walls and he placed the candle in the metal sink. When he looked out the window his own reflection appeared against the cotton night backdrop, the candlelight illuminated his chin. A father with crusty hair spears shooting out of one side of his skull and with lipstick spread around his mouth like an accident.

It seemed to David that regret and sadness must go into the melting pot just like anything else. No sudden weeping or self-flagellation. Nothing so dramatic or obvious. Instead it must seep into the stew with everything else and simmer, until it becomes part of the flavor of every single day. He put his hand inside his pocket.

He looked down and moved the lottery ticket into the flame. He pinched a corner of the paper until the fire licked against his painted nails, and then he dropped the ash into the drain and turned on the water. "Good for you," his mother would have said.

In the bathroom, he peeled off his pantyhose and scrubbed his face until it burned. The balloons moved and bounced on the bedroom ceiling, kissing one another and then drifting apart, again and again. Janet slept. On his side of the bed, hands behind his head, David closed his eyes.

The phone did not ring.

Conservation

I'll tell you how it is when you look straight at me and then at the full load of clean dishes in the dishwasher and then back at me and then at the dishes again. You are out of your mind with confusion or anger and your facial muscles are all tensed and contorted. If I look straight into your eyes, it's easy to see the gray clouds have turned to steel, smooth and impenetrable.

The truth is, they've been solid metal for a while now. And it is in this instant, right before you say something like "I thought you said, you'd unload the dishwasher before you left this morning." Which is not only true, but true for the third or fourth time in as many days, but before you say this, and before I respond with whatever I come up with, right in that gap of silence, in a single breath, you and I are eighteen years old, and we both have blond hair and we are going out, officially dating, in our first year of college, and we are in an eight week relationship that will end after Christmas Break.

You are quiet by nature, and easy going, and smart and you have a good sense of humor because you laugh at whatever I say. And you are very pretty. Also though, our connection is intense, too intense, but not physically—I don't think we ever move beyond a two-second kiss—but intense because we're so compatible or connected or whatever I start to call it. This is how I begin to tell myself the 'story of us'. We are separate clay; we do not belong to the lump of humanity.

I'm not afraid exactly, not yet. I look up spontaneous human combustion and worry that I'll explode into a firework rain before I figure out how to handle this seriously ridiculous desire. Do we feel slightly alien? Do we hint that our bond is supernatural, something other-worldly, unlike anything the mudslide of humanity has ever known?

You keep a level-head, and I am not too clouded to recognize that some of this nonsense is nothing more than the usual starry-eyed newlove gibberish, but this knowledge, this heroic awareness only confirms the extraordinary nature of our situation. I, for example, do not think of you in relation to sex, and this is the first time since age twelve that I apprehend a female separate from the sex movie running in my head. Maybe I think of you more like a goddess or some mystical creature way beyond my worth who I worship by pointing out my worthlessness.

I cannot stand being away from you. I experience actual heartache, an actual pain I my chest, and I'm running up the dorm staircase to the fifth floor absolutely every time I can, knocking on your door, revved up and filled with light. I am starving for you, the smell of your pillow, and your voice, and we talk all the time. But while I spout and spout, mostly nonsense, jokes, self-deprecation, you remain reserved.

You love that I can make you laugh. I am pretty sure that you're too good looking for me. And before I begin to self-destruct, before I plant the seed of breakup in your mind and then cultivate it into a certainty, I make an even more catastrophic mistake and plant a much more sinister seed, so deep that will take many years before it reveals its utter deadness. I decide that your quiet nature, your low key expression, your hesitance to divulge anything deeply personal, all of it, is due to the presence of a black velvet ring box that rests deep inside of you. It is easy to imagine this hinged box with its gold lips pressed tight, because mine is the same. Which is how I know what it contains: secrets and hidden passions, and those tender parts of yourself too delicate to be shown to just anyone.

I can imagine the hesitancy you must feel, your disinclination to open the box. After all, you have not learned how to defend the box with quick-wit comebacks or self-deprecating subject-changing jokes. Probably you worry about being ridiculed, worry that exposure to the heat of someone's gaze might dissolve you into nothing. I totally get that. But this box is exactly the best thing about you, besides your looks, because I have the same black box and the same fears of exposure. My obsession to be with you, the undeniable fact of this desire, proves that we are destined to flip open our boxes and exchange the brass figurines or seashells or whatever metaphor best suggests secrets and passions and suppressed desires.

Many years pass before you finally ask me, "What black box? What are you even talking about?" The irony, I try to explain, is that the very idea of a black velvet ring box dwelling inside a person is precisely the kind of secret that would be kept inside the black velvet ring box.

"Secrets? Secrets like what? Like bad things you've done? Like you want to screw the babysitter secrets?"

Exactly not those things, I explain, more like the ideas behind the bad things we've done, the reasons we tell ourselves, the version of the world we construct in our heads that allow us to do the bad things or cultivate the desire for, in this example, the babysitter.

You shake your head.

I offer a clear example from my own black box. This is not how I imagined the metaphorical exchange of our deepest selves would proceed, but I look straight into your eyes anyways, and I say, "Teleportation."

You say, "I don't have a black box. I don't have anything to hide."

I am not disheartened, because you are telling me something. You are telling me that your black velvet ring box contains rare and delicate components of your inner self. You are relying on our nearly mystical, sub-lingual comprehension of each other's whole being. I get it.

Over the Christmas break of our freshman year, I endure nonstop anguish. The weight of sorrow in my chest is absurd, my irritation all-encompassing, and I try to talk myself down on several occasions. People are enduring real grief, experiencing unspeakable tragedies, children are starving to death, and as always, the strategy fails to penetrate my consciousness as I roll and sink and twist in my swamp of misery, like a malaria victim in the grip of a fever dream. The phone calls from you are the reason I live. Trying not to speculate about when or if you will call on any given night becomes my primary occupation.

I had never before experienced the level of desire that I felt when I sat on the floor, next to my bed, in the middle of the night, and I attempted to transport myself through space. There was no internet then, so I couldn't look up teleportation and make sure I was doing it right. I had a book from a high school friend which suggested that people had meditated themselves out of their body and traveled.

I spent several hours each night, sitting cross-legged on my wooden floor and meditating. I worried about my ability to accurately and vividly hold a picture of your bedroom in my mind. I breathed, relaxed, and emptied my mind. Slowly, so as not to alert my conscious mind, I turned myself into a ball of yellow light. When I had become a large ball of light, dense enough in the center with blurry edges, I launched myself up through the bedroom ceiling, into the cold night air, where I stretched out until I was streaking across the sky like a single golden thread, until I touched down in your bedroom where I gathered myself into the more traditional and recognizable form.

I sat there in your bedroom, on the hardwood floor, and waited. I felt the tension return to my muscles like strings tugging a puppet to life, and I was exhausted. Part of me began to dread the effort required to try again while another part of me knew that I was sitting on the floor in your bedroom. I could even hear you breathing.

For some reason, I'd decided that successful teleportation hinged on whether or not I kept my eyes closed. The argument with myself began by questioning the value of materializing in your bedroom if I couldn't see you. The argument ended when I proceeded to open one eye, a millionth of a millimeter at a time, as if to trick the enforcers of the mysterious eyes-closed rule. The instant I registered the first glimpse of my surroundings, all was lost, and I would sit staring at the corner of the Candy-land game board protruding from under my closet door while I decided what to do next.

While each session began in earnest and with a sincere attempt at travel, failure had the effect of diverting my attention away from practicing teleportation to speculating about the potential consequences of success. What, I wondered, would happen after I appeared in your room in the middle of the night? Would I be able to transform your terror into joy? Did your father own a gun? Hugging would be possible, I imagined, and we would touch and still no sexual scenes presented themselves.

I reflected on how my supernatural ability would play in my favor, the inevitable appeal of having a boyfriend who was, or had the potential to be, a superhero. I decided that success would greatly enhance my desirability factor enough to secure us together and prevent you from doing what I constantly told you that you would do. Depending on the strength of the fantasy, I either went to sleep or began to try again.

Pulling onto the dirt road that led up to the house one night, I decided to try out a motion-based theory of teleportation. I was moving along the deserted road, eyes half closed, both hands on the steering wheel, when I suddenly smelled a burst of your perfume. My eye sprang pen and my vision instantly blurred. I tried to distract myself from the tightening at the back of my throat by looking around for the cause of the aroma. Stopped in the driveway, I knew I would not find anything, and it was while I was holding a tangled pair of rusted jumper cables in front of my face that I began to cry. I cried easily, in general. This would be one of the first secrets I let you see from my black box.

Instead of elation, instead of extracting the smell as evidence of success, I sat in the car and sobbed. I ached to be able to reach out and stroke your cheek with the back of my hand, the gesture that I would continue to do even after we broke up and dated the others and became friends. I don't remember exactly why or how, but I knew we would break up the instant I stepped into the dorm with my suitcase in hand. Of course it wasn't really over, not for good, not for real. Still, with the break-up I gave up on teleportation, and even worse, I put teleportation back inside my own velvet box and snapped it closed.

Then you refused to open your secret black box with me; you even refused to acknowledge its existence. I could think of nothing to do but to try and prove you wrong. I provoked emotional explosions and, like an army after a bombing, I tried to walk in and take the valuables that were left. For the most part the strategy failed; the single minor victory came when you decided to make a concession. Instead of moving us one step closer to a true exchange of our inner selves, your concession brought all possibility to an end.

You said that you had come to realize at last that you did have a black velvet ring box inside yourself, a box very similar, you confirmed, to my own. But when you told me that your ring box contained only one idea, one secret, I was sure I'd misheard. You turned your eyes on mine, and I saw your grave almost pained expression. Without a hint of mockery or derision you cleared your throat and said, "My box is empty." She repeated the phrase a few more times before clarifying, "That is the only secret my velvet rung box contains, the secret that there is nothing inside."

Now you see all of the possible reasons for my behavior, each one as unjustified as the next. Maybe out of hope or anger or disbelief or habit, I tell you that I will unload the dishwasher, but I do not. I see now, that the reasons are no longer interesting to you; you will not be provoked, you will not explode. I cannot compel you into any type of exchange ever again. The creased brow, the question mark face, the icy tone of voice: all of it has been smoothed over into a flat disinterested expanse.

You reach down and gently glide the clean dish racks back into the dishwasher. You lift the dishwasher door with one hand and press your hip against it while your thumb moves the lock. Turning the knob to the setting "Heavy Wash", you press the start button, and I hear a trickle of water begins inside the machine. By the time the machine's groan has peaked and the sounds of spraying water ripples through the air, you're no longer in the kitchen.

Dead Bugs and Disneyland

Arnold and Ruth were lying in bed with their backs propped against the headboard on the night of their twelfth or thirteenth anniversary. The overhead light cast a dim yellow glow over the bedroom.

Ruth gripped a book in both hands and Arnold stared at the ceiling, closing one eye and then the other, analyzing the perspective. A half glass of whiskey and flat soda water sat on his nightstand.

Ruth lowered the book; her fingers looked skeletal. One time, she slid over and rested her head on Arnold's chest.

"Are you bored of me?" she asked without turning her head.

"Why? Are you bored of me?"

"I asked first."

"Do you want the short answer or the long answer?" Arnold took the glass of whisky and placed it on his belly.

"What?"

"No," he said. "You?"

Ruth stared at the ceiling. "Maybe it's just, you know, regular life." Her voice cracked. "What was the long answer?"

Arnold stared at the ring of water on the nightstand. "Yes," he said. Arnold gulped the rest of his lukewarm drink. He wanted one with fresh clinking ice cubes, but he didn't dare move.

"It's good though," Arnold said.

"The American dream," Ruth said, her voice tight, controlled. "How long have we been saving for the trip to Disneyland?"

"'The family's dream destination'," Arnold said.

"Well I hate it," Ruth said. She violently threw her book on the ground where it thudded without drama and began to cry quietly into her fist.

Arnold decided that it was a good time to get a fresh drink. He slipped out of bed and said, "We won't go."

"Where are you going?"

Arnold passed by the vacant nursery, still smelling of fresh paint, cut and sanded wood. The air in the room sagged with tangible emptiness, its nothingness pulled at Arnold like gravity, like incredible disaster. He leaned, grasped the cold doorknob of the room and pulled it tightly shut. In the kitchen, Arnold coughed to hide the sounds of popping ice-cubes and guided them carefully into his glass as if they were bird eggs.

By the time Arnold returned, Ruth had stopped crying. She stood in the middle of the bed in the blue tee shirt that hung to the middle of her pale thighs. Shadowy veins mapped the back of her legs. She wore white socks.

"What are you doing?" Arnold asked. His drink chilled and warmed his body at the same time.

"They say that if you change your perspective, literally change it, then you'll start to see things differently." Ruth looked around with her hands on her hips, expectant. She rose up on her tiptoes and peeked into the light fixture cover

"So?"

"Dead bugs," she said ruefully. "A whole universe of them. All this time and I didn't even know they were here."

"What'll we do instead?" Arnold asked.

"Get the vacuum," Ruth said, stepping off the bed. "I'm not spending another night like this."

The Feast

"You were having sex on the couch," Erin's mother said. "I will not have this in my house."

"What are you talking about?" Erin asked. She felt prickly heat on her chest like thousands of tiny ants.

"You know what I'm talking about," her mother said.

"Stanley Pinkerton?" her father asked.

"We were watching a movie, not even holding hands," Erin said. She looked away.

"I know what I saw."

"Now Margaret," her father said. "Take it easy."

"Don't treat me like a child Henry," she said. "I saw them."

"Why don't you go take a rest," her father suggested.

"Are you blind?" her mother asked.

"First of all, the Stanley I know has integrity and plenty of common sense. And secondly, I'm sure that Erin is old enough to take care of herself."

Erin smiled at her father; he'd always been her ally. They testified on each other's behalf. They went to the mat for one another.

"She's seventeen years-old," her mother said.

Her father shrugged as he cut into his chicken breast.

Her mother placed her fork on her plate, stood up, and left the room.

Erin shook her head and sighed as if her mother's insanity was a burden that weighed on her body. And Erin remembered the night; she remembered thinking that someone had been watching her.

Stanley had rammed himself into Erin's body, and Erin bit her lip to control her noise. She was thinking at that moment that all of the traditional sounds of passion, the groans and gasps and urgent whispers were actually expressions of pain.

"You like to fuck?" Stanley whispered, out of breath, presumably mistaking Erin's grimace for pleasure.

Erin tasted blood from her lip and turned away. Stanley lowered his warm tongue onto her neck like a dog and Erin saw movement in the background. A shadow had disappeared, a form that had seemed permanent; a natural component of the backdrop had suddenly vanished. Had it been the outline of a human head?

Stanley bit into her shoulder until she pushed him away. He sat back on the couch, legs spread apart, glistening, and smiling at Erin like a satiated cannibal.

* * *

When Erin first arrived in *Magdalena*, the people behind the tables at the open-air market loved to talk to her. The swordfish butcher called her *Bambina*. The others latched onto the nickname and they never failed to smile and greet her. They often put a peach in her hand or a red tomato. She knew that's she'd found her new home.

The swordfish butcher was a bald older man with a muscular chest and thick arms. He smelled like tobacco and fish scales. His fleshy cracked palms and fingers looked as if they'd been dusted with chalk.

Erin spent most of her time near the fishermen and their bins of red, blue and sliver fish. White containers of slippery purple octopus stood next to mounds of black and green mussels. The smell of glassy-eyed fish felt more like life to Erin than the skinned rabbits that hung in *Magdalena's* meat shops, their bloody blue heads wrapped in plastic bags. The ocean's aroma stretched Erin out of her body; she floated in the vast ocean, weightless, and cool.

Signora Rossini was the mayor of *Magdalena*. She was a widow who wore black stockings, black dresses, and black scarves over her head. Her curly gray hair contrasted her younger face. As the older woman made her way from one table to the next with her wicker basket on her arm, the men and women vendors seemed to bow when they spoke to her, and they always spoke quietly. The hush traveled like an invisible wave through the market. The swordfish butcher said that she was not yet 50 years old.

"A very sad lady," he once said to Erin. "Her husband dead in New Orleans and her son," he gestured toward the ocean, "dead in the water, last summer." Then he leaned forward and whispered. "*La Monstra.*"

Inspired by an idea, the man sawed off the tip of a sword that surged up from the new white-bellied swordfish on the butcher-block table. The animal's large brown eyes looked like cloudy marbles.

"This side is good luck against *La Monstra*," he said and he ran his callused finger over the smooth edge. Then he barely touched the serrated edge and showed Erin the blossoming pinpricks of blood. "This side remembers the danger." He offered the tip to Erin and she placed it inside her backpack.

After Erin had been tested by the clinic and the fact of her pregnancy had moved beyond the ideas of missed-periods-due-to-family-stress and three faulty at-home-tests, the logical evidence regarding their course of action seemed obvious to Stanley and beyond any reasonable doubt.

"You're not even eighteen," Stanley said. He was taller than Erin, thin, and with black hair and dark eyebrows. He did not look at her eyes as he paced around her bedroom.

"Who has to be eighteen?" Erin asked.

"We're not ready for this Erin, not now, not like this. Do you have any idea how your father—"

"We're adults."

"We are not prepared for this. Your father wants to make me vice-president."

"So he'll make you vice-president."

Stanley looked at Erin like she had grown dandelions from her forehead. "Right. I'll say, gee Mr. Lockheed I'm really sorry about knocking up your teenage daughter, but how about we discuss my new office."

Erin felt the heat from Stanley's body.

"No," he said. "It's not possible—not now, not like this."

"You have a job, I'm almost done with school," Erin said. "It's not like we're on the street."

"We *will* be on the street."

"You're acting like we're 14 years old."

"You're his only daughter. You don't think he would prefer that we, oh I don't know, get married before you start—"

"You don't want to get married."

Stanley looked at Erin. "I never said that."

"You never said you did."

"Eventually," he said and paused. "Not now—not right this goddamn instant."

They were quiet and Stanley made his way to the bed to sit next to Erin. He calmed his tone.

"Look, I'm just not in the right position. I'm not ready for this." He put his hand on Erin's bare arm. "You know that I love you."

"I do?"

Stanley stood in a fury. "You're not listening. I said no, no way." He stretched his arms in the air. "This isn't happening," he said.

Erin looked away.

"Erin, I'm begging you," Stanley said. "Not now, not like this."

Erin sat quietly.

"It's just not logical, it's not right for us. There will be plenty of time," he said and his tone changed again. "Plenty of time to have a family of our own," he said, but he did not sit down. "We'll build a future together."

Erin did not look up at Stanley.

"I'll pay," he said softly.

Erin winced, but if he noticed, Stanley did not respond.

"This doesn't mean never. This just means not now." He walked over to Erin and her shoulder cringed under his touch. "I'll go with you, whatever you want, whatever you need. I'm here," he said. "I'll always be here."

Erin cried, and Stanley pulled her up from the bed and into his chest. "It'll be okay," he whispered as he stroked her hair, patted her back. "I'm here for you, I'm here."

Erin walked to the bathroom in the hall and locked the door behind her. She could not hear if Stanley said anything through the door before he left.

Erin stood at the pay phone on the edge of *Magdalena*'s main piazza and held the receiver to her ear. Her father's sentences slipped out from the earpiece and wrapped around Erin's neck. His tone wanted to jerk Erin back to reality through the tiny black holes.

The voices of the Sicilian boys kicking a soccer ball in the center of the piazza made it difficult for Erin to hear her father's exact words. Their laughter fell on the otherwise deserted piazza like flaps of metal from the sky. It was early morning and Erin stared down at her swollen bare feet. The ball skidded across the worn cobblestones with the sound of a street sweeper's broom and the boys were gusts of wind. The local bank had not made a mistake; Erin's father had not sent her any money.

"It's not about the money," her father said.

Erin pushed the tip of her bare big toe in between two black cobblestones and flipped a green shard of glass end over end.

"It's enough of this nonsense Erin. Do you understand that?" He spoke slowly, emphatically. "It's time to come home."

The toenail on Erin's big toe had lost most of the pink paint. Odd shaped flecks of pink dotted all of her toenails. She couldn't remember when she'd last painted them. She couldn't remember why.

"You *must* have money left," her father insisted.

"Yes of course," Erin said. Her ankle had become almost as thick as her calf. The top of her foot up to her knee was tan and covered with a thin film of black, as if she'd been walking through fine coal dust or clouds of ash. The *Pensione Florida* did not have a bathtub, and the water trickled from the rusty showerhead like broken rain.

"Stanley will be there by the end of the week, and he'll take it from there," her father said. Then he sighed heavily into Erin's ear. "I wish to God that you weren't making him do this. He looks like he hasn't slept in weeks."

Erin listened for any sounds in the air behind her father's voice.

"It's my fault," he said and he clicked his tongue. "I should have sent someone after you right away."

"Right," Erin said.

"Do you think your mother approves?" her father asked. "Do you think that she wants her only child to run away to some rinky dink Sicilian town like a ten year-old?"

The Sicilian boys had stopped the game and gathered in a tight circle on the far side of the piazza.

"I don't think so," her father answered.

The owner of the café approached the boys. He wore a clean white apron and the sleeves of his white dress shirt had been rolled up to his elbow. He raised his hand and yelled at the boys and they skipped away, throwing the dingy soccer ball to one another as they escaped. He turned and walked away.

"Do you know what your mother wants Erin? She wants you to carry on with real life. She wants you to live up to your potential instead of running away and hiding from the very people that love you. You have great potential Erin; you have a good head on your shoulders. You're smarter than this."

The shard of glass leaned against her big toe's callused flesh. It pressed into her rigid skin like a fingernail pressing into leather upholstery.

"You were just confused," he said.

"Right."

"Stanley will talk some sense into your head," her father said. "You have your whole life to live and it kills me to see you act this way. It kills all of us."

Erin drove her toe into the tip of the glass shard and the sensation of pressure remained constant as it sunk into her skin. No sting, no sharp prick; just a steady pressure, almost like a deep massage.

"I will see you when you get home," her father said.

"Right."

She lifted her leg and shook her foot until the glass fell onto the black cobblestone. No blood dripped from the tiny black hole. She hung up the phone and turned her back on the luxury hotel. Erin walked in the shadow of the towering *Hotel Paradiso*, and onto the main street that led down the steep hill to the *Pensione Florida*.

The unmarked flaking green door on the street opened into a dark cement room. Old televisions, computers, and radios had been piled next to broken wooden chairs and three-legged metal desks under the main staircase.

Erin walked up the three flights to the frosted glass door. "*Pensione Florida,*" had been printed in red on two sheets of computer paper and taped at eye level. She reached out and pressed a small button that was fastened to the door jam.

It felt like a pregnant suit clung to her body like plastic wrap and Erin wanted to unzip it. She wanted to pull it off and toss it like a wet blanket onto the hum of whispers that swirled around her like mosquitoes.

Erin pushed into the dim lobby and the door clicked shut behind her like a gate. Marco Florida sat behind the wooden reception desk wearing his glasses and flipping through a stack of yellow and white papers. He had slicked-back blond hair and a fleshy nose, wide at the nostrils.

"A friend will deliver money at the end of the week," Erin said.

Marco looked up. His stare shot above his eyeglasses on the middle of his nose. "There is no need for money," he said.

"To pay for the room," Erin said.

Marco smiled and then he shook his head as if an idea had suddenly gone sour. "You can't stay here anymore," he said. "I've told you."

"I'll work until then," Erin said.

"No," a woman's voice said from the darkened doorway behind Marco. Enza stepped into the light. She was a short and heavy woman with straight black hair and a mole on the tip of her nose the color of dried blood. She wore an apron with red and green smears around her wide waist, and she stood with her hands on her hips.

"It's better for everyone if you leave *Magdalena*," Enza said. Her eyes scanned Erin's pregnant suit.

"*La Monstra* has a thousand eyes in *Magdalena*," Marco said. "If you would have told us before, I would never have let you—,"

"The people of *Magdalena* will not tolerate the sin," Enza said.

Erin felt the last word hit her belly like a rock.

"I've seen a dead girl on the beach with red bricks tied around her bloated blue ankles," Enza said. "Her purple face frozen in horror." Enza made the sign of the cross and the voices of the couples' two young children floated out from behind her.

"Usually," Marco added gravely, "They are never found."

"I will leave," Erin said.

Enza clicked her tongue, shook her head, and waved her finger in disapproval. Then she turned and yelled at the children as she disappeared into the apartment.

Erin stared at Marco and for an instant, she saw behind his impenetrable stare. Once Enza had disappeared, his black eyes suddenly softened, became liquid.

"You're lying," Marco said.

Erin looked away.

"You can stay until the end of the week," he said, and he looked over his shoulder. "Stay out of her sight."

Marco sat back in his chair and his eyes hardened into onyx. He lifted his index finger. "Talk to Signora Rossini," Marco added. "She will convince you to go home."

Erin nodded and walked passed the front desk to her room at the back. The single window faced a red brick wall that was close enough to touch. The daylight reflected a pink hue that cast the room in a perpetual dawn or dusk.

Erin's two other outfits, a black dress and a yellow dress, were laid out on the ground in front of her mother's black backpack. They looked alone and forgotten, like museum pieces on display.

The backpack was the only piece of luggage that Erin had brought to *Magdalena*. The bag slumped against the wall like a stooped old woman, filled with Erin's collection of smooth black stones and rippled pink shells. It smelled like freshly killed fish.

Erin sat on the edge of her bed and laid back. Her belly was a small taut mound, beyond which she could see the two chipped gold cherubs who each looked up at the darkened light bulb they held above their head.

Erin had stood at the top of the staircase and looked down into the dining room. Her father might have snatched a lilac blur out of her mother's outstretched hand. It was hard to tell.

"Now am I crazy?" her mother had asked.

"You say things that make no sense," Erin's father said. "You see things that do not exist. Yes, I would call that crazy."

Her mother sat down in a chair and murmured a phrase that could have been, "How could you?" or "Who are you?" or "I know you."

"You need help," her father said. He noticed Erin at the top of the stairs. He put a hand in his pocket and shook his head slowly. He looked at her and shrugged his shoulders as if to say, *we are the victims. But what can we do?*

Erin left *Pensione Florida* the next morning wearing her heavy backpack and she walked down the cobblestone street toward the market. She wore the yellow summer dress that she'd bought when she first arrived and a straw hat that she'd found at the beach. The brim was split in the back but the shadow across her eyes made Erin feel slightly invisible.

The daily market was set-up on a stretch of boardwalk overlooking a public beach. Erin stopped and let the sounds of the ocean fill up her head. The ocean was as agitated as Erin had ever seen it. Four-foot waves smashed onto the beach and Erin could see the white caps rocking against themselves in the distance. She did not see Signora Rossini at the market so she walked down the cement staircase that led to the beach.

It was almost midday and the sand stung the tops of Erin's feet. She walked along the edge of the water and bent to pick up a smooth wet stone that caught her attention. The round black gem had a spider-web of white veins imbedded in the stone covering it like a net. She dropped it into her heavy pack and walked on.

Erin bent over to rinse a palm-sized black stone with orange streaks in a stream of retreating water. She turned her head and saw Signora Rossini standing at the edge of the ocean further along. The woman wore her characteristic black dress and a black scarf tied around her head. Her arm was looped through the wicker basket that hung from her elbow. Erin could see blurry impressions of the reds and oranges and greens inside the basket. Signora Rossini looked like a wet oil painting with the blue sky in the background, no land in sight. She looked as if she stood at the edge of the world.

Erin dropped the wet stone into her backpack and approached the mayor. Signora Rossini gazed out at the ocean and seemed not to notice Erin.

"*La Monstra* is upon us," Signora Rossini said. "And it will not leave hungry." Signora Rossini turned her head and set her even gaze on Erin. Her gray curls framed her forehead like frozen whitecaps and her cheeks and chin were as taut as sails. She nodded but did not smile.

"I want to stay in *Magdalena*," Erin said.

Signora Rossini shook her head with a grim expression on her lips. Then she turned and stared out at the ocean as if she expected to see something, as if motion had caught her eye.

Erin stared out at the infinite body of water and even as it thrashed and spit foam into the air with rage, Erin felt the waves rock her like a baby, like she was cradled in the palm of a gentle giant.

"My son died one year ago," she said, nodding her head toward the water. "I watched him from this spot."

Signora Rossini slipped the basket off of her arm and handed it to Erin. Erin followed her up the cement staircase and they walked up the main street.

Erin stood in Signora Rossini's kitchen and unloaded food onto the counter in silence. The widow put items in their proper place, creating still life as she went. A yellow ceramic bowl held two pears leaning into each other behind a fat peach in the center. Various nuts looked as if they'd fallen into the bowl from the sky. There were no crumbs on any counters.

The red and yellow ceramic plates with blue designs that hung on the wall reminded Erin of her childhood drawings of the spinning patterns that evolved from stars to flowers to complete circles of web. A strand of garlic hung from a nail on one side of the dishes and a string of dried red chili peppers hung on the opposite side. Nothing about the scene felt used or dirty or out of place—except Erin.

"I was like you," Signora said after the groceries had been put away and straightened and aligned in symmetrical rows. Signora Rossini had filled a stovetop espresso maker with coffee grounds and water and placed it on the stove over a tall and straight blue gas flame. "A young girl with no husband, no father for my baby."

Erin sat down in a kitchen chair.

Signora Rossini appeared with tiny espresso cups and saucers. She set a basket of warm rolls on the table, a glass dish of strawberry jam, and a dish of butter that had not yet been scarred.

Erin took a piece of crusty bread. She tore off a chunk and steam rose above the exposed tender flesh.

"In America maybe there are many girls like you," Signora Rossini said. "In *Magdalena*, no." The espresso maker gurgled and hissed on the stove as if launching from a pad. "In *Magdalena*, never."

Signora Rossini poured the rich coffee into the tiny cups, as black as oil and almost as thick. Erin spooned sugar into her cup until the mound pushed up from beneath the surface like the hump of a whale in and oil-slicked ocean.

"My father was mayor, and he went out of his mind to help me. He was afraid," she said as she stirred her coffee. "*La Monstra* does not feed on flesh, you see. It devours shame."

"Were you ashamed?" Erin asked. A flake of the hard crust cut into the roof of her mouth and she did not stop chewing.

"Not your shame, not mine—*Magdalena*'s shame. The ones who drown, they are girls like you, alone and with a baby. No man will take them and the town turns their back. For many of these girls they say death is a blessing."

Erin shook her head.

"The men do not have to step forward, and if they do, after it is too late, too visible, they are shunned by their own family. Few men choose this, and the girls, as you well know, they can't easily hide." The old

woman looked over Erin's pregnant suit. "My father decided to have a
ceremony. During the Feast of Maria Magdalena, he chose me to
launch the statue onto the water. I would send Saint Maria into the
ocean and return to the beach where my father would choose a husband.
In this way the men were protected, you see, they bore no responsibility
and they would gain honor—or so my father believed."

Signora Rossini put the small coffee cup to her lips and tilted her
head back to swallow all of the espresso like a shot of alcohol. She did
not eat.

"He chose a young man, Giancarlo Rossini, to be my husband.
But even after we were married on the beach, blessed by the priest,
witnessed by all in *Magdalena*, they turned against us. They would not
look at us, much less speak to us, and Giancarlo decided to move to
America where we could start again without the stares and talk of these
people on our shoulders."

Erin continued to spread the red jam onto the virgin white bread
and eat. The more she ate the hungrier she became. Signora Rossini
rose and returned with a pear that she proceeded to slice into wedges,
peel, and place on Erin's small ceramic plate. Erin slipped the bare flesh
of the pear into her mouth, one after the other.

"Luca was born in America, and he was only five years-old when
Giancarlo died. We returned to *Magdalena*, my young son and myself
and lived with my father. The people were not as cold, perhaps because
five years had passed, or perhaps because Giancarlo's death was
punishment enough."

"You escaped *La Monstra*," Erin said.

Signora Rossini stared at the wall of ceramic plates as if she were
looking through a window. "Luca had just finished his first year at the
medical school," she said.

The mayor rose and returned with the peach in her hand. Drops of
juice flowed over her thumb as she carved into the wet pulp

Signora Rossini nodded slowly. "On that night, we were walking
alone on the beach because he had something to say. He looked out at
the ocean. I saw the light of a boat speeding away, but Luca saw
something else. He ran into the dark water and swam; his head looked
like a shadow of an animal, a seal, bobbing up and disappearing, again
and again until I couldn't see him. I heard nothing."

Signora stopped with half of the peach in one hand and the knife in
the other. The knife seemed alive.

"When they found them, Luca's arms were tangled in the ropes that bound the girl's hands and feet. He was filled with water. The bricks on the ends of the rope had pulled them down together."

Silence draped the room like a cloak. Erin felt the texture of food in her mouth and had forgotten what she was eating. Signora Rossini wore a pained expression and her chin trembled.

"I lived, yes," she said at last, continuing to peel that last half of the juicy peach. "My own death would have been a blessing."

Erin stood and picked up her backpack. She felt hot. The air had thinned.

Signora Rossini looked up at her. "You must go home," she said, holding out the last piece of naked peach. "For you and for your baby, there is no other way. You must think of the child."

Erin bowed her head, turned away from the fruit that dripped from Signora's clenched hand, and walked out of the apartment into the blinding white sunlight.

Erin had sat up in bed early one morning and felt the warm patches of sweat that had soaked through her tee shirt. Something, it seemed, had knocked her on the head or clapped in her ear, some loud noise that had been replaced by a sudden vacuum, a noticeable lack. Erin strained to listen and a tempest developed in her stomach.

The first pink streaks of dawn streamed into the bathroom like laser beams and reflected off of the yellow shower curtain. Erin sat on the toilet with her head on her bare knees. Her stomach was settling, calming the waves. When she felt stronger, less dizzy, Erin left the bathroom and went to look for her mother.

The door to the basement was cracked open. The basement had long ago been converted into a home gym with a treadmill, a weight bench, and mirrors on the walls. Erin's mother always woke before dawn and Erin had the idea that her mother, with her newfound energy and stability, may have once again taken up exercise. Believing that she heard muffled noise, Erin opened the door wide and descended into the darkness.

The pink sunlight had turned red and poured into the basement from the half windows above the mirrors. The light illuminated the ceiling and spread the red hue so completely that it had an artificial look—an intentional rock-concert feel.

Erin's mother hung from the ceiling in the center of the room, her head forward, black hair covering her face. One of her black shoes had fallen onto the ground next to the overturned stepstool, and the other shoe hung precariously from her lifeless foot. Her father's black belt wound around her mother's neck like a dog collar.

Her mother was dressed in black stocking and a black dress, and Erin froze at the bottom of the stairs. She could not look away.

Erin stared at the hanging shoe, but it would not fall. Erin would not make it to the bathroom. She dropped to her hands and knees onto the carpet. Nothing came from her mouth except the harsh thrust of sobs. Her arms shook, her elbows buckled, and once again, Erin descended into the darkness.

Erin met Stanley in the lobby of *Hotel Paradiso.* She walked into the hotel with her few clothes draped over her arm and her mother's black backpack filled with her stones. She wore her cracked straw hat.

Stanley sat in a white leather chair and flipped through a magazine. The hair on the top of his head had thinned. He wore dark gray suit pants and a white business shirt with a solid blue tie. Blue, Erin knew, meant confidence.

He did not look up until Erin stopped directly in front of him, and when he raised his head, he did not smile. He glanced briefly at Erin's eyes before he shifted his attention to her stomach. Erin saw his jaw tighten.

"You look awful," Stanley said. He looked down at her feet with an expression of disgust. Then he stood and led Erin into an elevator.

Erin stared at Stanley in the elevator's mirror, but he avoided her eyes.

"When was the last time you bathed?" he asked.

Erin did not answer.

Stanley opened his hotel door and turned on the light in the bathroom. He held Erin's clothes as if they were dirty rags and he helped her off with her backpack.

"What the hell is in this thing?" Stanley asked as he lowered the backpack to the ground.

"The ocean," Erin said.

"Get cleaned up and we'll take it from there," Stanley said, as if it was the least she could do.

Erin stood naked under the warm water and opened her mouth to the streams. The warmth bubbled out of her full mouth and ran down her neck. It felt like a layer of wax melted off of her body and she looked at the dirty brown water that swirled around the drain by her puffy feet. She lathered all of her skin and her hair, and she wondered what Stanley was thinking. She wondered what exactly they would talk about, because certain events were always off limits. Erin wondered if she had become an off limit topic.

When she emerged from the foggy bathroom wrapped in a yellow towel, Stanley handed her a pair of his jeans and a tee shirt. She dropped the towel and Stanley turned away. Erin dressed and sat on the edge of one of the double beds, rubbing her hair with a small towel and running a comb through it.

"Feel better?" Stanley asked and he aborted an attempt to smile.

Erin let her eyes wander around the clean and well-lit room. Stanley had traveled with his black suit bag that hung on a portable metal rack in the corner. His suitcase was open on the small wooden table and all of his clothes were perfectly folded and organized.

"Your father doesn't know," Stanley said and he glanced at her pregnant suit. He lay back on the other bed with his hands behind his head and stared at the ceiling.

Erin knew that he was calculating, coming to the conclusion that Erin was probably five months along—almost the end of the second trimester. She slid back on the bed and fell asleep with the black comb gripped in her hand.

Erin sat across from Stanley at the restaurant table on the deck of *Magdalena*'s best restaurant, *L'Ultima Volta*. The sun hung like a solid orange ball, just above the horizon. The ocean rocked and slapped against itself under Erin's feet, and Stanley poured himself a full chalice of wine from a ceramic pitcher shaped like a red chicken. Red wine flowed from the open yellow beak, and Stanley gulped it down.

"I'm looking at a house about a block up from your father's place," Stanley said. Sweat stains had formed under the arms of his dress shirt. He had loosened his tie and unbuttoned the top two buttons, revealing the rim of a white undershirt. "Three bedrooms, two bath, and 1.4 acres. It backs up to open space."

Erin poured mineral water from the green glass bottle and took a sip. The air was still and the heat from the day lingered.

"We'll have to get new carpeting and appliances. The fridge is from the 1950's."

"I'm staying," Erin said. A thin gray cat appeared under the table next to Erin. The ribs pushed through the shallow fur and patches of the animal's bald white skin. It was six o'clock in the evening and they were the only ones at the restaurant.

"That's ridiculous," Stanley stated. "And you know it." He tapped his fingertips together around the stem of the yellow ceramic chalice. He seemed to want to strangle the cup. "You can't stay here. You don't belong here."

The waiter arrived with two pizzas. He placed the anchovy pizza in front of Erin and the hamburger and sausage pizza in front of Stanley. Stanley poured the last drops from the chicken's guts into his cup and gestured for more wine. When the waiter returned, he placed the pitcher directly in front of Stanley.

"I've talked to the high school and you won't have to completely repeat the classes. They'll let you join toward the end of next semester, where you left off. You'll graduate in December."

Stanley cut his pizza like a pie. He folded a triangle piece with his fingers and bit off a large part of the curved tip. Orange oil dripped down one corner of his mouth. He shoved the food into one cheek and drank wine while he chewed.

Erin stared at her pizza, and then reached out and tore off a piece of crust. She threw it toward the sick cat.

"Look how skinny she is," Erin said.

Stanley leaned forward. "Maybe by next summer, after I've settled in as VP, you've finished a semester of college just maybe, and I'm not promising anything, but maybe we'll start talking wedding bells. Anyway, I'm buying the house this month."

The cat did not move. Its big head and giant wide eyes stared at Erin, not even acknowledging the food that was inches away from its scrawny paw.

"I thought we could stop in Paris for a few days before we head home. Check out the sights," Stanley said. He nervously pushed another piece of pizza into his cheek and the chicken vomited more red wine into Stanley's chalice. *The sights* had sounded heavy coming from Stanley's mouth, as if the words were stretched thin over the top of a boiling kettle. A humid and heavy lie.

"And the baby?" Erin asked.

Stanley's face had broken out in sweat and he patted it with his crumpled napkin. "In Paris, we'll start over. We'll fix everything up there and return to the states just as soon as you're ready. I'm not here to rush you."

Erin stared at the cat and at the piece of tomato stained crust on the wooden slat. The cat blinked, and for an instant, she looked like a smiling kitten. The desperate expression quickly returned and the cat stared at Erin.

"I'm getting married here," Erin said. Only half of the sun remained on the horizon and Erin thought she could see it sink

"You're crazy," Stanley said, but he tried to swallow the last word by quickly adding, "What are you talking about?"

"It's a ceremony, a lottery ritual."

"Do they kill anyone?" Stanley asked and neither one of them smiled. When Erin looked under the table only the solitary crust remained. "Come on Erin, be reasonable. I'm here now and you're going to be alright. *We're* going to be alright."

"They think that children need fathers."

Stanley's expression became cautious. He continued to fork pieces of pizza into his mouth and drink wine. At some point, the chicken had begun to spout wine the color of weak urine.

"I'm the father," he said.

A chunk of chewed paste pizza fell out of Stanley's mouth.

"You'll be fine," he said with his eyes cast down. He attempted to smile. "I'll buy the train tickets for tomorrow night and in a couple of days, before you know it, our lives will be on track. We'll both be able to finally enjoy ourselves and you'll thank me for coming. You'll see." He did not glance up from his plate.

Erin had woken up too late for school. The knowledge that her mother was gone descended on her like an aroma. She had to pee. Erin walked out of her bedroom and as she stepped onto the bathroom's cool tile floor she heard sounds coming from her parent's bedroom down the hall. The door was cracked open and Erin cautiously approached.

For an instant, Erin hoped that the nude woman was her mother; it should have been her mother since it had been her mother's room. But the naked woman whose breasts bounced up and down as she straddled the man beneath her was not Erin's mother. The woman had long red hair and a freckled face.

The man lying on his back was, however, her father. There was no mistaking the top of his head or the round shape of his stomach. He had one hand on each of the woman's naked hips and he helped her bounce. The woman's eyes were closed, and her lips and chin were puckered. Neither one saw Erin.

Erin stepped into the bathroom, but her stomach was empty. Each eruption from inside her body brought images of the woman's wincing face, her father's fat hands pressed into pale white skin. Tears and sweat dropped like rain until Erin imagined that she had melted into the toilet.

A couple of hours later when Erin finally emerged, her father stood in her room dressed in his dark gray suit, white collared shirt, and a solid red tie. Red, Erin knew, meant passion.

"I thought you were at school," her father said. His face appeared without a hint of guilt, without a single crease of anxiety or concern.

Erin crawled underneath her covers and pulled them up to her chin.

"You're sick," her father said.

Erin did not look at her father and he sat on the side of her bed. He reached out and brushed hair off of Erin's forehead.

"We'll be okay," he said. "We'll get through this."

His fingers brushed passed Erin's nostrils. She swallowed hard, turned her head away, and let herself dissolve into the pillow.

The three-day feast of Maria Magdalena began late the next afternoon with a procession that started in the main piazza. The five-foot Maria Magdalena stood on a large wooden platform, dressed in the red plaster robe that draped down from her head to just above her feet.

Erin stood in the crowd. Stanley was on the telephone in the hotel room, trying to make an appointment for Erin in Paris. Erin wore a black dress and a veil over her face. The weight of her mother's black backpack pulled her closer to the ground, closer to the center of the earth. She felt sturdy—immovable and brave.

Erin thought Maria Magdalena's face looked sad and sick, but it might have been the irregular white spots on the plaster cheeks and chin. Maria held out her arms in a welcoming gesture, but her back was slightly bent forward and her eyes were cast down at her bare feet. She looked as if she were placing an invisible carpet down for a king.

Eight men wearing white undershirts and black pants took their positions by the wooden beams that were fastened under the platform. The two men at each corner bent at the knees, grabbed a section of pole, and heaved the woman saint onto their shoulders.

The local priest shouted words into a bullhorn and when the drums began to tap, the procession began down the hill. Erin stood behind the statue with other women who wore black veils. Many of these old women held pictures of the deceased in their wrinkled hands and walked with their heads bent. Erin saw Signora Rossini on the end, and she held a black rosary in her hand and moved her mouth in prayer.

As they proceeded down the main street lined with the residents of *Magdalena*, the men grunted under the statue's weight. Sweat soaked through the backs of their shirts and their legs seemed to tremble. The men halted and dropped down to their knees while the priest shouted prayers, and the residents walked up to the statue and taped money onto Maria and set flowers at her feet. Some reached up and touched the statue's hand and then kissed their own fingers. Some cried and others smiled. Young boys ran up and laughed as they threw handfuls of red rose petals at Maria, and many landed like giant tears of blood on the shoulders of the carriers. The men stood and continued.

By the time they reached the beach, the statue's feet and the bottom of her red cloak were hidden behind thick piles of red and yellow flowers, and money fluttered against her body like the wings of birds. The men steadily walked into the water, until the platform rested on the ocean's surface. They turned and bowed to the statue. The priest's words were swallowed by the arrival of the drums that brought up the rear of the procession.

Several women emerged from the crowd with thick white candles in their hands, followed by a young man who held a lit torch. The flame stretched toward the heavens changing from blue to orange to bright yellow, as if signaling to the pink sky, communicating to the sun that had fallen behind the horizon.

The women walked into the water and shoved the candles into holes on the platform encircling the statue. Then the young man walked around in water up to his waist and lit each one. The statue seemed to come to life with shadows and flickers dancing across her figure.

Erin stood with the other mourners and watched as the men pushed the statue out to sea. Maria drifted slowly backward, her arms outstretched, head bowed. The flowers looked brilliant in the firelight and the money flapped against her form like human hands waving from a departing ship.

The people of *Magdalena* stood on the beach with their heads lowered while the priest read the final prayer. The drums resumed their slow march and the priest led the people up the street and back to the church where they would have mass and then enjoy an enormous feast in the piazza.

Erin did not follow. She stood alone on the beach and looked through her veil at the retreating Magdalena. A hand touched her shoulder, but she did not turn around.

"You all set?" Stanley asked.

Erin let her head fall forward.

"Paris is ready and waiting. I got you in at one o'clock tomorrow afternoon."

Erin stared at her bare feet pressing into the sand.

"We've got about an hour. You sure you're okay?" Stanley asked. "I still have a little surprise for you, waiting at the train station."

"Bring it here," Erin said. She did not look up.

"That's a great idea," he said. "You wait right here and prepare to have your socks knocked off." He kissed Erin on the back of her neck and vanished.

Erin stared out at the statue. Maria Magdalena bowed to Erin and welcomed her with her hands. She looked so beautiful, so immaculate, slipping away into the hazy space between the sky and the calm ocean. The candlelight flickered in celebration and Erin was only vaguely aware of the water that had already crept up to her knees.

Erin's thighs dissolved, and then her waist. Maria Magdalena nodded. The sky had gone completely dark. The cool water sloshed against Erin's neck and she felt the security of her mother's backpack. Erin moved through the furthest regions of space. Her body disintegrated with each step, and her soul strained toward the heavens like a flame. Her feet never rose up from the bottom.

Erin tasted the saltwater, warm against her lips like tears. She turned toward the beach and closed her eyes. Erin opened her mouth and let herself sink back into the bosom of the endless body of water.

I am Not Friday

The cell phone vibrations do not blur the digital clock display: 3:13 am. I have been lying in bed next to my soon-to-be ex-wife, marking time at ten-minute intervals.

I scan Suzanne for any sign of movement, but she sleeps with her back to me, comforter pulled up to her chin. On the phone, my brother Derrick's voice.

"No one's dead," Derrick says.

For a second, I can't remember if he is in or out of prison.

"No?" My feet freeze on the floor and I move on tiptoes, like a cartoon burglar, to my closet.

"Meet me at Mile High in half an hour," Derrick says.

I stand inside my closet. For six years, my clothing has been put into outfits and hung according to occasion. All of it will be in boxes by lunch.

"The stadium?"

"Parking lot. We've got to do something about Ma," Derrick says.

There aren't many cars anywhere until I pull into the massive parking. Everywhere, trunks and hatches are raised, and people unfold tables and push up tents. I remember that Derrick is out on parole for armed robbery.

Derrick's dented and rusting white van looks like a perfect car bomb.

The minivan's door slides open and Derrick helps Ma into the far back. Ma wears a faded white nightgown and clumps of her gray hair sway in front of the red lipstick slashes across her face. I miss Ma. This is not Ma.

"Hi Ma," I say.

"I am not Friday," Ma says, not looking my way.

"Put this in the DVD," Derrick says.

I feed the disc into the machine and a bluish light appears on Ma's upturned face. Derrick places headphones with enormous black cushions over Ma's ears.

Derrick sits down heavily on a middle row seat and closes his eyes, breathing hard. He has a bald head with some black and gray along the sides, a thick black and gray mustache, and a beer gut that looks like pregnancy.

He pulls an envelope from the inside of his brown leather vest; his white tee shirt is soaked through with sweat.

I unfold the letter and stop breathing. It's the letter from Ma. Somehow, Derrick has broken into Suzanne's little metal box and taken the letter.

"How did you get this?" I ask. After I found it, I might not have read the whole thing. Suzanne can always tell when something of hers has been touched or moved.

"Through the mail."

"But it's from Suzanne's document box."

Derrick shakes his head. "It's addressed to you. It's a letter for you."

I watch a truck pull into the space next to Derrick's van. "Suzanne handles all of the official stuff—,"

"It's a freakin' letter to you," he says voice rising. He takes a deep breath. "Look, Ma sent us the same letter. Did Suzanne even let you read your own letter?"

"Of course," I say and then snort. I read and nod, like I'm reviewing the main points.

"Well, it's time," Derrick says.

His sweat smells like beer. I wonder what his parole officer says about drinking. Ma's wide eyes are fixed on the small screen. In the flickering light, she looks like an eight years old girl.

Derrick reaches out and grabs the letter from my hand. He searches and then reads out loud, "I am dead serious about this, boys. The instant I get to that point, you take me out somewhere and shoot me. I went through it with Nana, and I swore that I would NEVER put you through that hell— it was pure hell. If you ever loved me, don't think, save all of us and just do it."

"Do what?" I ask. "Shoot her?" I snort again.

Derrick takes a small silver gun from the fanny pack around his waist.

"Are you out of your fucking mind?"

"I am not Friday," Ma says, too loud.

"We're going for a walk, Ma. Be right back," Derrick says.

"How do we even know that she is at that point?" I ask, sliding the door shut.

"You know that she's been picked up twice now, right? Wandering around in the middle of the night? No clue where or who she is? Maybe Suzanne forgot to mention it."

I say nothing.

Headlights illuminate much of the parking lot. People stand with hands outstretched around the orange flames that leap up from a couple of barrels.

"Ma has no money for the nursing home. Everything comes to us after she dies. There is no way to get at it to pay for anything."

We stop near the truck next to Derrick's Van. A biker with a long black beard and a red bandana around his head steps up to Derrick and clasps his hands.

Three electric and two acoustic guitars sit propped and displayed on his table, next to two keyboards. A fully assembled black drum set sits in the bed of the man's truck. The man walks over, swings opens the face of the giant bass drum, and places Derrick's small gun inside.

When we return to the mini-van, I see two syringes with capped needle in Derrick's unzipped fanny-pack.

I open my mouth, but Derrick squeezes my arm hard.

"First, I can't be anywhere near this," he says. He takes off his fanny pack and drapes it across my arms. "The cops or my PO get a whiff of me around this and I'm all done."

The objections that occur to me dissolve in my mouth. "Second, you do not want to watch Ma turn back into an infant. It's a fucking nightmare."

Derrick's van disappears across the parking lot and into the orange glow hovering just above the horizon.

I hold the fanny pack to my chest, step up, and close the mini-van door behind me.

"Hi Ma," I say, moving toward her. "What are you watching over here?"

She says, "I am not Friday."

Experimental Fiction

Despite the vast differences that exist among the various types of experimental fiction, each type seeks to explore the less accessible, but no less true, areas of human experience.

They all operate on the principle that the limits imposed on realistic fiction, make it ill-suited to the discovery of the deeper truths about being human. Possibly the most enduring consequence of experimental fiction is that the work forces the reader to shift in their approach to fiction.

The reader is blocked from traditional interpretation and forced to look for the meaning of the story in a different place. Successful interpretation of an extreme story is dependent on the reader's ability to shift their focus and their expectations as they begin to read the story. This means that the reader must locate the place in the story which contains the meaning or at least, the author's intention.

A reader's approach to a story will determine whether or not the reader succeeds. This section attempts to present experimental fiction along with brief comments about the purpose and intention of four types of experimental fiction: Science Fiction, Surrealism, Absurdism, and Metafiction.

Science Fiction

Purpose: to tell a story that goes beyond the limits of natural law, human perception, and/or known truth.

Intention: to express ideas related to the following major themes:

The Nature of Human Perception- What role does Human perception play in human understanding? -What are the characteristics, the limits and the flaws of human Perception?

The Nature of Reality-What is Reality and what are the forces that affect reality?

The Nature of Time-What is Time and how does it affect human life?

What is Human Nature? The characteristic of being human. What will become of Human Beings?

If all fictional stories attempt to convey some truth about human experience, what kind of truth does science fiction attempt to convey? And how does it go about revealing the truth?

1. By presenting non-human, strange, and often grotesque characters (who are often thinking beings with varying amounts of intelligence and skill)--science fiction presents human beings with unique situations that reveal many characteristics of human nature.

2. While qualities of human nature are almost always the subject of fiction--we are better able to see those characteristics in science fiction because science fiction presents a situation which intensifies human action and reaction.

3. The truth that science fiction reveals is the truth of emotion. By creating a foreign and strange landscape and populating it with non-human characters, science fiction is better able to demonstrate the intensity of

certain life experiences. Major life experiences are intense, but realistic fiction struggles to accurately convey the intensity.

In realistic fiction, this may be shown as a young person traveling alone to a foreign country, or going far away to college. And while the sensation of loneliness or homesickness may be clear, the realistic story has difficulty portraying the intensity of the emotion.

Science Fiction distorts the outer world as a way to get a fresh glimpse of ourselves by placing human beings in unfamiliar situations to better see how and why we act as we do.

Technique A: Experiment on Humans

By creating situations entirely foreign to our current human situation, we are able to see our reactions from a different perspective—more intense—the unfamiliar surroundings keep us off-balance and so our reactions are highlighted, underlined—but essentially they are the same.

"Only under extreme pressure can we change into that which it is in our most profound nature to become . . . — Salman Rushdie (The Ground Beneath Her Feet)

Like realistic fiction, science fiction is mainly concerned with illustrating some form of transformation or change that takes place in the human being. But unlike realistic fiction, science fiction seeks to place human beings in strange, foreign and extreme situations in order to better reveal certain elements of human nature.

Scientists regularly construct environments and then observe the behavior of everything from mice to bacteria. In some ways this is science fiction's technique; create a particular environment so that we can observe how a person might act and react. By exerting extreme pressure on characters in a story, the reader is better able to grasp those human qualities which are forced to reveal themselves.

One other consequence of the situation created in science fiction is the possibility of viewing a common human quality from a fresh perspective. In realistic fiction, the familiarity may sometimes dull the reader's ability to grasp the intensity of a feeling or reaction. For example, we have all heard of the "football widow," a wife whose husband is so engaged by watching football that he pays her no attention during the weekend. But in a realistic story, it is difficult to grasp the intensity and complexity of the loneliness that this woman may experience simply because our familiarity prevents us from actually experiencing the depth of the emotion. Our minds have developed labels and categories for many aspects of this situation and unless the writing is spectacular or the use of language innovative and fresh, our minds will readily supply ideas and thoughts about the situation. Our expectations and assumptions are allowed to take over and dull the presentation of a familiar scenario.

Science fiction has the ability to allow the reader to encounter the loneliness and the entire situation as if for the first time, because the foreign and unfamiliar in a science fiction story, prevents our expectations and assumptions from capturing our attention. We must pay fresh attention to the situation in order to comprehend what is going on, and so we are rewarded with a fresh perspective or new understanding of human action and reaction.

If all fiction is concerned with revealing some sort of truth about the human condition, science fiction tries to do this by placing the human being in an intense and unfamiliar situation. It's as if the true qualities of humans will surface only when they are subject to extreme pressure. Because of this, as readers, we are able to view emotions or relationships that have become too familiar, from a new perspective. In this way, science fiction, despite its use of strange worlds, alien beings, and bizarre scientific laws, seeks above all else to expose the depths of the human being. And in doing this, science fiction gives the reader the ability to see humans from a unique and fascinating perspective.

Technique B: 'E.T Phone Home'

The second major technique for using science fiction to examine the characteristics of a human being is basically the reverse of the first technique. Instead of placing humans in a strange and intense environment, assign human-like qualities to very non-human creatures and place them in a very familiar environment. The effect may be even more extreme, but the goal remains the same: to view humans and human behavior from a new perspective.

By creating the alien character E.T, giving him the very human emotions of fear and abandonment, and placing him on earth with the familiar human-sensation of being lost, we are able to see the human beings ability for compassion in a new light. We are also able to witness the conflict between a child's compassion and adult fears. The environment and surrounding in the movie may be very familiar to us, but the alien at the center of the story is not, and this is how science fiction attempts to re-present those familiar human characteristics which are sometimes more difficult to see both in realistic fiction and in reality itself.

The Elements of Science Fiction

1. Characters in Science Fiction: Humans interact with non-human creatures-with an intelligence and perception equal to or surpassing human beings.

-characters still reveal themselves through dialogue, physical appearance, action and decision--BUT the question of whether these elements provide an accurate sense of a character is called into question.

Language might be impossible to understand-providing little info

Physical appearance may deceive, (ugly does not necessarily mean 'bad' or 'evil'.)

Actions and decisions may be based on non-human motivations or desires, not always accurately reflect the nature of a creature.

-Story may contain many non-human characters, but **MUST feature** at least one human being.

2. Setting in Science Fiction: The Setting in science fiction is always altered in a major and very obvious way. Other planets, different times, alternate planes of existence. No evidence of a recognizable human world is required (the story can take place in an entirely unfamiliar or alien setting.

-the setting plays a more active role in Science Fiction as it is often the cause of some of the conflict or difficulty which the human (s) faces in the story. Not merely a way to communicate emotion or set tone, setting can become a character in itself, an active participant in the action of the story.

3. Plot in Science Fiction: there must be a series of cause and effect episodes in science fiction as in realist fiction. Because of the non- human characters and the strange setting or landscape, the actions and reactions may involve very unreal elements. But the logic behind the sequence of action, reaction is very clear and very human-based on recognizable human qualities.

-Like traditional fiction, there is a buildup of tension and conflict that reaches a climactic moment which will irreversibly change the character by forcing them to do something, to make a choice (learn about themselves and their abilities) But Science Fiction often goes beyond the character change and transforms the entire physical situation, radically alters the setting and even the other characters (human and non-human) involved.

4. Structure: Unlike traditional fiction which follows a strict chronological path, (occasionally embedding brief and clearly marked flashbacks or memories in the main stretch from beginning to end) the structure in science fiction must conform to the idea or concept of the story--If the concept of time or memory is a focus then the structure must deviate from the standard chronological sequence.

5. Language: May deviate from usual and comprehensible to strange and impossible to decipher. Non-human languages help to highlight the sense of foreignness which forces the reader to be more alert and aware to the story.

The familiarity of realist fiction may feel more comfortable to the reader, but this can be an obstacle to experiencing the full impact of a story. It is difficult to notice or consider that which is familiar to us, whereas, to interpret the foreign and unrecognizable requires energetic attention.

Science Fiction calls into question, seeks to explore those assumptions and beliefs that make-up the foundation of realistic fiction.

Change vs. Transformation

A. 1st Degree CHANGE is a change in behavior that is consistent with your existing worldview, your existing beliefs, your existing "creation" (who you think you are).

EXAMPLE: If you believe exercise is good and you like to exercise and you have beliefs that lead you to exercise regularly—and then you learn about a different exercise routine that would be better for your health—you probably would start using the new routine.

1st Degree Change is Basic change-- a change in behavior that does not require a change in one's beliefs, in one's view of oneself, in one's "creation." It only requires information you didn't know before and a willingness to adapt to new situations with a change of behavior.

B. 2nd Degree CHANGE is a change in who we think we are in order to implement a change that is inconsistent with who we think we are.

Information and motivation usually do not result in change because often information is inconsistent with your belief system. And in the long run, it is difficult to act inconsistently with your beliefs.

So if we believe exercise is not necessary, that we don't have time for it (because it is way down on our

list of values), and that it is not fun, then learning about a new exercise or even learning that exercise is good for our health probably will not result in us using the new information we have gotten about exercising.

In order for that to happen, we need to change something about ourselves, probably our beliefs about exercise.

2nd degree change is a shift in your worldview, your beliefs, your "creation" —that opens up new possibilities for new actions that weren't possible before.

C. 3rd Degree Change. If 2nd Degree change is changing from one creation (our overall view of who we think we are) to a different creation, then 3rd degree change is Transformation.

As Flora Slosson Wuellner observes in *Transformation: Our Fear, Our Longing,* "Transformation "…involves much more than mere adaptation to outer manipulation. Transformation implies new being…new creation rather than change." This means becoming a fundamentally different person than who you were.

Example of transformation: being able to distinguish yourself as *the creator of your creation.* As such you have the ability to create a new creation at any time, which would create new possibilities and make any new information useable.

Little Black Blots

My first thought was that I was too mature to be racist—52 years old. Not to mention that I was the wrong gender, a member of the entirely wrong economic group, and clearly in the wrong profession.

After all, it wasn't like I had a horrid job that might naturally provoke such a response. I wasn't a prison guard or even a teacher in an inner city school with metal detectors and security guards and guns. Last year our parents raised over $100,000 for laptops, and the year before that, they sent the two sixth grade classes to London, Paris, and Rome for fifteen days.

And so like I said, I was shocked and appalled at myself as I stood in front of the class and stared at little Jamal. He'd huffed and rolled his eyes and refused once again to do his spelling words. They weren't even actual words yet, but sounds, pairs of letters that Jamal had not yet mastered—in second grade!

"I can't do it," he whined.

And just like that, without any warning I muttered, "Lazy brat," which was not like me at all.

Jamal's eyes drifted lazily up to me.

My face burned and my throat went dry. I forced out a cough.

His facial expression had not changed. His droopy blank face stared at me as if he'd only just noticed me standing there.

Mrs. McEilson had been the principal for the past three years. She sat behind her desk in a purple dress with designs drawn with what looked like wax. She was young, maybe thirty-five, with blond hair that she wore in a ponytail. Most of her dresses were from India and they were usually purple or green or rust-colored with the same ugly wax designs. She was the eleventh principal I'd worked for at High Peaks.

She didn't look up when I came into the room.

"Have a seat Louise," she said after I'd already sat down. She wrote on a small notepad as she examined the papers that were spread across her desk.

"How's the year going?" she asked.

"Not bad," I said. "Good."

"Jamal Anderson's parents tell me that he's having some trouble in your class."

"He's having trouble doing any of his work," I said, perhaps too forcefully. I tried to sound concerned. "He just refuses to try."

"I see," she said, but it was clear that she didn't.

"We've had our battles," I said with a forced laugh. "I'm hoping that the unit on Martin Luther King will get him more involved."

"And why's that?" she asked with an icy smile.

"Just something relevant, to him I mean." I smiled.

She did not look up. "His reading skills haven't improved since school began."

"I don't know what you want me to say Mrs. McEilson." I felt my cheeks burn. "It's only been three months—he might just be a late bloomer."

"That may be but his parents, well, they're concerned that Jamal is being overlooked; that maybe he isn't receiving the attention he needs. They're worried that your teaching style may not be well-suited to someone like Jamal."

"Someone like Jamal?"

"Someone with his racial background."

"You mean black? I've taught for twenty-five years and I've never had trouble with the blacks. It's ridiculous."

"I didn't say it was true; I said it was their concern."

"It's still ridiculous."

She glanced up. "His parents are not the type of people who take this issue lightly. Their two older children are high-achievers. Dad is a local attorney and mom works as a lobbyist for the State Bureau of Civil Legislation. It's fair to say that they're extremely invested in equality."

"Equality has nothing to do with it," I said.

"I'm sure."

"What do you want from me?" I asked. I stared at her and she turned her attention back to the papers on her desk. I felt the throbbing behind my eyes.

"You've taught long enough to know that the home life of the teacher can greatly affect the students, some more than others. We are all human Louise, and when a teacher goes through a tough time, for one reason or another, it can shut students down."

"What are you suggesting?" Sweat had formed on the back of my neck. I glanced at my watch, school started in fifteen minutes.

"I'm not suggesting, I'm simply inquiring. I would like to see this issue resolved before the district steps in—that's all."

"You can't be serious."

"I'm afraid that I'm very serious. The superintendent can already feel the potential heat from Jamal's parents and he's anxious to make this a non-issue. It may not be fair Louise, but right now, you're working under a microscope."

"This is absurd. I haven't done anything wrong," I said. "I teach the way I've always taught. Nothing's changed."

"Maybe you should take some time off. It's not just this Louise; a few teachers have expressed their concern as well. We're worried about you Louise, and in all sincerity, that's the bottom line."

"I don't need time off. It's the last thing I need."

"Promise me you'll think about it."

I knew that if I tried to speak I would cry, so I sat and stared at Mrs. McEilson until she finally told me to have a good day and dismissed me from her office.

It was hard to believe. I was a founding pillar of High Peaks Elementary and now, through no fault of my own, my neck had been stretched across the chopping block.

I had recess duty with Mrs. Sturtz that afternoon. Caroline Sturtz and I had been working together since the beginning. We stood together and let our eyes drift across the children playing on the asphalt playground.

"Do I seem different to you Caroline?" I asked.

She folded her arms across her chest. Her silver curly hair sat high on her head in much the same style as my own. My hair was curly and jet-black, it made me look a little younger than Caroline, but then again, her hair was real.

"What do you mean different?"

"I don't know, the way I act, the way I teach—something."

"What are you talking about?"

"McEilson brought it up."

"That woman," she said.

"I don't seem different?"

"I don't know. Maybe you seem a little tired—but who doesn't?"

I stared out at the playground without seeing anything. "Who doesn't," I echoed.

"Everything okay with you?" she asked.

"Edward left me," I said from inside my daze. I blinked and looked around. Caroline put her hand on my arm. "My God Louise, I'm so sorry."

"No, no," I said making myself smile. "It's fine, I'm fine—It's much better this way—much better."

"Do the kids know?"

"They know, but they're not surprised."

"Still, it must be an awful shock. I mean, no matter what, it's an adjustment."

"It's not that big of a deal. We've basically been divorced for the last five years."

"Even still. Did you hear about that young girl they found a few weeks ago? The one who hung herself in her apartment? Well, this twenty year-old girl finally leaves her husband after he hits her over the head with a burning hot iron. After six months of being free, she hangs herself in the living room with an extension cord. And can you believe this? She leaves a note saying that she can't live without him? Imagine that? She can't live without being hit with an iron?!"

I turned my torso away from Caroline and scanned the playground until I recognized a group of my kids. They were racing from one end of the playground to the brick wall of the gymnasium. Jamal led the pack.

I could sense that Caroline was looking in the same direction.

"I wish he'd put some of that effort into his work," I said. I'd probably sounded a little angrier than I'd intended.

Caroline put her hand on my arm and leaned toward me in a gesture of sympathy.

"Don't go beating yourself up," she whispered in my ear. "They just can't apply themselves very well," she said. Her eyes closed for an instant while she nodded.

They? A chill moved down my back like a snake.

"I had one last year. It was world war three just to get him to do the simplest math."

"He's not dumb," I said quickly. It felt like I was running out of air.

"Of course not," she said in a tone that suggested *wink-wink nudge-nudge you need say no more.* She squeezed my arm. "Of course."

I pretended to see something on the far side of the playground and I raised my hand in a vague gesture and casually walked away. My entire body felt sticky and hot.

A few days later, I was sitting on the couch surrounded by stacks of newspapers still in their green and orange plastic bags. The coffee table was hidden under crusty mugs, dirty glasses, and paper plates. I sat in my robe and flipped through the pages of a Woman's Day.

The caption read, *Are You Racist?* The quiz was brief, and it focused on exposure to other cultures. I thought I would do well since Edward and I had traveled through Europe on two different occasions; each time we'd been celebrating the successful end of my chemotherapy.

I worked through the quiz until I arrived at the last question, number 15:

"Have you ever had a blatant racist thought or uttered a blatant racist remark to yourself or to anyone else?"

A lie would only prove that I was trying to hide something, that I was not comfortable with who I was. Besides, everyone must have slipped up at least once, and they would figure that into the results. I answered honestly and when I tallied up my score I landed in the section that read:

"You are part of a large group of mainstream people who, despite your education and general intelligence, still cling to negative racial stereotypes that threaten to infect your perspective on the world and may one day come back to haunt you."

National Center for Perceptions and Awareness (oddly and perhaps purposely called NCAP) had placed a half-page ad just below the judgment exposing my latent racism.

Quotes from psychiatrists, psychologists and activist community leaders praised the Center's innovative approach to fighting racism. One quote read, "This may be the silver bullet we've been waiting for." They encouraged anyone who felt uncomfortable about the current racial climate to stop by for a brief evaluation.

If I'd had the energy I would have smiled. How could I possibly take a quiz like this seriously? How could anyone believe this pop-psychology muck? It was hardly scientific. It was probably just NCAP's advertising scheme—to get you in the door.

But then it occurred to me that there was an undeniable fact involved in this situation—my own words. I had said *lazy little black boy.* Those were not made up by the magazine or by NCAP. Those were mine.

After school on Tuesday I left school and drove myself to NCAP. To be honest, I was thankful for the diversion. As it was, I was staying at school until five or six o'clock, making photocopies, arranging, and rearranging my bulletin boards. In general, I dreaded going home.

NCAP was adjacent to the hospital. I had first glimpsed the brick structure when I was waiting for Edward after a chemo session. This was during my second episode, after they'd removed my left breast, and my legs trembled as I stood. Edward pulled up and it seemed to take forever for me to get into the car and sit down. After I caught my breath, I asked Edward if the brick building was a refrigerated room where they kept the dead bodies.

"Why do you always say the stupidest things?" Edward asked. "Try acting like an adult for once. They don't keep dead bodies at the hospital!"

"Promise that you won't let them put me there," I said. I was still bald. My hair hadn't had much time to grow back since the last time. I wore the short black wig that I'd used the first time, and it did not fit as well. I stared into the rearview mirror and adjusted it. I decided that I'd have to buy a new one; the hair seemed too black, almost like outer space with rich hints of purple.

Edward jerked the mirror back into place. "What's amazing is that you have no idea what you're talking about and still you just blab away."

"I don't want to be shelved like meat. I want you to take me home after I die. Just put me in the car and drive me home. You can get the pink dress that I've picked out and then we can drive to the—,"

"Why do you have to be stupid about every blasted thing?"

"I'm serious. I don't want to—,"

"Please shut up," Edward snapped. He huffed and turned up the volume of the baseball game on the radio.-

NCAP was a beautiful and large space with windows everywhere; wall to wall carpeting, leather furniture, and a giant indoor courtyard made to resemble a section of mountain canyon.

Small streams of water poured over the giant moss-covered rocks and actual trees with absurdly large leaves stood almost as tall as the glass ceiling above. Colorful stones were spread under the clear pool of water, and people had thrown pennies and a few dimes into the pool. A few of the pennies had turned black with moss.

I filled out paperwork about my history, the particulars of my 'perceptual issue,' and signed my name on a clipboard. I sat in one of the armchairs and picked up a Cosmo. I was feeling slightly distracted and spacey so it took me quite a few pages to realize that the magazine was in Spanish. All of the magazines were in foreign languages: French Ladies' Home Journal, German Glamour, Chinese or Japanese Modern Bride. I smiled and tried not to react. I had the idea that they might be watching me from behind a fake mirror or from a small camera imbedded in the mountain scene. Maybe I was being pre-tested. I acted as though I was reading precisely the Cosmo that I wanted to read. I sat in my chair like I was the kind of person who was open to anything, even advertisements for *tampones in Espanol.*

The counselor was a short man, maybe a little younger than myself, named Eric and he was Asian, but his English was perfect. He looked down at his clipboard and read from the form I had filled out. His lips moved slightly as he read. I smiled at Eric.

"I see that you're concerned about the way you view minorities," he said in a conversational tone. Maybe I had flinched or made a sour face because he quickly added, "Please relax, Mrs. Johnson, I've dealt with vigorous African-American-haters and violent homosexual-bashers. You, on the other hand, have not been ordered to my chair by the court. You are part of the group that I like to call the enlightenment-seekers."

Sounded Buddhist. Wasn't Buddhism an Oriental religion? I almost gasped out loud—who used the word oriental anymore? It was like Jap or coloreds or Negroes. I worried that I was worse off than I suspected. I imagined for an instant that the Center would detect a growing black spot on my brain—a black hole of tissue that corrupted my thoughts and compelled me to say repulsive words.

"And I see that you haven't assaulted anyone or even cursed a person to their face," Eric said with a smile. "I like to say that if you've never called someone a name, you're two steps ahead of the game."

"There's a boy in my second grade class—," I began.

"The one you called 'the lazy little black boy," Eric stated gleefully as he read from the clipboard.

"Yes, well I didn't say it out-loud to him, just muttered it to myself."

"I see. Fairly common."

"And he's not--"

"Stupid? Yes, of course Mrs. Johnson, of course he's not dumb, and of course you're not racist—not yet anyway. Still, I understand the concern, for yourself I mean."

"You do?" I asked. It made me anxious. I guess I half-believed that he would laugh at my concern, tell me to relax, and simply send me on my way. I crossed my legs and held my handbag close to my chest.

"The blot is still fairly small, but it's there. You were right to come here. If it grows unchecked, you'll soon have a major issue on your hands."

"The blot?"

"What most people don't understand is that 90 percent of racism does not originate from racist beliefs at all. Most of it is a manifestation of something else inside the person. If you call a black man a nigger for cutting you off in traffic, are you actually a racist? Are you subscribing to some complex and evolved theory about the supremacy of whites or are you mostly just angry?"

"Angry, I guess."

"Exactly. People just borrow the racist terms for their supposed power, in order to vent whatever particular issue or blot dwells inside them. Some of the guys who've killed gays, for example, turn out to be homosexuals themselves."

"What does this have to do with me?"

"You muttered a racist statement, but not because you have a certain belief about black people. You said those words probably because of the intensity of frustration you felt. And I'm willing to bet that your emotions run deeper than a disobedient little boy."

"So then I'm not a racist?" I asked hopefully.

"Not yet," Eric said. "What happens is that people fall into the habit of expressing their anger in this way. They start using minorities as objects for their rage and soon they become full-fledged racists. The more you utter the phrases and associate minorities with your rage, the more likely you are to start believing that they are the cause of your pain. You make them scapegoats for whatever you're holding inside. You never deal with your blot, and you start spouting racism without hesitation."

I thought about Caroline.

"Let me give you an example. A boy is sexually molested several times during childhood, and he internalizes all of the shame and fear and rage, pushes them deep inside himself and hides them away. Many years later he has a negative experience with a Mexican, maybe a bar-fight, or a car accident. In any case, the event cracks the shell that he'd created around his feelings about the molestation and they begin to leak out. It's only natural then for him to associate all of these horrible feelings with the object of the incident, a Mexican. In no time at all, this man becomes a vigorous racist because he wrongly connects the two experiences. He feels justified because until he's willing to face the past issue, an arguably difficult proposition, he can go on believing that Mexicans have done this to him, made him feel this way."

"I wasn't molested," I said.

Eric smiled. "Of course it's not only molestation. It can be anything really—any sort of trauma that has built up inside of you. One of our jobs is to locate the specific cause of your pain and to expose it to you. This lessens the chance that you'll make the same mistake of association."

"But my life has been pretty normal," I said. "If anything it's been fairly boring and uneventful."

Eric nodded. "You'd be surprised by how many people say exactly the same thing before Exploration. Sometimes they're stunned to find out that something they'd considered quite harmless is at the root of their pain. Something that had been staring them in the face every day."

I couldn't help but think of Jamal.

"It says here that you've had cancer twice," Eric said. "As I'm sure you know, once is extremely emotionally draining, but twice…do you have any fears of it re-occurring?"

I had trouble opening my mouth so I shook my head and shrugged my shoulders like the thought hadn't occurred to me. I felt the itch in my lungs.

"And your husband?"

"Edward has been great. He's been there for me, slugging it out. I was really lucky with him—he stuck by me."

"He's still living at home with you?"

I screwed up my face to halt the twinge of tears I felt rising up behind my eyes. "Why wouldn't he be?" I croaked.

"No reason."

"He's away on business," I added. I nodded my head. My palms were soaked with sweat.

"I see. I'm going to give you this workbook to complete in order to tailor a program to your needs. I urge you to be as honest as possible. In general we have a two-pronged strategy. The first step raises up the central issues of your inner pain and helps you confront the consequent emotions. This confrontation, while initially extremely difficult and upsetting usually results in a dramatic boost in your mood. The second step is a process of attaching these new feelings of freedom and hope to the minority in question. If all goes well, you will finish your program unburdened by your baggage, and you'll have a strong positive association with minorities."

I took the workbook from his hand.

"But you must answer honestly—can I count on you?" he asked with a smile.

I nodded and Eric left me alone to complete the test.

There were times on the couch when I could feel it grow inside my body. It reminded me of the first months of pregnancy when I was not supposed to feel anything, but I did. I detected a slight quiver, an expansion. I felt the tumors spread like mold. My lungs would itch and I'd make myself cough, checking to see if I might have dislodged the tumors and spit them out.

Edward hadn't come with me to the doctor's office. I'd already decided not to tell anyone else, and on the way home I considered not telling him. He didn't need to know.

But then I came home from the doctor, carrying the news like an iron bar lodged inside my chest, and at first, he did not say a word. He sat and watched television and I stood inside the front door and stared at him. I waited for him to say something impossible—a word that would erase the past five years, the past fifteen. A phrase that could've brought us back together, just for a moment.

"What's for dinner?" he asked.

I shouldn't have told him, but I did. I told him that they'd found new black dots on my lungs and liver. I told him that chemotherapy would have a 20 percent chance of shrinking the tumors. I told him that cure was basically out of the question.

A month later, on Monday, August 15th, while I was setting up my classroom for the school year, Edward packed up his life and vanished.

The rows of dentist chairs in the auditorium circled around a central stage on which several NCAP employees in white lab coats typed on computers, monitored medical equipment, and tracked progress on one of the several television screens.

The patients were buckled into their chairs and a few shouted, shook their fist, or tossed their head from side to side.

Each person sat in their own universe and confronted their own demons in an effort to become healthy again. It felt good to be part of a group that was wanted to change. It gave me hope about the future.

"Good luck," the assistant girl said happily, and she slipped the headphones over my ears. The sound around me disappeared, and I walked into my virtual world.

I was told beforehand that the virtual world would be programmed to be as familiar as possible, and I'd had the idea that any dealing with emotional pain meant dealing with Edward, but I was still shocked when I walked into our virtual house and saw him staring out the front window with a cigarette hanging from the corner of his mouth. He looked as real as he ever had. His mannerisms were the same; his clothes were ones that I'd washed dozens of times. Even the sweet smell of clove cigarette smoke belonged to him.

The sensation of the virtual world was similar to a type of dream that I've occasionally had. It was the dream in which I had suspicions that I was dreaming, but I wasn't confident enough to do anything too life-threatening.

Edward stared out of the living room window with his work-shirt un-tucked and unbuttoned. He wore only underwear and stood in bare feet. He was younger, but not much, maybe middle forties. I was about to say something when I heard footsteps on the staircase. A young girl, maybe 35, with long blond hair in a ponytail, hopped down the stairs looking ruffled. Her blouse was buttoned crooked and her cheeks were flushed. She did not look at me as she passed by and disappeared out the front door. She also smelled like clove cigarettes.

"Your home early," Edward said accusingly.

"It was a half-day," I responded. My heart thundered in my chest and I reached up and touched my forehead. I felt a few strands of my wig stuck to my sweaty skin.

"What's for dinner?" Edward asked as he let smoke trickle out of his nose. He had not yet turned toward me.

"Chicken," I said.

"There's a surprise," he replied. Then he turned to look at me with his dark eyebrows and foxlike face. He was still handsome and he smirked as he approached.

He stopped in front of me and opened his hand in front of my face. Tiny black spots dotted his palm.

"Don't just stare at them—take them," he said. "I made them for you."

The spots floated out of his hand and swirled in front of my face. I knew what would happen but I couldn't stop it and when I inhaled, they flew up my nose. I tasted them like bitter bits of burnt toast and I felt them lodge in my lungs.

I coughed.

Edward blew smoke in my face and disappeared.

Mrs. McEilson and Mr. School District sat at the back of my classroom, each with their own clipboard resting on their lap. They occasionally spoke to one another and glanced up at me. Mrs. McEilson smiled, but Mr. School District did not. He was a balding man who wore a dark suit and shiny black shoes. He sat with the tension of a person who had to go to the bathroom or to a very important meeting.

I was flustered, to say the least. We began writer's workshop. The children were writing sentences about vacations they'd had. Jamal held the pencil in his hand, which was more than I'd expected.

They were writing fine, but the silence in the room suddenly made me nervous. What if I wasn't performing enough, what if I wasn't proving that I could teach?

I started writing math problems on the chalkboard and asking for answers. Some of the kids kept writing and a few looked up and shouted out math answers. Jamal put his pencil down on his blank piece of paper and slouched in his chair with his arms crossed. I was afraid of appearing hostile toward him so I pretended that he'd shouted out some of the math answers. I congratulated him out loud and gave him a sticker. He stared blankly at the sticker on the desk.

"Jamal didn't say that," Marianna declared. "I did."

"That's not fair," Elvin whined.

I quickly held up pictures of dinosaurs and asked the kids to identify them. Some of the kids shouted out various osaurouses, while still others called out belated answers to the math problems on the board, and a few kept writing at their desks. I started to handout handfuls of stickers to everyone. Jamal let his pile up without moving a muscle.

I forget when exactly I saw that Jamal had fallen asleep. I ignored him, pretended that he was awake. Drool seeped out the corner of his mouth and onto his desk.

At some point the observers left. I didn't see them go; I might have had my back turned while I washed out the paint jars. I found a note on my desk from Mrs. McEilson telling me to come and see her after school. I promptly let the kids outside for a two-hour recess during which time I sat on a bench. I squeezed my sobs into small sounds that basically burped out of my mouth, and wiped the tears from my face.

"Have you thought about taking some time off Louise?" Mrs. McEilson asked.

"I couldn't," I said. "Now is not a good time for me to take a break. I need to keep focused, I need to keep working."

"I see."

"I know today, what you saw, was a disaster, but I was nervous— you understand. I guess I've been a little on edge lately."

Mrs. McEilson leaned forward and put her hand on mine. "Louise, I know you must be going through something very difficult right now, I can see it in your eyes. And if this were a factory or a restaurant I might agree with you, with your plan to work and keep busy. But education is not about teachers keeping busy—you know this. It has got to be about the children, about their needs. So while you're using them to work through your issues, they're suffering the consequences."

"I'll get it together, I promise. I'm going to therapy and I think it's starting to work. I really do. Please Diane, this is what I've got to do."

Mrs. McEilson sat back in her chair with a look of concern woven into her face. "The best I can do is hold them off for a little while longer, it's not much."

"Just this one chance," I said. I noticed that tears had been streaming down my cheeks.

"We test next week. If you can show that Jamal has dramatically improved by then, I'll make them re-examine your situation."

"Thank you," I said. "I really appreciate this."

"I'm not promising anything," she said as I stood up and left.

At first the virtual episodes with Edward seemed quite obvious. There was always an element or symbol of betrayal involved, usually another woman, along with a blatant reminder of my disease, usually black dots in some form. It was clear to me that I was supposed to deal with feelings of abandonment—a specific type of betrayal.

I'd often heard about how difficult it was for people to confront their inner pain, their blots as Eric called them, but I'd never understood why it should be so difficult. I figured that once you identified it, once you named the issue and acknowledged its power over you, then you would be set free. It should be a tremendous relief.

I couldn't quite understand why I continued to go through similar scenarios with Edward in which he betrayed me and in which I was ill with the black dots.

It wasn't until the fifth episode with my virtual Edward that I began to see that I'd misplaced the feeling of betrayal. I hadn't yet identified my true blot. It didn't actually have to do with being left alone—it had to do with something much worse, something that I could barely consider without losing my breath.

It was the first and only episode that ever took place somewhere other than our house. The classroom was identical to my real one and I instantly felt comfortable. I sat in one of the students' seats and faced the blackboard. My actual students populated the other seats and I turned and smiled at them. Edward walked in and set his floppy leather briefcase on the wooden teacher's desk. It was the same briefcase he'd used when he was the restaurant general manager and I was a waitress. He was thirty years old again, all black hair, and that was when I noticed my own age. I was in my twenties, and I still had my long brown hair that flowed down over my shoulders. It was good to feel my hair again and I combed my hands through it, reliving the sensation. I wore the restaurant's black apron and a white dress shirt.

Edward stared at the class. He opened his briefcase and took out handfuls of stickers.

"Now then," Edward said. "I'm looking for a certain stupid girl."

I raised my hand, and Edward walked toward me.

"Are you stupid?" he asked. He held up a sticker, but I couldn't see what kind it was. I wanted the sticker.

"Yes," I replied.

"Then open your chest," he said.

I pulled the front of my shirt apart and as I did my skin peeled back. I looked down and saw all of my organs in bright colors, as if I was a vibrant diagram of the human body.

He showed me the sticker, a small black dot, which he peeled and stuck onto one of my organs. It pricked like a needle, but the pain faded fast.

"You are an idiot too," Edward said and he applied another black dot.

Then we both began to age, but I sat quietly with my organs exposed.

Edward berated me in front of the class, proclaimed that I didn't know anything, couldn't understand anything, and after each statement he was right there to put another black dot inside my body. The wrinkles around his eyes and on his forehead had appeared. Meanwhile I felt my hair shrink away. The wig itched, but I didn't dare remove my hands for fear of being yelled at by Edward who was covering my organs with black dots.

I couldn't breathe.

"Take them off," I said at last. My throat felt stuffed with cotton. I gasped.

I came to awareness in a small white room. An NCAP doctor explained that I had passed out, and he continued to take my vitals and write them down on a clipboard.

There was only one realistic way for Jamal to show significant improvement on the test and that was if I took it for him.

The monitor, a parent-volunteer, came to our classroom at the beginning of the day on Friday to confirm on an official checklist which students were physically present for the exam. Jamal slouched in his seat with his head back and a pencil balanced on his upper lip.

The exam books were sealed and I put one on each of my students' desks. Then I gave them each an answer sheet. Just before the test began Mrs. McEilson stopped and glanced in from the hallway. She didn't wish me good luck or give me any sign. She looked at me as if we'd never met and then disappeared.

I read the instructions out loud and had them write their name in the large space provided at the top of their answer sheet. Then we started the test. A few kids needed help opening their sealed exams, and some immediately broke the tips off of their two pencils. It was a solid five minutes before everyone was working. Jamal had opened his test and was reading the exercises.

I returned to my desk and opened my planner in which I had stored and extra answer sheet and exam. I slid my finger under the sticker and popped it open. I began to fill in bubbles. I didn't know exactly how many right answers would put Jamal in the middle of the pack. I finally settled on a score of seventy percent. I finished the entire exam in the time it took my kids to get through the first part. Except for two short recesses and lunch, we tested all day.

I told the students to fold their answer sheets and slide them into their test booklets and then I went around and collected them.

"How did everyone do?" I asked the class, but by then they looked as though they'd been through a war—bleary-eyed and yawning. "I'm sure you all did great," I said and they picked up their jackets and backpacks and headed out the door.

I went through and separated the answer sheets from the booklets. When I came to the exam book without an answer sheet, I went back to see whose it was. Jamal's answers were missing. I checked and re-checked the pile. I looked around his desk, in his cubby, on the floor near his hook, but turned up nothing. I paced up and down the rows and bent over to look under the desks. That was when I saw the pair of legs just inside the classroom doorway.

I stood up.

"Looking for something?" Mrs. McEilson asked.

"Ah, one of the girls lost a bracelet and I'm just making a final check."

"Would it possible for me to get the tests from you?" Mrs. McEilson asked, though it wasn't as much a question as a command.

I walked back to my desk, debating whether to say something. If Jamal's test was missing he would be disqualified. Without a score, I knew that I'd be a goner.

I casually lifted up the pile of answer sheets with the one I filled out at the very bottom. I had written Jamal's name in my best imitation of second-grade handwriting, and I hesitated as I handed them to Mrs. McEilson.

"Something wrong?"

"No, I was just wondering if this would turn out to be the last time I ever gave one of these tests—that's all."

Mrs. McEilson reached out and took the answer sheets. She piled the exam books on top and left without saying a word.

"My husband did not give me cancer," I said to Eric.

We sat in his office and he reviewed the printouts of my past sessions. I had requested the meeting.

"I appears that you've made a significant breakthrough," he said. "This last time, when you passed out."

"Are you listening? My husband did not give me cancer—the very idea is insane. What kind of crap is that?"

"Mrs. Johnson, we do not accuse anyone. Based on the answers you gave, our computers synthesize and reveal perceptions that might not be readily accessible to the human mind—for whatever reason."

"The very idea that a person can make another person ill through words is crazy."

"Actually it's not the crazy. I'm not saying that it's true in your case, but there is quite a bit of scientific information that link physical illness, even terminal illness, with a person's distress level. But look, I understand that you're upset, and all I can offer is the advice that you stick with it, because this is all part of the process—this is all geared toward your best interests, your ultimate freedom from the blot."

"But it's not true! It's ridiculous. I think I would realize it if my own husband gave me cancer three times!"

"Three times?" Eric asked. "I thought it was two." He flipped through a pack of papers and scanned them, barely moving his lips as he read. "Yes, here we go—lung cancer when you were 40, which led to an operation and chemo. You were 42 the last time, and they removed a breast—then another round of chemo. I don't see a third, was there another time?"

I stared at Eric and opened my mouth. I would have told him, I was just about to say it when his emergency phone rang. He held up a single finger, pausing me, and by the time he'd hung up, the moment had passed. He asked again, and I simply shook my head.

"I know this is difficult for you, it's difficult for everyone who goes through it, but in the end it's worth it. Imagine how the young man feels when he discovers that his own father was the one who molested him all of those years? Do you think that it's something he takes with a casual shrug of the shoulders? This is rough stuff, Mrs. Johnson, and you are a courageous woman."

The first time I hit Edward, we were back in our house, in one of the familiar early scenes. This was the first time that I'd actually felt different. Instead of being off balance, like I was standing on one foot, I was completely in charge. The woman trotted down the stairs and out the front door.

"Who was that?" I asked.

Edward glanced at me, sucked on his cigarette.

"A friend," he said. But his tone did not fall heavy and sharp on my ears as it had in the past. Instead Edward sounded like a teenager, a punk.

"If I see her again, I'll kill her," I said. "I'll kill both of you." It was an outrageous statement but it sent a thrill through my body. I felt immovable, secure on solid ground.

Edward did not respond as he approached. Perhaps the people at NCAP had adjusted the virtual world, but for some reason I saw Edward's head and face, but I also saw what I guessed to be a giant tumor. His head was like one of those religious cards that you tilt one way to see Jesus' dead face and bend it another to see him open his eyes. I could see Edward and the tumor at the same time. The tumor was pinker than I'd ever imagined, like a tube of burnt steak still raw on the inside.

He stopped in front of me and opened his hand. He smirked. The black dots appeared, but before they could rise and filter into my lungs, I punched Edward as hard as I could in the face. He staggered backward, a look of shock on his face.

I no longer felt the desire to protect him, to save some image of our years together that was entirely false. In the virtual world, I yelled at him, I slapped and kicked him. They discontinued that aspect of my treatment after I lost myself in a rage one afternoon. Between my fists and the body on the ground, I disappeared into pure animal fury. I could not control my body at all, and I woke up in the small white room with the doctor taking my vital readings.

"We're going to have to pause treatment at this point," Eric said.

I couldn't believe what I heard. Finally, after all of this I had begun to feel like I was progressing. I wouldn't have said I was cured, but I could finally hate Edward. I let myself hate him.

"It's not that you're not progressing because we both know that you are, but I must always make this decision after the first phase of treatment. Moving on to the next stage requires a state of mind at which you have not arrived."

"But I've uncovered my blot. I've confronted it head on and beaten it back. Isn't that exactly what you said I should do?"

"Mrs. Johnson, you have come a long way, and you have identified your blot, but you are not yet free of its grasp. You've fought it, mentally and physically, and you've probably begun to understand it at some level, but you have not yet experienced the conversion that is required to enter the next phase. You haven't been flooded with the positive feelings that are essential to the next interaction with minorities."

I was stunned. I had shown up at the meeting with my calendar flipped open, ready to schedule the next batch of appointments. "But who ever experiences this type of joy that you describe? I don't know many people who skip around whistling all day."

"Many people who are in your position say the same thing. They cannot imagine what I'm talking about because they are still blocked, still attached to their blot. When the tie is cut for good, it is a true and ecstatic joy, an epiphany. Some people describe the yellow glow, the feeling of tranquility so powerful they feel as though they can float. They feel magical, holy, and completely at ease. You are very close, but as you yourself will attest, you have not yet arrived. We have done all we can do. I'm afraid that you must make this final part of the journey alone."

"You can't do this!" I cried. "You can't half-way cure someone and then send them back out on the street. It's malpractice, it's immoral. It's like helping the heroin addict temporarily suppress the craving and then pushing them out the door with a hearty handshake and a 'good luck.' I need this place; I need the virtual world to work out my situation. If I'm so close just give me one more chance to get over the hump. I know exactly what I need to do."

Eric paused and laced his fingers together on his desktop. "Tell me what you need to do."

"It's really quite simple. I don't know why I hadn't thought of it before. I need to kill Edward."

"Kill Edward," Eric stated as if it made no sense at all.

"Of course. By killing Edward I will destroy any remaining power he has over me. Then I'm sure I'll have that holy experience you mentioned earlier."

Eric sighed. "You can't just kill people. You know what I mean— virtually kill him."

"What you're not understanding is that there is danger involved. If you are simply allowed to come in here and beat up people or worse, kill them in virtual reality, it could have a drastically negative affect on you. I'm not simply brushing you aside." Eric paused and looked at me with a guilty expression. "I shouldn't do this, but I'll tell you the confidential reason that we've decided to let you go. During your last episode, when you let yourself rage like an animal, we inserted a small child in the place of Edward. It was a way of measuring yourself control, your ability to accurately perceive and moderate your behavior accordingly."

I could feel the adrenaline setting my body on notice. I bristled. "You slipped in a child while I was beating Edward and I didn't notice—what did you expect? In real life the subject rarely transforms in the middle of the scene."

Eric looked straight into my eyes. "Edward didn't even appear in that episode at all. It was in your own house, yes, but the only living being you came into contact with was a ten year-old little boy. You never once saw Edward, and you beat the boy to death."

I opened my mouth but no sound came out. I felt the adrenaline bubbling under my skin.

"It will be good for you to take a break for a while and get used to your new perspective on your blot which, I might add, is an incredible improvement from when you first came in here."

"You said that already."

"Goodbye Mrs. Johnson. I look forward to seeing you in the future. Think of it this way; you're halfway done with the program and there are millions of people who haven't yet begun."

I stood like a zombie, turned around and left.

"I wanted to discuss Jamal's test results with you," Mrs. McEilson said.

I walked into her office and sat down. I tried to read the emotion on her face as she stared at the computer printout.

"It looks like Jamal has really turned around," she said. "Not a genius, but back about where he belongs."

"That's great news," I said with genuine relief. "I'm so happy to hear that. Have you told his parents?"

"In fact they were just in here moments ago, but I must say, they weren't quite as happy as you seem to be."

"No?"

"No. They were a little confused because they'd come by my office to drop of this." Mrs. McEilson handed me a piece of paper. "It might be hard to read—it's the copy of something that went through the washer and drier. The original is much easier to read, but I'm sure you'll get the idea."

I looked at it and a dagger cut into my chest. It slipped from my fingers and fell onto my lap. I quickly picked it up and put it on her desk.

"My eyes aren't what they used to be," I said, making my voice steady.

"It's Jamal's answer sheet Louise. The one from the test he did so well on. They found it in his pants."

"How did he get that?"

"I guess the real question is how did he manage to score so well on the test, if he'd put his answer sheet in his pocket instead of turning it in?"

"Oh that one," I said. "He'd messed up on his name, and he insisted that I give him another sheet; so I did. I knew how important this test was."

"I see. Jamal claims that he worked on his sheet for the entire day and then decided to take it home because he wanted to finish it."

"Well, that's not exactly how I remember it," I said.

"Louise, is there anything you want to tell me?"

"What could I possibly want to tell you? I remember it one way and a seven year-old remembers it another."

She looked at me for an instant before her face fell into dismay. "Why are you doing this?" she asked, but it wasn't an actual question, more of a momentary plea.

"I'm not doing anything."

"After his parents learned about his mysterious score, they promised to sue. They called the superintendent from my phone and made photocopies of what they called evidence. They plan to have a handwriting analysis done to compare Jamal's name on both answer sheets. They said they'd even have the bubbles analyzed. They've had the feeling that we've been pulling the wool over their eyes, that we've been running some scam intent on making Jamal fail. They're talking about civil rights."

"Civil rights? Isn't this a little out of line? I mean—,"

"Have you've ever called Jamal a name?"

"A name?"

"Yes, a racial slur." Mrs. McEilson's face was pure red, but she was calm.

"Who would say such a thing?"

"Jamal claims that you called him a name."

"That's preposterous!"

"I've also spoken with Caroline Sturtz who recalls an off-color remark you made to her about Jamal."

"What?" I gasped. I put my hand on my chest. My blood was at a roiling boil and sweat broke out all over my body. It was difficult to see, but I used the edge of her desk to help me stand.

"Leave your classroom the way it is for now. I'll notify you when you can come and pack it up."

"I'm going home," I said in a whisper.

"I'll be in touch," she said without looking directly at me.

I stopped in my classroom and looked around. In the corner, half-hidden by a bowing poster, stood the trophy I'd received many years earlier for leading the most successful read-a-thon in the district. My class alone had raised almost $10,000 for the muscular dystrophy foundation. A miniature dark wood podium outlined in gold and holding a tiny gold book was secured to a three-inch thick white marble base. I remember how I had to keep putting it down to rest my arms during the reception. I had to hold it with both hands for the picture that made the newspaper the next day.

I stormed into my classroom and grabbed the trophy. I hip-checked the emergency exit and a shrill alarm blared that coiled my insides like a snake.

I walked home with tears burning my cheeks. But I was not sorry, I was not sad. I held the trophy with one hand, my fingers gripped around the podium, and my arms trembled.

I wanted more than anything to go back to NCAP and sit in one of those comfy chairs, sink into a virtual episode. I wanted to grab someone by the throat and throttle the life out of them. The more I imagined the scenarios, the deeper I bit into my lower lip. The taste of blood made my body ache.

The ache was familiar, it was the way I could get sometimes after Edward had been punishing me for something I'd screwed up like the checkbook, a lost gas bill, or burnt meatloaf. Months would go by and my skin would actually begin to ache for human touch. When I walked passed people in the halls at school I could almost feel my skin being drawn to them as if they were magnetized. I wanted a hug so bad that it made me nauseous.

The ache I felt as I walked up the path to the front door was similar to that, but of course I not only wanted to feel human skin, I wanted to crush it in my fist.

I walked in the door to the house and it was well lit. Someone had opened all of the shades.

Edward stood in the living room and stared out the front window. He wore a suit with his tie yanked away from his neck and he was pulling a cigarette away from his lips. Smoke leaked out of his nose. He turned and looked at me with a serious face, almost an irritated expression. He looked like an angry old man. "Don't make a big deal out of this," he said. It was his voice, always sharp and to the point—commands that any animal could obey.

"The house looks like crap—is this what happens? I leave for a while and you let everything go to shit?"

My lungs itched and I coughed.

"I'm not staying," he said. "I set up an appointment for a realtor tomorrow. You've got to do better than this if we're going to unload this dump."

"Sell the house?" I managed to say. My teeth were clenched.

"What did I just say? A r-e-a-l-t-o-r. Seller of homes."

This was when I experienced one of those moments; those sensations that I'd grown accustomed to. It was at this moment when I had to decide whether this was real or not, whether this was a dream or a simulation. Perhaps I was influenced by the distant hope that it was all fake, the Jamal situation, the Eric conversation. I checked my sensors, but with my blood already on fire, they were confused, unclear.

"Are you still standing there?" He asked as he bent down to tie his shoe. He clenched the cigarette between his lips as he tied one shoe.

It was too perfect—the bending down, the offering of his head—too scripted. I started to walk toward him. He must have seen my legs approaching.

He began to tie his other shoe, and he did not look up. "Look I'll leave if you can't handle—,"

I brought the marble base of the trophy down on top of his head as hard as I could, and Edward slumped forward.

The epiphany began as fragments. With each subsequent movement of my body, the glowing yellow revelation began to fit together.

My rage spent itself like gasoline, the gauge falling a little with each hit I made. But as I ran out of energy, my body began to fill with the Holy Spirit.

I was on my knees in a widening pool of blood when the overwhelming sense of peace descended on me.

It really was like Eric said, almost impossible to believe, this sense of lightness, of total golden ease.

The Truth About Spells

Like an anxiety bubble stuck inside the back of my head. Forgot to turn off the water, forgot to lock the door, load the gun, hide the bottle. Like that only much worse: my daughter is missing. Days pass, then weeks.

It's a stress that spreads and grows over time; it becomes the canvas of my life, the backdrop against which all subsequent action takes place. Tear open a bag of potato chips, twist open a bottle of soda, and there she isn't, my daughter, sixteen years-old. She's been kidnapped, drowned, buried, shot, sliced open and left to die in a field. Maybe she ran away and takes smack and sells her body and carries a pistol for protection. Some of this or none of it: I don't know.

Unless she's dead, my daughter turns seventeen and I update the missing posters in all of the gas stations, the supermarket bulletin boards, and the post office wall, but I don't have any current pictures, only different pictures, ones in which I think she looks older or more mature.

From psychics to dogs, from false sightings in Orlando to walks through the Portland State Park, this quest becomes the engine of my life. Right up until the moment I decide to cast a spell, and then everything changes.

I have cast spells in the past. I learned the basics like everyone else, sitting in a windowless high school classroom, though much of my attention was taken up by trying not to get caught spitting tobacco-juice onto the carpet. Because of this or whatever, I was always a less than average spell caster. I learned enough, the school hoped, to help keep myself safe and healthy and to avoid doing catastrophic harm to anyone; I'm definitely no wizard.

I flip through one of my old textbooks and in the section devoted to regaining a lost love I come across something called The Advanced Retrieval Spell. These were the ones that I routinely skipped over during my school years. It's accompanied by all of the usual warnings and cautions: you need to be at a certain level before you even attempt and so on. This is the first time I hesitate, and then I receive a sign that urges me forward. I answer the phone and am informed that the official search for my daughter has been officially called off.

It takes me a week to locate all of the necessary ingredients, but the main focus, the really important part, the book tells me, are the words I decide to use. This is where amateurs get into trouble, just saying whatever comes to mind and causing a chain of unintended dire consequences.

I put everything together, sitting on the floor, the candles in the right places, the amulets and feathers and colorful liquid in small vials. The first step is to hold the desired result in my mind. I know that I have to be clever about this; if I say that I want is to see my daughter again, I might end up getting a brief glimpse of her in the mirror that's on the ground next to my knee. If I ask for her immediate return, maybe I'd receive a cardboard box filled with her bones. This is when I decide to gamble.

Take me to my daughter. I build the phrase and cement it in my head.

If she's dead, then I'll die, but at the moment, the idea that my search will finally be over floods my mind with the sweetest relief. I don't care if I die, just to be calm again, at rest, not living in doubt or fear, not waiting for the right phone call, not anticipating the knock on the door. I'm increasingly confident in my choice of words, and I say this phrase over and over in my head as I begin to combine the ingredients, in the proper order, and then I speak the prescribed words out loud.

I wake up and it's the next day. I am not dead. I am still in my apartment and my daughter is not in any of the rooms or closets or cupboards. I shower and dress and drive to work. The roads are fairly empty for ten in the morning on a Wednesday. I drive to the office because I still have a job; one that I've been neglecting and ignoring to the best of my ability, but today, I feel like I've done everything that I can to try and find my daughter. It's like I've given in, submitted, and if my spell works, then it works, if not: I give up. There is nothing left for me to do. Maybe this is what it's like to move on.

At the office, the main receptionist is missing. I stand in front of her desk and survey the scene. Her mug of coffee is still steaming and her pen sits uncapped on a piece of paper. She's probably at the bathroom.

I ride the elevator to my floor. All of the personal assistants who are usually roaming the halls are absent.   I check my messages and my boss has left one that instructs me to report immediately to his office. By the time I arrive, he is not present, so I wait outside his office, near his empty secretary's desk. An hour passes and no one shows. I stand and walk back to my cubicle. Every telephone number I call is unanswered, and I don't have enough energy to leave a message on the machine.

By the time I stand up, most of the office staff seems to have gone home already. It's one o'clock in the afternoon. But their coats are still hung up, their briefcases still standing in their cubicles.

All busses and taxis are empty—no drivers no passengers. I see fewer than ten people walking on the sidewalks. No one waits for a bus.

The security guard outside of my building has disappeared, the doorman has vanished. But it's not until the roof of my apartment building disappears that I understand that something has gone wrong. No one at the office answers their phone; people have seemed to vanish throughout the city. This is when I decide that I need help.

If you're over the age of eighteen, then a visit to a Blind Photographer is bound to be at least a little embarrassing. It's like having to tell a doctor that you stuck something up your butt, and you can't get it out. During the visit your mind is crowded with possible reprimands, phrases that the doctor might be thinking: *What were you doing playing with your butt? You should know better than that*...etcetera.

As I drive on the empty roads, on which the stoplights have ceased to exist, I notice a single air current in the sky. At first I only see the motion, a water-like blurring high above my car, like a line of vapors from an invisible airplane's exhaust. Then the colors begin to appear, crystalline reds and greens and yellow and blues, rushing forward like tiny stars. By the time I reach the Blind Photographer's condo I can see this one giant stream of color crossing the pale blue sky like an agitated rainbow.

I knock on the door and it opens by itself.

"Come in," a voice says. "I'm making us some tea."

I step through the door and it closes behind me. I walk into a nice living room with two large comfortable couches and a black onyx coffee table. The walls are covered by hundreds of black and white photographs. At first I think that they are images of landscapes, until I recognize that the one of a single giant cave complete with stalactites and stalagmites is actually the inside of a single human nostril. All of them are parts of the human body enlarged to the extreme. There are many that I can't identify, but others are easier. The corner of an old person's mouth looks like sand-dunes disappearing into a canyon.

"Sit down," the voice says and a man, wearing the requisite black sunglasses turns the corner and approaches the coffee table carrying a tray with both hands. He wears a white suit jacket over a black tee-shirt and white pants. He's barefoot. "We begin with tea," he says and he pours a cup and hands it to me.

It tastes like sweetened cinnamon and rose and I finish the cup.

"I sort of made up this spell," I say, looking down at my shoes. "And I think something is going very wrong with it."

The man re-fills my cup and I drink, slower this time, but I have to force myself, the warm brown liquid tastes incredibly good.

"First, no one makes up spells," the man says. "They already exist, the spells," the man says. He keeps his chin up when he speaks, his head slightly tilted. "Do you even know what spells are?"

"Words that try to bring something into a person's life, like love or money," I say. "Or a daughter."

The man shakes his head. "Spells are souls, human souls, streaming through the air. The words and rituals are used to try and attract a certain soul's help; if it's money you need, and you make the correct gestures, say the specific words, a soul may respond. It may descend into you and help guide that part of your life."

"Into you? Like it possesses you?"

The man laughs. "I guess you could say that; it's part of your consciousness for as long as it believes it can help you achieve your goals."

"All I asked was to be brought to my daughter. Why is the world is disappearing all around me?"

"Yes, well, usually the less experienced spell casters," and here he lowered his chin so that I could look right at his black sunglasses, "they ask for love or money or good grades; they ask for other people to love them or else to succeed in some specific way. No one ever asks to be transported to another place."

"What's going to happen to me?"

"Your case is somewhat extraordinary. Instead of calling down the aid of a soul, it appears that you are becoming a soul. I assume that you'll flow into the main stream of souls and travel until you arrive at whatever location you asked for. I'm sure you must have seen the stream by now."

"And then what?"

"And then you'll be where you want to be."

"But *what* will I be? A soul? Can't you make it so that I turn back into myself, into a human being, into her father?"

"You will inhabit, or possess as you say, a person who is at the location you've requested. This is not physics; I have no way of transporting your body. And even if I knew how, you've progressed way beyond the point of ...."

The roof disappears and then the walls. I look up and see the stream of flowing souls, all of the colors, glistening in the light and for an instant it doesn't seem bad at all to swim with them, so high and together and safe. We stream through the air without danger, filled with hope and possibility.

I need supplies. I'm driving on a moonlit night down the main canyon road, and I'm suddenly grateful to be surrounded by the world on all sides. The silver river rushes alongside the road and the pine trees bend towards one another like groups of shadow friends. Even the headlights of the oncoming cars wink at me, letting me know that life is in order. I feel planted in the seat, comfortable, and I fish in vain for a cigarette among the empty packs on the passenger's seat. The gas gauge hovers above the letter E.

It's a Super-Go Convenience Mart and I park at a pump. I swipe my credit card, start the stream of gas into the tank and walk inside. A loaf of bread, a jar of peanut butter and milk. I need to get some beer. My eyes crawl across the wall of standing coolers. I see the twelve packs at the other end of the store and I start walking. I stop in the middle of the store, like my legs are paralyzed.

I'm staring at the picture of the missing girl with her long blond hair and full lips. She's smiling at me in an open way. I start to wonder if I should give her some beer, if maybe having a few beers would help. It's strange to see her picture; tears suddenly cloud my vision and I blink them away.

I walk out of the store with a twelve pack gripped in each hand and a plastic bag of food and cigarettes hanging from my wrist. I drop everything onto the passenger seat and close the door.

When I withdraw the gas spout from my car I hear a small noise, a tapping from inside the trunk. I think about giving her the beers right here, but the florescent lights are unbearably bright. Like standing on a movie set. I decide to pull over in a few minutes and toss a few cans into the trunk. Maybe she'll even be able to relax a little and she won't be so difficult when we get back to the cabin.

There's an ache in my heart as I drive away. It's a unique sensation, like a brief surge of sadness. But it's nothing that a few beers won't cure.

The Last Elf-Mite

The elf-mites were quite adept at latching themselves onto words as they left the man's mouth. They had undergone extensive training and carried specialized mechanical sanders and saws. The instant the man's words had been set upon the air, these elf-mites stuck to them like lint, worked on each one with professional attention. The elf-mites shined the grooved teeth marks into seamless curvature, hammered the blunt protrusions into harmless nubs. They ground the man's rough words into softer, less abrasive morsels.

This group of elf-mites had been dispatched to this extremely distant outpost on an assignment to work for the woman, the boy, and the girl in the house. Upon arrival these skilled elf-mites immediately divided into companies and fell into a rigorous routine. For weeks they toiled in the house with the discipline of soldiers. They sweated profusely and often skipped meals without the slightest concern for their own well-being, their own health. They were committed to perfection.

They expertly shaped, "What the hell are you babbling about?" into, "Excuse me, I believe I missed that."

They completely transformed, "You're an idiot," and presented "Now I see your point of view."

Some elf-mites learned to ride the words like horses while they scrubbed furiously with ever-thinning squares of sandpaper. Others clung to the sides of the words like mountain climbers and melted the syllabic steel spikes with tiny gas torches. They learned to mold sound into beautiful figurines and flatten the harsh intonations like rolled pavement over a bed of jagged rocks.

As time went on the workload began to increase. Frustrated by the fact that he was unable to accurately express himself, the man began speaking at a relentless pace. He fired severe tonal buckshot and sharply angled words without pause, sent them spinning through the air like razor-sharp Chinese stars. The elf-mites needed a ground breaking innovation or an evolutionary step that would help them adapt to the quickening pace, the increasing potency.

"You disgust me."

The miracle occurred one day on the woman's frontline. A particular elf-mite struggled, channeling all of his energy into polishing a particularly grotesque and dangerous deformity. His red-face trembled as the sandpaper moved over the sharp metal claws, and sweat poured from the elf-mite like a shower. The black hole approached out of his peripheral vision.

If he did not abandon the broken word soon, he would be pulled into the infamous dark void where capture and agonizing death awaited him. It was said that the unlucky elf-mite who slipped into the black hole would be tortured into denying his own existence by the cruel army of reason. The guards of the military council of logic patrolled the porthole. No elf-mite had ever returned from the black hole.

Sucking every last molecule of energy from within, this brave elf-mite scrubbed furiously and bled onto the razor-sharp word as clouds of dust rose into his face, up his nose. The rich black hole grew larger beside him, tugged at him as he entered its gravitational field.

Firmly secured to his word and unwilling to abandon his project, this elf-mite screamed in defiance. His body exploded. The word was blasted out of existence and the incoherent bits spun away in every direction.

Elf-mites on the front lines throughout the house stopped for an instant to absorb what had just happened.

"I'm supposed to eat this—?"

Another suicide explosion quickly followed the first, spreading the mist from a different word into oblivion. The woman heard the man's incomplete statements, the silent gaps in between his phrases, and she asked him if he might be losing his voice.

The suicide technique was quickly studied by the elf-mites, refined into a simple process, and then taught in re-training sessions. At a moment's notice any elf-mite could now combust while attached to a word. This discovery temporarily helped ease the increasing workload since it took much less time to bomb away the key words than it took to completely sculpt phrases. The results were no longer as eloquent of course, but the elf-mites knew that protection came first and artistry only if time permitted.

The explosion process became extremely popular and the elf-mites moved ahead uninterrupted with their work. The day arrived, however, when the elf-mites suddenly realized that they had made a grave miscalculation in their haste to adopt the new suicide technique. The elf-mite population was plummeting and they were the only group dispatched to the area. They might never receive re-enforcements, and most certainly not in time to avoid the imminent shortage.

The elf-mites shifted into super-overdrive in an attempt to maintain their schedule. They worked overtime, went without nourishment or rest for days, and they still could not keep up. Many of the young elf-mites were eager to become exploding white sparks, tiny puffs of honorable smoke, while many of the elders began to fall ill because of the increasingly hazardous working conditions. These elders could barely contribute to the various projects without fainting on their assigned words and diverting valuable elf-mite energy to their rescue.

Something had to be done and the solution, it turned out, required more courage and resolve from the elf-mites than they had ever given in the past.

They decided to abandon the woman. By re-calling elf-mites from that front, they would then have a sufficient number to continue covering the boy and the girl. On the day they withdrew from the woman, they felt a chill against their backs.

"Can you possibly be that stupid?"

The elf-mites looked over their shoulder and saw the woman's mouth open, her eyes widen with shock. She absent-mindedly brushed her long black hair against her chest and remained silent. The man shook papers at the woman.

"Learn how to read!"

The elf-mites turned away and joined the others. They re-grouped, counted off, divided themselves into new units, and set out to work exclusively for the boy and the girl. The decision had been made and the elf-mites focused their energies on fulfilling their re-assigned duties.

Initially it was not easy to watch the woman crumble. She grew increasingly skittish and nervous. Her black hair turned mostly gray in a matter of weeks, and she had taken up the habit of constantly cleaning whenever the man was in the house. Just before the family sat down to dinner, the woman stood in the corner of the kitchen and pushed handfuls of potato chips into her mouth. She never touched the food on her plate.

The man tasted too much salt.

The woman made a comment about salt.

"Why do you open your mouth when you have no idea what you're talking about?"

On more than one occasion the elf-mites watched the woman take a word in the stomach like a bullet. She lost her breath for a moment, and then agreed, gave in, obeyed, or promised, whatever it took to stop the man from speaking. She gradually learned to submit without resistance, as if immediate surrender might calm the air, her blood and nerves. Unfortunately, she never evolved from the most primitive defense strategy. She continued to move constantly, her face twitched, her eyes squinted, as if she might be able to dodge the lightning cracks of the man's words and crawl to safety beneath the live-fire.

When the woman began to fade and flicker, the elf-mites experienced their next crisis. The woman washed the brick fireplace with a wet sponge and hummed to herself. Quite suddenly, the image of her wearing a faded yellow robe and matching bandana flickered like bad reception. For a moment, pure static filled her human form and this new creature knelt on the ground to rub invisible dirt with her thumb. After the woman was restored, she looked generally faded and one step closer to becoming a hologram.

It would probably not end well for the woman, the elf-mites knew. If she were lucky she would simply disappear one day, dissolve into streams of light, and speed past the elf-mites into the possibilities of the universe. They could only hope for the best.

The elf-mite population had once again fallen to dangerously low levels. They were only barely able to keep up and provide the boy and the girl with protection. Whole words began to slip through unaltered, even with the elf-mites hurling their bodies onto them, detonating them into oblivion.

"Cut it," he said to the girl. "You're less ugly with short hair, less fat."

The girl rose from the dinner table, tucking her brown hair behind one ear. She walked upstairs to the bathroom, closed the door, and turned on the sink faucet. The girl dropped to her knees and threw up in the toilet.

"Watch It eat," the man said sarcastically, looking at the boy. "Can It even stop to breathe?"

The boy and girl fronts had grown miserably thin and exhausted. Weary elf-mites watched their failures zip by without the will to make a dent, let alone sacrifice themselves.

They had to cut the boy loose. All they could hope to do now was preserve the girl for as long as possible. She was clearly the weakest, the most fragile. The elf-mites believed that the man's words would actually snap her in half, shatter her thin bones into her bloodstream. The elf-mites withdrew from the boy under the cover of darkness.

The elf-mites were renewed for a short period of time with a sense of duty, of purpose and hope. They gathered all of their remaining equipment together, re-stocked their packs and belts, counted off with strong voices, and fell in line. They would save the girl.

At night, the man stood over the girl lying in bed with his arms crossed against his chest. With her body beneath the blue blanket, she closed her eyes, and heard the man say, "Daddy loves you." The elf-mites erupted in a cheer, danced in the air, and slapped one another on the back.

The boy handled the elf-mite abandonment as well as could be expected. He withdrew into himself and puffed up his outer shell to absorb the man's words, as if his skin were a bulletproof vest. The boy installed locks on the inside of his bedroom door, and he sat on the top bunk squeezing coffee cake in his fist and shoving the pastry ball into his mouth. He wedged a fan in the window and the soothing noise put him to sleep at night, successfully scattering the sound from the rest of the house into unrecognizable bits around his room.

The woman floated through the house like a ghost, always moving, getting thinner and grayer by the hour. If she were unlucky the elf-mites knew that the woman would end in spectacular tragedy.

A huddled mess, she would stutter and dodge and trip her way into a local pawnshop, constantly glancing over her shoulder. With eyes like a spooked horse she would point her trembling finger at the handgun gun inside the glass case and jerk her chin in an upward spasm; her request for the box of bullets stacked on an upper shelf.

The woman's muscles would suddenly relax, and she would stand tall. In one fluid motion the woman would pick up the gun, step back from the counter, slip a bullet into the chamber, and aim at her right temple. Before a word could be uttered in the pawnshop, the woman would fire the bullet into her head.

And though it would take some time, the elf-mites knew that the boy would eventually follow the path currently being cleared by the woman.

The girl, however, would not survive a single day on her own. Her body and mind had weakened as she watched the woman and boy slip away from her. They buckled and cowered under some invisible pressure, and they pushed the girl away when she asked them why. In her mind the man was her only hope, and if the elf-mites ceased activity, one word from him would certainly split the girl in half.

Meanwhile the situation became grave as the elf-mites continued to combust or otherwise disappear out of existence. Some simply broke into pieces from the persistent stress of their labor, the anguish caused by their increasing failures, while others calmly set the trigger and sacrificed themselves. Either way, they continued to pop into sparks and their numbers dwindled fast.

"You're as stupid as your mother."

The woman cleaned the brown heating vents on her knees with a toothbrush.

The man had finally beaten the elf-mites. Many of the most dependable and talented elf-mites would not surrender and so they suffered severe heart attacks while still attached to their words. Their lifeless bodies floated calmly into the black hole.

The girl was quietly left alone one morning, to be battered and bruised by the man's words in their roughest and rawest form, tumbling freely through the air like jagged chunks of gold ore.

Soon after the girl had been abandoned, the boy began to hear a voice in his head, but it was not a bad voice. It was a warm sound, coaxing and smooth. The pleasant voice gave him certain instructions and demanded that he tell no one or else the voice would vanish and never return. The boy quickly attached himself to the gentle voice and promised to please the voice in any way possible. The boy would have done anything to hear the comforting sounds of his only friend.

One night the boy broke through the window of a neighbor's vacant house and took a gun, which he unloaded, a stack of cash from an underwear drawer, and two tents from the basement.

The next day he brought the girl downtown to the bank and they each withdrew all of their childhood savings. The girl now kept herself together by wearing a yellow blanket tight around her shoulders, the two frayed corners crumpled inside her tiny fist. They walked across the street from the bank and the boy bought two long distance bus tickets for the next day. The children returned to the house.

It was a dangerous place to be for an elf-mite. Placed precariously at the entrance to the black hole, where even the slightest breeze could affect his balance, send him off the edge. Still, being the last elf-mite came with the greatest responsibility. He had suffered greatly in the struggles, being transferred from the woman to the boy and then to the girl. A true veteran. It took supreme concentration for this elf-mite to sit and cling to his place while he carved words and delivered them to the boy, directed his actions. The effort exhausted the elf-mite and he slept more and more throughout the day.

The boy and girl rose before sunrise on the next day. They dressed in the dark, gathered their pre-packed bags together, and took a jar of peanut butter and a loaf of bread from the cupboard. They made their way on tiptoe through the quiet house and opened the front door. The boy and girl stood next to each other on the front porch and took inventory of their supplies when they suddenly heard the woman clear her throat from the doorway behind them.
With their backpacks in place, duffel bags zipped and gripped in their hands, the two were prepared for the walk to the bus station.

The elf-mite struggled to stand and faced the dreaded moment with all of his strength. The woman could barely be seen by now, and she stood like an old movie image, flickering in the doorway, holding a toilet brush in one hand. The elf-mite took in as much air as possible and summoned every bit of energy that remained in his being. He crouched in place and waited.

The woman shook her head, a solitary figure standing like a ghost in front of the silent dark living room. She did not appear angry or surprised, but she shook her gray head with sadness. It was too late for her.

Fear rose like a beast from deep inside the woman and seized control of her body, tightened her stringy muscles. She gripped the toilet brush like a club and stared hard at the boy. The woman made one last attempt to avoid her fate, to pull that destined bullet back through her temple and into the cold harmless gun. Two words to try and suck the two children into her void and fill her with warmth against the spreading bone chill of loneliness. The woman opened her mouth to speak.

When the pleading words, "Don't go," left the woman's mouth, the last elf-mite heaved into action. He concentrated every bit of strength into one final jump, and leapt from his post to land with expert poise on the crucial traveling word. He could feel the black hole approaching from behind at an impossible rate of speed.

The last elf-mite held tight, closed his eyes, and ignited himself from within. In a single blink of the boy's eye, the last elf-mite successfully blasted the word "Don't" into a fine, silent mist.

Noah's Arc

In the sailor's quarters below deck, Noah stood in his cabin and stared at his face in the mirror. Hades, who now demanded to be called Captain, had said that they would be pulling into the next port during the evening. Noah hadn't shaved for months and the black hair had begun to creep down his neck and connect to his chest. He cupped cold water in his hands from the chipped wooden bowl and threw it on his face. Noah shook his head but he couldn't disrupt the image of the drowning boy's face.

The three boys had stood on the edge of the deck the day before and faced the water. Hades held a spear with both hands, and he spit juice onto the deck from a savage leaf in his cheek. He'd tied a red bandana around his head and had been drinking wine all morning. One by one he stabbed the boys between the shoulder blades and pushed their tense and skewered bodies into the ocean.

Noah' stomach sunk to the center of the earth when he saw the youngest brother's face in the water. The boy's sky blue eyes questioned Noah with the expression of shock, the incredulity of pure childhood wonder. The pale cheeks and nose moved in wavy distortion under the water bubbles and the boy's long black hair floated around him like seaweed. Slowly, with his pink mouth open, the boy fell away and dissolved into the deep green.

Noah shivered in his cabin and slipped on his canvas vest. He wrapped his leather belt around his waist, took his knife from under his pillow, and returned it to the sheath at his side. Noah pulled on his black boots and walked up the stairs and onto the deck. Prisoners called out and rattled against their cages. Noah looked up and saw the body of the old man still hanging from the highest mast. Hades enjoyed using his father's corpse like a flag. Birds circled and dive-bombed the sun burnt flesh.

Noah went into the meeting room and poured himself coffee.

Hades walked in shirtless, wearing the red bandana around his forehead. The tattoos on his arms and chest moved in animation as he took a cup of coffee and sighed.

"We've got a big one today," Hades said to Noah.

Noah almost asked where they would put the new arrivals but the thought made him queasy.

"We'll have to dust off twenty of these bums," Hades said. "Before we get too close to the port. People don't take kindly to dead bodies washing up on their shores."

Noah smiled grimly and looked down at his coffee.

"Why so glum, my boy?" Hades asked and he slapped Noah on the back, rested his big hand on Noah's shoulder. His yellow eyes shone like nausea. His wide, angular face, raised at the cheeks, his pointed nose and chin, all reminded Noah of a certain type of wolf. A wolf that gladly hunted his own pack. "We've got the world at our fingertips," Hades said, squeezing Noah' shoulder with a violent grip. "Money pouring in like seawater and women at every port getting hot at the sound of our names. Yes my boy," Hades said, digging his fingernails deeper into Noah' shoulder, "We've made it."

"The flood," Noah said.

"Come off of it already. Nothing but the old man's hogwash," Hades said. "And look where it got him." Hades let go and Noah stared with renewed intensity into his coffee cup.

"Rest up sailor," Hades said, pouring the rest of his drink down his throat. "We've got some celebrating to do tonight."

Hades winked at Noah and walked out of the room. Noah sipped his bitter coffee and heard the creak of the rope that held the old man high in the air.

On the day they pulled away from land with two Zebras, two cheetahs, and two vampire bats, Hades went out of his mind and slit his father's throat on the deck. Then the depth of his planning and organization was revealed. With a solid group of the bigger mates by his side, Hades stabbed two sailors in the stomach and had his thugs throw the shrieking bodies to the sharks. Hades wiped his blade on his pant leg, smiled, and asked if anyone else wanted to dance. It was a brief mutiny; Noah could still see the dock from which they'd departed. The remaining members of the crew were asked to bow down and pledge allegiance to the new captain.

With Hades' father hoisted up and hung out for the birds, life changed. Over the next several days, the animals were pulled from their cages and either slaughtered for meat or simply killed and dumped in the water. The cages were scrubbed and the ship pulled into the next port ready to take on a load of criminals. Hades had developed a scheme.

Town officials throughout the land began to bring their most violent and troublesome criminals to the docks and they paid Hades a considerable sum to take them away. Noah was one of the men responsible for escorting the prisoners on board and locking them up.

After Hades had managed to squeeze 8 criminals into each cage, he began to realize that the boat was overcrowded. If he hoped to maintain the flow of money, he would have to create more space. That was when he led the first three boys onto the deck.

Noah put his coffee cup down and stepped out into the harsh sunlight. The prisoners yelled at Noah as he walked down the rows and threw cups full of gray slop into the cages. A few men huddled like animals on the floor and rocked back and forth with their arms tight around their knees. Noah gagged on the smell of human waste. He swallowed, took several deep breaths through his mouth, and blinked the tears from his eyes. He continued his chore and managed not to vomit.

The ship pulled into the next port in the evening with three empty cells. After making sure the cages were secure and leaving two well-paid local men as guards, Hades led his crew into the town to relax and unwind for the night before they took on the next load. They stopped in a local bar and ordered drinks. As captain of the Prison Boat, Hades commanded respect from the locals and inspired a certain amount of fear. Waves of men parted as Hades carried his drinks to a table and women stood in line to sit on his lap and run their hands through his dirty hair.

Noah sat in a shadowed corner and watched his shipmates drink and gamble and dance like fools. One by one they passed out or disappeared with a woman through a velvet curtain. A knot tightened in his chest and Noah thought about the children who had come to see the animals. Their limber movements, cries of joy and shock. But he kept returning to the image of the young boy that Hades had speared. The boy whose open pink mouth seemed to dissolve into the sea itself.

A young lady walked passed a few over-turned tables and several broken chair legs. The bottoms of her feet crunched on a layer of shattered glass. She stopped in front of Noah and bent down so he could see her white breasts beneath her blouse.

"Howdy sailor," she said. She sat down in a chair next to Noah and smiled.

Noah stared over her shoulder.

The girls put a piece of gum into her mouth and placed her hands on his. "You're freezing," she said and she rubbed his knuckles with her thumb. "How about I warm you up?"

Noah looked at the woman without expression. "They'll drown," he said.

"Who's drowning?" the girl asked, her smile fading, jaw working her gum.

"The children," Noah said.

"You been on the water a while?"

"All of creation will be drowned."

The girl's smile had disappeared. "Why drown the children? What have they ever done to deserve that?"

"Nothing," Noah said. "Yet." He saw the drowning boy's black hair, swaying in slow motion, and the bubbles that distorted the boy's face.

"You're probably a little confused, is all," she said.

Noah gripped her arm and she stiffened. He looked into her light blue eyes. "The children grow into monsters," he said. "Who do you think slashes women's breasts, or sets an infant on fire? They were all children, they were all innocent, roaring at the world and laughing. And when you turn around, they've lopped off your mother's head, or tied your father to a stake in the middle of an alligator pit. They are children, these beasts, just regular kids."

Thunder shook the bar. The startled girl disappeared. Rain fell onto the roof like pebbles. The sound exhausted Noah. When he stepped outside, emptiness expanded inside him, as vast as the ocean.

The rain streamed down outside, stinging Noah' scalp, and rising quickly on the road. Noah let the water pierce him as he walked toward the ship. He boarded and barely heard the prisoners' shouts over the sounds of rushing water. None of the crew would come back until the next day. He unlocked each cage and stood aside as the men scrambled out and down the plank onto the land. At last he stood alone on the deck and he cast off. He'd gather as many animals as he could. The boat rocked side to side on the waves as it moved away from the dock.

Noah put one hand on his knife. He closed his eyes, tilted his face to the heavens, and filled his mouth with rain.

Eve exaggerated the sway of her hips as she walked toward the high school with her backpack slung over her shoulder and her black leather jacket folded over one arm. She wore a short black skirt and a black lace bra under her see-through blouse. The man stood in the parking lot across the street and leaned against his black convertible.

Eve stopped and pretended to scratch her thigh. She lifted up her skirt with her fingernail until the edge of her black silk panties crept into view. Without staring she could see the man's black hair, oiled and combed back over his head. Dark eyebrows. He wore a black leather jacket over his red silk shirt and he stood with his arms crossed in front of his chest—black jeans and the polished tips of black cowboy boots.

Eve let her jacket slip off her arm and bent over to pick it up. She paused and her long black hair fell around her face like a curtain. She felt his eyes on her.

Eve smiled in his general direction and walked through the black iron gates and across a patch of lawn. She walked through the metal detector with a police officer stationed on either side. By the time she turned around to look through the thick metal bars that covered the front windows, the man had disappeared.

This had been the ritual for almost two weeks and Eve began to feel as though she knew the man. He'd become the familiar opponent and she wanted to draw him closer.

Eve took her seat in the first class of the day and stared out the iron screen that covered the single window. The sun had emerged from the clouds and the day looked clear and clean. She could smell the ocean in the classroom.

The teacher entered and took off his jacket. He carried a black pistol in his arm holster and he turned to write on the blackboard in chalk. The classroom echoed with the sound of the mechanized lock that secured the door into place. The teacher stepped aside. He'd written, "Our Past, Our Lives," in giant white letters.

When Eve walked home, the man was nowhere to be seen. The sun had intensified and she felt sweat soaking her blouse under her arms. A jeep passed her on the street with several young Guardians standing inside, wearing black berets and tee shirts. Most of them were skinny teenage boys and Eve saw one boy wearing glasses on his pimpled face. All of them held automatic rifles across their chest as their eyes patrolled the neighborhood.

Eve walked on the side of the highway, and the town disappeared behind her. On her right, as far as she could see, hundreds of dirty white trailers and black plastic tents spread out over the fields. Across the highway on her left, the endless ocean rocked against itself presenting and submerging whitecaps in the distance. Several large ships had pulled into the docks and she saw men wearing pillowcases over their heads with uneven eyeholes cut out. They unloaded large black plastic containers and placed them in the back of several white vans.

A red bandana had been tied on the outside of the trailer's door, which meant that Eve's mother was working. Eve went to sit on one of the rusty lawn chairs that formed a circle under the clotheslines. A bent basketball hoop without a net stood at the far end of the pavement and a child's rusted tricycle had fallen on its side without a rear wheel.

Eve opened her notebook and continued with the drawing of the handsome man, standing next to his convertible. He smiled at Eve. She drew hearts around the scene like a frame.

Eve took a shower in a stall without a door and searched through her pile of clothes for her least wrinkled outfit. The trailer's only mirror was cracked across the center so she hunched down to see her face and apply her makeup.

The man was not in the parking lot and Eve felt her heart sink. It was as if a good friend had let her down and she panicked for a moment, considering the idea that he might be gone for good. How could she look forward?

"Hey," a voice called out.

The man drove slowly in his black convertible next to Eve.

"What do you want?" she asked as if she'd known him her whole life. As if she were punishing him for standing her up.

"You want a ride?" the man asked.

"I'm about twenty feet away," Eve said, staring at him, gently nodding her head in the direction of the school.

The man pulled over and stepped out of the car. Eve stopped walking and stuck her thumb under the shoulder strap of her backpack.

"I could take you there," the man said. He smelled like sweet seawater and he stared at Eve, hands in his pockets.

"I can manage," she said without looking away.

The man reached out and grabbed Eve's arm. A thrill charged through her body and she didn't pull back.

"Let's go for a ride," the man said.

"They might miss me," Eve said. She wasn't frightened. She stepped closer to him and stared at his rich red lips.

"Let them," the man said and he let go of her arm. He opened the passenger door and slid himself to the driver's side.

Eve could see the handle of a gun underneath his seat and the man smiled at her, nodded his head.

"Get in," he said.

Eve heard the sound of the engine and she looked around. She threw her pack in the backseat, stepped into the car, and slammed the door. The man put his hand on her thigh and they drove away.

When the Guardians brought Eve to the trailer door, summer had arrived and Eve was five months pregnant. Her black hair looked as if it hadn't been washed or combed in years.

The Guardians had flushed out an abandoned bus station in the center of town. The man had been dead for a while and his body was laid out on the cement floor next to Eve. She sat in a corner and warmed her hands above a small fire. Hypodermic needles, candy bar wrappers, and beer bottle shards were scattered on the crumbled cement floor.

The skinny Guardians wore black ammunition belts across their chests, and they guided Eve up the trailer's front steps. They nodded to her mother and drove away.

Eve's mother jerked her daughter into her chest and sobbed. Her body trembled and she hugged her daughter, stroked her tangled hair. She stepped back to look at Eve. In an instant she had slapped Eve across the face and embraced her once again.

"I thought you were dead," her mother cried. "Why would you do this to me?"

Eve's glazed eyes did not blink and she stumbled toward the couch to sit down.

Her mother went into the bathroom and began a hot bath.

Her mother undressed Eve in the living room. She stared at her daughter's belly as if it were a foreigner, an unwanted guest. She turned her head and clicked her tongue in disgust. "Get in the bath," she said, wiping her eyes with her hand.

Eve put her grimy black fingers on her belly and walked slowly into the bathroom.

Eve spent her days reading on the couch. Once in a while she would stop and stare out the window. Guardians stood on the beds of trucks and passed by Eve's window as if they floated in the air. Their boyish chest muscles were barely outlined by their black tee shirts and they moved their guns from side to side, their trigger fingers always in position.

The Guardians had recently begun to patrol the trailer parks and tent camps, looking for gunmen and bomb technicians. Five of her neighbors had been taken from their homes, loaded into prison trucks, and driven away. Not one of them had returned.

Eve sat on the couch with an open book on her lap. She drank seltzer water and ate carrot sticks from a glass jar.

The front door slammed and her mother stood in the entryway with a well-dressed older woman. The older woman's face had the look of artificial youth, and her rich red lipstick clashed with the dingy trailer walls. She wore elegant black high heels, which seemed to give her no trouble at all.

"Eve, I'd like you to meet someone," her mother said.

"Hello Eve," the older woman said, quickly glancing around, clearly uncomfortable inside the trailer. She spoke as if she were addressing a child or a dog. "How are you today?"

Eve shrugged and turned back to her book.

"This is Mrs. Susan Cantor. She wanted to meet you."

"You are a beautiful girl," Mrs. Cantor said. "How are your teeth?"

"Fine," Eve said, knitting her eyebrows.

"Good bone structure, and your mother says you haven't had any major diseases or genetic irregularities. Tell me about the father, was he a handsome man, intelligent?"

Eve felt her muscles tighten. "What do you want?"

"Mrs. Cantor wants a baby," her mother said. "Isn't that wonderful news?"

The healthy color in Eve's cheeks drained away. She stared blankly at her mother.

"I assure you," Mrs. Cantor said. "I will be an exquisite mother and I must say," she paused and glanced at the kitchen table, "The child will be quite well off."

Eve placed both hands on top of her belly.

"If I may, my dear, you are clearly in no position to raise a child," Mrs. Cantor said and she openly gestured around her as if she were smothered by evidence. "You are but a child yourself, a baby girl. You've no job, no way to support yourself."

Eve stared at her mother.

"That's wonderful news," her mother said.

"Has she taken vitamins?" Mrs. Cantor asked and before waiting for a reply she withdrew a crisp and clean stack of money from an envelope in her purse and placed it on the table. Her blistering fake smile radiated a discomfort that verged on physical pain. "Take care now, I must be off."

Eve's mother walked Mrs. Cantor outside.

Tears had started to fall from Eve's eyes, but she did not make a sound. She did not sniffle or sigh or clear her throat. She sat quietly while tears ran down her cheeks and fell onto her neck like raindrops.

A blue fire raged at the electrical plant and the hospital had been running on backup power for two days. The overhead lights had been set on the lowest possible setting, which cast everything inside the hospital in a soft orange glow. Eve's mother held her daughter's elbow and walked with her around the labor and delivery unit.

Eve stopped and gripped the wooden railing while her insides cramped like a fist and then released.

They completed two more laps around the unit before Eve decided to take a bath. Small electric candles had been set up near the medical equipment in her room so the nurses and doctors could clearly see the monitors. The bathroom's heat lamp was the only illumination and the rich red color turned the water to blood.

Eve took off her hospital gown and underwear. She stepped into the water and steam rose into her nostrils and filled her lungs.

When the doctor told Eve to bear down as hard as she could and push with all of her strength, her back arched slightly from the effort and her arms trembled. Her white knuckles tensed around the metal guardrail. Her mother wiped Eve's forehead with a cold rag and placed ice chips on her daughter's dry lips. The ice melted and dripped into the pool of sweat resting in the hollow of Eve's red throat.

At one point, Eve turned her head to the side and gasped for breath. She saw Mrs. Cantor in the next room. The woman sat upright in a chair reading a magazine and the hospital robe barely contained her bare breasts. She still wore her black high-heeled shoes. A transparent white infant's gown had been laid out on the naked bed, and a new car seat sat on the ground with the black straps open like arms.

Eve wanted to scream. Sweat poured down the sides of her face.

"I can see the top of the head," her mother said.

Eve groaned and squinted to keep the sweat out of her eyes.

The doctor pulled the baby out. With the support structure removed, Eve's body deflated.

"I'm so proud of you," her mother said.

Eve opened her eyes. A nurse dried the infant and the newborn stared directly at Eve. The infant's wide eyes locked onto Eve's and she felt a tug, a wash of sorrow. The tiny arms reached out and the baby began to cry.

"I'm so proud of you," her mother said again.

Eve's heavy eyelids closed and flickered open. The nurse carried the screaming baby into the next room and placed him in Mrs. Cantor's arms. The woman pushed the child's face into her bare breasts and began to feed the baby from a bottle.

"Rest now honey, just sleep."

Eve closed her eyes. She cried in her dreams and watched a nurse push Mrs. Cantor in a wheelchair with a bundle in her lap, down a black hallway and disappear.

Eve walked out of town and along the docks. A light drizzle had begun and the sky became a light gray. The ocean seemed calm and there wasn't a ship to be seen.

Eve walked in the drizzle. She felt the familiar ache inside her chest and wondered if she would ever feel whole again.

She stood on the dock with her back to the ocean and looked at the trailers and tents across the highway. Since many of the sailors had been grounded, her mother usually had a small group of men waiting their turn in the trailer's living room. They thumbed through old magazines that her mother had taken from the abandoned library and a small electric burner held a pot of water to go with the jar of instant coffee and packets of hot chocolate. She gripped her shoulders on the dock and shivered.

Eve heard the low sound of a motor and she turned to see an enormous wooden ship approach. She looked around her; the dock was deserted. The boat drifted toward Eve and she saw an older man with white hair and beard peer over the stern. He smiled and waved to Eve. She waved back.

The boat stopped and after a few minutes the older man walked down a plank and onto the dock. He wore a sea captain's blue hat and had a pipe in his mouth. A thin stream of smoke rose and Eve smelled the scent of cedar and pine.

"You ever seen a tiger?" the man asked.

Eve shook her head.

He reached out and touched her arm. Eve felt warmth ooze through her body and she did not resist. The man led her to the wooden plank and she followed him aboard.

Cages of animals lined the deck. The uppermost deck had been covered with a dome of mesh wire and birds flew back and forth inside, squawking and screeching. "I keep the fish below," he said.

Eve walked between the cages. A tiger paced back and forth in front of its mate and ignored Eve. Two baboons sat against the back of their cage like a fat old couple, and one of them stared at his hand as if he'd never seen it before.

"They're from all over the world," he said.

Eve walked passed a lioness who sat curled like a kitten in the corner of her cage. Her mustard colored coat was shiny and smooth.

They stood at the rear of the boat and looked at the ocean. The man stepped closer and put his hand on Eve's arm. She swelled inside her body and her cheeks radiated heat.

The drizzle slowly turned into large raindrops that tapped on the boat like coins and pelted Eve's scalp.

"I'll pull in the plank," the man said. Thunder rumbled in the distance.

Eve nodded and the man kissed her cheek. His lips felt as warm and soft as wet clay. Rain streamed like tears down his red cheeks and neck. Eve stared into his green eyes through a veil of rain until he turned away. She watched his soaking figure walk to the front of the boat, kneel down, and reach overboard.

Eve looked through the sheets of rain toward the blurred gray trailers and torn black plastic tents. White sparks of gunfire erupted and the flashes of light cast disfigured shadows across the soaking fields. Gusts of wind ripped the tents apart and rocked the trailers from side to side.

The boat moved away from the dock.

Eve turned away from the land and a hand touched the back of her neck. She closed her eyes, raised her face to the heavens, and filled her mouth with rain.

Absurdist Fiction

Science Fiction Techniques are used to highlight the intense transformation that happens when a person comprehends and accepts an aspect of reality which they previously knew nothing about.

Absurdist story techniques are used to highlight the way in which external pressures, expectations and influences, shape our behavior and decisions.

If stories want to convey a 'truth' about human experience, it is how external pressures of society cause our behavior: trying to communicate the feelings that result from this. How does it feel to have no free will? Trapped, controlled, hopeless, helpless----Stories attempt to help the reader feel these sensations.

Primarily, Absurdist Stories expose the following:
Exposes rules and conventions in society
Exposes our expectations for behavior
Exposes belief in cause and effect & the process of logic
Exposes contradictions between image and reality
Exposes the truth and lies of stereotypes

Character—abandons traditional character and offers figures that have no clear identity-Destabilize sense of character identity

Dialogue—call language into question by
1. Uses artificial language, empty of meaning, consisting of slogans and clichés
2. Language that mimics the style of educated or sophisticated speech

Plot—often abandons traditional plot. Nothing actually happens, or too much happens—various actions that do not develop in any sort of narrative or logical sequence.

Setting—often set in no recognizable time or place or the setting is overly cramped and confining

Absurdist Themes
Cruelty & Violence
Domination
Futility & Passivity
Language & Dialogue
Loneliness & Isolation
Materialism

Cruelty and Violence--Beneath the nonsense and slapstick humor of Absurdism lurks an element of cruelty, often revealed in dialogue between characters but occasionally manifested in acts of violence. On a less physical level is the cruelty hiding behind the apparently humorous dialogue.

Domination--Several well-known absurdist works feature pairs of characters in which one is the dominator and the other the dominated. Some of these are quite literally master/servant relationships. Others reproduce the master/slave relationship within marriage, or within the traditional teacher/student dynamic.

Futility and Passivity--The futility of all human endeavors characterizes many absurdist works; highlighting the idea that individuals are powerless to direct their own lives. The inability of even the most ambitious individual to make any headway against a self-perpetuating bureaucracy. Human effort is meaningless and leads to nothing in the end. Characters are ineffective and doomed to failure. Even decisions to do something or act, often results in either inaction or futile action.

Language--The failure of language to convey meaning is an important theme in the literature of Absurdism. Language is either detached from any interpretation that can be agreed to by all characters, or it is reduced to complete gibberish. Language often tries to sound familiar, to mimic a type of language, a standard philosophical discourse or the language of religious fervor, or uses clichés and slogans, from which all real meaning has been drained.

Loneliness and Isolation--Many absurdist works illustrate the loneliness and isolation of individuals, resulting from the nature of modern life and, in some cases, from the impossibility of effective communication between humans who are unable to achieve fulfilling contact, connection, or who are so isolated from each other that they fail to understand or know anything about the other character's in the story.

Materialism--Materialism is criticized by reducing relationships between family members to the terms of a profit and loss statement. Example: A woman marries a man she does not love simply because he is wealthy, and they buy a baby to complete their family. The baby dies, leaving them to mourn their financial loss rather than their emotional loss. Characters may worship things, may exclude all other experiences or else view them through the filter of monetary gain or loss.

Absurdist Story elements
No character identity
Absurdist Setting
No Plot/Resolution

Character: Absurdism often abandons traditional character development to offer figures who have no clear identity or distinguishing features. They may even be interchangeable.

Resolution: In conventional literature or drama, the resolution serves to tie up the loose ends of the narrative, resolving both primary and secondary plot conflicts and complications. Since so little happens in most absurdist works, there is little to resolve. Endings and plot action tend to be repetitious. Such repetitive actions reinforce the idea that human effort is futile, which serves as a prominent theme of Absurdism.

Dialogue: Since the ability of language to convey meaning is called into question by Absurdism, dialogue is of special importance in absurdist works. Artificial language, empty of meaning, consisting of slogans and clichés, is a hallmark of the movement. Many of the texts contain dialogue that appears to be meaningless but that mimics the style of educated or sophisticated speech. Often there is a marked contradiction between speech and action.

Plot: Absurdism at its most extreme abandons conventional notions of plot almost entirely. Although characters may engage in various actions, none of those actions are connected in any meaningful way, nor do the actions develop into any sort of narrative or logical sequence of events.

Setting: The use of setting is one of the most unconventional stylistic features of Absurdism. Typically, an absurdist story will be set in no recognizable time or place in order to convey the sense of emptiness associated with characters' lives. But the setting can also be cramped and confining, such as the claustrophobic single room.

MAIN Intention behind Absurdism
1. To expose the gap that exists between the internal mental landscape (the desired, the believed, and the acknowledged) and the exterior physical reality.

PURPOSE--HOW
How does Absurdism go about exposing the distortion gap in order to achieve its goal? Answer: Using the elements of story to develop certain themes-Cruelty & Violence, Domination, Futility & Passivity, Language & Dialogue, Loneliness & Isolation, Materialism

INTENTION--WHY
So what? What's the point of exposing this gap? Why do this? Which of the possible answers to you think is best for each story?
- To prove that a distortion gap exists.
- to expose the causes of the distortion- the forces that distort
- to show the consequences of the distortion-
- highlight the severity & intensity of the distortion
- to show how all-encompassing/widespread and inescapable the distortion gap is
- to assert that this gap shows the 'truest' truth about who human beings are and what they do- the truest version of reality

The Best Solution Ever

When you wanted to cry, you went to the hospital to walk up and down the halls or sit in one of the mini-waiting rooms and let yourself sob openly, simultaneously witnessed and ignored by everyone else. No one ever bothered you because crying belonged to the hospital: tears, in the hospital, made sense.

And when you were angry and needed to lash out, where did you go? To the airport, of course.

On your last visit, your fist shot over the airline's podium and stopped an inch short of the employee's protruding Adam's apple. You stood five feet and four inches tall, a full grown adult with short arms. Arms that transformed into a character defect in the 5th grade when Johnny Goluli used their length to orchestrate your character assassination. So when you could not even touch the employee's throat with the tip of your middle finger, your rage boiled over. After all, you've successfully punched airline employees before. Who hasn't?

You'd been told that the plane in question has landed and that it was in the process of taxiing to the gate.

"What, via Hong Kong?" you'd asked, but had received no reply.

You then watched each one of the sixty minutes pass before you approached Mr. Adam's Apple again.

"Dear God man, isn't there anything I can do?" you shrieked. You could feel the cartoon steam bursting out from your small ears.

But Mr. Adam's Apple, dressed in a maroon blazer, smirked. He tilted forward, and his oily forehead shone like a slip-n-slide. He tongued his flaky chapped lips.

"No sir," he said, "I'm afraid that's not our policy."

Which is when it happened: your fist, your comical short arms, and so on.

The situation quickly devolved from what should have been a simple and satisfying expression of fury into a more complicated and mind-numbing security interrogation.

But on your next visit, the policy has changed. This time, after you sign the waiver and hand the pen up to Mr. Adam's Apple, you fold your copy into the pocket of your windbreaker and push out a special door to a metal staircase that deposits you directly onto the tarmac. There, you join a small group of angry people like yourself and you pull on a fluorescent yellow vest and clamp huge stereo headphones over your ears. The members of your group twitch and flinch and open their mouths like they're screaming, but their voices are impossible to hear through your covered ears and the drone of nearby jet engines.

You are assigned a place in line by a man who wears headphones with a small microphone attached and who holds a florescent orange flag high in the air. He wears a pair of black gloves and you store that information away for the next time. When he drops his flag hand, you all follow him, jogging in a single file line. Just when you're concerned that running will ruin your anger buzz, you stop under the belly of a plane.   Envious passengers look down on you from their oval windows, obviously wishing they could trade places. You pick a spot near the nose of the plane and stand in the ready position, legs separated, knees slightly bent, head back and eyes that attempt to burn a hole into the bluish gray metal of the aircraft.

The Chainsaw Toothbrush

There once was a man named Harold who was pretty sure that he had been married at some point, and that children had been part of the so-called bigger picture as well. Whose children and how old and where they were, not to mention the so-called wife, well, he couldn't be expected to keep track of all that insanity. Keeping the seasons in line was difficult enough and he would need a good amount of firewood. Harold lived where winter was always approaching and anyway, who in these parts had ever complained about having too much firewood?

Harold lived in New Hampshire and in the frosty white winter, when the white townspeople placed white candles behind the white-framed windows of their steepled-white homes, the unrelenting and skin-splitting chill would sink deep into the white of Harold's bones and freeze him like a fly trapped in an ice-cube. Forced to endure the bloody lung taste of wind that stabbed like an ice cycle into his ears and nostrils, the misery would inevitably arrive and settle into Harold for the duration. Last year or else a few, several years ago, this despair had so depleted Harold's spirit that he was even denied that small relief afforded him by the ever reliable fantasy involving a dismantled safety razor, his wrists and a bathtub of cooling water.

So one day in late August, Harold decided that he would try to prevent this year's plunge into hopelessness by launching what he thought of as three-part preemptive strike. First, he would purchase a wood-burning stove. This would require him to buy new and powerful wood-cutting and wood-splitting tools. And finally, these tools would obligate Harold to perform several hundred hours of extremely physical labor that would, if all went as planned, guide him through the season by exhausting him daily to the edge of unconsciousness.

In this way, Harold would no longer have energy to try and identify the roots of his unease or confront that most unpleasant suspicion that he was simply an organism waiting around to die. The persistent muscle aches and a weariness known only to Harold in the form of a high fever would make it easy to ignore the abstract and meaningless anxieties that spun relentlessly, asking the unanswerable questions that have plagued human since the dawn of consciousness. No more incessant queries into the whereabouts of his wife and children. No more riddles about who had left whom and what did the bank plan on doing with all of the houses it was confiscating.

Instead, his exhaustion would stop the hamster wheel before it could start spinning out the random inquiries about whether the foreclosure sign referred to his property or to the river that bordered his property, and before he knew it, he'd have slipped into a sleep more akin to a coma than a powernap.

If Harold's mind proved more resilient than he expected, of course, there would always be the jugs of red wine; a few tumblers of the drink would put an end to any stray mental meanderings as quickly as a period ended a sentence.

Stupid thoughts. Useless mind chatter. Didn't there used to be a couch?

Luckily, in Harold's New Hampshire, shopping was a fundamental right that was known to cure depression and defeat terrorism. Because of this, each citizen was entitled to at least one credit card, no matter how many times they'd gone through each type of bankruptcy.

So, wearing his cleanest pair of underwear over the groin holes of his least ripped pair of jeans, Harold set out for The Hardware Dump, the largest of the retail chains that routinely sold complicated and specialized equipment to ignorant, testosterone-jacked weekend warriors. In Harold's New Hampshire there existed an odd belief that if something was sold in a retail store, then it was meant to be purchased and used by anyone with enough money. After all, the thinking went, if certain equipment was too complicated or too dangerous for the regular person, The Hardware Dump wouldn't offer it for sale.

It was while Harold was walking down the chainsaw aisle, contemplating the best length of bar and chain that he had the idea that would have, had the day gone differently, revolutionized society. He imagined a store that would be called something like MyMedco or Medicatropolis, where he would sell medical equipment and tools to the general public. An entire industry was ready and waiting to be embraced by a public who, armed with articles printed off the internet, could certainly handle stitching wounds, treating infections and removing their own teeth. After all, Harold mused, removing a kidney and carving a turkey probably had more in common than the high and mighty doctors wanted to admit.

But alas, before Harold could grow the idea into anything truly substantial, his eyes came across a very powerful but very lightweight chainsaw with an eighteen inch bar and chain. He ran a finger along the chain, and the instant that the razor-like metal tooth sunk easily into Harold's fingertip, he knew that this machine could fix his life. Just seeing the droplet of blood bubble up and streak down across his palm and passed his wrist, filled Harold with an enormous sense of potential. Suddenly, possibility turned out to be real, as did the whole concept of choice. Harold felt a surge of happiness at the knowledge that he had the power to act in a clear and definite way. Hope blossomed around him like a fragrance and had he not taken firm control of his emotions right there in the aisle, it's likely that Harold would have broken down and cried with gratitude.

A license for a gun? In Harold's New Hampshire, that was a big, though grudging, Y E S. But a license for a chainsaw? Of course not. The teenage clerk barely looked at Harold as he removed the various anti-theft devices hidden in and on the chainsaw. Along with the chainsaw, Harold bought a pair of gloves, the necessary engine oil and a set of clear goggles. Before he swiped his credit card Harold took a moment and bowed his head to give thanks.

It was a ritual performed by every decent citizen when they stood in a checkout lane anywhere across Harold's New Hampshire; Harold thanked the god of no sales tax and decided, for good measure, to thank the god of no income tax as well, even though Harold was pretty sure that he didn't have an income. He wished that the whiners and complainers who had been against closing the schools could see him at this moment, as he stood and gave thanks to these two gods. Maybe then the pro-school fanatics would finally realize just how much the absence of those taxes really meant to him.

Like a child coming to the end of a crying jag, Harold exhaled a shuddering breath and composed himself. With the plastic bag containing his smaller items in one hand and gripping the chainsaw handle with the other, Harold lifted his chin with pride and headed straight for a glass wall. The glass parted and he stepped onto the asphalt with a bright sense of renewed purpose which did not dim in the slightest as he returned home. His tree-cutting outfit required the addition of a baseball cap and over the ear headphones. Then he prepared his chainsaw, mixing the oil he'd bought with gasoline from a container behind the garage. With his new goggles fastened tight, Harold headed into the woods to exercise his renewed sense of purpose.

Harold pulled the ripcord once and the chainsaw immediately spun to life; the noise was soothing and elegant, unlike anything Harold had expected. The whizzing hum sounded more like a jacket being unzipped than a car without a muffler. Harold thought that if they ever got around to making laser saws, they would probably sound exactly like the one he held in his hands.

A tingling sensation passed from his hands, up through his arms, and cascaded down his back causing a strange feeling, as if the saw was simultaneously creating and relieving an itch down the length of his spine. His delight intensified when he discovered how easily the chain moved through the wood. It seemed to Harold that he only had to aim his saw, and the wood parted like soft cheese.

Harold was no lumberjack. By the time one large maple had fallen onto the garage, crashing straight through the roof and onto the cement floor, and another maple had nearly smashed his leg into oatmeal, Harold had learned several techniques and sequences of cut that were best avoided. Soon enough he turned his attention to the fallen trees and began slicing through the logs he was cutting off chunks of butter. Like a light-saber, he thought at one point, more than a chainsaw. There was no better tool, Harold thought to himself, than a brand new chainsaw.

After six hours of cutting, and a careless swipe of the churning blade that shredded through a section of pants and left bleeding tooth marks on the side of his shin, Harold paused to admire the number of rounds that lay on the ground all around him. It might've taken him ten weeks to split all of it into useable pieces, but as he'd worked, thoughts about returning to life gradually pushed into his head. He was surprised to find that the ordeal of splitting the wood felt as remote and unlikely to him as if someone had suggested that he might one day live on the moon.

He took off his goggles and with the nearly soundless chainsaw still spinning, he made his way toward the collapsed garage. He looked around at the splintered two-by-fours and gallons of spilled paint and decided not to shove his precious new chainsaw into one crevice or another. Yes, the garage was where he stored his tools, but the structure was in no condition to house such a fine instrument. Instead of leaving the power tool somewhere outside, Harold decided to bring it into the house.

Only after he heard the zipping noise echo inside his empty living room did he remember that the chainsaw was still spinning away, quietly humming. The sound had become so familiar and comforting, so connected with the sounds of peace and quiet that Harold feared turning off the tool would create an audible deficit, a frightening and gravitational silence. For now, he decided, he would leave it running.

He needed to take a shower, but he couldn't just lay the running chainsaw on the living room carpet, where he'd never hear it while he showered. And what if it snagged a tiny thread and jammed, or if the vibration caused it to rotate and move across the floor until the chain cut into a wall outlet? So Harold decided to bring the chainsaw into the bathroom with him and set it on the tile floor where the worst it could do, he figured, was bump up against the toilet base.

In the new, much cleaner, and much whiter setting, it was difficult for Harold to imagine how powerful and beastly the saw had been in the woods. Humming gently, it resembled something like an electric can opener or a toaster. Naked and caked with dry sweat, Harold brushed away the tiny wood chips and dust that had accumulated around his neck. Fortunately there was only cold water and before Harold stepped under the stream, he saw that he needed a new bar of soap. He found one under the sink and after several attempts, his wet hands failed to pry open the plastic wrapping. Harold found himself staring at the chainsaw and its blur of metal teeth as he contemplated giving up. He slowly stretched out his arm the way a person might try to feed a stray dog, and lowered one end of the soap onto the blurring chain. ,

When the chainsaw bucked, it not only tore open the soap and shredded half of it, but the metal teeth had momentarily brushed up against Harold bare foot and cut away his little toe.

The shock and the beginning of pain were of no consequences compared to the overwhelming rush of relief that flowed through Harold. Like everyone else, he'd heard about those troubled kids who were said to cut themselves intentionally, but never in a million years, would Harold have connected them to his own life. He couldn't tell if it was the sting or the sight of the growing puddle of blood, but it felt as if his blood had been suffocating inside his body, and now it could finally stretch out and breathe.

The water in the shower began cold and never warmed up, which happened to suit Harold perfectly. His exultation from the cut had probably jacked up his already overheated body, and the ice cold water wrapped Harold in a numbness that added to his sense of relief and well-being.

There are the types of itches, athlete's foot for example or poison ivy, which seem to provoke the sufferer into a frenzy of scratching so violent that they may not cease until actual skin has been torn away. This type of itch was the first sensation Harold felt after exiting the shower. In the center of his back, a burning and itching that summoned him, but no matter how many different doors he tried rubbing against, the itch seemed to grow worse, spreading out from the center of the spine until he could reach the very outer rings with his hand, an effort that only fueled the itch's core.

Determined to ignore the itch and the tears filling his eyes, Harold returned to the bathroom.

He might have turned off the chainsaw before he used it to scratch his back, except by the time he was using both hands to lower the tool behind his head, he not only sought relief, but he wanted to punish the itch. He had personified the itch, turned it into an enemy as real as any he could have imagined, and part of his intention was to teach the stupid itch a lesson it would never forget. Guessing at the correct position, he tapped lightly against his back.

The itch was instantly erased and replaced by a sting that drew into Harold's body, a wave of relief more powerful than the first.

He felt liquid running down his buttocks and the back of his legs. But even in his state of weak-kneed relief, sensing within himself the addict's insatiable appetite for relief, Harold was not foolish enough to go on pressing the tip of the chainsaw into the center of his back. He lifted the saw from his back, up over his head and crouched to place it on the ground.

Feeling a little buzzed and woozy, Harold surveyed the walls which were speckled with red. It was possible that Harold would not have to clean it up, since the patterns and swirls of the red freckles looked quite artistic. Chainsaw as paintbrush, was the thought that convinced Harold that the smears and puddles of red color all around him actually was paint.

He could not see his back and the side of his foot was already submerged in a pool of red, he could conclude nothing else.

Harold's face in the mirror remained unmarked by blood enough so that his first thought was that he needed a shave. An uneven black and gray beard coated much of his neck, his cheeks and under his nose. It had been a while but he suddenly felt way too drunk to trust himself with a razor. Or the chainsaw for that matter. One slip and he'd cut his throat. And anyway, going without a shave had never bothered Harold.

He needed to take a nap.

But nothing upset or distracted Harold more when he tried to fall asleep than the taste and feel of an unclean mouth.

He opened the wooden cabinet beneath the sink and found the orange box, half-filled with a solid brick of baking soda. Harold's mouth felt sticky and tasted like gasoline and oil. Probably he'd breathed in too much chainsaw exhaust. Smacking the baking soda into chunks and dipping his finger in the dust, Harold began to brush. Immediately he remembered that there was nothing less satisfying than finger brushing, he might as well have used his elbow for all the good it did.

This time, Harold had not intended to turn off the chainsaw since the whirring chain reminded him of a dentist's tool. But this made it difficult to load on the baking soda chunks, since they vaporized on contact. At last he picked up the box, let a few good sized chunks roll into his mouth and chewed until the powder turned into paste.

Without looking down, Harold squatted unsteadily, found the chainsaw's handle and very carefully, stood up. Using both hands to guarantee precision, he brought the tool closer to his mouth. Harold saw himself smile in the mirror. Bluish glops of paste and saliva coated his grinning teeth. Some spilled over his bottom lip and down his chin. He felt a tiny breeze.

Harold did not see but felt his grin widen as the chainsaw tore into his mouth.

After it's Too Late, but Before it's Over

Heidi's pig wasn't just any pig, it was *Destiny: The World's Smartest Pig*, and Alan had spent an entire afternoon painting exactly those words, in bright pink, on the side of the star's trailer. It looked like an advertisement for Barbie.

The pig was the size of a small dog. It wore a studded leather jacket and sunglasses and rode a small tricycle in circles. It shot a rubber basketball through a hoop by stepping on one end of a tiny seesaw—just like a dog. But the pig sure as hell didn't smell like a dog, not to Alan. The pig smelled like hard-boiled eggs and diarrhea.

"Otis told me that you can buy a woman's eggs online," Alan said as he drove home on Saturday afternoon. "Just like cyanide and dildos."

"Don't be sick," Heidi said.

"Anyway, I looked it up, and he's right," Alan said. "About the eggs, I mean."

A tiny blue Yugo appeared next to the truck. A fat man with greasy black hair and glasses honked and gave a thumbs up. He barely fit into his car. His car swerved slightly into Alan's lane as the fat man honked again and waved. He mouthed the words "Big Fan."

"Slow down," Heidi said. She sat in the passenger's seat and waved like a prom queen with a fixed red smile on her powdered face. She wore her shiny pink prom dress with puffy sleeves and a diagonal white band across her chest that read *Destiny* instead of *Miss California* or *Miss Idaho*. Her black hair was shaped into two stubby ponytails that stood erect off either side of the back of her head.

Alan fed the engine and they surged passed the blue car.

"Alan!" Heidi snapped. She clicked her tongue in disapproval and continued to wave and smile from her imaginary float.

"Seriously," Alan said. "These egg-women list if they have cancer in their family or insanity; if they smoke or drink; if they act or sing—all that. It's like you could pick out a future movie star if you wanted."

Heidi held her hands in her lap and stared out the front windshield. "I think she needs more calcium in her diet," she said. "We should try giving her whole milk."

"And they're not that expensive," Alan said.

"What?"

"The eggs."

"Are you deaf? I'm talking about her limp. She can barely finish her hula."

Alan glanced at his side-view mirror and then at Heidi. Her clenched jaw and mouth—she looked like a skull. "There's this one blonde," Alan continued. "She has a killer back, super-tight legs, and a Ph.D. in biology. She'll sell for ten grand."

"Don't be a monster," Heidi said.

Alan guided the truck off of the highway and into the spot next to their trailer. Heidi disappeared from the truck before Alan had pulled the gearshift down into park.

Alan walked into the storage shed next to the trailer—his workshop. He pushed a button and his computer creased to life.

Once again Alan scrolled through the information on the blonde with green eyes. She was 23 years old and had never been hospitalized for mental illness or drug abuse. She'd scored in the upper 3rd percentile on her SAT exams. He carefully examined the picture of her nude and basically fat-free body. Her tan thighs made his mouth dry up.

Alan had been looking at this woman every day for two weeks. He half-hoped that she would sell her eggs already and disappear. He wanted fate to step in.

With sweaty palms, Alan typed in his background information. He guided the little black arrow onto the word SUBMIT and paused. With the click of a button, Alan made an offer.

Otis worked the northbound lane and Alan the southbound from ten until six in the morning. The air was chilly, but not too cold, not yet, and Otis stood on his chair and tied one end of a rope to the metal beam that went across the tollbooth.

"Well, it won't be long now," Otis said. "My brother's getting me a job on a highway crew—twenty bucks an hour for holding a stop sign."

"Sounds thrilling."

"It beats the hell out of having to listen to you and your problems with that shotgun of yours."

"She's my wife—you can say wife."

"Your shotgun wife."

"No. No shotgun—we don't even own a shotgun. We don't have anything to do with shotguns."

"The hell you don't," Otis said. He began to tie the other end of the rope into a lasso. "But you're right about one thing—a shotgun wedding doesn't need an actual shotgun—not anymore," Otis explained. "It used to though—you know, with pa in his overalls in the middle of the night sayin', 'You git o'er there Jethro and murry my pregnint daughter.'" Otis neatly coiled the rope around the neck of the lasso.

"But pa never really blew Jethro to smithereens."

"Sure he did—blasted his bloody guts all over the preacher's good book, and his wife's nightgown. But I'm just talking about the idea anyway—of being forced into it." Otis poked his head through the noose and yanked it to the side with one hand. He closed his eyes and stuck out his tongue.

"We weren't forced into it," Alan said. "We were planning to do it."

After the fetal pig, Alan wasn't yanked from his stupor again until his senior year of high school. In between he'd muddled through a life of gray oatmeal and occasional and only vaguely familiar nighttime ejaculations. When he finally came to awareness, Alan was drinking canned beer and sitting with a pretty girl on a picnic table. She proved that she wasn't wearing underwear and Alan was born again, thrust onto her body and into the sensation of being alive.

Sounds and smells bombarded him and he howled, Heidi told him later, much like a coyote—caught in a trap. Still, the moment had shot Alan out of his canon and into the fresh air. Heidi's cheeks were red and she smelled like peeled fruit and afterward, Alan pounded on his chest and jogged around the table with his shorts around his ankles.

"Give me a break. What were you, eighteen?" Otis asked. "You don't plan anything when you're eighteen, you just do—and you went ahead and did." Satisfied with his creation, Otis sat on his feet in his chair.

The noose hung perfectly still.

"We had already talked about the future," Alan said. "Way before that," he added, and he couldn't help but wish that it was true. It seemed like a good idea, to talk about pregnancy, to plan it, before.

"So you're telling me that you planned it?" Otis asked. "A couple of horny eighteen year-old kids sat down one night and over a cup of coffee and before they guzzled beer and humped on a picnic table they mapped out their future together? "

"It just sped things up is all," Alan said. "It was a blessing in disguise."

"A major disguise—a disguise so complex that you still haven't figured it out. Whether you know it or not, your strings were pulled, my man—she danced you like a puppet—straight into saying 'I do.'" One of the problems was that Otis did not believe in love. He had told Alan before that love was basically a passing sensation, similar to heartburn. It felt endless and intense when it was happening, maybe even like it might never go away, but voila! after a short while and without any reason, it simply faded and vanished. And when it was gone, he noted, you kind of missed the familiarity of the pain, but only an idiot would make it come back on purpose.

"What's the big deal? People get married every day," Alan said. "There's a guy, probably like twenty of them getting married right this second, somewhere." The major difference between the fetal pig incident and the picnic-table night was that Alan did not sink back into his state of lifeless graydom—Heidi wouldn't let him. And when this became clear to Alan, for the first time in his life, he started to panic.

Alan freaked because he suddenly felt exposed and vacant, like he was too light inside, too empty, and so he desperately looked around for filler. Everyone seemed to have some type of filler or focus or future. People's lives seemed to be about one thing or another. During his search Alan witnessed a guy playing second base, a girl blowing a trombone, and another girl blowing a trombone player.

These people, it seemed to Alan, had their hooks into life; they had themselves filled up with something. They were solid, grounded human beings and they were probably never overcome with Alan's fear that he was teetering on the edge of a vast black hole that waited to suck him down and away forever.

But fortunately for Alan, Heidi was ready with her stream of talk about baby names like 'Eduardo' and marriage tips like 'never go to bed mad' and station wagon trips to Disneyland, and so Alan braced himself and simply swallowed and swallowed until he too was full up with pregnancy heartburn, ultrasounds, and write-your-own marriage vows.

They were married in a courthouse when Heidi was seven months pregnant.

"Bless those sad sad souls," Otis said and he faced the noose with his eyes closed. He raised both fists to his mouth like a trumpet and blew a funeral dirge.

Probably the whole egg idea triggered Heidi's maternal instinct.

The pig waddled into the kitchen for breakfast with a diaper around the hindquarters and a pink bonnet tied under the chin. The pig brought with it the pure animal smell, the rolling in manure and urine smell. The black beady eyes reminded Alan of a rat, and the hairy snout left discolored wet spots on the floor.

"What do you think?" Heidi asked when she came out of the nursery. She stared at the pig. She wore an infant front pack on her chest.

"Don't let it into the kitchen," Alan said. He could imagine the tiny teeth sinking into his calf like cobra fangs, puncturing straight into his vein and ushering thousands of vile bacteria into his body. The thought made his body itch.

"Don't be stupid," Heidi said. "Destiny is as clean as a house cat. Besides—,"

"I know, I know—pigs are actually very clean and extremely smart," Alan said in a mimicking tone. "So smart that they end up on breakfast sandwiches all around the world."

"You might be kind," Heidi said with an irritating good nature sound humming through her voice. Alan half-expected her to begin singing the next line of dialogue. "She'll be a big star someday."

Heidi bent down and spoke baby talk to the pig as she lifted it up and slipped it into the front pack.

"What are you doing?" Alan shouted. "You'll never get out the smell."

"What smell?" Heidi gazed down at the small animal attached to her chest and when she opened her mouth the pig strained to lick Heidi's tongue.

The next morning, the pig sat in a high chair and wore a pink bib. It stared at Alan and he thought he could detect a slight smile of victory on the hairy face.

"I'm not eating with this, this—" Pig was the only word that came to his mind.

"What has gotten into you?" Heidi asked. "She's just as much a part of the family as either one of us, now sit down and behave."

The runny snout pushed a plastic red bowl around the tray and the tongue sucked up something that looked like oatmeal. Alan smelled a whiff of farm, of animal tang.

Heidi barely glanced at Alan. She smiled at the pig and reached over to wipe the animal's slobbering mouth with her own napkin.

"She sleeps with the pig?" Otis asked with a laugh. "How about that, Mister Farmer in the Dell? The pig takes the wife!"

"It's nothing—it's just like a dog or cat."

"Who takes the cheese again?" Otis asked. "Because I'll take it—I love cheese."

"I'm just worried, that's all, I'm worried about Heidi."

Otis made the obnoxious sound of a buzzer. "Wrong answer. She's doing just fine. You're the one to worry about."

"Why me? I'm not licking the snot off of a grimy little animal."

"Bingo! The pig is not a grimy little animal to her. Don't you get it? The pig is her baby," Otis said. He sipped from a styrofoam cup through a straw. "How long has this been going on? How long have you been kicked out of bed?"

"I haven't been kicked out of anything," Alan said. "I don't sleep in the bed. In case you haven't noticed, I work all night."

"Please tell me that it hasn't been *that* long."

"So?"

"Well, let's see. The baby dies, an infection wrecks her body, and then a week or two later she starts to train a pig."

"And?"

"And now the pig eats at the table," Otis said. "It's called emotional transference."

"She's probably just practicing," Alan said.

"Right. Most women work out all the kinks with a farm animal before they go for the real thing. Hell, my mom breastfed two goats before she had me."

"She's been through hell," Alan said. "This is not your typical situation."

"Look, whether you know it or not, you've got a baby. In her mind, the pig is her own little baby, see?"

"She knows it's a pig," Alan said.

"No. She knows it's an animal. But babies are animals too, and they're very dependent—actually it's not that different, if you think about it. She trains the pig to obey certain sounds, a language, if you will—we'll call that education. She dresses the pig up and takes it to the park, maybe lets it play with the other children—there's your socialization. She sleeps with the pig—either nurturing or incest, depends on the state."

"Are you high? It's a freakin' pig!"

"Maybe you could teach it to play catch," Otis said.

Alan left work early. He felt like a secret agent as he crept through his own home. It was barely five in the morning when he pushed open the bedroom door.

The smell of pig shit almost knocked him over. It was like sniffing a bottle of moldy ammonia. Heidi was still asleep with the pig in their bed. Heidi looked much as she had in the hospital, her face relaxed, pretty and smooth, her cheeks red and healthy. It was clear that she didn't smell a thing, and if she did, she was used to it by now.

A chill moved through Alan as he wondered what went on while he was at work. The block of time suddenly seemed dangerous to Alan; as if entire schemes were being carried out without his knowledge. It was absurd, almost as if he'd discovered an affair.

The pig was dressed in an infant gown and it had nuzzled itself into Heidi's neck.

A small pile of greeny-brown pig shit sat on the pink comforter at the foot of the bed. Alan believed that he could see steam rising from it. That was when he gagged and felt the burn in his throat.

He closed the door and stood in the hallway. He stopped his vomit by picturing flowers. He imagined the floral perfume that came from wreathes of pink and white flowers; the same kind that had arrived at the hospital after the baby died. He felt a familiar panic rise in his chest.

Alan walked straight into his workshop and fired up the computer. He leaned like a hacker over the keyboard and reviewed the blonde's information for a while. The familiarity calmed him down. Her green eyes and bright smile (all natural teeth) made Alan feel like things would work out in the end. To be fair to the unborn child Alan tried to look at other women, but he always clicked back to the naked blonde. Finally, he wiped his palm across his shirt and took out his wallet. He held his credit card with one hand and slowly typed the information into the computer. With a single, barely audible, and anticlimactic click, Alan spent ten thousand dollars.

Alan and Otis sat quietly in the center tollbooth with stadium electric lights humming outside. It was around three in the morning, and as usual they could not see any stars at all. No cars were coming or going.

Finally, Otis filled his mouth with vodka and gargled out the phrase, "Happy anniversary."

"One year," Alan said somberly.

Otis nodded his head and swallowed. "I bet it seems longer, doesn't it? Hell, you should've been divorced by now."

"I don't get divorced," Alan said. Sometimes the Blah nipped at Alan's heels; grabbed an ankle or tugged on the collar of his shirt. He knew that it wanted him back, wanted him to march in lock step through the vast nothing of everydayness. He felt it swirling, and he feared being sucked in alive.

"But of course, please excuse me." Otis raised his voice and lifted a finger into the air. "Sir Alan will not be having even a small piece of that creamy and satisfying divorce this evening. The nineteen year-old male at the peak of his sexual potential would rather have a nice big slice of that crusty pain and salted misery instead."

The dim yellow glow in the nursery came from a night light behind the closet door. Alan didn't see clearly when he first walked into the room.

He was prepared to finish painting. A finished nursery would help buffer the ten thousand-dollar surprise he was going to announce to Heidi in the morning. He held a hammer in one hand and a new gallon of pink paint in the other.

Heidi sat in the old rocking chair, head back, eyes closed. Her shirt had been unbuttoned and she wore no bra. Her relaxed face looked beautiful and young again. She looked like she didn't have a single worry on her mind.

Something moved on Heidi's chest.

Slowly, the form of the pig emerged. The pig's head bobbed slowly and Alan saw the tongue slurp and lick around one of Heidi's nipples. Heidi breathed quietly while the pig snorted and salivated.

Alan gagged again and felt his stomach acid rise; his chest burned. The room smelled like it hadn't been aired for weeks. The fleshy animal stench clung to Alan's nose like a thick fog. No matter how he turned his head, the thick, almost bloody smell continued to assault his nostrils.

The animal's smacking and sucking almost sounded like words, like an infant's language. The noise was playful and while Alan fought to control his gag reflex, the pig suckled like an infant.

Alan's veins filled with ants. His body itched, his eyes watered, and he felt sweat stream from his armpits down his sides. Alan needed to control himself. He lowered the new paint can onto the ground and took careful steps toward the beast. He held onto the hammer.

Alan wrapped his free hand around the pig's belly and lifted it off Heidi's chest. She did not move. The pig's eyes were half-closed and Alan felt the fat hairy body quiver against his palm. The pig lethargically tried to free itself and Alan tightened his grip around the belly and pressed the animal hard to his chest. He wanted to crush it right there.

Alan's other hand trembled. He searched through blurry vision, blinked hard, and forced tears onto his cheeks. Holding the pig tightly against his chest, Alan bent and hooked an empty paint can with his pinky and then gently closed the door behind him.

"It's weird, that's all," Otis said. He was positioning a book in his window as he spoke. The title was, "The Idiot's Guide to Suicide."

"What's weird about it? An animal is an animal," Alan said.

"So you left the bedroom door open *and* the front door?"

"That's weird? The room smelled like death—I couldn't breathe."

"And the pig just up and runs out the door, never to be seen again?"

"Animals run away everyday—probably twenty animals ran away just while I said that."

Satisfied with his book display, Otis sat back down and took a roll of gauze and a pair of scissors out of his drawer. He fired a stream from his water bottle into his open mouth and let the sound linger before he swallowed.

"How's the old lady?" Otis asked.

"Better now. She was out of her mind at first—I must've spent twenty hours just putting up Lost Pig signs all over town."

Otis cut pieces of gauze and wrapped them around each wrist. Then he took a red marker and pressed the tip onto his wrist. The color slowly bled into fabric.

"We chased a few leads—people calling and saying that they thought they saw a pig running under someone's porch or through a garden. One guy said he saw a pig come out of the movie theater."

"But you weren't going to find the pig, were you?" Otis asked without looking up. Then he spoke in Marlon Brando's raspy voice, "I axed the pig for a little respect, a little friendship, and what do I get? Shit. On my bed." The red patch had spread across both wrists and was beginning to look dark red, almost black.

"We didn't find the pig," Alan said.

"Course you didn't," Marlon Brando said. "Nobody sees the pig, nobody hears from the pig—the pig disappears, like magic."

"And whose idea was the funeral?" Otis asked. He temporarily capped the red pen, wrapped another piece of gauze, and repeated the procedure.

"It was a memorial service," Alan said. "And it was my idea. We just buried a symbolic little coffin, played some music, cried—it worked out well."

"I'm sure you cried a river," Otis said.

"She seemed to feel better," Alan said. "You know, after the ritual."

"And then, while she's still emotionally wrecked, you take advantage of her grief and present the egg idea. Which is way more than just an idea by then because you've already spent the ten grand. It looks like you're saving the day, like you're doing something to help her focus on the future. Not a bad plan, if I do say so myself."

"I didn't take advantage of anything. It just worked out this way. She knew it was the best thing."

Otis had finished wrapping his wrists. He lifted them up and showed them to Alan. "See? Just enough blood coming through so people won't mistake it for a tennis or handball injury."

"Anyway, she's doing great, and I've been out of my mind, getting the room ready and taking her from the doctor to the nutritionist to the mall."

"I guess it's really weird," Otis said. "Because you don't even want the kid."

"What are you talking about? Of course I want the kid—I'm the one who bought the egg!"

"Yes, but that doesn't mean you want a kid. That just means that you want her to be pregnant."

"And that's not the same thing?"

"Not at all," Otis said. "You need her to be pregnant because that's why you married her in the first place. Without pregnancy, you have no reason to be married, probably no reason to live—no offense. I'm just saying that when the baby died you were faced with big questions like what you're all about and why you were married. And you probably always drew a blank—you need her to be pregnant."

"You're cracked. We're in love, first of all."

"Let me ask you this. How many times have you imagined yourself with the baby, holding the baby, teaching the little kid to walk or catch or any of that?"

"Are you kidding? I haven't had time to just sit around and imagine bonnets and rattles and all that crap. And besides, you're forgetting that we had already planned—,"

"Right, right I know—a blessing in disguise. I'll tell you one thing, you better get your mind straight on this because no matter what, she can't be pregnant forever."

Otis reached out of his window to give change with one of his bandaged wrists and he pulled in a prayer card, which he then proceeded to read like Count Dracula.

Heidi was five months pregnant and beginning to show. One night, while Alan was a work, Heidi must have been kneeling on the nursery's carpet and folding clothes into certain piles and then into the baby's dresser. The piles were still there by the time Alan got home. The drawers were still pulled out.

Anyway, at some point, she noticed the dirty white blotch on the wall behind the crib. A spot that Alan had missed with his paintbrush.

It was a small patch, barely noticeable, and the old Heidi could have easily pushed it out of her mind for good. But the new Heidi was a bit more of a perfectionist. She had decided that all things having to do with the baby must be done to absolute perfection. She may have been under the impression that sloppiness and disorganization called forth the devils of tragedy and distress. By putting her universe into exact and precise order Heidi felt she could protect herself and her baby from the demons of the unknown.

Still Heidi was Heidi. She might have folded another pile of clothes before she stopped and stared at the blemish on the wall. Even if her newly established fascist perfectionism was irritating her at the moment she could have easily rationalized the painting as a kind gesture to Alan who had worked so hard and been so supportive of her—especially after Destiny's disappearance.

Heidi needed to go into the shed and scan the shelves of paint, most likely looking around the crusted rims for evidence of the color inside the can. The pink paint can was in a cluttered corner, hidden under a rug and some of Destiny's old toys. Heidi probably needed both hands to lift it. Heidi walked out of the shed and up the three steps to the trailer's front door.

Maybe Heidi stopped and leaned against the banister at the top, trying to regain her breath. After all, hadn't the doctor had repeatedly warned Heidi not to stress her body?

She might even have considered leaving the can on the porch for when Alan came home, but inevitably her strength would return and she might have remembered that she was doing something nice for Alan— she was using this paint as an opportunity to thank him for all that he'd done for her.

Again kneeling in the baby's room with the paintbrush next to her, Heidi needed to loosen the lid with the hammer. Then the easiest way would be for Heidi to stick one of her fingernails under either side of the lid and pull up and away.

Heidi might not have immediately recognized the pig. A black fault line ran down the middle of the bloated purple head, and shreds of gray snout had lodged inside the eye socket holes.

Nature Takes its Course

About two weeks after I cut off my finger, Big Dog came to visit me at my apartment. He brought a 12 pack of beer and a bottle of butterscotch Schnapps. We sat on a green couch I had found by the dumpster and watched Olympic volleyball on TV.

"You could've just quit," he said, motioning to my cast with his beer.

"I know."

Big Dog was a veteran of the kitchen, middle 30's, with the barest hint of Asian in his face. A big-boned man with a giant torso and stomach. He wore a baseball cap over his short black hair and occasionally barked at the ceiling with rounded lips.

"Crazy son of a bitch," he said.

Since Kelly left I'd been going to an acupuncturist for my mental health. I didn't feel better, but I carried around the sensation of a pin driving through the top of my skull.

I'd lived in the apartment for less than a month and open boxes lined the living room walls. The TV sat on a black garbage bag filled with blankets and the VCR lay on the ground nearby. The whole place was bare except for the photograph that hung by a magnet on the freezer door. I took the picture of the three of us when the baby was still alive. Kelly lies on the bed with the baby cradled in her arms, her brown hair splayed on the pillow behind her head. I lean into the picture with my mouth open like I'd been hit on the head. He must have seen it hanging there, but Big Dog didn't ask any questions. Instead he took beer from the fridge and told a story about the 19 year old cook who'd quit the restaurant to sell drugs. He made $5000 a month.

"And still you work," I said.

He looked at me, pretending to be shocked. "It's my life, James."
He raised his beer and barked at the ceiling. "It's how I stay good." Big
Dog was engaged to be married, another thing we didn't talk about.

"You ever hear voices," I asked him.

"No," he said, drawing out the word like he was trying to be funny,
pretending to be frightened.

"I wish I did," I said.

"What, like God?"

"At least voices tell you what to do."

Big Dog swallowed and shook his head. "But they don't tell you
what *not* to do," he said.

"It'd still be better than the sounds. All I ever hear are sounds," I
said. "Plates smashing on the floor, dogs howling, people crying. It
seriously makes me crazy."

Big Dog cupped a hand around his mouth to change the sound of
his voice. "Get beer from fridge," he said.

I laughed and obeyed.

A few months after Kelly gave birth, we made anywhere from $200
to $500 for internet sex videos depending on the quality and length.
We were saving money for the baby's college and the language of our
lovemaking completely transformed. "Scene time," or "Let's do a hot
audio," became our whispered foreplay. Up until the baby died, I don't
think we did it once without cameras on tripods, without considering
edits as we moved through the scene.

I remember looking through the video camera with Kelly lying on
the bed in her underpants and a white halter top. I was trying to choose
a distance so I kept zooming in and panning back.

"I'm fat," she says to the camera. She pinches the skin around her
belly.

"You're gorgeous," I say. Then I see myself crawl on the bed,
wearing boxer shorts that looked like leopard skin. I kiss her on the
forehead and then we both stop. Kelly gets up and leaves the room and
I lay on the bed. After a few minutes she comes back with the baby, lays
down facing me and starts to breast feed. The two of us just lay there
with the baby sucking away. I remember being impatient, and I even
move my foot back and forth like I'm irritated, like I'm waiting to get
on with the scene. At some point, I place my hand on her thigh and all

I can hear is the baby eating. It's my least favorite video and I watch it all the time.

I still hear the sounds that came out of the baby monitor on the night he died. A sucking hum that made me think about whether the audio on our last scene was any good. The sound of rubbing fabric, moist mouth noise. We were paid the most when the audio was great, if you could hear dirty talk or narrative fantasies while the camera captured thighs or pubic hair or wetness. The talk and groans and orgasms always fetched the most cash, even compared to those beneath the body angles I found so intriguing and inventive. In just under 2 months we had made over $3,000.

The doctors said the sounds I heard were probably nothing, maybe the pacifier in the baby's mouth. After all it wasn't like we woke up to find a cord wrapped around his neck or his face planted in a pillow. They said the fact remained that he died from SIDS. But I still hear those sounds and of course I wonder if things would have been different if I had gotten up to check on him. If I had investigated those sounds instead of placing a hand on the back of Kelly's neck and whispering, "Great scene tonight," even though she was asleep.

Things were not going well on the day I cut off my finger. I worked the egg station and Big Dog was out of the groove, calling out the wrong orders, slapping his metal spatula against the grill in frustration. My over-easy eggs broke in the pans before I had a chance to flip them. They oozed yolk all over the place and I'd smack the pan against the counter until the broken eggs fell into the garbage. I swallowed my anger and sucked the sweat off my upper lip.

I had felt this day coming on, like the flu, since Kelly left. A day I had tried like hell to escape, but with each broken yolk I stepped closer to a gorge. Like I was on the verge of being sucked down into darkness, vacuumed away.

Big Dog kept screwing up and I heard his first beer can open during the mid-breakfast rush, around 10:00am. At one point he tossed me a beer and said, "It's a wonderful life." I swallowed 12 ounces in a single gulp.

Not much visual description of the main event from my perspective. A pinky that may have had something to do with equilibrium and balance, but beyond that it seemed the obvious choice. One minute I'm looking at the deli slicer, choosing a thickness, pushing toward the blade, and the next I'm lying on the floor smiling quite stupidly. I remember a blast of pain like ice water and my apron getting heavy and sticky with blood. The vibrations of the metal blade continued to hum through my bones and my vision spun while I laid on the floor. I probably threw up. I heard Big Dog bark above the chatter of the ticket machine and I remember wondering for a moment how the entire scene would've looked on video.

Someone must have picked up the top part of my finger, severed just above the first knuckle, and probably wrapped it in ice since that is what they do on television. And then I remember crying when a waitress was kneeling next to me, supporting my head, and brushing my hair with her hand. Her name tag read **Beth** in black marker and she looked like she was 18. She had black hair with maroon highlights cut close to her head and she wore a stained pink dress shirt beneath her apron. It was unbearable to have someone so beautiful helping me. All I could do was smile and cry. She let my head rest in her lap while an ambulance made its way to the restaurant. She said, "You're doing great," which was not true at all, but I remember not wanting that part to end.

Awake at the hospital I saw Big Dog looking down at me.

"I guess you'll live," he said to my face. And then he whispered, "They sewed your foot onto your hand."

"Funny," I said. My throat was as dry as paper.

Beth stood in the corner and I heard Big Dog say that I should have given my two weeks and quit in the regular way. Beth and Big Dog drove me home with my hand wrapped up and in a cast.

"You'll be okay," Beth said. She looked around at my virtually empty apartment. I saw her glance at the photograph on the freezer.

"Sure," I said. "No problem."

She let her hand linger on my shoulder and then left with Big Dog. I found a few beers in the fridge and opened one. I sat on the couch and cried for a while, watching gymnastics on television.

Beth and I progressed in a regular way. She brought a plate of cookies and I kissed her on her beautiful mouth. "Lips like cherries," I said and she rolled her eyes.

"You can't be serious," she said, but her cheeks flushed anyway.

She had that peculiar attractiveness, a boyish look to her face and when she brought me a bottle of champagne after my cast was removed, we spent some time on the couch sliding our hands underneath each other's clothing. My hand could close completely around her bare ankle.

"Are you married," she asked. She had pulled away from me and straightened her clothes. Her feet were on my lap and my hand was still wrapped around her ankle.

"I think I'm divorced," I said.

"But you're not sure."

"It's hard to tell."

Beth tossed her head and combed her fingers through her hair. "I don't sleep with married men," she said and she tried to pull her leg away but I tightened my grip.

"That's funny. I only sleep with married women."

"That's a pity," she said and she squirmed out of my hold to put on her sandals.

When I lifted my head off the table I was shocked at the number of acupuncture pins sticking out of my skin. Hundreds, it seemed, quivering along the length of my naked body. The three inch pins on my torso felt like they pierced straight into my organs. I thought I saw a single drop of blood rise out of my belly button and my stomach went into spasm.

On the visit when Beth brought a large pizza and a 12 pack of beer, she wore a baseball cap and a white tank top. I pulled two bed sheets from a cardboard box and draped them over the couch. We covered ourselves with one of the sheets and using a flashlight I found a small tattoo of a dolphin on a patch of skin beneath her bikini line. I whispered secrets to the dolphin and Beth moved her hips. For a while everything inside our fort smelled like melted cheese and beer.
"Does this mean that I'm married," she asked. "Or that you're not?"
Her chest was red and sweat pooled in the hollow of her throat.
I moved to ask the dolphin this question, and felt her skin rub gently against my chin. Beth made perfect audio sounds. We fell asleep in our tent, with my cheek against her belly and her hand resting on the back of my neck.

Things went well until Big Dog threw a dinner party. His fiancée was there and a few people from the restaurant with their dates. Beth drove up to the house and parked.

"I'm not going in," she said. "What time do you want me here?"

I walked around to her side of the car and opened the door. I took her hand, raised it to my lips and then bowed, gesturing for her to step out of the car. She pulled her hand back and slowly stepped onto the pavement. I slipped my arm around her waist and we walked to the front door.

Big Dog had been famous. The video of him played on one of those special shows that catches people in the act. There he was, standing in his snowy gray and unfocused world, leaning over a tub in some generic stockroom. His forehead was against the wall, keeping himself still. You could barely see any liquid going into the tub on the ground, but you were persuaded by the commentator that Big Dog was urinating into a vat of sliced pickles.

The commentator wanted Big Dog to experience a sort of shame and humiliation that would drive him from the business forever, make the world safe again for the rest of us. The commentator actually chuckled a little and said something like, "He'll have a hard time finding another job anytime soon," and he said it like wink wink nudge nudge *ain't that the truth.* When in fact, Big Dog told us, two days after being fired (which were his first two days off in a row since age 14) he was hired immediately by The Breakfast Place. They hired him, he joked, because they didn't serve pickles.

And as for shame, *he* was the one who showed us the tape before dinner. We sat in the living room drinking gin and tonics and laughing at the tape while he served slices of bananas that had been fried in bacon fat. It turned out that he was an excellent chef. I'm talking Cornish game hens stuffed with figs and raisins, glazed with peach nectar and served with asparagus spears, homemade hollandaise, rice pilaf.

Dinner went smoothly at first. Drinks, small conversation, jokes about cutting off my finger. Big Dog's fiancée and Beth did not get along. The fiancée would offer me more wine and completely ignore Beth or else she would look past Beth and strain to be polite. Big Dog was standing constantly, bringing out more food or toasting to one thing or another.

There was a quiet moment, the calm I suppose, when the only sounds were of forks and knives getting to work on the game hens.

People were murmuring about how delicious it was, but they were saving their comments, waiting for Big Dog to return to the table.

Big Dog did not return to the table. Instead his fiancée appeared at the head of the table holding what I first thought was a black silk scarf. "I believe these belong to you," the fiancée said, and she threw them at Beth. As the panties passed in front of me I could see the lace around the edges.

Beth drove the car to my apartment and I was still drunk. She looked at me each time she moved the stick shift.

"You're mad," she said.

"About what?"

She glanced over at me. "Anyway, it's over," she said. "It was just a couple of times."

"Good thing he wasn't married," I said.

In my apartment, Beth sat on the couch with a drink while I searched through boxes for the video equipment. She crossed her legs beneath her black skirt and talked about Big Dog and how bitchy the fiancée was, and how sweet I was for understanding. Then she stopped. "What are you doing?"

"Setting up." I had placed two video cameras on tri-pods aimed at the couch. I set a couple remote microphones on the floor by Beth's feet. The videotapes had been loaded and the red lights were on, everything was set.

"Okay," I said, pulling off my shirt and taking her drink away. "I'm ready."

"What the hell are you talking about?"

I unbuttoned my pants and stood in front of her in my underwear. "Action," I said.

Beth stood and instead of removing her blouse or pushing down her skirt, she backed toward the door.

"Do a sexy audio," I said. "Tell me what you want."

She opened the door and left.

I filled the cassette tapes with images of me drinking on the couch and watching the high-jump on television.

There's nothing you can do. I never understood about "nature taking its course" until I recently lost a fistfight with the wind. I was standing in an open field leaning forward into the gusts of wind and like any reasonable person, swearing at its persistence.

"Do you want to go?" I screamed. "Do you?" I bent over and picked up a rock. Standing firm, head down, feet spread like a major league pitcher, I hurled the rock as hard as I could, and the wind subsided for a moment.

"Is that all you have," I taunted. "Oh no, I'm so scared, someone help me, please help me from the big bad wind." I bent down and picked up another rock.

The wind has taken my breath away in the past, but this time it reached into my throat and seized my lungs. Then it gathered up strength and sent me running backward until I decided to fall. By then, of course, it was too late. I was cradled in a section of barbed-wire that cut into my calves and dug into my back. I lay like a crucified cowboy as the wind tossed weeds and pieces of garbage into my face. With my back curved like a fish and my chest caving in, I fully expected to be speared. I could not breathe and I waited. I prayed like an idiot that I would wake up dead.

The best thing about waking up one morning and finding a blue-faced baby in the crib is that through the miraculous transformation of death, the child only barely resembles the one you remember. Like a doll of the baby. But still it's startling enough to shock you and send you running for the phone and all the rest.

The woman on the telephone told me how to perform CPR, which I had learned at some point in high school, though I remembered very little. And so I did the pressing with my two fingers on the chest and the small puffs of air to inflate the lungs. Sudden Infant Death Syndrome. Now there's a catch all phrase.

I held the baby before they took him away and cues were offered, hints as to the way I should've felt, the way I ought to have reacted. But for some reason I kept missing the mark. For example, I was worried because I had never dealt with funeral arrangements before and it seemed like a major hassle.

And then I said, as they took him away to be readied for burial, I said to Kelly, "Good for him."

I've spent some time wondering at my intentions at that moment. I even had them explained away as shock by one of the nurses at the time who had taken an interest in our situation. But at that moment, it only made sense to me that this person's life had ended and that was some sort of accomplishment, like finishing a marathon or an Olympic gymnastics event.

"I've lost everything," was Kelly's response. I'm sure it was meant to highlight my lack of understanding.

"Yes," I said. "You have." But I did not intend for my words to be spiteful or mean. I even used a tone I thought would convey a certain solemn respect, a degree of empathy for this poor woman having to see her own child disappear. Having, I knew, to go through the hassle of leaving her husband.

But my reaction might have been why a police officer arrived at the hospital and asked to speak with Kelly and I, separately. And also why a grief counselor described my reaction as an indication of denial. But even if that was true, I said, there certainly was no law against being in denial and I wondered why the officer stood in the room with his arms folded across his chest.

They detained me in the hospital for the evening while they prepared the boy for burial. I was released without any charges filed since the baby's body had been found physical-abuse free.

I have escaped acupuncture.

My therapist asked, "Thoughts of suicide?"

"Not that I can remember. Not intentional, I guess. Drinking a twelve pack of beer and going swimming up by the dam as an example of the unintentional."

"Imagined violent scenarios in which you would die a heroic death? Perhaps saving someone from some imagined evil?"

"Sort of."

You can see the suppression of joy in the human being most obviously in the jaw muscles and small wrinkles at the corner of the mouth. The eyes too, of course. The shiny happy eyes.

"What are some of the details you can recall?"

"In high school I imagined a girl I liked was being pulled into the car of a mobster, and I ran after the car. It was slow because she was not all the way in, only running along with her head inside. And I was able to somehow punch out the driver, kick some other faceless thug in the groin, and eventually receive the love of the young woman. The physical version, of love I mean."

"But you didn't die in the process."

"No."

You can see disappointment most obviously in the throat, a swallow, and in facial tics, various creases that resemble a wince.

"And that's the only one you've had?"

"I used to have those all the time, but with different girls."

"And now?"

"I couldn't possibly catch the car now, no matter how slow it went."

Kelly and I drove home together, after the service.

"You're not living up to my dreams," she said.

At first I thought she meant her view of the future, her dreams as in her aspirations, how years ago she must have seen herself turning out different somehow, other than married to me, her son dead, and so on.

"I mean my actual dreams. You were so much like a sponge in my dreams, taking me in, the baby, surrounding us in a good way, a nourishing way."

"How can I be like in your dreams? I don't even know your dreams."

"I know."

It's not the first time someone had been disappointed in me, but I was hurt I guess, and still a little confused.

"You're not even in my dreams," I said which was nothing but the truth, and something I wished to have stricken from the record.

I groped for my cue cards. The phrases and words I had filed in case of emergency or conversation. The appropriate sentences that would allow the ride to level out, smooth into a glide. I couldn't find them anywhere and so I burst out with words, like animals crashing through a gate.

"I'm sorry that I can't read your mind."

After a while Kelly said, "My father gave me a plane ticket for tomorrow morning."

"That's good," I said. "I'm glad for you."

"He is dead James. He is gone forever."

"I realize that."

"No, I don't think you do. I don't think you have the faintest fucking notion of what is going on right now."

"You're not even *in* my dreams," I said again.

"Goodbye James."

Fifteen minutes later we arrived home and the next morning she left without a word.

The title of the book? The Smell Of Baby's Hair.

What are we, a bunch of idiots? Of course you smelled your baby's hair and bathed yourself in the universal tenderness of such a moment. And yet, when you're sitting there on Oprah's book club with a glass of wine, you are compelled to lament. I'm not blaming you, after all you were probably chosen for the book review dinner because of your high lamentation potential. Still, in front of millions of viewers you lament, saying that you too wish you would have treasured the smell of your baby's hair. Whatever the hell that means, quantifying treasure or treasurement. As if you are able to flip your wrist and say, "Enough of this, I have treasured it." Possibly meaning buried.

And these book club people nod. They talk about time passing and about tragedy, until people are blubbering into their drinks. As if to say, fuck it (gulping wine from smeared glasses) if it's going to be like this, all fleeting and shitty and dead babies. Soon arms are launched around necks and weeping takes the room in waves, gradually building with that embarrassed laughter that comes from passing a box of Kleenex.

I sit on the floor of my apartment that afternoon, also drinking, also lamenting. When I see you crying on television it seems that you have somehow succeeded, that you have come out the other end of this darkness with a wine glass in your hand and a tissue crumpled in your fist.

I put in the videotape of you breastfeeding the baby. I try to remember what it was like to have you laying near me, to feel your body heat. I close my eyes and let my hand rest on the floor next to me, I pretend to squeeze your thigh. When I look again you're touching the baby's forehead, kissing his hair.

It wouldn't have changed a thing. That's the sad part. But if you had left ten minutes later on the morning you flew away, you would have seen me shouting and crying into my pillow on the couch, gripping it on either side as if it were an anchor. As if I was a piece of debris refusing to be spun away.

The Giant's Crust

A Giant sits on his enormous couch and eats a huge chicken potpie, which is a common enough activity for Giants, as we all know. He holds the potpie, which has cooled sufficiently, with his two giant hands as if he were eating a sandwich. The tin pie pan lies on the ground next to the big toe on his giant right foot.

He eats. It's a deafening sound, though only barely recorded by his own ears because he watches a television that roars in the room, filling his world with what to an average human being would sound like the constant thrust of jet engines. It happens that a portion of the potpie crust falls from the edge of his potpie and back into the pan. A significant distance for the crust itself, though the impact does little damage and the crust manages to retain its complete shape. The size of an adolescent boy, maybe bigger. The whole event goes unnoticed by the giant since, as we know, Giants are not famous for becoming anxious over the small, trivial details that make up their Giant life. Nonetheless it does happen. The crust falls into the pan and lays there curved like a skinny young artist sleeping on the floor of a cathedral. The rippled edges of the crust appearing much like the bumps on a starving man's spine.

Now this crust, having met its new fate, still contained some innards of the potpie as well. Some of the golden gravy in which a few green peas, a couple squares of carrots, and even a triangular shaped chunk of white meat. Blocks of food that could easily keep the starving human artist alive for hundreds of years. The crust lay on its side in the pan and wonders what is to become of it, though in its gravy gut it knows that there is nowhere else to go but into the dark and dank waste-bin, which by the way, could serve as a duplex housing project were it tilted onto its side.

Giants require what they require, and bits of crust, remnants of simple feasts are not one of the things they require. So the crust, faced with this inevitable fate, decides that for once in its short life as its own independent crust, it will not suffer the inevitable demise without a fight of some sort, some kind of resistance or active response to its admittedly difficult situation. Laying there the only thing the crust can think to do, with the sound of the Giant's masticating thundering above, is to try and eat itself out of existence. One can hardly blame a pot pie crust for entertaining such a self-mutilating, cannibalistic thought, having been created accidentally from a situation which was clearly made to be eaten in the first place. The fact remains, that mastication and digestion were precisely what made up the crust's very narrow view of the world at the moment that the crust made the decision in the tin pie pan.

It seemed the noble thing to do, a more honorable fate than being simply discarded into the dark of the waste-bin to rot and fester and mold its way out of existence. Rather it seemed a completion of sorts, a realization of the potential it carried in its brief time as an individual of sorts. And so the crust begins with the insides first, curling a bit and munching away at the vegetables, swallowing the gravy. Yes, the crust decides, this is the way to go about it, and finds that it is not altogether unpleasant. The plan is to consume from the inside out and after the crust has been cleared out, work begins on the shell itself. The entire process was only barely interrupted by the sound of the Giant's belch, a noise not unlike the violent crash of a motorcycle into a tree during which the gas tank explodes, and the fumes engulf the surrounding area.

The damp inside crust goes down the hatch and the crust is spurred on by the idea of eating oneself from the inside out, consuming oneself out of existence. It seemed to be rather poetic to the crust, and delicious as the crust made its way over the browned bumps of the spine.

Finally the Giant finished his potpie and noisily licked his fat fingers. He picked up the tin pie pan and walked into the kitchen with a refrigerator the size of a scraper that did not quite touch the sky. Perhaps the dimensions of a building in which a moderately successful insurance company would do business. He opened the waste bin by stepping on a lever with his gigantic bare foot and was about to drop the flying saucer sized pan into the dark when he paused. He had the idea for a moment that something in the pan had moved and when he focused again, which took some amount of time since it is not a short distance between a Giant's eyes and the tips of his lowered hand, he saw nothing. So he dropped the tin and thundered his way through the enormous house to the bathroom where he took a piss, which would've probably required five firemen just to steady the stream.

Eclipsed

This was before my mother-in-law Henna had passed away, about the time she began her final decline. Henna could hobble well enough and her husband Jim helped her outside on the night of their 40th wedding anniversary to look up at the darkening moon. Everyone was outside, standing on the front lawn and looking up at a moon already partially covered by the earth's shadow. I remember thinking that there was no way for any of us to prove what was really happening, that we all were relying on what we'd heard in grammar school or on a recent newscast. For all I knew, my brother-in-law, regarded by all as a brilliant electrician, could have strung up a spotlight in some distant tree and been maneuvering a disc using pulleys or remote control.

"It's so beautiful," my wife Andrea said, which is exactly what someone would be expected to say on such an occasion. People murmured in agreement. Andrea was eight months pregnant at the time, which probably gave her some sort of mystical cache.

"I don't know," I said.

"It sure is," her father Jim said, stepping on my words.

Most of the thirty or so people were talking to each other about regular life subjects; it wasn't like we were all awestruck. A blurry darkness moving across a moon may have been really exciting at one time, back when people assigned all sorts of magical meaning to the event, but because I knew I could go inside and pull up a much more impressive computer simulation of the event, a much more realistic and detailed image, it all seemed so forced and phony and boring.

Then the full eclipse occurred. The moon was blocked out completely and the night was as dark as those nights when the sky is cloudy or when there is no moon; basically, it wasn't dramatic at all.

That's when Henna said, as she stared up at the moon, "Look at us; there we are."

"It's true, I know," Jim said and I knew that he didn't have the slightest idea what his wife was talking about. But he'd been through a long illness with his wife of forty years and I'd learned that most words were empty to him; they were used to eat up awkward silences or to iron over the sadness.

Henna was staring up at the missing moon and when she said those words, I figured out what the big deal really was. We live on planet earth, but it's not like we can take a quick trip up into space and look down on the planet, at least not most of us. So the eclipse was pretty much the only proof we common people had that it was all true, that we lived on a planet that turned on its own axis, revolved around the sun, etcetera. By casting a shadow onto the moon, we affirmed that we did indeed exist.

Henna died a month later and two weeks after that my daughter Emily was born.

But it wasn't until I was fired from my line cook job that we had to sell our house and move into my wife's childhood home.

The first part of me that I replaced was my arm.

This was a few days after my father-in-law had bought Emily a four hundred dollar toy castle and seventy-five hand-painted cast-iron figurines. I used a red flannel shirt, and I stuffed one of the sleeves with plastic grocery bags. The idea came to me late one night, after I'd failed to put my nine-month old Emily back to sleep at three in the morning. I could sit up straight on the rocking chair and reach over the wooden bar of her crib and place my hand on her stomach or chest.

My hand was about as big as her chest. But I couldn't do this for too long before the pressure under my arm would cut off blood flow and my hand would go numb, and if I lifted it, even a little, before she'd completely dropped off to sleep, her eyes would spring open and in a few seconds she would be sitting or standing in her crib and crying. So I decided that all I needed was a fake arm.

I slept fitfully the next night, waiting to hear her cries through the baby monitor; at around one in the morning I got out of bed, excited to use my new invention.

I sat in the dark, my real hand pressing on top of the end of my fake arm. I thought that the fake arm wasn't heavy enough so I grabbed a few smaller stuffed animals and jammed them in among the plastic bags. The rest of the empty shirt hung down the outside of the crib acting as a perfect counterweight. I tried to make my real hand as heavy as possible; my idea was that the fake arm would somehow retain the pressure. After unsuccessfully attempting to escape three times back to my own bed, I decided that the fake arm wasn't convincing because there was no hand.

I picked up Emily and walked down the hall into her designated playroom. At the time we'd been living in my father-in-law's house for almost a year, and the creaks from the wood floor and the clanking from the heat had not yet begun to feel familiar.

With my drowsy daughter pressed to my side, I knelt next to the open toy box and searched with one hand until I felt the bald rubber head of a baby-doll that could become my fake hand.

Back in Emily's bedroom, with the fake baby's head shoved through the arm of the shirt and popping out at the end, I managed to successfully put her back to sleep. The baby-doll's eyes remained open, staring up at me from Emily's back, as I crept away from the crib, even afraid to breathe too loudly. Before I closed the bedroom door, I saw the remainder of the deflated shirt almost touching the wood floor. She slept through the rest of the night.

A year passed before Jim asked Andrea to sort through her dead mother's clothes, which were good quality and easily more expensive than we could've ever afforded. Since Andrea and her mother were a similar build, Jim urged Andrea to keep as many of the clothes as she wanted. This process seemed quite innocent and normal; I could work through the situation logically in my head and so any unease that I felt at seeing my wife in her dead mother's clothes, I kept well hidden. Jim and Andrea were both still grieving after all.

And then one day I walked into my dead mother-in-law's room and saw Henna, the dead woman, standing with her back to me, looking at herself in the mirror. My wife had put on one of the brown haired wigs (also of top notch quality) left over from her mother's chemotherapy and she stood in one of her mother's outfits, a pale green skirt and white blouse and matching vest, smoothing the fabric against her body, turning to look at one side of her reflection and then the other. When she saw me she did not rip the wig off of her head and look away, like she'd just been caught, but she smiled at me and I saw her as the little girl she must have once been, red cheeks and wet green eyes. Only a monster would have insisted that she remove the wig and so I turned and left the room.

"I bet you'll have a great first day of school," Andrea said to Emily as she changed her diaper one day on the floor. "Wearing your pretty pink dress with your hair done up."

"Pink? She's not wearing a pink dress," Jim said. "We're not turning her into some prissy wuss of a girl."

"Would you like that," she asked the baby, "Your own backpack?"

"She's not going to be some limp-wristed girly girl," Jim said. "An airhead who giggles at nothing and pretends to be stupid in math."

The next part of me that I replaced was my lap. This idea came about in much the same way; back when we were still sleeping together my wife used to say that I had a magical lap. She'd said that my bouncing knee could put our daughter to sleep under any circumstances. The idea came to me as my daughter slept on my lap while I watched television and drank a beer. It was about eleven in the morning and my father-in-law had taken my wife out to see a movie for her birthday. I really had to pee, but when I tried to put my daughter on the couch she woke up crying and squirming. That's when I thought that it would be ideal to have another set of legs, wearing my pants of course, onto which I could transfer her while I went to the bathroom.

By the time anyone came home, I had hidden all of my beer cans deep in the trash barrel and my daughter slept on a headless dummy, red flannel shirt and blue jeans. The plastic baby's head still served as one hand, and a green plastic dragon's head had become the other hand.

"And when you turn thirteen, you'll have your ears pierced," Andrea told Emily. "You'll go on your first date wearing jeans purposely torn at the knees, and a new red blouse that matches your lipstick." Emily sat up on her pink blanket and looked around her bedroom. She raised her hands to her face and sucked on her knuckles.

Jim spoke up; he said that at age thirteen Emily wouldn't be dating for another three years. "And lipstick?" he said. "Your mother never wore lipstick. She won't need any of that—she's not going to be some glamour whore."

"A friendly date," Andrea said.

"A group outing," Jim said.

"Then there's your first kiss," Andrea said.

Jim said, "I'm not hearing this, I've got to get another towel." He almost knocked me over when she walked out of the bedroom. He did not smile.

By the time Emily turned two years old, I had trouble sleeping; this worked out well for my headless twin. First of all, he couldn't have cared less that he was sleeping in Andrea's childhood bedroom where all sorts of rites of passage had taken place. The dummy was immune to images of his wife making out with other guys, her hand down their pants, her lips on their lap. And fortunately for him, he was also immune to images of his daughter Emily doing the very same things.

Plus, in order to be effective in tricking Emily into sleep at night, I had once explained to Andrea that the dummy had to smell as much like me as possible, so it was important to make sure that whenever I wasn't in bed the dummy was there soaking up all of my essence. This worked out well, because when I started drinking I usually snored pretty loud which used to irritate Andrea, back when we were still a family; not so much the noise, I think, as the fact that

I spent much of the day drinking. So there were many nights when I would get up, tuck the headless body into my place and go down into the basement to watch television and snore alone on my futon.

The time that I walked into the kitchen and found the group of them engaged in a family hug was probably one of the worst single moments that I experienced. My daughter had grown fond of the headless dummy and so even he was included in the huddle. He was like her blanky, my wife had once told me.

"I'll bet you're voted prom queen," Andrea said. "I saw the most gorgeous aqua dress today, it's a classic twenties style; it looked like it was fringed with diamonds, and when you walk into that gym, the whole world will stop." By this time, Emily could stand on her own, but she wobbled and hadn't even tried to take a step. "You'll have your hair done just like I did, professionally of course."

"Why does she have to be Prom Queen?" Jim asked. "What about Valedictorian? Or do you want her to turn out to be a beautiful giggling brainless priss?"

"You can wear the same necklace your mother wore on our first date," Jim had said when he first presented Emily with the treasure. Of course he meant to say your grandmother, Henna, not your mother, who was still my wife. Now I may have been intoxicated, but it didn't take a genius to interpret the slip of the tongue.

After the first snow of the following autumn, my father-in-law bought my daughter stuffed snow-bears. He went shopping with my wife and bought her a new blouse and a pair of pants. He complimented her on her new haircut and agreed that our bedroom would look better painted a sky blue. The two of them painted the room one weekend.

Meanwhile, I had perfected the talent of urinating into empty two liter bottles just so I wouldn't have to walk upstairs and accidentally walk in on any family bonding.

The idea to put a head on the dummy came to me one afternoon when the house was empty. My father-in-law had taken Andrea and Emily out to a farm to pick apples and pumpkins for Halloween. After that they were going to have a hayride dinner picnic.

The dummy's head was much more difficult than the rest of the body and after several failed attempts, during which I tried a lampshade and a plastic jack-o-lantern bucket I settled on a brand new pillow that I found on what used to be my side of the bed. A thick and sturdy white pillow that I folded in half and stuffed down the neck of the shirt. The front was a smooth surface, while the major crease in the back made it look like his head had been bashed in. I dragged him down the stairs and laid him on the living room floor. I used a permanent black marker to draw eyes and a mouth. I was afraid that any nose I drew would look ridiculous so I left the space blank and added eyebrows instead. I sat the dummy on the couch and he did not fall forward or slouch. He sat perfectly upright, but he did not look pleased—probably because he was bald.

I found the shaver in the bathroom cabinet. I'd bought it one summer when I'd decided that paying for haircuts was insane considering that all I ever wanted during those months was a shaved head. It took me less than ten minutes to shave off all of my hair. And even though it had nothing to do with the dummy, I actually lathered my head and shaved it bald with a razor. The white skin was frightening, a pale color beyond death, almost inhuman and too smooth.

I glued the hair onto a section of a pillow case that I found in the hall closet and successfully fastened it to the dummy's head. He looked better, but still not complete. I drained the last of my father-in-law's scotch and decided that the dummy should be changed into a new outfit. After all, he'd been wearing the same flannel shirt and jeans for a few months now. I undressed, removing my khaki pants, my underwear, my green flannel shirt, my shoes and even my socks. I had to take the dummy apart, pull out his insides, toss his old clothes into the blackened fireplace and stuff the new clothes with the plastic bags and stuffed animals and dish towels that I could find. Also, I struggled to add the socks and shoes, but after I found a ball of white string in the utility drawer they finally stopped falling off.

I sat my stuffed self on the couch and he looked great. The hair was long enough to hide the fact that it was glued to another piece of fabric. He looked stronger in the upper body than he had previously and he'd developed what could've passed for a six-pack in his abdominal region.

I sat naked and bald in the rocking chair in the corner with my glass of scotch positioned on my naked flabby gut and waited for the family to return.

They came into the house through the garage. My father-in-law carried two shopping bags and my wife carried my daughter. The sun had gone down and they turned on the kitchen lights as they entered the room; my corner remained in total shadow.

Doing his Best

Jeremy stands on a long, narrow, and elevated balcony. A cruise ship-type balcony; there are several glass doors behind him that open onto this balcony. His white belly protrudes slightly over his pair of long blue shorts and his buzzed hair has been bleached white.

A lengthy lump hangs down from the balcony in the shadow off to the far side.

"You can use almost anything; an extension cord, a length of rope. Here I have a section of clothesline." Jeremy raises the white coil and pulls a section of it taut between two fists. "Strong."

"Where did you get that?" Jeremy's father has emerged from one of the glass doors. He wears a white tee-shirt and he has combed strips of shining black hair across the small dome of his head. His thick black eyebrow extends across his forehead and knits into a V-shape.

"I cut it from the balcony."

"Cut it? What? From my laundry line? Where's your mother? Janet—get out here would you?" He yells over his thin shoulder. "What are you doing in there? You've ruined the clothesline."

"The backs of the chairs work fine for drying."

"Ha! That'll be the day. Chairs are not at all good for drying wet clothes! The water destroys the wood, see? Get out here—Janet!!"

"I always use the chairs to dry my clothes when we come here."

"And you're always an idiot when we come here—Look at that! You can see the stains, all splintered and raw. Janet!!"

"Now then, the anchor-knot is key. I mean that's the most crucial part. I'll tie one end around this stone pillar."

"You need a beam, like the one across our bedroom ceiling. Something with plenty of room around it. This way it's useless, it'll just snap. What the hell are you doing in there? Janet!"

"Maybe she's resting. Now, you make a solid knot—,"

"Are you listening? I said it'll rub against the stone railing here and snap. It needs to fall straight down, not against the building."

"A good solid knot—,"

"Who taught you how to tie knots? Go get your mother. Just let me do it—you've already screwed it up."

"No—,"

"Stop touching it, and just let me do it. Tell your mother to get me a knife."

"If you just wind it around—,"

"Get. Me. A. Knife. Janet!!"

"Around the post and secure it well."

"I don't know whose stupid idea this was."

"There now, nice and secure. Now at the other end, you're looking to tie a loop, kind of like a lasso that tightens around the neck of a calf—before the cowboy leaps down and knees the calf in the gut and ties the hooves together in the air."

"A calf weighs 50 pounds—you need a different rope altogether. This is a piece of crap, and the clothesline is ruined."

"Calves can weigh up to 300 pounds."

"Don't be stupid. I've never seen a calf that weighed more than 50 pounds. You think that'll hold?"

"I've thought a lot about this."

"And still you're screwing it up."

"Just make the loop, any size since it's adjustable, but this knot also has to be secure. It's probably the second most important knot."

"I'm getting your mother."

"The balcony makes the most sense. Just slip the lasso around the neck like so. Pull it to make sure it works. Nice—see that, see how it cinches up. And it's strong, this cord, nice and strong, with good knots."

"Your mother is hanging from the beam."

"She's probably just resting."

"She's not resting you idiot, look. One of her shoes has fallen off and the other is just about to fall. Help me get her down—she looks ridiculous. I need garlic for dinner."

"I'll help in a second, let me finish. Then you stand up here on the stone banister with the lasso around your neck like so, nine stories above ground."

"Are you going to wear those shoes to dinner? You look like Bozo."

"Spreading your arms is optional. But it is dramatic; probably creates the sensation of flying. And so I prepare to fly."

"We're out of garlic, and I need green beans for dinner, quartered tomatoes, and don't get the crap green beans, but try to get edible ones this time—beans that are actually green, for example."

"Then, quite simply, too simply, you jump—"

"The bread is as hard as a rock and there's probably only enough for one person, tastes like crap and of course she bought the most expensive wine and drank the whole bottle before lunch. I said buy if from Franco, but she doesn't listen to a thing I say, just walks around town, oblivious, stupid, spending money. Are you listening? Are you?"

Blood Brothers

Arlan and Jake used to punish themselves by falling from the enormous tree behind Jake's ranch house. Sometimes they didn't even make it halfway up the tree ladder before God struck them down, jerking their bodies to the side and sending them carefully to the ground. They never spoke while they acted out their punishment and each boy wore a solemn expression.

They climbed and dropped like apples until Jake uttered a genuine cry of shock, followed by a few tears. At this point of the ritual they have absolved their sins and may return to the fort.

Jake rubbed his elbow and winced. He looked up and said to the older boy, "God's probably gonna kill us one day."

Arlan inspected Jake's bruise. "No," he reassured him, "We'll be alright." And then he kissed Jake's arm.

Arlan has been living with animals in his attic for almost 3 years. He knows now that it's at least one raccoon, maybe a whole town of them by now, judging by the noise in the walls at night, like a goddamn family reunion. At first he was determined to fight the invasion and he would run up to the crawl space just as soon as he heard a noise. But things must have already been wrong with Arlan by then, because when he peered in and saw those beady eyes in the corner, he reached into his pocket to grab his Swiss army knife but found that he had actually grabbed a red pen from his desk instead of the knife. And he crouched in the crawl space wondering what the hell he was he supposed to do, red-pen the thing to death?

Soon he gave up the battle and started leaving a little dish of cat food and water inside the door to the attic, which he did until a week ago when the thing almost bit him. He was trying to feed the raccoon with his bare hand, thinking that he might as well make his peace with the thing, when for no reason it leaped forward and just missed taking a chunk out of Arlan's palm. Since then Arlan has been too weak to fill the cat dish anyway, which is fine with him since now he hopes the damn thing starves to death.

Arlan swallows the last of his beer and puts the can in the brown bag next to him on the porch. He sits outside in his lawn chair and spreads old photographs out onto the blanket that warms his lap. His cat crouches on the porch and growls. At one point Arlan turns to look at the foothills, comforted by the dizziness in his head because he knows he will be drunk soon. Arlan glimpses the ribs of a solitary coyote trotting toward him and then standing still. This summer they starve and Arlan often hears their howls dividing the night into patterns, their yelps leaking into his fitful dreams. Just as quickly the animal turns and disappears into the landscape.

The problem with photographs for Arlan is that you never capture the most important moments in your life. Those times when the whole world seems to vibrate around your head, and you're afraid for a moment that something crazy might happen, like you'll explode or just plain vanish. If those were caught in a picture, you could just put them in an album and forget about them. But instead, these moments are always kept inside your head and each time you remember them they grow and exaggerate until, one day, you see that they've gotten way out of proportion. They've become a whole circus of events and monstrous images, careening through your mind and the next thing you know, your whole perspective is out of proportion. When that happened small things started to seem big and also the other way around. Like borrowing Jake's gun, for instance. Today it seems like a small, easy, perfect thing to do.

The cat starts to yowl and twitch, and Arlan knows that this is a sign in a series of signs that have recently appeared to let him know the right things to do. The cat's body jerks like a single muscle that flexes and twists and relaxes. Arlan struggles to stand, which is ironic to him since he's 6 feet tall and only weighs about 100 pounds anymore, and he lets the worthless photos fall to the ground. He goes in to get more beer, hoping that the cat will be already be dead by the time he comes back. Arlan has never thought to buy a gun of his own and he glances at the knife block in the kitchen. What a major messy production that would be, to do it with a knife. The black handles sit perfectly aligned and set into their slits. When Arlan steps outside, the sensation of fur against his leg freezes him. The cat brushes against him like a kitten and then falls over and dies. After a moment she lies still.

Arlan 13, Jake 10. Before penance, before the mattress and the sleep-over, before the fire and the fear and the fucking, there has always been the wind. Hot wind that rushes down from the mountains and blazes across the land like invisible fire. Power lines snap and whip like snakes, sometimes sparking fields of hay. Roof tiles fly like birds.

An afternoon windstorm tried to get at the two boys in their brand new fort. They had claimed the old chicken coop that morning and spent most of their time imagining additions, such as an elaborate second floor, and piling old wood boards next to small hills of collected rusty nails. The wind came at them in an instant and inside their fort they both knew that no one could come looking for them, even if they wanted to.

The heat rose outside and the fort shook and creaked with potential. They talked about being picked up and landed in Oz while they crouched in a corner and sweat. In case that happened they promised never to leave one another and they cut an X on their thumbs with a nail. They pressed their thumbs together until blood seeped out the side. Violent gusts vacuumed air away and Jake looked up at Arlan with blue animal eyes, nervous and wide. They moved closer together.

"In some tribes," Arlan told him, "Chiefs seal promises by hugging each other and kissing on the lips." The wind thundered outside but could not touch the two boys in their fort.

Arlan is dying and he has made a space in his body for the disease. He learned to actually live with it, sort of like a roommate. Once a week Jake would walk up the road to Arlan's house and bring him something to eat and maybe a magazine to read. For a while Arlan got along fine, just him and his roommate, with Jake as the only visitor to the small house. But that was before the roommate began to get out of proportion. Hogging everything, all of Arlan's energy, his fluids, and leaving him so weak that he would sometimes even shit in his own bed. Arlan began to suspect that he couldn't live with a roommate like this for too long, before something had to be done.
Arlan struggles to walk down the road, pausing every few steps, and trying to convince himself that he can do it himself. Just borrow Jake's gun and walk home. The road reminds Arlan of an ancient riverbed he's

seen on TV. The pink dust rises with each step and the smooth rocks make spiral patterns in the potholes, laid there by the spring run-off. One half mile takes him and hour, but he only vomits once and only barely splatters his shoes.

Standing on Jake's front porch Arlan catches his breath and sees the vacant spot where their fort had once stood, down the hill behind Jake's house. Now only a few pieces of charred wood lie on the ground near a patch of straw-colored weeds. They had once painted the wall inside of the fort with a stolen bucket of brown stain and Arlan thinks that he can still smell those walls.

Arlan leans into the screen door and knocks. He hears a grunt and gathers his breath to speak.

"Jake, you in there? It's me Arlan." He puts his hand on the screen door's handle. "I need your help Jake."

Arlan pulls open the screen door and waits.

Jake opens the door, but he looks across the room at the TV. Arlan stares at the side of his head, his neck.

"Who? Jesus Christ Arlan what are you doing here?"

Jake hasn't shaved. He wears a baseball cap backwards and holds a beer can to his belly. The bottom of his jeans are stained the color of mud, and Arlan remembers Jake as a boy with dark blue veins under the skin of his arms and legs. This man has nothing to do with that memory.

Jake glances at Arlan and then turns away, back to the TV.

"I need help Jake. Today, I need your gun."

Jake turns and looks at Arlan with his nervous blue eyes, still beautiful. "The game's on," he says. He glances at Arlan's throat, "The World Series."

"Right," Arlan says and he leans into the house. The couch is draped with flannel shirts, dirty socks, and wide open magazines. A pair of old boots crusted with mud stand under the wood coffee table, and an enormous tool box sits open inches from the door. Jake stands barefoot.

"Yeah right, come in for a minute," Jake says. He leaves the door open and goes into the kitchen.

Arlan sees the baseball game and stands in the doorway.

"A beer?" Jake asks.

Arlan steps inside and takes the can from him, pops it open. Jake helps Arlan sit on a familiar stained wooden chair.

"Isn't this a chair from our fort?" Arlan asks.

Jake turns to him and shrugs, then goes to sit on the couch. They watch the rest of the game in silence.

Arlan 15, Jake 12. Jake's tiny bare arms helped Arlan pull the old mattress down the hill to the door of their new fort. Their faces shone with sweat and Jake looked up to Arlan for instructions. They struggled to fold the stained beast through the doorway, and after positioning it in the corner Arlan decided that they should take off their shirts like highway workmen sometimes did. They lay on their backs with fingers locked behind their heads.

The plan was to sneak out of their houses at midnight and meet at the fort. They wanted to live in their own house for a night and they deserved it, Arlan said, after all the work on the fort they'd done. Jake would bring orange juice and Arlan would make sandwiches.

That night, poised at his window for escape, Arlan hesitated at the sounds of the coyotes. The howling and yelping echoed off the mountains and the sound moved across the empty fields, everywhere at once. Arlan convinced himself that they could never catch him and he jumped down from his bedroom window and didn't stop running until he saw the fort.

Jake sat on the roof with the crescent moon forked in the branches behind him, shadowing his face. He sat in their designated guard post. Arlan held up his paper bag of sandwiches and Jake scrambled down to meet him.

"The good thing about having your own fort," Arlan whispered once the boys were inside, "is that you can do whatever you want."

They sat across from each other while they eat peanut butter and honey sandwiches and swallowed orange juice. The mattress felt clean enough and Arlan said that he always slept without clothes in the summer.

"Besides, who needs clothes out here anyway, right?" Arlan pulled down his underwear and added it to the pillow of clothes.

"Right," Jake said and copied Arlan.

Both of them lay with hands behind their heads, staring up at the ceiling. Arlan's body hummed and for the first time in his life he smelled sweat.

Jake slept perfectly smooth and naked and Arlan's body swelled until he ached for warmth, ached to be swallowed whole. Arlan moved carefully at first, sliding his body until he rubbed up next to Jake. Then he pressed into the boy. Jake jerked to move and Arlan's muscles took hold of the boy, set him still. Soon there was nothing to Arlan but the noise inside his body. They moved, it seemed to Arlan, in slow motion. The blood under their skin pumping in timed, staggered moves.

Arlan dressed to the sounds of yipping and screaming coyotes outside. He left Jake curled on the mattress and ran home barefoot through the fields, crying and yelping at everything he couldn't see.

The two men push through the wooden gate and past the weeds onto Arlan's property. Jake holds the gun and stares at his feet while he walks. Arlan holds Jake's other arm for support. The cat lies dead on the porch with her eyes clenched open.

Jake looks at the cat and shakes his head. "You don't need to do this," he says.

Arlan says they should do it out in the field so Jake won't have to drag the mess across the porch. Arlan picks up the cat and her dead eyes stare past him. Jake holds the barbed wire fence for Arlan to duck under.

They both watch the ground for cactus as they walk, stepping carefully. They head to the coyote's dirt path and stop. The mountains stand like a gigantic poster backdrop, and when he stops to vomit, something on the mountain makes Arlan squint. In the gravel quarry at the base of the mountain he sees a black cave he's never noticed before. A hole as black as lead sits near the center of the pink quarry and Arlan shivers. The shiny black color of a crow. He suddenly feels as if something important and dark and wet has always been alive inside the mountains, and now it's as if he finally smells it seeping out from behind their costume faces. Everything seems unmasked to Arlan, and the air reeks of rotten fruit.

"An accident," Arlan says. "I'm trying to shoot my cat and put her out of her misery." He stares into Jake's eyes for a moment and then turns and gingerly kneels on the ground, dropping the motionless cat in front of him like a sacrifice. When Arlan motions, Jake hands him the gun and Arlan wedges it between the coyote's dirt path and pushes the nozzle into his belly. Arlan rests his finger on the trigger.

Arlan 16, Jake 13. The fort burned down on the day they built a fireplace with rings of stones and constructed a chimney out of wood boards. Smoke rose out the window, but more filtered through the cracks in the chimney and hung in the air. Skin tasted like smoke. Everything tasted like smoke, even the glasses of water Arlan poured with flakes of black ash. Ash everywhere and Arlan painted on Jake's white back. He drew faces and arrows and circles of ash. Tiny crosses that smeared away when they wrestled.

The roof started to melt and part of it fell into the fire. The boys dressed and poured the last drops of water on the flames, but the roof had already begun to fall down in chunks by then. The tar paper melted and stripped away like plastic wrap. They stood outside and watched the flames turn everything around them into a wild dance of shadows, sending up a smoke signal. Jake turned and went to hook up the hose to his house. But by the time Jake reappeared, Arlan had run away.

Jake says something about helping, about doing it so Arlan doesn't have to suffer.

"It has to be this way," Arlan says finally. "This is how I want it to be."

The crack of the gun sends Arlan onto his back, a few feet away from Jake. This was his plan. Pain explodes through him until it becomes everything around him, until it becomes more than him and then it disappears. Arlan's stomach goes numb and he feels blood leaks onto his arms, gather at his sides.

"Now get out of here," Arlan tries to shout. "Go away." He chokes and turns his head to look down the coyote trail.

Jake kneels next to him for a moment.

"Go," Arlan whispers.

Arlan 17, Jake 14. The two boys avoided each other in high school and at home. They took separate walks in the foothills where the trees had grown into clumps of pine forest in certain spots. One evening at dusk, Arlan walked into a clearing and saw Jake sitting alone on a giant pink boulder. He stopped just as Jake's head snapped up like an animal. Jake let himself slide off the rock.

Jake didn't sprint for Arlan right away, but he started moving toward him, measuring his steps and focusing his eyes. Arlan stepped back into a wrestling crouch, hands poised. And then he sidestepped into the forest. He didn't want to turn his back and he back pedaled over rocks and between trees, navigating with glances over his shoulder. The sun disappeared except for a pink haze high in the night sky.

Jake's figure slipped behind trees and crept around boulders. He jumped and swung himself from branches, landing on his feet like a cat, swiveling his head.

Arlan's neck burned with sweat and finally he turned and ran, hearing the steps crashing behind him. He stumbled from running side to side, scraping his arms against bark, and he twisted his foot. He fell.

Jake stood above him, sweat drenching his face. Jake lowered himself and pressed one knee into Arlan's chest. One hand gripped onto each of Arlan's shoulders and made him still. Only the sound of breathing. Jake's eyes blazed. His lips moved as if he might speak, but he made no sound.

Jake bent forward and pressed his lips into Arlan's neck. And then everything tasted like sweat salt and pine. The silent trees turned to shadow.

Arlan 28. Night arrives and Arlan presses his cheek against the ground, his eyes closed. Jake has left and the pain returns, in a dull and throbbing way. *Listen for them,* he thinks and he feels the cold blood sticking on his elbow. The howling begins in the foothills and hangs like a mist, and he tries to smile. Arlan waits. He waits to hear the coyotes come down the path. He waits to feel them nuzzle his side with moist noses and lick his neck. He waits to be swallowed away.

The Floating Zoo

People were lined up at the dock, mostly locals, a few tourists. I scanned for Angela and I saw Chuck, the band's bass player standing at the front of the line. He worked at the only Italian restaurant in Porter, and he'd practically pop out his eyeballs and set them into Angela's cleavage every time we ate there. He nodded his head and gestured with a sweeping motion of one hand as if revealing a great wonder of the world, and I saw the speedboat transporting people from the dock to the giant ship anchored near the mouth of the inlet. I smiled and nodded and took my place in line.

I analyzed Chuck for signs of depression, for an extra slump in his shoulders or a particularly weary stride, but he seemed to bound onto the empty speedboat that had pulled up to re-load, smiling and laughing at the people around him as he reached out his hand to help others board.

I stood at the head of the line, watching the speedboat spit up water and buzz like a chainsaw toward the main ship. It must have been a giant oil tanker at one point or an aircraft carrier.

When I stepped into the transport boat I saw that there was another one speeding toward land with people aboard. Their faces looked dull and bored and I wondered if it was disappointment or plain nausea. All my life I was always the first to get sea-sick in the group. Whether it was a high school dance or a friend's wedding reception, I would be leaning over the guardrail long before anyone else, barfing my brains out. Maybe that's why I never cared enough to learn about the types of boats; if you've vomited over the side of one, you've vomited over the side of them all.

Fortunately for me, the ride to the zoo was quick. We were instructed to climb up a wooden ladder that had been attached to a floating wooden platform. In high school, we used to try and swim out to this platform. I was an average swimmer, but I could never find the joy in swimming.

The top of the ship had been extended by a huge canopy of chicken wire, stretched over a landscape of trees and rocks and even some manufactured streams, a small waterfall. Birds flew now and then from one tree branch to the next and the noise forced our guide to shout out his introduction. His name was Arnold and he managed the general store in town, but he refused to give any familiar looks to the townspeople. Instead he tried to assume the character of a very mysterious and wise older man. He gave us each a small map and explained that the ship had been divided into four levels. The birds, the mammals, the amphibians, and the fish (some of whom were also mammals, he pointed out.) It was a very liberally guarded zoo and so we must exercise extreme caution at all times. The lions, for example, would bite off our arms without hesitation.

As he spoke I watched a couple of sight seers in the upper deck, crouching to take pictures of the birds that seemed to be dive-bombing their heads. The screaming and shrieking birds reminded me of medieval torture, and I decided to skip the first staircase that led up toward the bird death chamber and continue along the main deck. That was where most of the main attractions were kept.

The ship must have been the length of two football fields and the main deck had been lined on either side by huge cages. A white rope had been strung down the center to help maintain the direction and flow of the crowds. There were probably 20 other people scattered about on this level, peering into cages of lions, tigers, bears and orangutans.

I saw Angela sitting on a small platform at the tip of the stern. She waved at me and gestured for me to come toward her. She had her shoes off next to her crossed legs, and she was beaming. If she were facing out to sea she might have made the perfect Mermaid ornament in her tight shimmering gold tank top. I had no idea what I was about to say, so I meandered toward her taking my time to notice the tired, yellow eyes of the tiger fixed on some distant point behind me.

"Isn't this spectacular?" she asked.

"It's pretty amazing," I said. I was probably the only person on the boat who could sense that we were on water. It moved my insides, ever so slightly, and I decided that if we were eventually going to have a serious talk, I would be better off on the ground.

"Come on, I want to show you something," she said. She slipped her shoes on and glided off the platform in one fluid movement. She held my hand

The next level down had some sunlight from Plexiglas windows that had been fastened into the hull, but the light still reminded me of those basement windows that barely peeked over the surface. Like prison, I'd always thought.

It was a cabin, not unlike a cruise cabin, with a shallow bed and a nightstand. Blue curtains hung in front of the same plexi-glass windows. "There are four of these on the ship," she whispered. That was when I noticed that someone lived in this one. There was a small wooden desk scattered with papers and open books. A few leather bags stuck out of a small closet in one corner.

"I want you to meet someone," Angela whispered.

"Who's there," an old man's voice boomed out. We walked toward a corner and through a door. I saw an old fisherman with a white beard and mustache sitting at a larger wooden desk. He had turned around to face us and was straightening his black fisherman's cap.

"I want you to meet someone Daddy," Angela said. "This is Jacob, the man I was telling you about. Jacob, this is Daddy."

I shook his strong and rough hand, trying my best to steady my balance. The lower we were, the more I could feel the ocean's waves working on my blood, in my blood.

"Pleased to meet you," I said. "You have an amazing thing here," I said feeling ridiculous as I gestured to this room that was about as big as a closet.

"Don't tell me what I have," he said. "You don't know the half of it." Daddy took a pipe from his jacket that was draped on the back of his chair and carefully filled it with tobacco.

"You didn't tell me your father ran a zoo," I said to Angela and she winced even before her father spoke.

"It's not a goddamn zoo Mr. Jacobick. It's a goddamn Ark."

I expected him to say, "Ahrg," or "Me maties," at any moment.

"You didn't tell me your father was crazy," I said to Angela.

Daddy stared at me with red cheeks and a forehead that looked chapped all over. After a minute he smiled and began to laugh. I though his cheeks might crack as his laughter eventually turned into a violent hacking cough.

He cleared his throat. "Very well, Jacobick. I admire a man with a strong sense of humor. It gets you through some of the worst times of life." He offered me a pipe of my own and I took it, knowing that without a doubt, one puff would send me running for the bathroom.

"The world's disappearing Jacob, bit by bit, going down. People think it's a biblical myth, they think that since it was written many thousands of years ago, it must certainly be hogwash by now. But I don't think that. I know that each year California loses 1.1 million tons of sand into the ocean. I know that the polar ice caps are pouring 14 million gallons of extra water into the oceans each year. India will be the first to go, then California. It's coming Jacob, make no mistake about it, we are going down."

Angela was leaning against the doorjamb with her arms folded across her chest. "I grew up here," she said. "On this boat, when I was a little girl. Of course we didn't have as many animals then. We transported goods all around the world. Packages, cars, helicopters, food, books, everything. Just me and Daddy, acquiring the animals, bit by bit, one at a time. We've got most of them by now, don't we Daddy."

"Sure as shit we do," Noah said. "I deliver animals for the most part. To zoos around the world and sometimes they pay me with animals. Anyway we keep the best animals for ourselves, unload the others. The sickly ones."

"So you're trying to get two of each animal?" I asked.

"That was the idea at first," he said. "But we've had to make compromises, sacrifices just like in any other business. After the flood, you won't be seeing elephants around too much, just to give you an example."

The tobacco smoke had started to make me dizzy and I was using all my energy to keep from falling down.

"I think I might need some fresh air," I said.

"You're looking a little green around the gills there Jacobick," Daddy said.

Angela led me out of the cabin and up the stairs to the main deck by the arm. The air felt warm and not particularly refreshing.

"He's a good man," she said.

"No doubt about that," I said, keeping my head trained on my feet.

"You don't believe him?" she asked.

"No, I do believe him. I just don't care much. I mean we are talking generations before any of this actually impacts us. I'll be long dead by the time India goes under."

I was hanging my head over the railing and it felt nice. The monkeys in the cage next to me were hooting and swinging inside their compact African world. I didn't feel well at all, but the churning that had begun in my stomach had slowed to a crawl. I wondered if they'd remembered the snails, bugs in general.

"He's been away a long time," Angela said. "I wanted to surprise you with the good news."

"I'm surprised alright; I just can't lift my head to express it."

"Do you love me Jacob?"

I had to look up for this one. "I love you Angela, I love you and that is my problem."

"Let me show you our cabin," she said.

Suddenly, my nausea evaporated, as if the breeze had delivered a secret tonic. I jerked up and stared at Angela.

"Where we'll sleep," she said.

"Here?" I shrieked, but paled in comparison to the captured birds above us. "What do you me here? Actually here, like on this boat?"

"My father is an old man Jacob, he knows that he will be dead soon. He's come to pass it on to me. And I want you to be with me, to sail across the globe, to prepare."

"Angela, are you fucking crazy? We can't live in this pit, with these disgusting depressed animals. I meant being together, on land, like regular human beings. Walks on the beach, wine, dinner and a movie. Those things. Not slinging steaks into cages or spraying monkey shit off the deck. Please Angela, tell me you're not serious."

After a moment she began to sob and speak at the same time. All she wanted was something, something to love, to be with that special someone, something something, together and living, something, apart separate souls. Then I lost the transmission completely.

"Okay, okay," I said rubbing her shoulders. "Calm down, let's just talk about this like two reasonable people. "You want me to live with you, the male human mammal counterpart to you, on a giant floating zoo. And I want you to come with me back to land where we can move in together and order pizza anytime we want."

Angela had stopped crying and now pressed her balled up fist into her lips. She shook her head. "We have a spark," she said. "We have a love and a bond, and I think this was meant to be. God is not going to have me pair up with just any sperm shooting son of a bitch. It has to be special, chosen. And you, Jacob, have been chosen. You have to believe that you are the one."

I began to see myself on this god-awful vessel. Walking down the corridors with my plastic buckets filled with steak, stopping to vomit every few feet.

Angela took my hand and we began to descend to the very bottom of the boat. It held tanks of fish much like I'd seen at the aquarium. And they were lit from behind to simulate the idea that they were swimming through crystal blue water. The aisle between the aquariums was narrower than the one upstairs so we had to walk in single file. Angela came to a stop in between the dolphin's tank on one side and the hammerhead shark tank on the other. The light blue glow highlighted her face and I couldn't help but be taken aback by her sudden almost holy beauty.

She wore her black hair long, to the middle of her back and was always tucking it behind her ear when she spoke. She had a Mediterranean look about her, with dark black eyebrows and eyelashes, her lips perpetually red. At the moment she appeared to be as glamorous as any model I'd ever seen. But she was a small woman, thin, with small but gorgeous breasts and the hips of a teenager. I stared at her, as if I were hoping for some secret sign, some celestial event to take control and tell me what to do. Then she leaned forward and kissed me.

In the bowels of the giant barge with me behind her, my hands on her bare hips, it seemed to me that my thrusting motion was causing the boat to rock. The giant 800 ton tanker was moving to the rhythm of my hips. Right. Water in the aquariums was spilling over the top, all due to my outrageous desire for this beautiful woman. And then it occurred to me. We were moving.

We dressed ourselves again and I scrambled up the stairs to the main deck. I did not panic, because I figured that as long as I acted quickly, I could probably swim back.

"To what?" Angela asked. Her cheeks burned pink.

"To my life Angela, that's what."

She tried to take my hand, but I pulled it away. I thought about my truck and how much it had cost to have Soft Serve Handyman painted on the side.

I looked at her, feeling helpless, like one of the animals. "I don't know anything about boats," I said.

"You'll get used to it."

"To not knowing anything?"

"I will teach you."

About two weeks into our adventure, while we were still going along the Eastern coast of the United States, Noah died. It was on a day when the sun glowed a burning red as it rose into the sky. I could not remember what that was supposed to foretell. Doom, I suspected, but then again my state of mine hadn't been the best over the past two weeks.

Angela had been busy with the sea charts and instruments, learning the course we would be taking and becoming familiar again with the various dials and gages. There was a giant wheel, but it looked more like a huge truck steering wheel than the type I'd seen in movies about boats. But since those movies also usually involved a shipwreck of some sort so I was calmed a little by the odd looking wheel, as if it's modern shape would somehow keep us safe.

I had been down on the lower level by the freezer wearing bloody yellow gloves and cutting slabs of partially thawed cow with an electric hand held circular saw. The light from the sun streamed down from the upper levels as if a giant red spotlight had caught us in its beam. Then Angela appeared. I hadn't heard her over the sound of my saw and when I looked up she was suddenly there, standing with her feet together her eyes looking at me.

I had to gather up the nets and prepare to feed the fish. The camel had chewed through a corner of its pen and I was pretty sure that one of the monkeys had been killed and eaten by his own family. That is to say, I had a lot on my mind.

"My father," she whispered. "He's died."

And so I put the saw on the wooden table next to the pieces of meat, took off my gloves, wiped my hand on my apron and stepped forward to hug her. It was a long embrace and all I could think, was that I had somehow been duped by Noah. As if he had planned it all along, to bring me aboard and then die all of the sudden.

"What do we do?" I asked.

Angela handed me a note that Noah had written, instructions for how to deal with his body. We were far enough away from the mainland and I had immediately assumed that we would simply dump his body over board. But Noah had left precise instructions.

I read the note.

"Was he joking? Surely he wasn't serious," I said. The note detailed his desire to be dismembered and fed to the various carnivores on board the ship. We could dump a few pieces of him in the ocean, but the majority of his body was to be consumed by as many animals on board as possible. "This is impossible," I said.

Angela looked up at me in shock. "Of course it's not impossible Jacob. It's quite easy, especially for you. After all he was not your father."

But I had talked with him on several occasions, smoked a pipe with him after dinner. He had been sizing me up, checking to see if I was up to the task of helping Angela run the show. And apparently, up to the task of slicing his body apart.

Noah had once said, "You'll learn more about life on this boat Jacob, than from any college in the world. It's all here you know, the Garden of Eden, the fall of man, original sin. Just getting through the day, feeding the animals, spraying the shit off the decks, watering the trees in the aviary. This is living." He drew a puff of smoke from his pipe into his lungs. "Those birds will claw out your eyes if you let 'em."

"I can't do it," Angela said to me. "I can't take a saw to my own father. You have to do it Jacob, he wanted you to do it."

"I know he wanted me to do it and that makes it even worse. Like he's pulling my leg from beyond the grave. I'll probably be dry-heaving for weeks."

We walked up a level and then down the corridor. When we stepped into Noah's room the sun had turned everything yellow. He lay on his bunk, with his hat on his chest, eyes closed. I walked over to him and tried to prod him, hoping that Angela had been mistaken, and that maybe he was in a deep sleep. His skin had started to turn cold and I knew it was hopeless. If I jumped overboard now, I would most likely die before I could swim to land.

The two of us carried Noah down the flight of stairs and put him on the butcher block table next to the saw. "Get me some vodka," I said and Angela left. Over the weeks, I found that alcohol helped to steady my insides. I was the most coherent when I was drunk.

"You stupid fuck," I said in a desperate attempt to insult him back to life.

Angela returned with a bottle of vodka, her father's sweater, and an electric lantern. Then she put on the sweater and undressed her father on the table. After he was laying there in all his glorious dead nakedness, she slunk back and crouched in the shadows. I started the saw. She had disappeared into a corner of sorts, everything except for the tip of her white sneaker. It was that rubber white tip that I would seek out every so often, mainly when I stopped to drink again from the bottle.

I cut his leg first; just a minor abrasion to secure the knowledge in my head that he was indeed deceased. With a butcher knife and the hand-held circular saw I, to put it crudely, went to town.

"They have to do this for medical school," Angela shouted out from her corner, trying to help prop me up when I began to slow down, to lose focus.

"Good for them," I replied, feeling the vodka run warm into my stomach.

His head had been the first to go and that had been the hardest. But I made myself believe that I was simply cutting meat for the animals just like any other day. Until I saw his wrist watch. I pulled the watch off his arm and put it on my own. Noah's flesh looked blue, almost like blubber, and the lifeless blood, leaked like water onto the table and the floor. I turned and saw the tip of her tennis shoe, and continued.

I put Noah in buckets and dragged him into a nearby corner. I hosed down the table and the floor. Water had leaked into my shoe and my sock was soaking wet. I took one bucket in each hand and made my way to the main deck

I repeated the ceremony until Noah had been equally distributed to all of the carnivores on the ship. Angela had spent the time in her corner, not bothering to look up at me when I came to retrieve the next bucket. Afterwards I took a shower and lay on our bed with my hands behind his head. Eventually I fell into a deep sleep.

When I woke I was immediately nauseous. It only took me a moment to figure out why. The boat had stopped, and it felt as though my insides had continued moving. I staggered up to the deck with the hope that the air would revive me, and with the faint hope that perhaps, by some miracle, we had returned home.

"We've anchored and we're off the coast of Maine," Angela said. She sat on the same platform at the stern of the boat with her legs crossed. "Guests should be arriving within the hour."

The last thing I wanted to deal with was a bunch of gawking morons, but as I stood with my head hanging over the edge I tried to compose myself. I stared at Noah's watch.

By the time the first speedboat arrived with curious visitors, Angela had slipped her shoes on and joined me at the entrance. I had changed my clothes and was wearing Noah's old fishing cap, his pipe in my mouth. A young boy and girl were the first to arrive and their bodies hummed with excitement.

Surrealist Fiction

Absurdist story techniques are used to highlight the way in which external pressures, expectations and influences, shape our behavior and decisions.

Surrealist philosophy is based in large part on psychoanalysis originator Sigmund Freud's theory that human behavior is motivated by unconscious thoughts.

Freud used dream analysis and free association to unveil the unconscious. Surrealists try to express unconscious thoughts and feelings in their works. Various techniques are used in Surrealist art and literature to unchain the imagination from conscious control. The most frequent approach is psychic automatism, which is spontaneous drawing, painting, and writing without conscious self-censorship of aesthetics and morals. Surrealist writers, using automatic writing to mine the unconscious, disregard literal meanings of words and substitute implied or associative meanings.

Resulting works are very difficult to comprehend, relying as it does on symbols and interpretation.

Surrealist Art embraces and incorporates primitive art and the art of children. Surrealists appreciate the untrained artist for having greater freedom to express the imagination without any constraints of conscious aesthetic and moral conventions. The uninhibited functioning of the mind's instinctual urges is paramount in Surrealist Art.

The surrealist story expresses the subconscious mind of at least one character. This exposure of the subconscious mind is an attempt to understand the hidden impulses behind behavior. Remember, in this context, behavior is more significant or meaningful than obvious action (running, hitting, etc.) i.e. Lying is a behavior; Hiding information is a behavior, etc.

According to surrealists, the thoughts, ideas, emotions, or desires of the subconscious are the true cause of human behavior, and if art intends to express the 'truth' of our human life, art must express the power of the subconscious. We all act in response to these deep and hidden impulses.

Interpreting a surrealist story is an attempt to examine the subconscious motives behind certain actions. What is the true cause of why someone acts the way they do?

To interpret, you the reader must change your mind set before you begin to interpret the story: you must aim your focus/attention in a certain/non-traditional direction.

You are not trying to figure out what's happening as much as you are trying to figure out what is behind a character's actions.

You are trying to figure out what unfiltered emotions, thoughts, or ideas are causing the behavior.

You are trying to get at the 'true' cause of behavior or action--what is being expressed underneath the surface of the plot.

Example: Red Blossoms-the narrator tells a story about encountering two drugged out kidnappers and shooting them in the back of the head--

--it turns out that this is not an actual event, but probably a story in the narrator's head. To interpret then, the question is "what does the story tell us about the narrator?"

--it is a revenge fantasy of sorts so he must be seeking revenge of some sort

--the dying child in the revenge fantasy seems to have an impact on him--so perhaps the revenge he seeks has something to do with the child--revenge against those who harmed a child?

If science fiction asserts that the depth of human nature can only be explored by juxtaposing the familiar and the unfamiliar, then Surrealism expresses a similar idea. The very major difference between the two has to do with where the unfamiliar comes from and how it interacts with the realistic.

Science fiction draws much of its unfamiliar material from two main realms: advances in human society and invention and discovery or interaction with other planets and alien beings. In any case, it is the relationships that form between human beings in a foreign place, or between human and non-human, that develop the unique perspective that science fiction wants to present.

Surrealism pulls its unfamiliar material from an entirely different place: the subconscious of the human being. Science fiction focuses on relationships between the self and the other while Surrealism focuses on the relationship within the self, the relationship between the conscious and subconscious.

Science fiction asserts that humans can only be understood when characters are subjected to intense pressure and the unfamiliar. Surrealism, on the other hand, believes that the truth about human beings can only be found by tapping into the subconscious and expressing what is found.

Surrealist story techniques are used to highlight the way internal/subconscious impulses, emotions and thoughts affect the way we behave. Surrealist stories try to expose the subconscious feelings and connect them to the way we act.

If stories want to convey a 'truth' about human experience then Surrealist stories not only want to communicate the 'truth' that subconscious emotions cause behavior, but how those subconscious emotions feel-Example: Trying to communicate how jealousy feels by breaking out of structure--using dream-like/symbolic images. To cause the reader to feel the emotion.

Surrealist story techniques are used to highlight the way internal/subconscious impulses, emotions and thoughts affect the way we behave. Surrealist stories try to expose the subconscious feelings and connect them to the way we act.

How to interpret a surrealist story:
1. The surrealist story expresses the subconscious mind of at least one character.

2. This exposure of the subconscious mind is an attempt to understand the hidden impulses behind behavior. Remember, in this context, behavior is more than obvious action (running, hitting, etc.)--Lying is a behavior; hiding information is a behavior, etc.

3. According to surrealists, the thoughts, ideas, emotions, or desires of the subconscious are the true cause of human behavior. We all act in response to these deep and hidden impulses.

4. Interpreting a surrealist story is an attempt to examine the subconscious motives behind certain actions. What is the true cause of why someone acts the way they do?

5. To interpret, you the reader must change your mind set before you begin to interpret the story: you must aim your focus/attention in a certain/non- traditional direction.

6. You are not trying to figure out what's happening as much as you are trying to figure out what a character is doing and why they might be doing it.

7. You are trying to figure out what unfiltered emotions, thoughts, or ideas are causing the behavior.

8. You are trying to get at the 'true' cause of behavior or action-- what is being expressed underneath the surface of the plot.

Red Blossoms

On a particular Thursday for no particular reason, I make love to a young woman who I meet at the library. Her blond hair is pinned up, librarian style, and when she lets it down the clip snaps and lands on my notebook. When I pick up the clip and offer it back, she smiles with the whitest teeth and asks if I want to get coffee. So I follow her through the library's revolving doors and when I step into the sunshine she whispers in my ear something about screwing and we take a turn toward her dorm room.

I lie naked on her bunk and smell the fragrance from the pajama top kept under her pillow. While she undresses behind the closet door, she asks me general questions about myself that I have no interest in answering because a poster pinned to the ceiling has startled me quite a bit. Where one might expect to see the glistening muscles of an athlete wearing a bikini bottom that strains with his penis, there is instead a scene from what looks to be a black and white foreign film. A movie poster with only the fewest bits colorized.

Apparently a beautiful French woman plays an ordinary housewife in this film and she looks out at the viewer, in this case me-- a naked man about to commit adultery-- from behind enormous plant leaves. Like a gigantic houseplant has been grown in the backyard of her perfect white house. A flash of light off a huge knife blade can be seen in the reflection of the house's only window and I can tell that this does not bode well for her. The woman's smile seems particularly wifely to me and her black hair cut to the shoulder and rounded at the bottom reminds me, (can you guess?) of my wife of course.

When the blond settles on top of me and begins raking her fingers through my chest hair, I notice the colorization in the poster. The housewife's eyes are tinted the slightest green and formed like the typical cat eyes with dark slits down the center of them. Then I notice a small crescent of bright red on the breast of her gray housedress. Most of her body is shielded behind the gigantic plant leaves, (and I speak possibly of the largest in nature, at least six feet tall and four feet wide, and curling a little around the edges making me think of plants swallowing humans). But a corsage of some kind, maybe a single red flower, sticks to her chest and I focus on that while the blond girl heaves and sweats and tears at me with her fingernails, trying the whole while to get off on me.

In this way, during a single three-hour period of time, my normal life comes to an immediate end (the life in which I was married to a lovely, wealthy woman) and I know I have shoved myself off into foreign territory. The blond had gone out of her mind with copulation and could barely nod when I asked if I should ejaculate or not. In any event it was definitely a good scene, but I am intelligent enough to know that my wife would find out, (because I know I'd confess it all) and that because of this I would have to move my stuff out of the house. And I wonder for a moment how will I ever find a woman like my wife ever again. Sterile and perfectly stacked without a single mother's instinct in her blood.

So the depression I cultivate leads me to a nearby bar where I proceed to drink light beer and chain-smoke. I had let my wife down before so this was nothing new or particularly interesting, but probably enough to qualify as a last straw. I think about emotional pain in general and how it must belong to anyone just as much as happiness and maybe ten times more. And while it's nothing to be exceptionally proud of, I decide that both my wife and I will grow from this experience. A terribly nice and tidy thought.

I explain my enlightened point of view to a guy sitting next to me with long brown hair and a tattoo of a giant human eye on his bicep. The bloodshot eye has produced a single blue and green tear, which has been made to look like a marble-sized earth. It is because of this tiny blue planet that I am confident I can explain myself to this man, a person who obviously knows something about compassion.

"You want to see something fucked up," he asks after I buy him a second light beer.

"Sure," I say and cringe at the tone of my own voice. "By golly."

We drive into the city and I'm aware that it has become night and that I am still have not returned home. Soon we are no longer cruising through the best neighborhoods, but I am convinced that whatever happens it will serve me right. A sort of penance.

To pass the time I say, "I nailed a co-education today. A woman hockey player as sweet as honey." My tongue slides free and loose and I'm certain I could talk my way out of anything. Meanwhile, my new friend opens his glove compartment and pulls out a real gun. And then a second one, after tossing the first gun onto my lap.

"I've never shot one before," I say, lighting a cigarette. "Is there much kick?"

"If you need it, just aim and start popping. Otherwise keep it quiet and next to your dick. I need to show you this little girl."

We pull over in front of an empty parking lot next to an abandoned elementary school. Small tornadoes of barbed wire lay still on the ground, surrounded by enough brown and green beer bottle shards to coat the playground with a version of snow. The pavement underfoot has turned into chunky black crumbs that disappear into puffs as we walk over to the school. My friend motions me to stay quiet. I've never floated before, but that was as close as I'll probably ever come. We peer through a crack in a plywood window.

A guy and a woman sit on a filthy green couch smoking cigarettes and passing a bottle between them. They watch a black and white television with terrible reception. Without knowing much, I instantly know that this scene is all about drugs, and hardcore drug addicts from the look of their withered arms, their slack skin faces. At first I assume the little girl on the floor is dead, but then I think I see her head moving slowly. I can see no wounds on her body at all and I decide that she sleeps. My friend offers a quick nod and opens fire, taking aim at the sky. The two people scatter and scramble around on the floor, whispering loudly to one another and it's like hearing fits from inside of a coffin. Then I hear a motorcycle start on the other side of the building.

The little girl, my friend tells me, is definitely dead. But when I lift her up, her mouth moves and she clenches her jaw, showing her tiny teeth. In the back of the car I hold her in my lap and feel her flesh cooling down. The skin around her eyes and mouth have started to turn purple, and noise comes from her as if she were suddenly humming a tune.

"This kid is alive," I say, and my own skin begins to feel uncomfortable.

"They just pumped her full of shit is all," my friend explains. "She's as dead as they make them."

Her nasal song creaks along through her grooving clenched jaw until finally she freezes still.

"Sons of bitches," my friend says. "Goddamn."

I think that when you're not anyone in particular and you die, then you're probably lucky if a couple of chumps find you and take the time to put you in the ground. I strain to lower her into a shallow grave we dig in a field. She weighs practically nothing and still I am sweating and grunting as I lay her down.

I help push the dirt in with my sneaker and I look at my friend. For a moment I wish I hadn't screwed that blond college sweetie. I should have simply pleasured myself in her bathroom and then left for home, where meatballs and sauce were waiting. But then I think about the dead humming girl I'd just held in my arms and I'm sort of glad I did what I did. When I picture her baby teeth grinding across each other and her tiny blue lips, I begin to cry. I stare at my friend.

"Goddamn," he says again and I want to hug him.

We sit in what must be the last diner in America, eating eggs and pancakes with blueberry syrup. Crispy brown sausage links and fatty bacon. Neither of us speaks and, to be honest, I have little on my mind except the shape and size of the next forkful.

Suddenly my friend stands and says, "There they go."

I pull out my wallet, leave cash on the table, and follow him out the door. The motorcycles have stopped at a corner and we follow them downtown in our car.

They park against a curb and walk into an Italian restaurant. I watch the restaurant door while my friend buys a couple of ice cream sandwiches from a vendor. I lick melting ice cream from the wrapper and know that if I'd never seen that girl's blond hair fall to her shoulders in the library, I would never have found myself in this situation. The gun tucked into my waistband makes my penis sweat and itch like nothing I've ever felt. Then I wonder about disease and the blond who had squirmed excessively and clawed at me like a cat gone ill, but I decide that her smell on my fingers was healthy enough. The dead girl's two evil-drug-parents eventually come out of the restaurant and decide to stop for ice cream across the street. We follow them as they stroll for a few blocks out of downtown, enjoying their ice cream down to the last bit of cone. When they duck into a pale blue building that flakes paint, we follow them.

We stand behind them and my friend says, "Now you are both going to die." They stop and stand shoulder to shoulder in front of their open apartment door, heads bowed, hands reaching up for the ceiling. There is something beautiful about justice, about passing judgment and enacting punishment on the guilty. Especially when the guilty are actually caught and turn out to be so perfectly wretched and despicable. My friend's gun jams, but the soon-to-be-dead parents must think that he is loading it because they don't move a muscle. In fact, I think the very same until I look over and see him having trouble.

"Goddamn," he yells and throws his gun on the floor. I raise my gun and for the first time I notice our victims. The one I aim at wears a gray uniform that reminds me of a prison guard's uniform complete with a shiny black belt. I pause and think, this will be my only chance to kill one of these bastards, ever.

I pull the trigger and blood shoots out from the person and their body seems to leap forward. The legs jerk once on the way down, or maybe it only looks that way because the foot trips over a peanut butter jar on the floor.

My friend takes the gun from me and sends a bullet into the back of the other person's head. Then I turn and run like a fucking crazy man.

I sit with my wallet open on my knee in the attic of a residential house I climbed into a few hours ago. I heard the people downstairs making normal people noises, mostly saying goodnight and checking locks. A crescent moon illuminates the window and the picture that keeps me company is one that has been ripped out of a magazine. A 1950's housewife woman, doll size and with a perfect complexion, stands in a black and white backyard staring out from underneath giant pieces of hanging laundry. I think it may be about the Incredible Shrinking Woman. The laundry, mostly flannel work shirts, have been lifted by a breeze and they curl a little like they are tempted to wrap up a human being.

The woman seems bored by the fact that she is only two feet tall. I stare at her and think that she could be my mother, or anyone's mother I guess. She's definitely somebody's daughter, somebody's little girl. It may have been advertising toothpaste or feminine hygiene or even special tropical laundry detergent that makes clothes wrap up human beings in ways to better help them sleep, or I suppose, to suffocate them.

I picture everyone in my little daily drama all wrapped up by these flapping laundry arms and hanging above the tiny woman. My wife, the naked blond, my friend with the tattoo, the dead little girl, the person I shot, and that starts me crying again. I carve on my wrist with a piece of glass and my one hand is completely covered with blood. I cry and hope that I am dead by the time they find me here with my shrinking woman, my advertisement for laundry detergent.

As I finally drop off to sleep, from which I'm sure death will follow, I think about being honest. For a fluttering moment I think that if I have to, *I will make it perfectly clear that I did kill somebody, and so I do deserve to die.*

***

There was no attic. I sat in a cell that sucked mightily, but since I'd never been in one before, what did I know? My friend with the eye tattoo sat silently on his bunk with his hands folded in his lap. He missed a young boy named Joshua.

We were part of the segregated convicts, the fag block even though much of the HIV had to do with drugs and not penis. My truth, which will not be a shock, is that I had never even come close to killing any man or any little girl for that matter. Instead I arrived home on schedule, without the scent of blond thighs anywhere on my being, to a pan of burning meatballs and blackening sauce. My wife sat on the sofa in a kind of daze, shock I guess. I almost said the child's name because our one year-old girl lay on her lap, clearly dead, with her blue mouth open. The first thing I did was turn off the stove and open a window. I pushed the burned meatballs and red garlic sauce through the kitchen screen the best I could. Giving me time to think. Meshing it like steaming play dough through a sieve, and burning my hands until most of it dropped onto the floor at me feet.

My wife said, "It's probably better this way." She meant because we had the HIV, and because of us, our daughter had the HIV too.

Had I, as one expert witness said at the trial, exhibited the barest amount of human compassion I would immediately have called for an ambulance. And I never had the chance to say that the girl, dear expert dumbfuck, was absolutely dead-- any idiot could've seen that.

We loaded into the car and drove to a small farm that turned into a petting zoo every summer. We only took the girl there once before, but

I drove past it so often that it seemed familiar to me. The main house with the owners was set back further from the road underneath a small forest of trees and lilac bushes. You could barely see the chimney through the leaves. We walked and I aimed for the small white pig barn around the bend, and out of view.

We wanted to do it together. She stood without speaking, holding the girl like a doll on outstretched arms, and I got to work. The sunlight began bright around my wife's head and changed as it set. The color turned orange and darkened, dripping down her face onto her throat and across her arms until, for an instant, she glowed completely reddish orange and held the girl like some sort of an offering to the sunset. For a moment it was beautiful and then she turned to shadow.

The whole while I jammed away at the ground with a shovel we'd brought. I finished in the dark on my hands and knees digging like a dog, with grit under my fingernails and the smell of my sweat and animal piss all around. The hole was almost done when my wife started to cry and shake so much that she had to kneel with the girl across her lap. I dug like mad to finish, clawed as fast as I could, and because my wife couldn't speak or gesture or do anything but rock back and forth, I had to lift the ghost of a girl off her lap and gently fold her body into the ground.

Medical doctors testified that there were no visible marks of trauma on the little girl's body. Which was obvious to me since what could possibly be visible about dying alone in a crib? We couldn't manage the charges against us, as best I could tell, because we chose to bury this little girl ourselves. Because we forgot how to react in a "logical, reasonable, and humane manner." We went down together, so to speak, my wife and I because we couldn't think of a right way to explain what had happened. Doctors testified to the possibility of some amount of suffocation, but they could not say what may have caused it.

What the jury believed: the jury believed that we had tried to save our little girl from having to grow up and live with HIV (with which she had been born), by first killing her and then discarding her corpse in what amounted to a pile manure.

What the jury needed to send: but they needed to send a message, the foreman said, that this was not the way to deal with an admittedly difficult situation. A message that clearly said to the world, **It is NOT okay to dump a precious child in a barnyard hole**!

Back before the riot they used to bus the infected prisoner women over on Thursday afternoons to those of us infected prisoner men who were married to them. CAC: Criminal AIDS Couples. I think this idea had less to do with keeping marriages together and more to do with keeping down the spread of disease by promoting conjugal visitation. At first I thought that a surprising number of us were outlaw couples until I learned that many were getting married after they've already been in prison. It definitely gave people a reason to look forward.

Usually, we met out in our designated courtyard and talked and petted. Occasionally some of us would cry or scream too much and have to be separated. Right there in the center of those cement walls, it was like we performed theater for the guards in the towers. And like a giant tainted playgroup we made believe in real life every Thursday afternoon, until That Thursday.

It rained That Thursday, forever a gray spot in my memory. The cement walls surrounding the courtyard stood undarkened by the rain, and the smooth gray sky held still over us like a dome reflecting off the faceless men in the towers with their bodies of gray mirror. I remember at one point in the confusion my wife walked toward me with the most brilliant red growing from her chest as she approached. I'm no longer sure if it happened this way, but it is the image I still see sometimes when I'm lying in my bunk at night. She shattered the single plane of gray with a point of the deepest red, blossoming out of her blue-gray uniform. At first I thought it must be a rose, but as she stepped closer I could've fainted and indeed, I sunk to my knees. The rain intensified and pulsed for minutes like clogged plumbing, and she placed a warm palm on my cheek, tilted my head up. It was absolute beauty. Her pure smile like electricity through my blood and the rain made me cry. Goddamn.

That Thursday when it rained, at first we all pressed against the stone walls and tried to speak to one another by shading our faces with our hands. But our mouths quickly filled with water and no could be heard over the sheets of water falling from the sky. So one huge Mexican guy lifted up the skirt on the short woman standing in front of him, (I remember that she had the longest hair I've ever seen-- hung to the back of her knees), and pulled down his pants. A burst of rain hid them from view but her laughter echoed and dropped down all around the rest of us. I saw this Mexican's bare ass grinding into the woman pinned to the wall, the heels of her feet like hooks.

Soon we were all performing and grunting and shouting out words like, "Oh," and "God," and "yes," as loud as we could. I pinned my wife to the wall and for a while there was this amazing rhythm in the courtyard. An "Oh god, oh god, yes baby, yes baby," rhythm and I felt so absolutely free around these couples, everyone coming like liberated gunshots. Some of us called out, our tone begging the rain to let us screw ourselves to death. The rain poured down, melting all of us into pools of sound. Sounds like birth and rock n' roll. Screams and firecrackers. Sounds like well-protected riot-geared men peeling people apart at a high school dance. And then clubs began to hit people and knock them down.

The riot began because someone tried to have sex with the wrong woman. That was the spark. And then one guy started doing another guy and everything went to hell, turned to gusts. Guards swarmed down like flying monkeys with batons and I saw the insect tattoos around the Mexican's slick neck crawl while he shouted and kicked and twisted in the brawl. He shattered a guard's jaw with the force of his naked backside thundering down from a height of three feet. Some prisoner men were even warding off the guards by walking backward and waving their hands drenched in their own infected blood.

That Thursday, when more than one prisoner was beaten unconscious by a helmeted gray soldier wearing rubber gloves, one woman was accidentally shot dead. I watched the blood growing from her blue-gray uniform chest, at first like the tiniest star. That's when I almost fainted, and I fell to my knees with the rain shrieking in my ear.

They pulled me away and I screamed, "That was my wife you fuckers. You killed my goddamn wife you stupid motherfuckers!" I couldn't see or breathe or taste anything since the snot and tears clung like a mask to my face. There was a blurry walk to my cell where I eventually grew tired of screaming and thrashing against the walls, and I curled up alone in my room for over a week.

With compassion I was eventually given trash duty and I had to stand in one place and empty small trashcans into bigger ones. Like a robot I dumped out rusty buckets that came from God knew where and I only barely noticed that no one seemed to use the bathroom to piss anymore or toilet paper to wipe up their semen.

As time passed at least we all agreed on one thing; guards, prisoners, administrators, more guards, laundry workers, delivery people, ammunition checking people, soda machine stockers, occasional journalists, a volunteer teachers or two-- we all agreed that if you smoked in prison, big goddamn deal. If I'm lucky enough to die of lung cancer, I want to be buried with my little baby girl, so llamas and goats and sheep and chickens and one cow and two Shetland ponies and fat rabbits that never move and a parrot named "Aquifer" can all shit on my dirt pile and help compost me back into the earth and into that little girl-- from whom now in some strange way, it seems like I was born.

Once, sitting with the boy Joshua at the Dairy Queen, my cellmate saw a huge cylindrical tank on wheels being pulled by a city truck. On the side of the truck was the phrase "Gravity System." Shortly thereafter he became convinced that the only reason we all remain connected to earth, spinning around, was because the people in these trucks filled up underground tunnels with gravity. Some secret gaseous substance, he explained, that reacted with the center of the earth and hardened something that made our core unbelievably heavy. He hoped one day to sabotage these trucks and agencies because he wanted our core to evaporate so he could fly off our planet and float forever, or so he thought.

"You'll burn up into a tiny piece of charred toast crumb," I told him, but he was not in jail for this theory. He also believed that pedophilia would become socially acceptable long after he'd died. After fags had been digested by society, he said, pedophiles would be next. They'll publish articles that say children in close communities and families that experience early childhood sex in a supportive, positive environment, perform much better on standardized tests than those who must spend their life overcoming the wrong that has been inflicted on them.

"Bullshit," I said.

He said they'd already done scientific studies in secret communes, and change always followed scientific proof. He loved and hated this with a passion. He'll miss out, he said looking sadly at me, but at least others will be freed.

When we fucked that night he whispered that the gravity system idea was really Joshua's and his tears poured onto my lower back, forming small rivulets down my thighs.

When the guys in the fag block finally beat the shit out of my friend with the eyeball tattoo, I defended him. I stood on a table in the food

court and told everyone to shut up about revenge. I glanced at my
friend retching on his knees. Maybe he should fuck little boys, I said,
and maybe he shouldn't. But what do we really want to kill, what do we
hate more than his puny little prick?

I ordered them to go back to their cells and be sad, and for once
they should shut the fuck up about kicking ass. Learn to be sad, I
shouted, learn to be alone. Listen, I said and I tapped on my chest, hear
yourself. For an hour they took turns beating the hell out of me and
someone pushed a paper cup so far into my colon that it had to be
removed by a surgeon.

The hospital had always been a tricky place for me, a sort of slippery
slope because I never knew if I would be coming out alive. But now it
just seems to always have been part of my life, a place like any other that
you might often visit. During one stay, I learned that on the horizon
there was a procedure that will enable doctors to pull blood out of your
body through a tube in your neck, run it through a virus killing machine
and then re-introduce it into your body through your thigh. Of course
you wouldn't be able to eat or drink or have sex in the hospital bed
while the procedure took place. Up to 24 hours. When I heard this I
thought, *others will be freed.*

Since my prison sentence was commuted to time in this house, I've
grown to dislike attempts to freeze time. I am quickly agitated by still
photographs and what they often propose to be "saying" about one
thing or another. I hate them simply because they are frozen images,
still and quiet, inviting us to hurl private meaning or verbal conjecture at
them like nothing else I know. And they need not respond, resting
satisfied and smug in their eternal representations of one, most often,
choreographed moment. They are nothing to do with life and the only
one I have in my room I tore out of a magazine and tacked onto my
ceiling.

A black and white picture of a mother and teenage daughter in a
backyard. Their black hair looks identical and the mother's arm pulls
her daughter into her side as they pose. It looks like no one is taking
their picture, as if they've set the camera on a rock or fence post and
have been waiting for it to go off. They begin to appear bored. Leaves
come into the picture from below and enormous dandelion heads
partially block their legs. Maybe the camera was set on the lawn.

Now what any of this had to do with the designer pens advertised was beyond me, but the absence of a cameraman was not. For an instant, when I first saw them, I imagined that the women were actually staring at me and I even thought, *It could have been me.* I could have taken their picture and I envisioned the scene with the three of us in our backyard, teasing each other and laughing and saying silly family words. That's when I ripped it out of the magazine.

All of the typical responses to my own life wait daily in the wings of this room, as if I may somehow decide to regret or beg forgiveness or end it all with a broom handle. As if for me there is decision involved anymore.

Now, after a bath or a calm nap I still like to rest on my bunk, but I rarely consider the picture on my ceiling anymore. Lately, I am able to look straight through the image and past the ceiling and see the night sky in wonderful swirls of star clusters and galaxies. I take a tour from my bed on those nights and I choose the light of my next star from the field of sparks and hesitating lovelies. It's where I'll go when my core gravity eventually gives way and I'm finally tossed from this tiny blue earth.

Performing Art

One morning, she stops him on a sidewalk that runs by the university campus along the main street.

"Excuse me, are you Aaron Hessler?" S/he wears a curly wig, dark brown, and lipstick smudged around her mouth like a clown. S/he hasn't shaved the black stubble from her square chin and rough cheeks. A blue plastic handbag hangs across her chest.

"I'm sorry, but you're not Aaron Hessler are you," she asks. A pause. A quick but violent shake of the curly head. "No, no of course not. Of course not at all. He's dead, I'm afraid, still quite dead." A sigh and a pat against the blue plastic handbag. "No, but you do resemble him, I guess I should say did, when he was alive. How can I know about any resemblance now, I haven't seen him since the funeral. Were you at the funeral perhaps? A close friend? No, of course it's quite impossible. An extremely private funeral, almost no one there but myself. In fact, no one there but myself. Aaron's dying was as simple as flushing his license down the toilet and putting on a wig." She touches her curls.

A glance down and a stomp of the foot. "They're always doing that though, aren't they? People. Every goddamn time I turn around, dying goes on. Always, always, always indeed."

A quick, timid shrug of the young man's shoulders. He scratches his black beard and thumbs his overalls. A cramp in his stomach makes him think about the Chinese food he ate the night before, and more specifically, about the two small chunks of uncooked chicken he'd found. Although he only ate one piece of the pasty pink meat, sour belches continue to erupt between hiccups.

A slow car passes on the street with the window rolled down framing an adolescent boy's face, prepared to spit.

"But who can I blame? I mean really? It's the only way we know how to do it, isn't that right, dying I mean. Change and all the rest of it. I guess there really is no other way, unless perhaps you know another way?"

A silence.

"No, of course not, nothing. Never you mind what I said about resembling a dead man. I meant when he lived, when he was alive. And he was an upstanding fellow, handsome Aaron was, but he didn't care too much for his penis, you know. I guess that's how some men are. Well anyway, he's truly dead and we live so I suppose we must go on. We must start fresh on this glorious day. Take care of yourself Aaron, if you don't mind me calling you that, it was good to see you anyway."

The sound of a solid, nasal-crunching discharge, spit from the car and landing near her feet.

"Take good care," she says after pausing a moment and gazing beyond the bearded man. She winks and says audibly, but to herself, "I know you will." She walks away without avoiding the phlegm that squishes nicely under her pointy black high heel. Black hair presses through her pantyhose.

The young man shivers, slides his hands deep into his pockets, and walks back across campus toward the library, belching quietly to himself.

"Hey Dad, watch this."

Dad slows the car. Son leans out his window even though the air-conditioning has been cooling the inside of the car. The family has been driving leisurely down the main street of the college town and Dad believes he has seen as many firm tan bodies in this one place as he's seen in his life. He believes the campus crawls with tan thighs and he thinks about bikini lines while he slows the car.

Son stretches his arm out the window and points to the sidewalk.

Mom turns to look out her window as she feels the car slow. She knows that Dad has an erection while he drives, but she has almost successfully forgotten this. "What," she states.

Honey, the one who will be starting college this fall, wants not to pay attention to anything her idiotic younger brother would see, but the car slows and her mother's movement have prompted Honey to lean over and look as her brother points out his window. She's been considering her boyfriend Fritz, whom she's left in a town where she lost her virginity to a janitor, learned how to play pool, and drank cherry flavored vodka until she threw up (what she thought was blood) all during the night of her going away party. She believes, and feels soothed by this, that she may be starting to despise Fritz. She sighs heavily in response to her brother's voice.

Son points to the ground, so Dad slows the car more, almost to dead stop. There are no cars in the rearview mirror.

Dad scans the campus; he sees skirts, imagines women crossing their legs without underwear.

Mom squints.

Honey wonders for a misty moment about her period.

On the ground, just inches from a man wearing a wig, lies a fist size, lime green pool of snot that has just come from Son's mouth.

Honey reacts. "Did your brain leak out?" she says sitting back in her seat

The mother turns back to watch the road, feeling the car pick up some speed. She feels like a mother, but remembers being in a car with her college boyfriend, the one before Dad, and leaning over on the highway to help him unzip his pants.

Dad has choices to make. To be the father figure and set some kind of example, or to be the young man he has been remembering. The college man who would say, "Check *this* out," and proceed to hawk the biggest spit wad he could muster straight onto the inside of the car windshield. That college superstar, he reflects, would have had his erection taken care of long before now.

"Now son, let's try not to embarrass your sister too much," he says, smiling weakly at his wife who nods without turning her head. "You have enough on your mind, don't you Honey?"

Son rolls up his window and sits back in his seat.

A long silence and the smell of a rental car, until they stop at the next streetlight.

A large disrobing woman strides across the crosswalk in front of them, and lays her large bra on the hood of the car. It is by far the largest bra Mom or Dad has ever seen and the edges are discolored. The four family heads turn to watch the bounding topless woman as her skirt falls and then her wide panties scoot down her trunk-like legs. Her massive whiteness moves around the corner, just as she pulls something onto her head.

Dad and Mom will do it up against the shower stall in the hotel while the water steams the mirror. Son will practice in his room across the hall with a magazine displaying the hottest summer bikini fashions. In a few days, Honey will be a freshman and will meet a library janitor who will say his name could be Aaron Hessler.

On the first day of family college orientation Jo steps onto the grass with her chin up, but her eyes scan to see who checks her out. And as I expected, many do. She's naked and fat for one thing, and she wears a red clown wig.

At first I don't watch her, though I know she does this because she is my roommate, my sometimes lover, and she told me that today was the day. Today, she said, would be about art that moved on two legs from one suffocating university building to the next. It would be a day for smothering reason with her swaggering belly, and shadowing the quest for meaning with her curly hairs. Performance art.

Instead of watching her I look at the new students, some sit with younger siblings or parents in small groups on the library lawn. Tentative friends talk in groups of two or three, tanning their legs on the grass.

My own wig makes my head sweat so I take it off and shove it into my handbag. A brown curl catches in the zipper teeth and I remember, as I always do around zippers, that I still have a penis and probably always will. But today I will not despair because I have given the old Aaron Hessler's identity to the handsome young man I met earlier with indigestion and a black beard. I will choose a new name. I begin fresh today, penis and all, a happier and healthier person. I shout, "I love you," and people barely glance at me before returning to watch Jo.

The whispers multiply as she makes progress toward the library and I see many pairs of wide eyes. Cheeks and faces of the new students flush and make them all appear suddenly attractive and healthy. Frisbees fall to the ground and roll like tires while boys without shirts grope for them without taking their eyes off Jo. Giggles and snickers and a few ill-concealed pig snort noises bring a smile to my lips. The humming and subtle commotion remind me of one thing so I shout again, watching my roommate's bare feet tread toward the library I shout, "I'm alive."

Then I freeze. Jo walks up the pink slate steps toward the library door. For a moment I do despair. I think, *Not the library Jo, for goodness sake, those people only want to be left alone.*

But when I see the white moons of her butt eclipsed by the closing wooden door, I am flooded with warmth. It will be fine for those people, just as it was for everyone out here on the lawn. All of the new friendships adhered and glossed together in the wake of Jo's strutting body. The families radiating and blushing inside their embarrassed bodies with something as raw as birth. Through the library window I see the red clown wig, strangely out of place and maneuvering above her like it was its own head.

I applaud.

***

I catch the thought after lunch, after the woman with biceps and hairy arms mistakes me for a dead man. I step into the library and think, *now we're getting somewhere.*

Anyway, I don't usually pay so much attention to a single thought because I catch them all the time. Sometimes I have to write them down on the walls of the johns in precise, small red letters just to get rid of them.

Sure, it's rare. I'm no psycho; I'm not tuning into little blips of the future or anything. Probably, I pick up the thoughts people try to throw away. It's definitely electric, when the thought collides with my reality.

I was leaning against the pay phones, sliding a toothpick in and out of the gaps between my teeth when I saw a gorgeous leg and had the thought at the same time. I focused on a patch of brown thigh that pressed against a hole in her jean shorts. The swirl of blond fuzz on her skin spins and spins and sucks me into a revelation.

Bullet holes through her dead brother's jeans. A blood soaked tee-shirt, up against the trash can in the mall, still filled with his dead body. A couple of bullets had entered his jeans and one hole frays in the cutoff shorts his sister now wears, revealing her brown thigh to the world like an advertisement for maturing steel.

The terror might have sent me into a comma or set off a stroke or something if my view of the jean girl hadn't been suddenly and totally blocked by a wall of white human flesh. I watch the huge naked woman as she fills the nearby loveseat with her body. I have the thought, and I move to touch her rubber wig with the tight red curls.

"Hello," I said as I leaned over to kiss her cheek. "I am Aaron Hessler and pleased to make your acquaintance.

A Pervert's Orientation

A good many of the adults who hung around campus during freshman orientation were perverts like myself. We sat at random tables, wearing dark sunglasses and pretending to read. Men, except for Jack who was the group's only woman, began perverting each day with the first girl we saw who bent over and we ended with the last bare-skinned frat brother to tuck a Frisbee under his sweaty armpit and stride off for dinner. We tracked and recorded exposed skin on them all, we celebrated flesh, and on a more emotional level, we lusted.

Shuffling our books and backpacks, clearing our throats and blowing dry noses, we excelled at disguise. We generated feelings that we belonged on campus, that there was nothing out of the ordinary about our sitting at these tables or on these lawns, while we stared hard and traced underwear lines with our eyes.

When I saw the new college kids, the freshmen, the fresh year students, the cliché hit me (not literally and not even metaphorically since it seems that clichés are always just resting there). I saw how lucky they were: these sexy girls with their tan mothers and solid boys with attentive fathers. Each student, embarrassed by their genealogical donors, but also decidedly with them, by their side.

One heterosexual fantasy went something like this: A small-breasted freshgirl wearing a short flower dress and no bra rises from a table in the food court where she sits with her slit-skirt, red-lipped mother. The mother goes bare-fingered, wedding ring-less, sporting fashionably cut hair, died black to match the daughter who steps up to my table and speaks.

"Do you know where the library is," she asks.

"Indeed I do."

"Could we find a place to screw?" she asks.

"Indeed we could."

But I began by describing the cliché, the bit about the piece of luck these kids carried around with them during the first week of orientation. All of them quieting the terror of leaving home, and strolling nonchalantly about, guided by a massive sense of inevitability. This, they must have thought, was how it was meant to be: even if they stood on the edge now, on the verge of being stranded. Honey awaited them, as well as crickets and a desert to traverse wearing Jesus sandals, and they clutched the glow that was their parent's undying love.

Okay, the love bit may be too slippery, even if it was mostly true, but the fear wasn't. Fear grew out of these kids' minds from a seed that had always been there, waiting to be named. It was their lucky seed because it forced open their eyes.

Families looked around. Everybody appeared lost but walked with purpose, glancing at campus maps without being caught. Except for some of the heavier mothers who stood with feet apart, staring at the map pinned to the wall by their thick hands.

Question mark foreheads aimed forward, then at each other, then away again. Because someone around here knew the answer to their question and this engraved many question marks deeper into the fathers' foreheads. If only they could ask the right person the exact question at the perfect moment.

I'd been in a few disagreements with my fellow perverts over the years, but we'd always found a way to make things work, until the university sought to have us destroyed by stripping us of our dignity. That could have really bonded us together, but instead, it destroyed us and we scattered, forced to pervert alone.

It had been a good year for innovation. A spot on one roof afforded the best view of all the main grass on campus. The primary patch was spread out below me, and I'd sit on the roof with a book in my lap, gazing out from behind my sunglasses. But my little secret wasn't a secret for too long, and soon the others started muscling in. It got so bad that we were all running through the early morning alleys until we reached the dumpsters. Then we scrambled up the pink slate walls, nudging for handholds and footholds until we could pull ourselves onto the clay tile roof. Then whoever won, would sit in the lawn chair (the one I had originally brought up for myself!), while the others sat on the roof tiles and pouted. Well fine, I thought.

I decided to bring a new lawn chair for the next five days, until there was one for each of us. That began to cement our bond. It's amazing about lawn chairs, and how we started helping each other scale the wall. Discreetly whispering to one another when we'd spot someone's skirt up with the wind, or boys streaking naked across the lawn with red hearts painted on their butt cheeks. We became a sort of family sitting in our chairs on the roof and staring out from behind our dark sunglasses.

One day up on the roof, I could tell everything was going well. Each one of us was juiced up and horny and this itch just sort of hung in the air. We must have been a sight that day, all coughing and book flapping and throat clearing, saying things like, "YEEEOWWW, HOLY SHIT!" All to distract attention from ourselves and our fevered state. The bodies on the lawn were charged as well. The tan skin was everywhere with men and women shining with sweat from flipping Frisbees or wrestling on the lawn. We had just reached the pinnacle of our day, where we'd try to cling as long as possible, letting the current tickle our insides before we eventually began to calm down and notice our sunburns. We were at the climax of the day, practically swimming in skin soup, crossing and uncrossing our legs, coughing, muttering, drooling, gulping, and swallowing when Jack screamed, "Oh God."

It's about a five story fall to the ground and she clung to her chair as she went, landing on a metal spout that stood erect spurting water in the center of a dozen drenched college kids who'd been wrestling and slipping in and out of their bathing suits. It wasn't the spout, but the fortunate snap of her neck that killed her instantly. But apparently her death wasn't enough for the university community.

No, instead it became an all-out campaign against perverts. There were speeches in which the state of affairs at the university was somehow clearly illustrated when you had "perverts falling from roofs all over campus." A solution needed to be enacted, people said, something had to be done. Of course, as with much public policy, a compromise was reached after Jack's touching funeral.

Jack's family had stood in support of her, had said she was an excellent and honest mother and wife who only wanted to elevate humankind by paying the closest attention to these flesh cases into which we'd all been born. To adore skin by watching it, to cultivate the sexual longing that it stimulated within us. Sacred and holy. Her husband, two daughters, and young son all stood naked by the grave, heads bowed and hands folded casually in front of their genitalia (which was fortunate for the newspaper photographer). It was this picture and the printing of their speech in the newspaper that forced the university to the bargaining table.

The administration made a show out of recognizing perverts as part of the university community, and designated an area for our viewing in which a plaque in memory of Jack was planted in the ground. They seemed satisfied with themselves. They shook my hand on opening day and left after pouring themselves a few generous glasses of wine from our small reception table. It was all so grand and generous, so how can I now, you may ask, resume my incognito pervert routine in good conscience?

It's a two part answer. The first has simply to do with the unbearable location of the official perverting section. And the second, well, I assaulted an officer with perversion and quickly became a wanted man.

The fact remains that they relegated us to the single lousiest place on campus. We occupied a small plot of lawn with three benches forming a horseshoe around Jack's plaque that faced the smoking section of campus. And it's not like I didn't give it a chance at first. I sat for over a week on those stupid benches, staring at the smokers as they huddled together (many wore long sleeves in May!) or stood apart and gazed at the dumpsters. Some of these college kids were only taking a break from more serious self-medication and they squinted up at the sun like they'd just been healed by Jesus. Pasty white skin, pale lips, healing cuts, and yellowing bruises-- a pervert's hell!

The sexy smokers, I found, avoided their designated section. The ones in cutoff jean shorts and golden brown chests were smoking any damn place they pleased and so I began to fantasize. I imagined myself a lone wolf again, perverting wherever my dark sunglasses led me.

Then one day someone stole my bike and in my attempt to recover it, I ended up as a wanted pervert with a horrible sketch of my face plastered throughout campus.

The man sat in a security uniform behind a large wooden desk.

I said, "Excuse me sir, something's happened. I can't seem to find my bike where I left it this morning."

Without looking up, he asked, "Locked?"

"Yes, I had locked it. Here's the key, but the bike isn't there. I'm sure of it because I've looked three times. A whole row seems to have vanished."

Still not looking up. "Quite possible," he said. The folds of fat under his chin rippled when he spoke.

"Why?" I asked.

"Why what? Do you mean why are they gone?"

"Yes, why? Because at least one of them was mine."

"Because someone wanted them."

"Why?"

"Don't be simple, boy." He looked up at last, and stared at me with a smirk. "To have the bikes or else to sell them. Anyway it's been stolen and I am quite certain of that. You can fill out this report form if you'd like." He indicated a stack of yellow forms on the desk.

"But if it was mine, why on earth would someone take it?"

The man smiled. "Come on now. Haven't you ever wanted something that wasn't yours?"

"Well, sort of."

"So you see then, it's as easy as that. Someone just like yourself perhaps, wanted those bikes. Quite basic really. For example, what was it that you desired that did not belong to you?"

"A professor in the visual art department, a painter."

"So see, you would have swiped her I'll bet, stolen her straight away if you could have. Wouldn't you have? By chance, was she married?"

"I believe so."

"Even better still. You'd have done it then, stolen her. Admit it."

"But I only I performed cunnilingus on her. One night in her office for 36 minutes with only one drink of water in between."

He looked impressed and smiled broadly. "See then? Stolen just as surely as I sit here speaking to you. You understand this business about your bike a little better now, eh?"

"But I didn't steal her, I don't have her. I only performed-- well it happened like I told you. Imagine, only one drink in 36 minutes."

"Yes, imagine. But that's as good as stolen my boy. Good as any stealing I know."

"But I haven't anything to show for it, a sweaty memory perhaps, but she goes along now much the same way she did before that night. Before I serviced her."

His face darkened and his eyes narrowed. "I see. You must excuse me, but what did you just say?"

"Before I serviced her. Serviced. It wasn't stealing. A favor perhaps, a pleasant moment shared by the both of us. But as far as having, I assure you sir, I have nothing."

An expression of disgust crept into the man's face. "I see. Serviced." He said the word as if it tasted awful. "How dare you refer to that sacred and beautiful action as merely 'servicing?'" He glared at me, visibly upset. "A pervert," he almost shouted it. "Leave me be, you pervert. Your bike is gone and luckier in my opinion, than the rest of us who must remain and tolerate your filthy presence. You perverts are a disgrace to the college." He made the sound of gagging.

"I'll go, but I must thank you anyway for this little talk. Do you mind if I have a draw off your water bottle there?" While he answered I reached over and lifted the water bottle from the desk.

"The art form, the holiest of holies, the sacred right, the treasured field of sanctity and pubic hair," the man was saying. "Serviced." He spat the word at me and reached for his telephone.

"Thank you for the water. That makes one swallow of water during our 16 minutes conversation, not bad. Not bad at all. Thank you, again."

"Code PVT," he said into the phone. "I've got a major pervert here."

I ran, and I've been forced to pervert covertly ever since.

If you glimpse a pair of sunglasses aimed in your direction, know that the eyes behind them may be peeling back each piece of your clothing with hard-staring eyes. You might feel the sensation moving like a feather along your warm bare skin. You may hear the person clear their throat or see them cross and uncross their arms. You may even glimpse their hardness pressing against their jeans. Out of respect to Jack and all of the others who have been forced to pervert from the shadows, I ask you not to turn the pervert in. Instead, I suggest that you remain still, close your eyes, and feel the sensation as it moves up and down your body.

The Suicide Painter

They call me late at night, or sometimes during the day, depending on when they want to die. Some of them have thought it all out, and some of them seem to be winging it, one step at a time. There are always reasons to go out during the nighttime, that's the most usual. It's the time of the spirit, the time when souls are awakened and so it's as if someone will be around to check them-in on the other side. I've heard stuff like that. The daytime ones are usually more dramatic, more frantic, like get me out of here before I change my mind type of thing. And people change their mind too, by the time they see me pull up, they've had a change of heart and they apologize, maybe give me some money for my time.

I don't do it for the money, though I can't deny necessity. The paintings are selling like crazy lately and so I guess I can't complain. There's a wait list for my paintings which is like saying there are people waiting for other people to die.

I get the call at night. I slip out of bed and dress in my old brown monk's robe splattered with years of paint. My easel and my case of paints sit by the door and I pick them up on my way out. It's chilly out, and the sky is as clear as it can be. I get in my car and follow the directions I have written on a yellow sticky pad.

I don't know why all of them want to do it. Some don't even tell me hello, it's like they're already in some other space. But the others, the ones that talk to me before, they see it as leaving one final mark here on earth before they journey on. Almost as if, one guy told me, as if he were using the painting as a porthole to the other side. They know that other people, wealthy people, are buying these paintings but that doesn't seem to bother them. In fact it's almost as if they believe that being hung on a wall will ensure them immortality.

I arrive at a cabin in the foothills. I park my car and follow a small footpath up to the door. I knock tentatively, hoping not to startle the young man who called.

"Come in," a voice says and I step into the cabin.

It is a single room cabin fairly well furnished with a couch and two rocking chairs. A young woman sits in one of the chairs and a man stands to greet me. He shakes my hand and gestures for me to step through the doorway. A fur throw rug lies in the center of the floor. Sometimes they bring people to watch, the ones who do it cleanly.

"We're going together," the man says. I see that they have brought a black bag with them and I see that the woman has already prepared herself to shoot heroin into her arm. I arrange them so that they are both sitting on the couch together. I move the chairs out of my way and set up my easel.

They drink whisky for a while and offer me some. I decline trying to keep them alone in their space together, keep myself out. It needs to be as if I'm invisible. The room is dark maroon, brown and the two figures are turning out to be yellow with some orange. They shoot up and drink more whiskey. The woman is sobbing at one point and he holds her. They're both shaking uncontrollably and I'm hoping that they do not expect me to step in. I never step in. If they are unsuccessful then I simply call for an ambulance, pack up my painting and go home.

They've settled down a bit and have removed most of their clothing. This is something many people do before they die. It must be a biological thing because way   more than half the people I paint have died naked. It looks as if the two of them are trying to make love or else they're simply trying to keep themselves together, keep themselves attached to something.

She has long black hair and delicate white skin. You can see the veins in her arms and legs as if in the depths of white marble. He has short blond hair and a tattoo of a black sun around his belly button. Her seizures begin first and the guy tries to do something, but he cannot lift his head. The two of them have slumped onto the ground before the couch. But she has fallen onto the floor and she twitches uncontrollably, her mouth open, eyes rolled back into her head. It's almost as if he decides to mimic her. The two of them twitching and I'm moving fast with my paints, my brush sweeping back and forth across the canvas. I am capturing this, I think, I am capturing something.

The silence is the worst part, always. The end when everything has gotten still and you can still hear the rustling noises from moments before. Or even hear the words they spoke just before they could no longer make speech. I slow down, until I'm barely making any brush marks at all. Then as quiet as I can, I pack up my belongings and close the cabin door behind me. I know that this painting will be hanging in someone's living room before the paint has dried.

It's wrong, what I do, by the way. The same people on the waiting list have no problem condemning me as the most immoral of artists, a scavenger of the human soul. And yet they have not seen any of these people, they have not talked to them. They do not see that I am providing a service to those in need. These people want to be documented, counted, and yes, they want to die. But I do not kill them with my paintbrush. If anything I keep them alive with it, and still, I have been called a purveyor of filth, a murderer.

When I was twelve years old my mother hung herself in the basement. I remember waking early and standing in front of the basement door on that morning. Everyone else was asleep and I had recently gotten into the habit of drawing. I used to get up in the mornings and spend a few hours sketching in a notepad before I had to go to school. As soon as I opened the basement door I knew something had happened, and as I descended the staircase she came into view. I froze. Her body hung in the center of the room. A chair had been knocked over onto its side and one of her shoes hung from her foot, just about to drop.

I fixated on the shoe as I completed my descent into the basement and walked to the other side of the room. She was wearing a wide-brimmed black hat and her face was covered by a black veil. With my back against the wall I eased myself into a sitting position on the ground. Then I opened my sketchpad and starting with the image of that precarious shoe, I began to draw. It was as if I couldn't believe that it was my mother, as if by drawing I would discover who it was. Later of course I knew it was her and I would paint the image several dozen times, always trying it from different angles, trying to capture something.

I've been dating Amanda on and off for over two years. Sometimes we date each other exclusively and other times we exclusively do not date one another. It's a tricky relationship, often subject to the variations in our moods. As if we can't quite get a handle on each other and so we wear ourselves out trying. Then we retreat, pull our forces back and regroup. I had not heard from her in over three months until the evening when she called. Her voice sounded serious and she told me to come over to her apartment and bring my paints.

"You can't be serious," I said.

"As serious as cancer," she said.

So I hopped in my car and drove over.

"What's this all about," I asked after she'd let me into her apartment.

"I want you to paint me," she said. "Killing myself."

She was a tall woman with long red hair and dark blue eyes. I stared at her for a moment, my mouth agape.

"It's what you do isn't it?" she asked.

"It's what I do," I said. "But I'm not going to do it for you."

"Why not? You do it for total strangers."

"I do it because they're total strangers. You've got to be kidding me."

She did not sound desperate or hopeless. She had not set up her room with a noose; there were no bags of pills lying around. It looked like an ordinary apartment.

"I'm going to sit on the couch and I want you to paint me eating these hamburgers," she said and she held up a brown paper sack that had been stained in places by grease. She smiled.

I set up my easel and she took off her clothes. "People die naked, isn't that right?"

"I miss you," I said. I began to paint.

She sat on the couch with her legs crossed, eating the burgers without a napkin. Juice from the hamburger and streaks of ketchup rolled off her chin.

"You never call me," she said. The grease on her fingers reflected in the light of the apartment. "I call you, but you never call me back."

"I've been sort of busy lately, painting and everything."

"I mean how are we ever going to make it if I have to kill myself every time I want to see you."

I had painted her before but each time was a treat. She lay out on the couch and put the bag of burgers on her naked stomach. I didn't have an answer for Amanda. I just kept painting.

"How am I dying?" she asked.

"How are you what?"

"Dying. How am I dying in the painting?"

"I don't know. I guess you overdosed, because you're just lying there with your arm hanging down, your wrist bent against the floor. Maybe natural causes."

"No," she said. "Definitely not natural causes. Maybe an overdose, that seems about right. Would you ever do it?"

"Do what?"

"If I called you and I was dead serious would you ever paint me killing myself."

"No."

"Even if I begged you, if I swore to you that it was the thing I wanted most of all, to be painted and to die with you by my side, you still wouldn't do it."

"Amanda you're being ridiculous. You know I could never do it."

"What if I threaten to go to one of the other guys?"

"Those monsters are a bunch of hacks. They have no sensibility at all, you might as well hire a photographer. They don't capture anything, no emotion, no intensity, nothing."

"But if you left me no choice then I would have to go to one of them."

"Why do you want to kill yourself? I can call more often if that's what you want."

"Why does anyone want to kill themselves?" Amanda asked.

"Lots of reasons," I said. "Pain from a disease, pain from living, to get to the other side. What about you?"

"I'm exhausted. That's why. I'm tired of going on, day to day, playing out the games of school and work and relationships. I'm always looking and never finding anything. Always trudging around."

"But what about us, we used to have some good times together."

"And nothing ever came of it, that's what I mean. A life full of false starts and I'm getting tired. Did you bring another canvas?"

I told her I did, but I felt happy enough with the one I was completing. And that was when she showed me the gun.

"Holy shit Amanda, be careful with that thing, it could hurt someone."

She was kneeling on the couch and waving it around as if it were a make believe airplane. She was even making the noises of the make believe engines. "Set-up your next canvas," she said and she said it the way an announcer would say "Start your engines."

"Amanda, please don't do this. I'm begging you, just please put the gun away and we'll go out and get a few drinks."

She put the gun to her head and made the sound of a fake gunshot. I tried to walk closer but she aimed the gun at me and I froze. I couldn't tell if she was on drugs. The grease and ketchup had smeared on her chin and together with her make-up made her look like some crazed army sergeant. "Set up your next canvas."

I walked out to the car trying to decide what to do. I had no telephone and I couldn't think of who I would call anyway. I realized that the real danger was in how long I remained outside. With each passing second Amanda could give into a sudden urge and then in an instant she would be dead. So I got the canvas out of the back of my car and ran back into the apartment.

Amanda lay on the couch drinking wine, the gun nestled in between her breasts.

"Paint away Mr. Painter man."

"I'll only paint if you give me the gun Amanda."

She eased the barrel of the gun into her mouth and I began to paint. As I worked I imagined different scenarios. Leaping over and grabbing the gun while she poured herself another glass of wine. Creating a diversion by smashing a window and then stealing the gun away. But all I could do to keep her still was to paint and keep painting. Whenever I stopped she aimed the gun at various places on her body. She smiled at me as if were all a big game.

Then it went off. The gunshot echoed in my ears and I looked up. Amanda was dead.

You get used to seeing death. After a while it had become routine for me and so even as her body lay there naked, it did not cause me to throw myself on her wailing. No, but it caused me to stop in that eerie quiet and wait. I could hear myself talking to her, promising to call her, promising her that life was not simply a series of false starts.

But then I know she didn't believe me. I didn't believe me. Eventually I made a few last brush strokes and then I packed up my belongings and closed the door behind me as I left.

Being An Easy God

What was Juliet anyway, fourteen? When I was fourteen my older brother handed out condoms to his friends in the Catholic youth group. Actually, only one friend got the rubber. During the group we talked about Jesus and about how he used to take a shit, just like us. Pretty much no one believed that.

About how Jesus believed that we all had God inside of us, and so we were all part of the organism of God, of eternal life.

At first, my brother's friend with the condom made me promise not to have sex until I was married. Then one time at the drive-in he said that I was too delicious and that he could swallow me whole. He refused to believe that I took shits and this made me hug him and laugh and almost cry. I loved him before anyone and I married him to Jesus in my head. The blond one, with the blue eyes, and the humor in his body. Jokes that made me feel good and the sound of his jeans unzipping.

Catholic youth group. My very first time and you drove me crazy for a while, like a generator had started in my body, sending vibrations beneath every patch of my skin. All I wanted was to dissolve into you, to stay in there forever. All you wanted was to have a good-time-Saturday-night. We drank, we got drunk, and you hurried on top of me, believing that if I had a chance to think, if I suddenly came alive I'd probably halt your big expedition. Inside my cramped pain I was learning to be permeable, learning to be part God and part human all at once. I would learn that I often lost parts of myself inside other people and that I should never expect to be whole again. They missed us at church on Sunday morning. I left blood on you and you tried not to gag while you washed yourself in the sink, in front of the mirror. I apologized. I have since learned that blood happens.

You think it's easy being a girl but my moods change. I ride my bike to campus and some days I must crush the grasshoppers on the path. On colder mornings they're slow and it's almost like I'm harvesting. If they jump away they live, and if not, the rubber nubs of my tires are doing a service. Nature taking its course. The crunching becomes a type of sustenance and by crushing one after the other, I exude.

My skirt rides up my thighs and since I'm wearing biking shorts anyway, I think about hiking it up around my waist. Laying it all out there in black spandex and dissolving the mystery the college boys seek from their car windows. But instead I pedal and leave everything just the way it is.

You watch my legs and your eyes travel up my biking body. From your car window you must think I have it all figured out. You've already matched my breasts to your secret images, to your private movies, and you think I'm in control because I can make it happen. You think I can make you real with the nod of my head, like a genie.

But you are no mystery to me college boy. I saw you look down at my naked chest and avert your red-rimmed eyes. You rolled off and tried to muffle the sigh that started from your chest, that leaked out like air. You were disappointed and empty, and suddenly my skin hurt your eyes so you said something like, "We'll freeze to death like this." You dressed yourself like an old man, hunched away from me on the side of the bed, and I waited to fill up again even while you cooled so close to my heart blood. I remained on the bed after you left and let the humidity dissipate like steam off my body, turning to lukewarm drops. I wiped you away with my underwear.

Other days I can't imagine being that person, the grasshopper killer. So eager to crush the tiny creatures. Instead I weave around them, in between them. Especially the fat ones that sit with their legs perfectly poised, petrified. I sing songs to them, and I call them my little pretties.

Maybe you really had it tough because you had a leather jacket and an old motorcycle you fixed yourself. Because you were a young renegade man, a traveler, a free spirit. You had two tattoos, one on each shoulder and you had that thing between your legs leading you around, I said, poking it. Being dragged all over the country by such a silly looking thing.

Your face dimmed.

Big, I said, but still strange looking. Huge, in fact, the biggest I've seen, fine. You had it tough because you thought that if you could get me done first, then you could move on to other things. After you'd gotten me squared away, the rest would fall into place. I stretched out for you because you were a beautiful boy, and you told me about your plans for a giant tattoo of the planet earth to be done in the center of your back. Your black eyes gleamed and you knew exactly what to do. And for a moment I believed in you. I turned my cheek to the pillow as you made delicious lies about love and God and yes.

I talk easily to dead animals. At the end of my road, next to the row of mailboxes lay my two raccoon friends. Hit together on the highway and left to dissolve into the dirt. Only once was their stench too bad for me to hold a conversation while I checked the mail. It rained and now their skin looks like the rubber beneath Halloween wigs, their fur a light fuzzy color. I ask them how they are, and if it's a drag to be stuck, wasting away in the same spot with nothing else to do. I want to make them into puppets, make them talk, but I am afraid to touch them. I'm sure I'll miss them when they finally disappear.

Men, you said to me, fucking men. You said it because you knew how your kind was, how they could be. Pigs, you said, little more than pigs. After all you were in a college fraternity before you graduated and became the successful professional that you became, a salesman of some sort. They wanted one thing and one thing only, and we both knew what that was, right? But since you were alive to the seediness of your kind, you wouldn't fall into the same trap as mostmen. For starters, you were more intelligent than mostmen. You were certain that mostmen did not notice the things you noticed, or use the same, gentle words you used. Lilac and chamomile. Mostmen would never have stroked my face or treated me like a princess or touched me like a rock star. Fucking mostmen.

You felt a little sorry for me and what, by nature, I was forced to put up with. The pawing, the shouting, the star roles in mostmen's private movies, sized up like a beast in mostmen's lust for female skin. Believe it, you told me, because you knew those fantasies, you'd seen them. For you though it really was quite different because sex was making love and not just banging some drunk chick behind a gas station with her skirt pulled up, her underwear ripped and wet. Making love was filled with the pillowy images of a castle resting on a cloud and spires that reached up to tickle God's belly. You lied to me, but at least you were not the same one who bruised my neck.

I don't usually ride too fast. The idea that my wheel will come off and the image of my body tumbling down the hill causes me to slow down. But on this particular day I don't care. I pedal as fast as I can, inhaling in sharp bursts, my thighs burning. Then I begin down the steepest part thinking that maybe I want to wreck. The moment I see the squirrel lying on the road is the same instant that I run across its plump body. Chills flow up and down my back and I grip the handle bars trying to keep control. I scream over and over, feeling the squishable lump replay vibrations beneath my skin. I do not wreck on the patches of gravel and when I finally stop to lean against the fence post, I try to sing calmness into myself between shudders.

Here is what you explained to me professor, you said that women were nature. Giving birth, bleeding, they were the liquid pools of creation, human style. And meanwhile, back at the Hall of Justice, man worked out his rational world and assigned roles. But in the process, man maintained control of nature and of women.

He dammed the water, so to speak, set up views and charged for access.

At first, you explained, woman gave little shit about the roles man invented. But now woman gave a shit. Well, you said, you were all for it, it was time to change the roles and the rules. You said Amen to this, and you even had ideas about how to re-order the world. About how you would go about the whole process of re-assignment. It made me wonder about changing roles.

I asked you what would happen to women if all men didn't mind being fucked in the ass.

Please, I said one night into your beard, please fuck me into being, and you were startled, but not enough to stop trying.

I squish a housefly inside a tissue and throw it away. This is how life will go, always one person or another. The barrier between the boys, the grasshoppers and my self, a wet onion skin, a translucent membrane.

With each boy a petal inside myself falls away. I am forced to create and re-create myself, shed the old as best I can, and I continue to live.

The Death of Count Roger the Marionette

A significant contributor to Count Roger's distress is the uncertainty as to the fate of his son Jordan. Only five hours have passed since that trouble on the beach, but the count cannot remember if he's killed Jordan or whether, as he knows is the case with his son's pitiful accomplices, he has spared Jordan's life and gouged out the boy's eyes. By the time Count Roger had finally arrived on the beach, he had changed his mind several times, which ended up wrapping both options in the sense of familiarity the count relied on to discern truth from lies.

The muddle develops inside the Count's mind like a weather system gathering strength. He felt the clouds on the horizon of his awareness darken, senses their inky black tendrils stretching to block out the horizon of his mind. No idea of sunlight or imagined candle-flame could halt the steadily approaching front and this time, the Count knew that death meant to swallow him up. All at once, his nerves pulled across his breast like leather straps and his stomach seemed to spread, to snap open into his chest like a sail caught by a furious gust. Slowly, with eyes closed, the Count grips the edge of the table with each hand and sweats while he waits.

He sits at the table of honor in the re-conquered village

The table of honor extends across the length of the piazza. The uneven, misaligned row of tables, workbenches and wooden fish crates have been covered by a patchwork of fabric, a multi-colored insult to the elegant linen that usually graces the tables of royalty. Everything from a fisherman's overalls to the golden-laced velvet tapestries of the church cover the head table, giving Count Roger the impression of sitting behind the corpse of an enormous African snake. The Count digs inside himself and tries to pluck out the root of his unease, but each time he pinches the nub of a cause, it slips back into the murk of his mind, leaving him slightly more conscious of the unusual disturbance spreading like black ink throughout his being.

He starts violently in his chair. The moment he becomes aware of the hand on his shoulder, it has already been withdrawn.

Count Roger hears himself speak. "I must have fallen asleep".

"Not unless your lordship has perfected the art of sleeping with your eyes open," the advisor, Jeremy of Norkington says. This strikes the Count as the perfect description of a dead man.

In all likelihood, the Count is about to be assassinated. Or perhaps he is half murdered already. The sick itch in his bones must be the premonition that comes upon all of the greatest leaders in the moments before the blade slips in between the ribs or the throat swells closed from the poison. But how could he know about such things; how could anyone?

The Count pushes his plate of half-eaten food away to wait for the poison to take effect. Without a word, the Count reaches out for the man on his right, his most trusted advisor, Jeremy of Norkington. Count Roger's fingers close around the man's skinny wrist and the Count senses how easily and precisely, with a single sharp twist, he could break both the present moment and the man's bone.

Jeremy's knife, speared to the hilt with burned and bloody chunks of meat, drops quietly onto the table. Jeremy cautiously turns his face, frozen in a wince of a smile, to the Count. The advisor's watery blue eyes dart back and forth from the Count's grip to his face.

"Do you feel that, the heat?" the Count asks. He pulls Jeremy's arm closer until his hand presses against the Count's throat.

Jeremy has risen partway out of his chair. He makes noises of jovial protest. Like an animal trying to conceal its attempts to break free, Jeremy struggles to keep himself from turning and soliciting help.

"Right there," the Count says, pressing the man's palm against his throat. "Feel how hot it is? Right there. Feel it?"

The advisor nods furiously, and Count Roger drops the man's hand with a grunt of disgust. Jeremy draws his hand back, still nodding, and folds back into his seat. The Count stares out over the piazza and tenderly presses fingertips into his neck. "That's the spot," he says. "Readying itself to receive the arrow." The Count finds that he's disappointed by what will probably be his final words, but expects they'll be sufficient to trigger his end. He moves his hand to his lap and feels his muscles stiffen; he listens for the wind whistle that will precede the tiny sting, barely a pinch, that he'll feel before he falls into total blackness. After the Count is not slain in his seat at the banquet, the King and Queen most in charge of his thought these days, irritation and anger, return to their thrones. He should signal to Jeremy that the spell has passed and the panic subsided, but allowing his advisor to twist and jitter with anxiety gives the count pleasure.

Having concluded that the Count's insanity had passed or had at least sunk back underground, Jeremy dared to make a suggestion. "Perhaps the strain of today's events have taxed and exhausted your lordship. May I suggest that your lordship turns his attention outward, perhaps to focus on the remarkable stage before us? It would better serve your lordship's health I think, to pause the spinning inside the head and attend to the performance that will begin momentarily on the remarkable stage before us."

"A performance given in my honor," Count Roger said without expression.

"Quite right," Jeremy replied.

"And yet no one dares so much as a glance at me. As though I am a pox riddled demon who must be ignored lest I send a pock from my body into their blood."

"In honor and gratitude," Jeremy said.

A short distance away, Count Roger's ship is being readied for the following morning when he will embark on his doomed voyage. Why doomed, the Count wonders. What sickness is it that can seize a man's thoughts instead of his body? He thinks about his son Jordan and wonders if ever there existed a more devastating affliction than the misbehavior of one's own child.

Whether the arrow arrives as expected or as a surprise will not, in the end, affect the result, and this tiny submission relaxes the Count. He surfaces from the black muck of his thoughts, rises from the swamp like crocodile eyes and sees for the first time the details facing him from the beginning.

More than one Messina official has expressed gratitude to Count Roger for his unexpected return and re-conquest of the town, but not one of those men have looked into the count's eyes. The people too, even the children haven't glanced at the Count. But it's not like everyone has forgotten about him, instead it's like they are all remembering not to look at him. Seated in the center of the head table he is flanked on either side by his advisor, several of his best sailors and the unexecuted members of the town administration the Count had appointed.

Regardless of what the people believe, Count Roger is not sorry for whatever he's done. He holds onto this thought as if it were an iron bar. Would he have proceeded to cut the eyes out of those men even if one of them had told him the reason for his son's flagrant and irrational disobedience? Of course. Without a doubt. Even if they had known and even if they had told the truth, the Count would not have spared a single eyeball. This was treason, after all, and was he not already sparing their lives? It was a simple message: betrayal would not be tolerated. It was unlikely that anyone in Messina would soon forget the lesson. And then he'd stood above his son, kneeling on the sand, the sea air around them smelling of blood and carrying the shrieks and groans of the men writing in agony farther down the beach. The son of a whore, but his all the same, and needing every last relation of the royal family as the kingdom grew.

A shadowed figure glides from the darkened wings toward center stage and stops. As more candles and lanterns are lit around the stage, the count sees the profile of a knight in silver armor posing as though for a portrait. Behind him, the painted backdrop of a forest appears by degrees. It takes count Roger a moment to recognize that while the knight is very probably the size of a person, the movements suggests that he is in fact a giant puppet.

The puppet-hero stands in the posture of a conqueror, one foot forward, a hand placed on the hilt of his sheathed sword, chin up. He wears no helmet and his curly black hair rests against his armored shoulders. Traveling up the profile, the Count registers the exaggerated size of the Adam's apple, the severe jut of the protruding chin, and the steep angle of the long nose. These signs, along with the hair and the black mustache, signal that this is no ordinary knight. This is Count Roger of Sicily, the puppet.

A peculiar quiet begins in one area of the piazza and spreads until the silence seems to shriek in the Count's ear; it is the sound of many people holding their breath at the same time. All together and all at once, they audience, including those seated at the Count's table, do not turn to look at the Count. Everyone present seems rooted and resolved not to glance for an instant at the real Count Roger. More and more light confirms the puppet's identity, and no one dares to turn and witness the count's reaction to the puppet. No doubt many are wondering who exactly might die as a result of this insult, if it does indeed turn out to be an insult. There are some, most likely those concealed above, the ones with their hands on the ropes, who have already divided the blame, portioned it out, and they wait, chests tightening, wishing themselves invisible.

Despite his quick victory and the gesture of a grand celebration in his honor, Count Roger doubts he has given the impression of being a man in high spirits. On the contrary, he's been acting like a man who lacks the energy to refuse an invitation to help a farmer clean out a pen swamped with pig excrement, enduring each part of the ceremony with the attitude of a slave who teeters between the fear and desire of being struck dead where he stands.

Risking an outburst or sharp reprimand, Jeremy leans to whisper to the Count. "It is the highest form of flattery and respect. It is a great honor in these parts your lordship, to have one's person immortalized as a Marionette. It is a form of homage, a pledge of allegiance to the royal family."

The sliver knight moves slowly and suspiciously, taking long, exaggerated steps and turning his head from side to side. With a quick hop the puppet count faces the audience and scans the faces as if trying to locate someone in particular. The thick lips are bright red, shiny and slightly turned up at the corners. This mouth along with the eyebrows and the deep grooves etched across the forehead present a malicious visage. The knight blinks and the long eyelashes rest for an instant against the polished pink cheeks.

Despite this so-called honor, Count Roger decides that he's had enough of Messina without having to endure an idiotic presentation of himself as a doll. The Count's departure ought to begin by leaning forward, and then pushing himself back from the table. But he cannot move. The immobility is so complete that even his struggle is not expressed and goes undetected. Fear needles him and sweat surfaces along his hairline: droplets begin to slip down the front of his forehead. Some make it all the way to the tip of his nose. If he panics, he will suffocate to death. He gathers up all of his attention and directs it at the stage. He thinks, this is the highest form of flattery and respect. He thinks, it's the peasant's way of pledging allegiance. He thinks, a moment more and I'll be dead.

The Count Roger puppet swaggers across the stage, as loose-jointed and unsteady as a drunk. He stops and while his feet remain planted, his body moves in circles. After another blink his eyes remain half-closed. The puppet stops moving and slowly bows his head until his chin presses against his chest, in what might be an impression of sleep.

When the marionette jerks to life, pretending to have been woken by a sound, the real Count Roger hears nothing. The puppet's head tilts to the side in the pricked ear imitation of a listening animal. But the puppet's head does not stop tilting and then, perhaps due to a broken string, the puppet's head collapses to the side. A listening pose has transformed into a hanged man's pose, a lolling head on a snapped neck.

The puppet's head has not been properly or thoroughly severed. After several unsuccessful yanks and twists from above, the marionette turns to the audience. The head hangs next to the puppet's knees. One of the hands rises to about where the forehead would be and gives a quick salute. Then the marionette is jerked into the heavens and the curtains close.

Metafiction

The process of the narrative has always privileged one method of communicating and comprehending human experience over any other. Telling stories has been part of human culture, we have been told, from the very beginning. It would not be surprising therefore to understand the narrative as one of the primary ways in which people have sought to organize and understand themselves and their life experiences.

As John Gardner suggests in The Art of Fiction, "Human beings can hardly move without models for their behavior, and from the beginning of time, in all probability, we have known no greater purveyor of models than story-telling" (86).

One might even suggest that the narrative has been the most comfortable way of deriving meaning from our actions and those of others; as we grew familiar with the elements inherent in narrative we began to be able to assume and expect. We categorized personalities and searched out characteristics in order to praise the heroes and condemn the villains. We attached our minds to the increasing tension and suspense, waiting for the climax, the resolution, the moral.

This method of storytelling helped ground our own consciousness. Narration made those boxes available into which we funneled our own personal experiences as well as the information to which we were exposed (…and we place trauma here; disillusionment goes over there, just slip it next to epiphany. Fiction writers have, for a long while, been creating box after box, attempting to fill it with new and exciting things.

Metafiction challenges those narrative components by highlighting the concept of process over the idea of product. Specifically, Metafiction seeks to expose the mechanisms of the narrative: the reader's expectations, character development, plot structure, the form and language used to deliver a story, and finally the writer's role as creator.

By exposing the ways in which these elements worked and the intent with which they were used in the past, Metafiction accomplishes much more than an investigation of the craft or writing. By exploring how and why a story is made, Metafiction helps to reveal the way in which reality is made, the constructions of everyday life such as the role of the father or the rules governing the worker/employer relationship. The consequences of Metafiction expand beyond literature and directly into the way in which we process and comprehend human experience.

Metafiction has problematized the inherent value which was once assigned to the notion of fact and calls into question any conventional understanding of a separate and objective reality. In her book Metafiction, Patricia Waugh details one of the main impacts that Metafiction has had on the world outside the pages of a book:

> ...for metafictional writers the most fundamental assumption is that composing a novel is basically no different than composing or constructing one's 'reality'. Writing itself rather than consciousness becomes the main object of attention. Questioning not only the notion of the novelist as God, through the flaunting of the author's godlike role, but also the authority of consciousness, of the mind, Metafiction established the categorization of the world through the arbitrary system of language. (Waugh 43)

This emphasis on the process of construction, through the unstable system of language, serves to upset the very idea that there can be a clear separation between fact and fiction. Communication and comprehension rely on too many variables and versions of perception to be categorized purely as one or the other; the truth, it seems, comes from a perpetual blend of both the factual and the fictive. In this context, the function of the imagination becomes clear; this state of mind and the processes contained within are particularly suited for precisely this task of combining concepts or ideas into a meaningful whole.

The focus shift from the outcome to the process has led to destabilization in many arenas of human discourse. It has become virtually impossible to know if what we read or see is true or fictive, or both at once, and bit by bit the distinction is losing relevance. If I tell you that I heard or that I read somewhere, in some magazine, maybe Time or Newsweek that thirty eight percent of all fifteen year-olds in America regularly smoke marijuana, what is your response?

Do you immediately sit down at your computer and look up the facts to establish the veracity? Or instead do you check the information against your own perceptions, your own beliefs, and the bits about the topic that you've heard or read or seen or experienced? And maybe the next time you find yourself in a conversation about drugs and teenagers you offer this bit of speculative information, since perhaps it seems reasonable enough to you.

The process, or the burden of decoding the overwhelming amount of information that we are exposed to each day has begun to shift squarely onto the individual whose effort or lack thereof determines what is believable and what is impossible.

The imagination is being called into service more and more often as individuals wade through the waves of information, make their own distinctions and develop their own personal meaning. Understanding the ways in which Metafiction has shaped the act and consequences of storytelling will help identify those ways in which many people through their imagination consciousness have begun decoding and assembling their life experience and establishing their own worth and value and truth in the face of the deterioration, universally speaking, of those very same values.

Metafiction began as a critique of the assumptions and expectations that traditionally accompanied the process of narration. By first drawing attention to the gap between the created artifact and reality and ultimately confusing the two into, for example, the genre known as creative non-fiction or in some cases, journalism, Metafiction began to highlight the implicit biases and ideologies inherent in the Realist's approach.

> Any text that draws the reader's attention to its process of construction by frustrating his or her conventional expectations of meaning and closure problematizes more or less explicitly the ways in which narrative codes—whether 'literary' or 'social'— artificially construct apparently 'real' and imaginary worlds in the terms of particular ideologies while presenting these as transparently 'natural' and 'eternal'. (Waugh 40)

If Metafiction could expose the inner working of fiction and reveal that the Wizard of Oz author was merely a human being with a particular set of desires and sensibilities and filters, then who was supposedly providing us with the true history, the true statistics, the true scientific theories? What if the earth really wasn't the center of the universe?

Because of the crossover success of the idea of constructing reality, the techniques of Metafiction have grown out of their place as a side-show cultural experiment over the past thirty years and into mainstream culture. The genre of creative non-fiction is not the only popular medium to have adopted many of the techniques; the so-called reality television shows mimic Metafiction in their elaborate and self-conscious constructions of what is presented as spontaneous reality.

The techniques of Metafiction, which have been liberally adopted by these genres and others, serve to remind the reader that our reality is a construction, born from the accomplishments and failures of our own imagination and that much, if not all, of the meaning of our experience as human beings is based exclusively in our mind.

Metafiction breaks down the narrative model which relied on the differentiation between fact and fiction. The narrative model, because it seeks to use fiction to show the real and uses the real to create fiction, was also absolutely invested in the idea of truth versus imaginary. Without at least a cursory belief in this distinction the narrative process of comprehending our experience would not have been so popular or so comfortable.

It was important to the success of each, fact and fiction, to be able at any time to identify the difference, to ultimately separate the two. Form is just one example of the impulse to solidify the distinction: a newspaper article did not look the same as a short story. The process of narrative itself did not distinguish between the two; history was told using the narrative model, as was myth and fable. It was important therefore that there be a supreme authority or some sort of objective omniscient editor that could perform the task of sorting one from the other.

Metafiction has unlocked a mode of perception, comprehension, and communication based not on a historical formula and not on the distinction between real and fake, but on the ability of our own imagination consciousness to perceive, develop, and assign meaning to our experience.

Metafiction and You, Dear Reader

One of the first objectives of Metafiction was to expose the expectations of the reader and the process of reading. This exposure resulted not only in a better understanding of narration, but also in the awareness of the inherent expectations we had as human beings in all situations of our experience.

Our understanding of what makes up a story had become so ingrained in our way of understanding that it had become buried, fixed, and perpetually reinforced by our natural preoccupation with the past. The first and most obvious way that this 'fourth wall' (as it was often called by playwrights) was broken was when the author spoke directly to the reader from within the text. John Barth makes it quite clear to whom the narrator is speaking in this story "Life-Story":

> The reader! You, dogged, uninsultable, print-oriented bastard, it's you I'm addressing, who else, from inside this monstrous fiction. You've read me this far, then? Even this far? For what discreditable motive? How is it you don't go to a movie, watch TV, stare at a wall, play tennis with a friend, make amorous advances to the person who comes to your mind when I speak of amorous advances? Can nothing surfeit, saturate you, turn you off? Where's your shame? (Funhouse127)

The reader has now become as much a part of this John Barth story as possible. They've called to mind the television, the idea of tennis and associated knowledge, the concept of amorous advances and associated images, reflections, desires and memories. While John Barth attempts to berate the reader into participation, Italo Calvino applies the opposite technique in If on a winter's night a traveler.

> You are about to begin reading Italo Calvino's new novel, If on a winter's night a traveler. Relax. Concentrate. Dispel every other thought. Let the world around you fade. Best to close the door; the TV is always on in the next room. Tell the others right away, 'No, I don't want to watch TV! (Winter's 3)

This conversation between author and reader has several consequences. The reader can no longer act as a passive voyeur or receptor of information. They are drawn into the story and expected to, on some level, provide the missing elements in order to extract the meaning that had traditionally unfolded before their eyes. Their imaginations have been provoked and their perspectives readied to mesh with what the story has to offer. In many ways this effort reveals the

Metafiction writer's ultimate desire to make their created thing into a living experience.

While the 'Dear Reader' device had been employed by many of the omniscient writers in the past, it had not demanded much from the reader, and had operated more as a narrative guide than as a provoker of thought.

As is characteristic of Metafiction, the overabundance of an element serves to destabilize the traditional arrangement. Over plotting occurs in an attempt to deflate the common power that used to come from the climactic moment. The movie Forrest Gump is one such Metafiction which bounds from one climax to the next, thus defying the traditional story structure. But Metafiction is also quite adept at eliminating expected elements in order to disrupt the narrative. Breaking the form of narrative is another way in which the reader is prodded out of their passive role.

As the boundary between author and reader (and consequently between reality and fiction) becomes more visible, it becomes more and more possible to understand human experience as a narrative, to view reality as a series of narratives made up of history and memory, both of which are stories that require a reader's interpretation. The idea of reality as narrative, the notion that our experience is the ultimate novel from which fiction was created adds a dimension to the way we think about life. John Barth once said that while traditional fiction was said to mimic life, "Metafiction is a novel that mimics a novel." How much more consequential is that statement when viewed from the perspective of life itself as a novel?

This is a quote by Carole Maso taken, as it were, out of its first context and applied here to highlight a point:

> Writing, for me, is a significant human adventure; it is about exploration and investigation and meditation. It's about the search for a legitimate language. It's about the search for beauty and integrity and wholeness. For meaning, where maybe there is none. A work of fiction should be a genuine experience, I think, and not (as it most often is) a record of an experience. (Maso)

The desire to make literature that can exist as a living experience requires, above all, the active engagement of the reader. Without the animation of the reader's mind and the additions that come from their perspective, born from their personal experience, a story exists as words in a book. Only if they can be incorporated into a person can they be said to be part of a true living experience.

Types of Metafiction

<u>Type 1</u>: Make the reader aware they are reading a story by addressing the reader directly as 'you' or, "As you sit there reading these words...." Or by using characters who are aware of themselves as characters in a story.

PURPOSE/MAIN THEME: The meaning of a story depends as much on the reader as on the writer. Make clear the reader's role & participation in the story process. The reader assigns meaning to a story, they interpret stories (decide what he meaning of a story is) based on their own limited perspective and life experience. A story, therefore, cannot contain precisely the same meaning for every reader.

<u>Type 2</u>: Show that a story is a constructed thing, put together from a single point of view to achieve an effect. Raise questions about where characters in stories come from, and how they reveal more about the writer's mindset than about the character being portrayed.

PURPOSE/MAIN THEME: Life vs. Art—which is real and which is made up? By exposing the inner workings of story, the role of each story component becomes more evident and raises the question—do stories actually reflect life or does life reflect story. Plot is a fabricated series of events, created and presented by a writer in order to push their story forward. Life does not contain such clearly crafted and sequential events with meaning. In fact, we often try to fit real life into this model—a major event occurs and we weave a story around it to explain it. So if our understanding of life is organized by story and story is unreliable, our understanding of life is unreliable. Characters also, are much more comprehensible than any real people. But we understand people in the same way as we learn about characters

Type 3: Draw attention to the writer or the teller of the story-question the motivation of the writer/teller—their biases and agenda--

PURPOSE/MAIN THEME: Story can only reveal the storyteller's narrow life perspective, which means that learning any sort of general/objective truth from story is impossible. We can be persuaded to believe one story more than another, but this is due to a trick of language and not due to any actual objective truth. Making something sound objective does not mean that it is objective. The writer has an agenda, wants a reaction, or wants you to think a certain way.

Type 4: Draw attention to the nature and use of language. To show where meaning in language comes from—the reader's job to make word have meaning

PURPOSE/MAIN THEME: When used, Language is being manipulated to achieve a certain effect. We can be persuaded to believe one story more than another, but this is due to a trick of language and not due to any actual objective truth. Making something sound objective does not mean that it is objective. Language can be and is manipulated whenever it is used. I am using it right now to try and persuade you to believe what I am saying. Using the 'correct' words does not refer to being accurate, but to achieving a certain effect.

Type 5: Draw attention to the concept, effect and role of story in life, in the relationship/interaction between the Inner and Outer story.

PURPOSE/MAIN THEME: The way a person reacts to a story can reveal the way a person views life. Much of our behavior comes from models provided by stories we've heard or read or seen. Is there a certain way that college students are supposed to behave? A certain way that a father or mother should be? If we say someone is a good mother, what are we basing this on? Some idea of motherhood that comes from where?

Words Fail

In my study I put my index finger on the floor and then my body floats up, sometimes spins around. This is my answer to the, 'are you in touch with reality' question. Meaning, I am touching it, what else do you expect?

Words fail, of course. In the car I drive and speak to my wife, sitting beside me. We drive in a bathtub it seems, a shower scene because when we stop at a light and I turn to the car next to me, the gentleman looks like, hey man I'm a little busy in my shower here. So I look ahead. All of this intimacy and so I say certain words in order to communicate my good will toward her, my affection.

She responds in accordance, also making familiar sounds, forming words that have lost meaning. As if to say, right back at you. Love.

And we drive on.

So I begin to look instead for secret signals, gestures that I hope can communicate something true, not warped or distorted by hollow words that can no longer be filled up. When we were young I wanted to make up a new word for love, a way to break with the past, since we'd both already used it enough. God knows. And then I thought, why not a new language altogether, our own secret code. But after one usage the words fell like cellophane smeared with mayonnaise. Gave up on language, so it was obvious the next step. Physical signals, what has been termed body language. But the gestures that resemble the familiar have lost meaning, only the secret ones, the unconscious ones matter. You can take those to the bank, or so I thought.

Let us say that she has a laugh, a certain laugh that you are able to withdraw from her, as if with a special trick of the hands, a magic manipulation of the wrist. A note of shock, if you were forced to describe it, a delight in that sound that transmits the knowledge that you have a place inside her body. Somewhere in there, you dwell, you matter and effect. A joyful noise which you alone can elicit, it is a hook into her, a grounding of sorts which maybe count as connection.

And so we say that you hear that laugh, as if a moment had opened up, a hollow in time from which this sound rises and strikes you. In your study you've been busy, distracted, one finger touching the ground, your feet treading on the ceiling. An open book in one hand and you read. But then you hear it, the laugh, and she talks on the phone to an old friend. Your body falls as it does on occasion, a balance has been upset perhaps and with your skin pressing into the floor perhaps you sense the motion of the earth on its axis. Perhaps you don't. In any event you wait.

Do you hear it again, or at least believe that you do? One more time, the sound scurries like so many microscopic mice and under your door and into your ear canals. And you itch because of it. Because of the secret signal, which was not a secret signal after all. It was only a normal signal, a noise that she, as a creature, makes with her vocal chords in response to some stimuli. A regular noise like, "I love you too." Empty for you, and you reel in that hook, which you see was not a hook at all, but more like a lead ball bearing that you must have heaved into her at one point and then forgotten about. Mistaken for a hook after time had passed, when really it just sat in there, sloshing around. You were tricking yourself again you silly goat. Tricks are for rabbits.

But you've heard it twice now, no? Breaking the plane of your concentration. You might not have even noticed it at all; perhaps it would have been better this way. Believing in the hook, in the connection, but you are forced to reel it in under the door and think yourself a silly man for behaving this way, for concerning yourself over the sound from a young woman, whom you amorviate, as you once called it.

Let us not stop there. Let us also say that there is a peculiar look, an arrangement of her facial muscles, completely involuntary, unconscious and so not tainted by plans and intent. A look of adoration you might say, angelic as if in the portraits of the Madonna which you have seen. Holy and beatific that you orchestrate into existence, not unlike a conductor. A secret recipe that you yourself could not write down, which means of course that it is real, that it signifies. You maneuver based on intuition, based on direction provided by impulse and the gods. As if you stood over a caldron on the correct day of the year and stirred with a broken broom handle and happen to look into the pot at precisely the right moment and there it is, her look, the facial muscles stretching the skin in order to show this, this connection you have. This numb mastery over the workings of her blood, and hormonal release. You could not detail it, who could? but you know it and you have seen it appear over the table as you cracked a lobster claw and she held a glass of wine in her hand.

Sure you must often use generic words in the dance of elicitation, fabricated gestures, planned revelation of sentiment. You dance on the court, elbowing what you must, dodging and spinning and then pulling and there it is, coaxed into existence, your reward, your certification. You dwell in her, how else can it be?

And so it appears, the look, slowly coming over her face, not unlike a weather pattern, but you have done no work at all. You sit side by side, and you think as you watch her that perhaps you've grown so expert at the process you can make the look appear just by the pulsing of your blood, through the invisible transmissions of your body heat. But you see that she watches television as she sits next to you and does horror excite your blood? She does not look at you, but at the images, the millions of electrical impulses that make up pictures, that then fabricate drama. And her look is aimed there, at the screen, at the appliance and you do not move for fear of dissolution. A television drama has pulled the look from her, that same look, of this you are certain, more certain that you care to be.

Do you make a list? Do you write down every possible physical signal, every indication that the two of you dwell in one another? Can it be that there is no such thing as dwelling, as hooking into souls, as connecting? But words have already failed, you plead in your study. At least there is this, right? RIGHT?

And do you take out that list every so often and cross off another gesture? A list that already contains phrases and words which you have had to abandon by now. A notebook, really, with pages full of words crossed out. One by one they fall, the gestures, the secret signals, until at dinner you sit over a piece of cooked chicken. Why don't new signals arise to replace the old? Can it be that the infinite pool of gestures has by now, been exhausted, emptied and infected. Only silence reigns now and it has a difficult time confirming anything.

"We never talk anymore," she says. And the sounds of the words, the way in which she holds her fork, they are like lightning flashes and you cannot look, you must close your ears to the thunder.

"I love you," you retaliate. And already you can see through your hand, your arm. Rising out of your seat like a helium balloon. You think, I am connected to nothing.

"I love you too," she says and then she displays what used to be the look, she puts it on her face like make-up. Obviously you must be a television show, you must be a fabricated bit of drama. Put together with blocks of meaning, sewn together with proven ways to elicit emotion. No anchors at all now and your head bangs on the ceiling but she does not notice or does not comment. What could she say after all?

Just a Story

The story begins with you, in bed, relaxed and comfortable and completely unaware that you are about to ruin the rest of your life. With the same careless and subtle inattention that accompanies some of the most catastrophic errors, you are about to slip out of living and into the story of your life. Like the distracted eye that turns away from the road, or the bare foot that lowers onto the slick smear of soap, the time it takes you to make this mistake is nearly immeasurable while the consequences are eternal.

A pillow supports your back against the headboard, and you read a well-paced story. Not a thriller or a romance, not one of the 'I-stayed-up-all-night-and-couldn't-put-it down' varieties. You do not completely disappear into this story; you do not suddenly look up to see that four hours have mysteriously vanished. Instead, you pay just the right amount of attention. Your eyes glide seamlessly from one sentence to the next, and the story develops.

Eventually, you are lulled by the rhythm into a peculiar state of mind, a delicate state of dual-awareness; you are in bed and you are in the story.

To stay aware and in touch with both places at the same time, you must not stop to think, but simply continue to read. This is how you'll make the mistake that ruins the remainder of your life.

You read—

"The dying college president heard the hinges of his bedroom door groan open, and the fresh white pillow materialized like a featureless ghost, hovering in the threshold. The pillow hesitated for a moment, as if steeling itself before pushing into the bedroom air that had, at some point, begun to feel like part of the president's decaying body, as drained and dry as his deflated hairless legs. When the pillow finally crept toward President Marshall, he might have been dying in his bed for twelve days or twelve years.

"Moments of disorientation were nothing new, but the pillow's sudden appearance cut the president's last tether and set him rotating like an impotent astronaut. In a single instant, the levitating pillow had demolished the president's daily routine and in so doing, the pillow had also highlighted the intensity of his reliance on a daily routine.

"Linens were not changed in the middle of the night, but now he could no longer be sure that is was the middle of the night. It seemed like it ought to have been. Perhaps he had forgotten that he'd vomited onto his current pillow or maybe there was daylight that he could no longer see. The unsettling appearance of the pillow eased the president as close to the physical world of his bedroom as he'd been in a long while. He felt a black and white spray of fear settle on his face like mist from a shower scene; he noticed the moist heat on his skin and knew that the sweat had, at some point, become his normal state of being. He was both intrigued and horrified by the sensation and the knowledge. President Marshall lay in bed with his right cheek pressed to his pillow; he stared in the direction of the open door and saw the ghost advance. The president could not turn away."

While you read, part of your mind notices the heat in your bedroom and it responds by imagining the cool night far above your own head. A white spark falls across the dark sky and disappears.

"But what could President Marshall do about time? He constantly slipped in and out of his bedroom life; lately, more out than in, and only peripherally aware of his body's ongoing erosion. Decades ago, it seemed, he'd lost the ability to speak in any meaningful way. President Marshall had spent much of the time living inside memories of himself and his life experiences; only occasionally stopping by to visit, what felt to him like, the memory in which he lay dying in his bed. Words no longer made much sense to the President; he'd begun to think of them as fairies, and he could no longer understand what they wanted from him.

"Perhaps they were simply gathering in his room, around his

bed, waiting until there were enough of them to take him away. One afternoon he suggested this to his son Peter.

'Urp ung aul,' the President had said.

'Save your strength,' his son had replied. "You don't need to speak. There is nothing left to say.'" This flurry of fairies swarmed around the President's face, so that he'd had to close his eyes and let his head fall away."

When your own grandmother was dying, she couldn't speak at all by the time they moved her to the hospice. You had never been to a hospice before, and you learned that it was a facility that provided the amenities and atmosphere of a hotel for the family members; maybe as a type of shield against the drooling ugliness and unnatural muscle contraction of dying. You remember that the foyer and hallways smelled like bacon, and you wondered what gave these hospice workers the right to make bacon; the smell of salted and smoked flesh seemed beyond inappropriate, almost evil.

You did not really know the dying old woman; she was not the type of grandmother who lived nearby, who you saw every week for Sunday dinner, and so you didn't really form any sort of emotional attachment to her. So it surprises everyone, yourself included, when you find yourself sitting in the front passenger seat of a car, sobbing all the way to the cemetery. You cry uncontrollably, with a fist in your mouth, trying to control the shudders. Your silent and solemn cousins must be wondering what the hell is wrong with you. Especially since each one of them had a much closer connection to the dead woman. And when the oldest cousin puts a hand on your shoulder and causes you to cry even harder, you feel the need to explain. You manage to say, "So sad."

But they cannot know what you mean. You are not crying for this dead old lady, whose passing was as far from tragic as a death can be. You are trembling and crying because all of you are trapped inside this story. This is not an 'everyone will die' revelation, but more an understanding that her death is the best-case scenario, the best possible outcome. If all goes well, perfectly and without surprise or accident, each person standing near you, staring up at the dead woman's particular shelf coffin, will die just like this. This is victory, the first place finish, the death that we should all desire.

There is no better way out.

In bed, still reading the story, the undercurrent of your thoughts rolls on and you review the scorecard: you and your wife each have a grandparent on deck in the dying circle, including a ninety-seven year-old grandmother who, when she hears that she has outlived another person, probably leans out of her nursing home window and shakes her blue-veined fist at death. Maybe she yells, "Bring it on, you cowardly bully!" For her, death has occurred out of order too many times to count.

Chronologically, you wife's parents should die before your own parents, and by then, all of your uncles and aunts should be dead. This is the plan if all goes well, that is, if nothing extraordinary happens. If your wife doesn't miscarry and your young son doesn't slip off of the diving board and drown. If you don't start drinking again and this time, manage to swallow the entire three-month supply of sleeping pills.

If all goes well, perfectly, death will happen in natural order. The new baby shouldn't die in her crib, for example. But nothing ever goes perfectly. None of this is explicit; none of this projects onto the screen of your consciousness as you read.

"At the moment that the pillow appeared, hovering like a sentient being just out of reach, advancing slowly toward President Marshall's immediate future, he knew what was happening.

"Moments of clarity were unpredictable, and they were not much to his liking. Despite a desire to be confused, he recognized the pillow for what it was, and he also knew the identity of the blurry figure carrying the pillow toward him. He tried to scramble back onto the platform of uncertainty, but it had vanished.

"It should have been one of the home health nurses who had rotated in and out of the presidential villa. It should have been Kara or Tara or Maura or Laura, and she should have been coming to replace the soggy excuse for head and neck support that lay under his head like a deflated and smelly balloon. It should have been, yes, but it wasn't.

"President Marshall knew that the pillow carrier was his son Peter. And he knew that the pillow was not meant to rest under the back of his head, but on top of his face.

"Had the President retained the motor skills or even perhaps the desire, he might have made a noise, he might have called out

no matter how garbled and unintelligible he would have
sounded—no matter how unprofessional the gurgle might've
sounded coming from this once distinguished leader of the
community. Embarrassment aside, it would have been enough
of a noise to summon the sleeping night nurse, (surely someone
was still being paid to watch over him?) but instead he made no
effort at all. President Marshall lay in bed, seventy three years
old and dying, while the pillow fairy eased solemnly through the
air toward him, becoming brighter and whiter than anything
the President had ever seen."

Part of your mind leaks out of your skull and ascends through the
bedroom ceiling and into the cool night sky. The peculiar sensation has
developed slowly, beneath the radar, but then all at once, the book-
world has achieved equal footing with your world, but not in any
hallucinatory or fantastical way. You do not shrink and fall into the
pages and find yourself sitting at a tea party or suddenly find yourself in
a forest clearing astride a white horse with a sword in your hand.
Instead, the weight disappears.

Your hands dissolve and your head no longer rests on a pillow. As
if you are supported by angels, you rise into the sky and look down on
humanity; you observe the human race from a distance. You view both
stories with this semi-detachment, yours and the old man's, as if each
one belongs to the world of make-believe.

"Would this moment never end?

"The shining black smear above the floating pillow might
have been the rich and luxurious center of the spirit world,
casting out this pillow fairy to be his guide into the next life.
But it was not. The slick blackness was the oiled hair of his
only son Peter, and of that the president was unhappily certain.
This was no exchange of linens, but a surrender of spirit, or
even grittier than that.

"The pillow hesitated in the air, perhaps somewhat shocked at
the president's quiet posture. After all, the president's eyes were
open, his head resting on one cheek, and he stared directly in
the pillow's general area. President Marshall had not been a
quiet and complacent man by nature—he had been a fighter,
and the nurses had repeated this at the beginning, a real bear of

a man whose strength of will and brilliant vision for the future would see him through to recovery. He was still a young man, they'd said, still had so much to offer the community.

"But they were paid, his son had remarked more than once, to kiss his ass. At the moment of the pillow's appearance President Marshall was no longer a bear; he weighed less than ninety pounds and his outer skin shed so frequently that a special dustpan had been placed at the foot of his bed."

You empathize with the old character, the fumbling human who trips and bumbles and skids into death and you think that it is a shame that these humans are so obviously doomed. One way or another. Wouldn't it be awful to be one of them?

As a watcher, you feel weary and sad, but in the same way that a person might switch off a depressing movie, or click away the disastrous evening news, you experience a moment of opportunity, an instant of choice. Closing this book will shut out this old man and his tiny human world of mistakes and emotional harm. You can turn away from this world and get some rest, no longer burdened by the line of family members waiting to die in chronological order. No longer waiting your turn.

You're so relieved to know that you will not have to die or watch others die or hear your daughter's gargled scream coming from the river. As you walked or sprinted or slid into death, it would be awful to reflect on your failures and review your empty goals, your volumes of wasted time. You taste the old man's unrequited life like bitter almonds on your tongue. And you are overcome with relief.

You peer down, an observer—you are sad for them, the humans, in the same way you might've been sad for the red ants when their hill was doused with gasoline and set on fire with a single match. Watching them scurry and burn, you felt a little sad, but mostly you were grateful not to be one of them.

"The fabric of the clean pillowcase slowly covered President Marshall's face, falling like individual snowflakes across the bridge of his nose and then his cheeks, his chin. The cool cloth seemed to enshroud his entire head. The gentle touch would only gradually increase in pressure, eventually, and the sensation at first would not prove to be at all savagely painful or grotesque.

"Somewhere in the president's mind, large white swans flicked across a black pond."

It is only a story. How had you been so foolish as to take the stories seriously? This is the thought that hangs like a banner behind everything else in your mind. At the moment, you are not consciously tricking yourself. You are not consciously doing anything. The fact of the moment is that you are free to close the book, turn off the light and disappear.

These poor humans in the story, on the other hand, are doomed to live out their destiny. They are forced to watch their mothers and fathers contract cancer and wither away; fated to stand in the cold night air, bare feet pressed to the gravel, watching their house burn to the ground.

There is only one way out of their life. And they must go through it. No matter what.

Young daughters become pregnant and uncles shoot themselves in the head, and these human people must endure or take matters into their own hands. Either way it's not a pleasant situation.

You shiver for these humans, these characters in the story. You pity them.

This book-closing decision is not imaginary; it is not make-believe. You do not think wouldn't it be nice if I could just shut this book...No, such is your state of mind that your freedom, your epiphany, is as real and as inescapable as gravity: it is only a story.

With one simple motion you'll be able to turn away from this putrid world and sink into your pillow-world of eternal safety. Once you close the book, the story is over. You are swimming in the relief, embracing the sudden knowledge that you no longer have a long way to go. You are not trapped in the story, you are not fated; you are not destined to experience any of this human misery. How had you missed this realization for so long? Why had you believed yourself to be one of them? Reality has re-arranged itself, as your eyes have been moving along the words, and it is clear to you, beyond doubt, that they are both just stories. Being human is only a story; it is only make-believe. And thank god for that.

A vaguely familiar fear quiets and you enjoy a particular sensation, an exhausted elation, as if you'd remembered your back-up parachute just in time. Pull the cord, shut the book, and you are no longer afraid. You will not have to do your time. It will be okay after all.

This all happens in a single, elongated instant—a century wrapped in a second. You hold safety in your hands. You are about to escape. And you finish reading with a light heart, wrapped in a safety that must have slipped your mind. It is only a story, you think, and as your eyes move over the words, the first itch of the impending catastrophe makes its presence known. Somewhere far away, you sense the unpleasant tang of something not quite right, waiting for you. Your only clue is a thought that flashes too quickly to be understood, like the flare of red neon just before the sign goes black. You are left only with a single question, which is the story? The answer waits for you to finish and you read on:

"President Marshall knew that at one time he would have been able to explain his son's action. There was a process by which he could surround moments with words and assign meaning to a situation. He'd done it all the time, but now he could not even recall the first step. It seemed bizarre to the President now, this impulse to pad words around a moment; had it ever really worked? Words as thin and as transparent as fairies, zipping around an action; what could they ever have possibly accomplished? Moments simply happened, like this one, and no wheelbarrow full of words could do anything about it.

"This was the idea that occurred to President Marshall as he smelled his son's cologne—a sweet mixture of pine and rose. And it was this truth that prompted him, at long last, to cry out into the fabric that at first settled gently on the tip of his nose. Not in order to save his life, but to make an argument against words. You see, he would say to his son, there is nothing that can be said; there is no need for framing or posturing with babble. Already I'm beginning to loosen inside my skin like a foot inside a snow boot, ready to slip off.

"Just then, President Marshall felt his body, against his wishes, begin to resist the pillow.

"It was a sad fraction of an instant and President Marshall attempted to calm his body, to send signals through his nerve endings into his skin and physically convince himself to succumb. This was the best ending he could have hoped for, and he worried that it would slip away. He moved suddenly, raising one hand to his face where he felt his son's hand gripping into the pillow. The warmth from Peter's hand felt like his own, as if he'd touched his own skin. The action must have startled Peter and for a fraction of a moment, the pillow-pressure on his face relaxed. No, the old man thought, and he might even have made a sound—but the only fear rising in his heart at that precise moment was that his son or the pillow would fail to finish the story and retreat prematurely into the blurry corners of his bedroom."

Maybe it's a fruit fly that bobs drunkenly in front of your eyes. Or the heat that comes on with the crackle of metal or the refrigerator's compressor that clunks to life in the kitchen. Perhaps your pregnant wife gets up to go to the bathroom.

Whatever the specific cause, in a single breath, you have fallen back into your head. Your hands shake as you close the book and lay it on your chest.

Fear ignites each cell of your body and your skin flushes with fever heat. You peel away the blanket and the bed sheet. You feel the sweat soaking into the pillow behind your neck. Your heartbeat pounds like a sprinter in your ears. In one instant you understand that there is no parachute, let alone a backup.

The heat inside your chest moves up, tightening the back of your throat, and burning behind the bridge of your nose; your eyes fill with tears. You open your mouth wide and struggle to catch your breath. A mantra from childhood repeats in your mind, It's not real, It's make believe, It's not real, It's make believe. Instead of cooling your fear, the words feed the furnace. Your story was not real. Your ability to escape was make-believe, just a tiny bit of impromptu fiction put together in your imagination. Terror sinks deeper into you like a black cat settling into a favorite cushion.

Even though your lamp is still on you are powerfully and uncontrollably afraid of the dark. You blink hot tears down the sides of your face and they pool in the hollow of your throat. You are so goddamn scared that your stomach churns and juices with anxiety, but you are unable to move.

"Enough of this nonsense." You say this out loud to break out of your paralysis and put this childish sensation in its place. You have to work in the morning. You turn to look at the clock on the bedside table; if you fall asleep immediately, you can get a solid five hours. You lean to place the book on the nightstand and click off the lamp. You stretch your arms and legs; you shrug your shoulders, and tilt your head from side to side.

You settle into bed, on your back, and after a few moments, you place one palm on your chest and take a deep, shaky breath, but your body won't relax. Your muscles are tensed to run and your heart gallops in your ears.

The story ends with you in the dark, on your back and sweating in bed. You stare wide-eyed at the ceiling; tears rise like a tide and overflow down your cheeks.

There is nothing you can do.

The Writer's Struggle

I walk down Main Street one afternoon dressed like a bum. Details like torn flannel shirt, scraggly brown beard, curly brown hair (unkempt), cigarette in my mouth. I squint into my palm and write in a small notepad.

A tuxedoed fat man with a gray goatee and a top hat strolls to a stop; a buxom young woman hangs on his arm. He grips the hook of a polished mahogany cane and looks me over. The woman (probably about my age) could be, but clearly is not, his daughter. A diamond tiara glitters on her ocean of blond hair. An emerald choker attaches her head to her body. She wears an ivory Cinderella ball gown, fringed with lace.

"I say, my word," the man says. "Look dear, what have we here? My, my, a real struggling writer—a live one indeed." He lifts his cane and prods my side with the fat rubber tip.

The woman stiffens, smiles, and pulls herself closer to her father-like date.

The man reaches into his breast pocket and withdraws a dollar bill, pinched in between his fat thumb and forefinger. "You there," he calls to me. "I say, my good boy—do me a favor and struggle a little for the lady."

"Honestly, Harold," the woman says.

He looks at her and strokes her hand. He stares at her, a little too long, and says, "Isn't she precious?" He turns and aims his shiny black stare at me. "What do you say, a little struggle on this fine day?" He waves the dollar bill. I could lunge forward and grab it with my teeth.

His date watches me intently; her eyes widen, her red lips part, her choker bobs once when she swallows. "Do you think he's drunk?" she asks in a false whisper.

"Come now my good man, that's the way," the man says and he bends a little at the knee, dangling the money off to the side, showing me, persuading me.

I collapse onto the ground. I roll on the sidewalk with my tongue out of my mouth. I groan and gag and spit onto my chin. I flail over the curb and onto the street. My shins slam against the back tires of a parked car. I growl at the air and pretend to weep. It actually feels kind of good, this writhing, this fake crying. I scrape my chin squirming back onto the cement.

I barely hear them as they walk away.

The struggle doesn't end, but after a while, I roll over and pick up the money. I sit for a long time with my back against a brick building, the dollar crushed in my hand. My body shudders while I watch the people pass by.

I see my notepad under the parked car.

The fake crying goes on and on.

Behold This Man

In a small garden villa on the coast of Italy, a young man and young woman stand naked and face each other. Her dark hair down the sides of her cheeks and over her shoulders, the curly tips like seaweed pressed against her skin. Freckled chest, nipples red and tender and stiff, a tiny egg traveling down into her uterus and pausing, perfect hips and clean shaven legs.

Always sunny on this coast of the world, always-blue skies, actual blue water layered down into the deep.

His shoulders wide, stomach bloated. They have just eaten a midday meal that lasted for five hours. He gags into his mouth, swallows, and goes to brush his teeth. His butt cheeks chill while he bends over the sink because even though it is always sunny, their villa is composed mostly of cool stone and cotton sheets and cottage style windows.

This is cinematic.

When he returns from the bathroom, she puts her arms around his neck and strokes his hair. She says, "I want you to make love to me like never before." She says it softly since neither of them can breathe too well, having just stuffed their stomachs with fish in a red sauce, bread and wine.

Her fingers, slender and strong, eventually work him into somewhat of a lather and lead him onto the bed.

"No pressure, no pressure," he whispers. He places the knuckles of one hand on his forehead and lies on his back, eyes closed. He groans.

Neither one mounts the other-- no one gets off or gets themselves off. No sweaty climax. They sleep separately on the bed and their palms touch.

Outside the villa a stone path leads down through gardens of flowers, lemon trees, and olive groves. Down to the lava rock beach that ends abruptly with cliffs and a fifty-foot drop to the ocean. A crater blanket of lava, a dead moon's surface that rolls and slopes like a petrified ocean.

The young woman walks ahead wearing her light blue bikini and a pair of brown hiking boots. The young man carries towels from the villa folded on one arm and pauses to yell after her. The wind mixes his words, steals them, but his tone is clear. He wants to marry her and he wants never to see her again.

White birds share their crusty beach. Jumpy white birds that fly and circle and land and peck over and over while the young man tries to get it off his chest, tries to lay it on the line, take a stand, get to the point-- here on the lava. He thinks, when I see her face I'll know.

She turns and squints. She shouts, "What?" Raises her hands to shield the sun.

He pauses and wonders if it's supposed to be like this. The warm wind whips her hair and a dark strand sticks to the corner of her mouth.

"What?" She shouts again.

It's a good possibility that she is *it*, that if there is an *it* she could very well be *it*. The two of them, the *it* of eternal promise-- togetherness. Why not?

And now facing each other again, holding hands, with a sore on his lip and a pimple on her forehead. Sleepy genitals. Stomachs digest the best they can under the circumstances and blood pumps although there is no visible proof of this at the moment. He asks, "Will you marry me?" He tosses his head to move hair that is not in his face, to do something.

At first her face brightens-- then dims. She says, "You're practicing, right? You look around at the blue ocean and the birds and the lava beach, here on the coast of Italy and you think why not? You picture my legs, you see me straddling you and you think this must be as good as any, as real as it gets. Here with everything besides cameras and directors and with me who loves your lips and you ask me, for practice, to marry you? Is that it?"

He nods and tries to maintain his composure. As if it weren't for his skin, he'd pour out onto the rock.

"Well then, for practice, I say yes. Yes I will marry you and now we have the moment. Now the scene is complete. The time you proposed to the pretty girl on the Italian coast, the time I got engaged standing on cold lava rock. Yes, now we have it and now we have instant visions of Christmas. Together with my family, all of us gathered by the fireplace, sipping wine and eating cheese cubes. The men dressed in sweaters and slacks, shiny black dress shoes. Darling cousins with bows in their hair. We have a mountain of well- wrapped gifts and a lush tree and a family argument about tinsel, about whose turn it is to put the angel on top."

They kiss. Eventually they guide themselves onto the lava and maneuver on their sides. They pull away dry swimsuits and scrape their skin. They bleed onto the rock, imprinting the moment beneath their flesh. They press deep, urging cells to group together and multiply inside the woman's womb.

                                        *

In the Laundromat the slow whine of airplane take-off rises from the new washers, the more expensive ones. Our clothes occupy the older models; the ones that thump and shudder like motel room sex. All around me the sounds of water, pipes filling and draining, shooting like tiny fire hydrants, springing leaks. An orange light goes on above the words *UNBALANCED SIGNAL* and I must sit on one of my machines to close the lid enough and satisfy the washer. I feel a horse's body, the way it grooved beneath a leather saddle just moments before he tossed me into the dirt.

I remember being bucked off one December at the age of seven but my mother says I just leaned to the side and slid off like a cartoon. Either way, the *UNBALANCED SIGNAL* has gone dark and I've achieved *MACHINE IN USE* satisfaction.

Santa Claus, dressed in a gray tee shirt and sweatpants, walks over to me and stands looking into a nearby dryer. He says, "Electric." He strokes his long beard and shakes his balding head, white hair carefully combed over his pink dome. "Horribly inefficient." His reading glasses have slid part way down the bridge of his nose. "Machines probably before the war," he says.

I nod like he's not joking, like he's really telling it like it is.

My clothes spin under me. Across the street there is a gym behind large glass windows. A young man with his legs outlined in black spandex climbs a simulated rock wall. The rocks come down from the ceiling and disappear beneath the climber's feet. His perfect butt muscles flex three feet above the ground.

"Going home for the holidays?" Santa asks.

"My wife's family," I say. "How about you?" I wink. I can't believe I actually wink at Santa Claus.

"Work," he says. "If I ever get out of here." He wipes his brow with a folded handkerchief. "Damned inefficient."

Now a woman takes her turn in the gym, climbing the wall. She chooses particular rocks and lets others pass by. Legs of muscle. Butt of steel.

"My wife is pregnant," I say. I guess Santa is sort of like God that way, inspiring. I mean if you had something to tell, he probably has a list or already knows or something like that.

Santa asks, "Boy or girl?"

"Doesn't matter to me," I say. "Just as long as he has 10 Caucasian heterosexual male fingers and 10 Caucasian heterosexual male toes." Again, I wink.

Santa shrugs. He says, "Could be here all day."

When I stand *MACHINE IN USE* continues and I am free to stretch my legs. It sounds as though my machine may be filling with water for the third time. I stretch my calves. It really wasn't anything like that bucking bronco I rode.

Santa pulls his clothes out of the dryer and sighs. He folds his pants and slides his collared shirts onto wooden hangers. He stuffs black socks, wide underwear and towels into a fishnet bag that expands. He hauls the bag over his shoulder and nods. He says, "Good luck."

"Good luck Santa," I say.

He turns and walks away. He limps a little and pushes through the glass door, pausing to watch the rock climber across the street. Sweat down the perfect bare back.

At midnight mass on Christmas Eve I fall in love with a young man. *I could kiss him*, I think, *without a thought*. I want to kiss him and I picture him naked without hesitation. I would have to say that as we sing Christmas carols before mass begins I am technically a homosexual. A homosexual standing next to his pregnant wife and just a few feet away from his in-laws.

The young man stands with his girlfriend or sister or whoever in the pew behind me and at one point I glance over my shoulder, catch his eye. I pour meaning into that glance because we are saying prayers that I don't particularly care to indulge in at the moment. I infuse that glance with all sorts of sexual positions and assumed secret desires while the prayers remind us of our sinfulness. The prayers call out for guidance from a God that dwells above this church steeple. I want to point out that I am God, as is my wife, and the young man in the pew behind me. The singing begins again.

I spot Mrs. Claus in the next pew over with her face made up to look whiter than flesh and her red lipstick. Powder white hair and reading glasses. For an older lady she sings with power, and closes her eyes every so often to shake her head.

There is a part of mass that I know well, but on this night it presents itself to me in a completely different light. It appears on this night as a once in a lifetime opportunity, when usually it is only about praying for the suffering, the poor, the ill. I can't say what causes me to stand, but I believe Mrs. Claus winks at me and nods her head as if to say, yes, it's your turn. I am aware of my state of mind, but somehow that doesn't seem central. My wife grips my arm when I stand, but I free myself and move down the pew toward the center aisle. My in-laws must think that I am going downstairs to pee.

I was married in this church some months ago, but no memory surfaces to halt my steps toward the microphone. When I reach the altar I step up to the podium as the woman finishes praying for peace in the New Year. I begin.

"I am God," I say. People generally sink and squirm into tight balls with red faces that turn from person to person, looking for my leash. "You are all God," I say and this forces one of the more dignified men to stand. Then another one stands, dressed in a suit. I can tell they are not following my particular line of logic.

"Our eternal life is happening now. In here," I point to my chest, "is the kingdom of God."

The men have moved up toward the altar and look at the priest for a signal. This has become a military maneuver, an overthrow at the church podium and they almost crouch when the priest signals them to wait. This man may not be harmful, the priest's gesture seems to say, we can wait him out.

I hope he is right.

"Our paradise is sorrow," I say. "And joy, and buying groceries, and falling down, and dying, being born. It is not what we want, but it is everything that happens."

People are waiting for me to finish and return to my seat. In fact, I am waiting for the same thing as I hear my words through the speakers.

"I stand before you at this moment as a homosexual with a pregnant wife. In the next moment I may be a heterosexual carpenter, an animal, an exterminator. Eternal life flows through me because I am God as you are God."

After I said the word *homosexual* the men began to nod at me as they stepped forward, coaxing me with gestures but not with their eyes. I finished speaking and they escorted me down the center aisle. No one had come to meet me at the back of the church so I walked out the double doors and made my way to the in-law's house in the cold.

There is a photograph at my in-law's house. A family portrait taken two days after my wife's high school classmate shot his girlfriend and himself in the head on Christmas day. She says she was sick to her stomach while she stood in the simulated forest setting and posed. I guess people do thing like that, plan and pose and smile even if they don't want to. People always do things.

Something is getting into me on Christmas day. A nameless sensation, perhaps a type of seasonal disorder suffocation and I gulp three well-mixed holiday drinks with my eyes closed.

I stand alone on the front lawn of the in-law's house.

Inside the house Christmas continues in the right way. Well-dressed clean people cut pie with the sides of silver forks. Buttery crusts dissolve on tongues. Brains are touched by liquor, as are words, and fire reflects off polished dress shoes. General words are spoken and drift above the people, pressing down like a fog.

When I scream, my eyes shut tight, I hear a patch of blue sky rip open and fall to the grass, steaming before me.

When they come outside I am on my knees, eyes closed, and my hand grips the dessert fork handle. The prongs are buried halfway into my left breast. Blood seeps into the shirt cloth around the puncture and I remember a small piazza in the town on the coast of Italy.

I remember the post-engagement dawn, kneeling on cobblestones in my swimsuit. Sunlight brightens the sky to the sounds of a scraping broom. The fountain water rains behind me, tickling itself in the basin.

A beggar's feet walk in front of me, torn brown boots, callused skin streaked with grease. Everything swollen and misplaced. Then a plastic garbage bag, black, dragging over each stone. A laugh. Somewhere the sun and I hear and taste and see my breath, the air. There is nothing else.

"What has gotten into you?"

"There is nothing else," I say on the lawn. A hand on my shoulder and I'm sure it's my wife. Quiet on the lawn, a Christmas quiet. Death and birth locked in one second of stillness. "There is nothing else," I say again. My breast throbs. Only this.

Be Good

Jenna's father drove her to the airport. She was on her way to study in Rome.

"Be good," he said.

Jenna will meet the Italian policeman at the Trevi Fountain. He'll take a picture of her throwing a coin over her shoulder.

"Be good," he said by which her father meant, *"I know those men. You better not find yourself buzzed from a few glasses of red wine, riding in the passenger seat of an Italian man's police car in the middle of the night, driving up some dark road and expect it to end well."*

Jenna will sit in the policeman's passenger seat. When the police car stops, she will not recognize where they are—somewhere outside the city.

"Be good," as if her father meant to say, *"Don't move into the backseat, even if that's where he keeps champagne, or flowers, or whatever other weapons he's brought. All I ever wanted was pussy. I'm part-Italian. I brought pills and vodka—to slip those panties to the side, just for a second."*

And he'll be on her, in the backseat: the nice Italian police officer with the stiff black hair and generous smell. Perfumed dress shirts. Smooth dimpled chin and black eyes, greedy eyes. Thin lips that'll suddenly swell when she begins feeling his tongue.

"Be good," by which her father intended to mean, *"I don't care if he hands you a copy of his AIDS' test, if he's circled the numbers and words and he's smiling at you with a fistful of rubbers like this should close the deal. There is no deal. Nothing is exchanged—there are no bargains, no gains. You can't expect to turn back now."*

And the nice Italian police officer will move his expressive hands, his artist's hands with thin fingers that wander, that grip her shoulders and set her firmly in place; hands that will soon slip and claw with sweat.

"Be good," her father said as if to warn her; *"Don't let yourself become a project that he finishes, a chore that he squares away before he begins another part of his life. I'm part Italian. I've completed my share of girls, nailed them to the wall, fixed them in place so that I could get my bearings, so that I could find my way and move on to something else. He's lost, we're all lost."*

A drop of Italian sweat will fall onto her cheek. He'll be inside of her and then, a quiet slow-motion moment. Before any emotion matures, before her brain collects the details and meaning arrives on the scene, a flicker eases gently into her mind, a thought passes. Her eyelids close—half a blink.

"Be good," her father had said and after a long silence he added, "And don't forget to write."

They'll fuck and just like the reader who suddenly thinks, *I do not need to be reading this*, Jenna's eyelids will open and she'll think, as she swallows tongue, she'll think: *This does not need to be happening.*

But by then the story will be over.

The End

Once upon a time Snow White rode to campus on a skateboard, her bra strap showing, sunglasses on. In mere moments she found herself pressing into a dark corner with Prince Charming. When his hands flattened on the brick wall behind him, Snow White saw the glint of his gold wedding band. But they were beyond that, the two of them. They were not creatures of the earth, not bound by the rules of gravity, of molecular composition, of matrimony. What could hold them down?

They were supremely connected, each allowed to probe into the other, to experience the brilliance of intimacy, the sheer power of falling into another person. And without articulation, without ruining everything with words, they maneuvered like private shadows in the dark corner. Snow White saw herself kneeling before Prince Charming, with his face unclear in her mind except his eyes. The color of Alaskan blue ice, the texture of a rose petal, round and perfect.

What could be said? The cosmos had smashed them together and so they sat next to one another at a séance. Body heat radiating from their thighs, exchanging themselves through their shared skin, and agitating their minds. They trembled for no reason and Snow White showed the other guests her quivering hand. The two of them existed in the presence of the impossible, the miraculous. On the way home after the party, traveling down a dark road, they pulled far off to the side. Nothing to say, how impossible to express. Snow White straddled the driver. Prince Charming's warm hands moved beneath her dress and up her body to communicate with her breasts. Heavy breath, sweet breath, fogged the windshield. Rain tapped all around and the front seat lowered back, as far back as it went. They were delivered unto one another.

So it happens that Snow White would not die from her desire to consume and be consumed by Prince Charming after all. The spell had broken and she sat in a bathtub of water turned cold. A coffee mug of urine sat in the sink with a pregnancy stick showing baby. In the garbage, three other sticks had shown baby as well. At that moment no little worker elves had ever existed nor any such bird that helped string up laundry on the clothesline. Prince Charming occurred to her as a simple man, not to say unattractive, but simply a man like any other. A slight headache accompanied that moment and her eyes burned. "The Fever," as she once called it, had run its course, presumably having burned up the contagion which she once called "Love." Even the episodes with Prince Charming seemed to dissipate into the air around Snow White's head. Becoming steam-like images clear enough in tone, but visually hopeless.

What's more, Snow White tried to believe that everything would still come up roses. She had finally descended from cloud nine and at that very moment, through the most remote regions of her complex being, Snow White moved on with her life. Decisions were being made, plans formulated, perhaps even, lessons learned about what she never called an "Affair." Snow White raised both hands and felt her waterlogged fingertips press against her face. Sadness treaded through her body, peaking like labor pains in her chest, and yet she thought to herself, only roses for me, only roses.

Then there was telekinetic hopeful, Prince Charming. He sat at a wooden table across town eating forkfuls of egg burrito with fresh tomato salsa. He drank beer. More often than not he practiced moving the world with imagined mental powers. With his eyes closed and a quick flick of the wrist, he attempted to wave doors shut or float beer bottles to his mouth. Precisely nothing happened. He wanted to dissolve himself into particles of light and pour into Snow White.

Not exactly your typical Prince Charming, he didn't even have a horse.

He rode to town on a tiny stunt dirt bike, his low-rider bicycle-- hands perched on handlebars at his eye level. He wore a baseball cap backward. On a street corner he gripped the handlebars and swung the bike around and around beneath him, jumping over it like rope. He rode onto campus tilted onto the rear tire. Prince Charming stopped in front of the university library, locked his bike and re-oriented the world to his height. He was five foot six inches tall and for him, at that moment, everything was Snow White.

The way information is anymore who knows what really happened, but while reading in the library Prince Charming suddenly had the impulse to see Snow White. A usual enough occurrence considering their psychic connection. While he gathered his books, Prince Charming reviewed his situation as he had done so many times before. He rented a house in a nice neighborhood with a brown-haired young woman for whom he had certain feelings, a woman whom his parents adored and to whom he had often made love. Enough love so that he found himself in a marriage ceremony not so long ago, enjoying each moment and committing it to memory. But now he had a promising career as a professional bicycle trickster, magician, superhero,..and on and on. Everything seemed possible to Prince Charming, especially being with Snow White, and especially happily ever after.

But today when he stepped into the sunshine and unlocked his bike to go see Snow White, the tone of the world had suddenly changed. Instead, the sun shone like florescent light, smacking off the sharp corners of his bicycle, his hands felt sticky, and the air seemed conditioned. Something was changing and he knew he must ride immediately to her house. He put his hand to his forehead, and felt only the barest warmth. He feared that what they called their "Fever" was receding.

What were once called "gods," Snow White liked to call "Readers" since all along it seemed they'd scanned her life for imperfections, for character flaws that would inevitably lead to her spectacular demise, her narrative unraveling like a failed rocket launch. And if the Readers had heard any of this out loud they might appear and look her straight in the eyes and say, "What? You do some guy in a car, get pregnant and that's it?" Which is not enough for the Readers, and which is precisely the reason Snow White had been crying for so long in the tub. She couldn't make them understand because they were only interested in details, and those disappear. She grew furious and asked herself, how did you expect it to turn out? "Love" could not keep it together.

Snow White's illusion, her elaborate fiction. After all, cars don't really transform into giant search engines of the soul. Clouds don't descend from the sky to cushion two people virtually levitating inside the car. Now crawling into the backseat, now ripping through pantyhose, now rocking.

Snow White put her hand on the hot water nozzle, cold metal. She turned it on and water fell, more or less warm at first. Then cold, only cold. The well outside the cottage was not the deepest so a Reader might think that she would've turned off the water when it started to overflow. Instead, water moved over the side of the tub in small waves, forming puddles on the floor. "Are you going to keep the baby? Do you have health insurance? Aren't you a little young to be a mother? Babies need plenty of attention."

Prince Charming's wife, a sweet woman indeed, who had for so long remained beside the point, had instantly become the only point left. Which for Snow White made the situation all the more tragic. Snow White had fallen, had become the 'other woman.' But they had existed beyond all that, hadn't they? beyond all of those gritty normal terms and phrases. They had dwelt in a castle, souls at play, in fusion. So he must never know about the baby, he must never learn how many times Snow White will have to get up at night to feed the baby, or to soothe the baby. Instead, they have been extinguished, and that was that.

Snow White: pale white skin, watermelon colored lips, black hair spilling out of the bathtub. Her bathroom floor spreads with water, leaks under the door into the hallway. It'll be into the living room carpet within minutes, the dark orange color darkening, soaking like a sponge. In this way though, she knows she could never drown. She would have to slip under or knock her head against the side of the tub and sink to the bottom.

Prince Charming rode up the bike path into the mountains. His mind recalled events of the week as if gathering evidence, trying to prop up his world, trying to focus on the good times. But they blurred almost beyond recollection. Episodes that once carried tremendous weight, that were clear evidence of "True Love," melted as he sweat on his mini-bike. He wondered in a panic if this Snow White existence was somehow genetically engineered to fail. He pedaled through the dissolving fog of her skin, and touch and smell. Soon, he could not even recall Snow White's face.

As he strained to re-ignite his feelings for Snow White, the events from the past week suddenly presented themselves as omens, as warning signs that had clearly foretold of this doom. The end, (what an idiot he'd been!), had been especially obvious just the day before, during his intramural softball game. A ball had been hit high and Prince Charming backpedaled. Even though he played short stop he moved back, deep into center field shading the sun with his glove. "I got it, I got it," he shouted. The ball landed firmly in his mitt with a satisfying smack. The girl who actually played center field looked at him with a hand on her hip and said, "Nice work, Bully." Better safe than sorry he thought but when he threw the ball to the pitcher he saw the umpire holding a red handkerchief in the air. Prince Charming was called for male dominance and the batter was allowed to trot to second base. Who ever heard of male dominance in softball?

Yes, it was coming clearer to Prince Charming and terror tickled his body. The momentum of his life shifted and he knew soon that Snow White would disappear and he would no longer attempt to move the world with his mind. He left his bike by the creek and ran up the path to the small house. He was frantic by the time he pounded on the door. How could it end like this? What could he possibly say?

Words were a dilemma for Snow White at that moment as well. Her lips had gone numb. Such a trap, such a vulgar and impossible web of meaning to navigate if you wanted to tell about how it was, if you wanted to expose their beauty together. Always when she looked at Prince Charming it was as if his skin melted around the edges, as if they were actually enchanted, floating.

It's all about metaphor, she thought. Their whole romance boiled down to a goddamn metaphor, lived in virtual spaces, with fantastic notions. How terrible it felt to recover, how wretched. Too bad mental telepathy failed, she thought caustically and shook her head. What kind of ridiculous illness could've made them believe that they were capable of speaking into each other's brain, of breathing from inside the other's skin?

Snow White used to organize her day around Prince Charming. She would calculate distance and time in order for them to meet and walk together. She would kick the skateboard into her hand and walk beside him. Together they felt like a fountain, nourishing and whole. The water from the faucet had turned a rusted red color and spread in the bathtub like clouds of Easter-egg coloring, definitely draining the bottom of the well. Maybe three inches of water sat on the bathroom floor, less in the rest of the small house.

Grape soda pop did not come out of the faucet. There were exactly zero magic queens or talking lions in this scene. No one cast a spell on anyone else and magic potion saved exactly no one. It seemed to Snow White that kissing would do about as much.

Prince Charming had never broken down a door in his life so he walked around the cabin looking for a window to open, or if necessary, to break with a rock. When he came to the bathroom window he looked down and saw Snow White lying in the tub with her head tilted back, eyes closed. Her cheeks and lips had seemingly drained into the blood colored water. He ran to the front door and tried the knob again, still locked. This is real, he told himself. He rested his forehead against the door and thought, this is real, and I should do something.

Snow White was freezing by then and decided to stand. Liquid trickled from the faucet, pure rust by now. She wrapped a towel around her body and walked through the water into the bedroom to lie on her bed. She closed the door. It was clear to her by now that Prince Charming had vanished.

Prince Charming removed a screen and lifted the front window. He went in head first, and let himself down gently onto the couch.

One night, Prince Charming had bitten Snow White's neck on this couch. The memory of this, of his desire to taste her blood, receded like sound and he couldn't exactly recall what had made him want to do that. In fact, it didn't make any sense at all. He felt his head screw on straight and he knew that there was precisely nothing vampiric in his body anymore. Even the flavor dissolved and he remembered it like flowers. Since when does blood taste like flowers? Who could he ever tell this to?

He walked on the soaking carpet, trying to be as quiet as possible. All of the doors were closed except the bathroom and he looked in. Someone had taken the body. He stood next to the bathtub and water soaked through the bottom of his shoes, into his socks. Her clothes were wet rags in the corner and he picked them up, lifted them to his face, and dropped them in a pile at his feet. When he glanced at the sink, he saw the coffee cup of urine with the pregnancy stick showing baby, and it was clear to him that Snow White had disappeared.

Behind him, she cleared her throat. "Excuse me," she said, "are you looking for someone?" She stood in her doorway, a gray towel wrapped up around her breasts, arms crossed. Hair wet and tangled.

This woman's eyes were red and her skin had wrinkled into that of an old woman. No symphony struck up. No musical interlude, no lovers embracing and grooming each other like saved souls. Nothing but drips into the tub.

"No," he said. "No. They must have taken her away."

She shrugged.

No last kiss. Only the sounds of his sloshing footsteps and the closing of the front door.

The Fireman

1.   Joe the fireman said, "I'll give you a quarter if you make me a promise. If you promise me one thing, I'll give you this quarter here." Joe sat on the morning bus wearing a flannel shirt and torn jeans. His retarded friends sat in the seats near me and my friend T.J in the back of the bus. In school we learned not to make fun of these people and I always managed to control myself better than T.J. "Promise you'll never become a fireman," he said to me, and he pinched the coin above my open palm. And well, I promised.

2.   I promised to vacuum the living room, even though I'm allergic to most everything, while my angry wife drives herself to the grocery store. She has just threatened to leave me again, and we are both exhausted from trying to make something between us work. Trying to save ourselves. I vacuum on my hands and knees, pushing the nozzle into corners and brushing up clumps of cat fur. "Waiting around to save things will screw with your head," Joe told me once as his hand stroked his long gray beard. "It'll throw your imagination out of whack and before anything else kid, you have got to save your imagination. It's the only place where everything balances."

3.   The only place where everything used to balance for me was inside a bar named JUICE, with one dollar draft beers and chicken wings that dripped red hot sauce to the sound of snapping tendons. Life moved into perspective there mainly because it was blocked out by the silent big screen TV, endlessly showing football highlights. Then the waitress in the short black skirt stopped in front of my booth. "My feet are killing me," she said and she slid

into the seat opposite mine. Her blond hair was pinned on top of her head and she smiled. Her white shirt stretched across her chest and framed her neck and face as if she were a sculpted bust of a woman. She crossed her legs and wrote down my order on a pad of paper. "I'll carry you," I said and her head fell back with a laugh. But I did not even smile and I gazed at her throat as I put a green bottle of beer to my lips.

4.   My lips moved, but hers did not. I wanted to be honest with my wife and so I said that the affair was over and that in fact I was sad about that, which turned out to be the wrong honest thing to say at the time. Now I have trouble concentrating in the university library when I see couples walking outside in the snow and strolling behind a giant tree traced in white, like a pen and ink portrait. Branches sag under accumulation and I have trouble reading the book in my hand. I can't seem to focus on anything having to do with the present, with formulating a plan. Instead, I simply sit and watch frosted people make words, watch them gesture to be let into one another as their breath freezes and evaporates.

5.   Breath evaporated on the bus and fogged the windows. Joe sat across the aisle and explained something to the retarded man who always wore a blue hat and sweatpants in the winter. When Joe jiggled his balls with his hand T.J. laughed and whispered in my ear, "Did ya see that? I told you Joe was a retard." I said, "So what, George is a retard, too." T.J put me in my place by saying, "George was on TV." George sat quietly in the back of the bus holding a clay horse model on his lap. We knew from television that it was on its way to be dipped in bronze. The horse posed on its hind legs, and the body strained up with the front hooves clawing and twisting into the humid air.

6.   The humid air clings to my skin like hot breath. I turn off the vacuum and stand on the front porch. It could be that my wife will not come back from the store, and even this fails to provide a spark in my mind. It's like I'm dead. A coyote trots up the driveway, smelling the dirt and when it stops, it considers me. I try not to blink. George never said a word on the bus, always offering his agreeable smile. He was an autistic man, which T.J took to

mean 'good' retarded, and on 60 minutes George's mother showed his work to the camera. A pair of coyotes with straining leg muscles pulled meat from the remnants of an elk's body. A bronze horse dragged a man with a tangled rope around his neck, his hat lying on the ground. Emotional power, the interviewer said, horrifying and beautiful. But George, he marveled, such a peaceful nature, such a delicate hand.

7.   With a delicate hand positioned beneath her, I carried the waitress. My body compressed, and I was sweating like an Italian cradling a five-foot tall Virgin Mary. At one point I rested beside her on one knee, the sides of my crew-cut drenched, my whole body feeling like I was on fire. She took another order, and looked down at me kneeling next to her. Our eyes connected, but neither one of us smiled anymore. I rose to my feet like a knight, swept her up and walked to the kitchen window. Maybe she was as exhausted as I was because when she stabbed the order onto the metal prong, she stabbed the palm of her hand. She shouted between clenched teeth and my arms trembled.

8.   Joe's arms trembled, but the woman's did not. When I was a kid I always had trouble finishing my homework when I saw people coupling together in the library. The shelves of books rose to the ceiling with a ladder to touch the top. One day after school I saw a retarded woman wearing a straw hat, black sunglasses and a lemon colored dress standing toward the top with her back against the ladder. Her arms were secured around the neck of Joe the ex-fireman. With white knuckles and forearms quivering, he climbed the ladder and nuzzled his head into her lap. He continued his ascent and for the first time in my life I smelled people in the library.

9.   People in the library used to let T.J. and I watch appropriate movies after school. But Joe the fireman helped us find certain adult books. "Nothing dirty about it," Joe said. "Making babies is about the only thing we haven't screwed up." The pages felt heavy from being turned by so many hands, and we flipped through diagrams of the internal reproductive systems. One day, T.J. told Joe and I that a man in the bathroom had shown him what

semen looked like. He had barely been able to see it in the library's urinal, but he thought it looked like spit. Joe said, "It's the only thing men can do by themselves."

10.   The only thing men could do by themselves was die. Joe said to think about death just like anything else. That just because we didn't know what happened afterward didn't mean we should go around being afraid of dying. He said, "It's the only story we have to look forward to. The only ending we don't already know." Joe the fireman was beaten to death and left to drown in the creek near the library. A photograph of two jean-covered legs, twisted onto the river bank accompanied the article. In my room I cried for literally two hours straight when I found out. And so I did not become a fireman.

11.   A fireman, maybe, but I was no fireman. Her bandaged hand showed the barest amount of red soaking through, and I carried her through the restaurant while she balanced a pizza pan on her chest. "It's burning," she said and she tried to keep the pizza revolving touching the pan with her fingertips like butterflies, like gasps. On television I saw quarterbacks pass footballs like blessings into outstretched hands, connecting for an invisible moment with their receivers. Players danced through tackles making the other team bump into each other and fall down like comedy. Highlights and replays went on and I drank ice water, down on one knee again, while she served pizza onto the plates. Our eyes connected. All facial expression except determination had drained. I stood and swallowed.

12.   I swallowed, but my wife didn't. I definitely have trouble concentrating when fighting breaks out in front of the library. My wife had come to see me in the library, to surprise me with some news that had instantly evaporated when she found me. I stood with my back to a ladder in the book stacks, and the waitress knelt before me. By that time, her hand that rested on my naked thigh had completely healed. My composure during our fight in front of the library had to do with my throat, scratching, holding, massaging, swallowing. Hers had to do with feet position, arm crossing, and hair tossing. She yelled, "I don't want to hear it

anymore," and the force of her anger set her back a pace. "I don't give a fuck what you want," I said. My throat burning. One night long ago we had painted each other with finger-paints and made love until pools of sweat formed on her belly and streamed purple and orange onto her sheets. Sheets that will probably never come clean, and that were at that very moment, seriously changing in value. She yelled, "Get a fucking life." I said, "I will." And then she backed away.

13.   The woman backed away from the unmarked grave and I stood in the shadow of a nearby tree. Baby's breath cushioned the three carefully arranged red roses that she had brought to put on the mound. The retarded woman wore her straw hat and black sunglasses. She did not cry or seem to notice the dirt stains on her bare knees. She carried a purse over her shoulder and crushed cellophane in both hands as she walked backward, and finally turned away. On TV they rehearsed Joe the fireman's death for a few days and then dropped it. Nothing ever came of it, except I guess, that final ending which we can never know anything about.

14.   We can never know anything about the miraculous. My wife returns with groceries and for the rest of the afternoon there is a strange calm in the house. A silence that is, if not comfortable, at least not as oppressive. I fold laundry in the bedroom. It's like I've always waited to step inside the only place where everything balanced and made perfect sense. And now I have stepped into my imagination and found that my balance and my perfect sense will always have very little in common with the world outside of me. Little to do with my wife's delicate hand, tucking hair behind her ear, or with the humid air around our bed. I will never finish with Joe because I feel him inside me, guiding my perspective. He swallows and touches his throat standing naked in a beautiful young woman's bedroom, and his arms tremble with lust and desire. My wife approaches me and when I sing to her, his lips move. Joe said that to be a fireman was to put our (human) life before everything else, to kill our imagination and keep ourselves in boxes. Wife, husband, father, mother. I make love to my wife on the bed, and for the rest of the day we are repaired. Eventually I will appear unbalanced and deceitful to my wife precisely because I never

became a fireman. My imagination has taken over and I dwell in a balance of my own design.

The Black Madonna Miracle

No sound. The opening scene is usually nothing but the endless expanse of dark water. Clearly the rich green and black sway of a deep ocean; the eye focuses on a hesitant white-lipped crest when it briefly appears before dispersing back into the endless push and shove. But unlike a camera lens that endlessly adjusts and re-adjusts, struggling to identify and focus and lock-in on some thing, the eyes quickly tire and settle on the wider view.

The sloshing, rocking rhythm hypnotizes the conscious mind until, growing weary of perceiving even this general ocean blur, the halt happens. The ocean's movement slows and slows until the image freezes into a giant oil painting. The flicks of a brush that tricked the eyes are exposed, and all at once, motion is as impossible here as it is on a canvas, as irretrievable as the artist's own memory of the moment. Your own existence, the reality of being alive and strapped to a balloon basket, holds its breath, turning you and your experience into art.

There is a tightening, a suffocation of sorts, when you become part of this suspended animation. To not die, to avoid becoming so much dried oil paint on a two dimensional square requires movement, a powerful push, but you cannot find purchase anywhere and you spin noiselessly, like a car tire rotating silently in an icy rut, only an insistent rocking that gathers power will be able to rock the self out of this rut, but you are fixed tight in place, unable to move even your head. Nothing to do but wait and make believe that expectation or will or mercy will transform the art back into life.

Trapped. Dead. Or at least dying, you face the timeless spread of quiet ocean, and your panicking mind casts out and reels in, again and again, snagging nothing. When the mind cannot catch, when no grappling hook shoots out of you to wrap around something, anything, the hungry mind does not react as the eyes have, it does not enter peacefully into a petrified state of surrender. Instead, the human mind turns on itself. Whirring like a dying computer, searching and researching, the mind scrapes for the tiniest bit of data to process. This deprivation causes the mind to move into the water itself, and to keep itself stimulated, it begins to strip an ocean of life and churn out images of rusted spears, rotting nets and bloated corpses.

Not unlike the dancing silver fish at the bottom of a green mesh net, tugging and flipping and trying to propel itself toward the water's surface, the mind wriggles and spasms and strains toward knowing. Creating and delivering questions to a consciousness nearly out of power. When is this ocean view? Noah's flood? Amelia Earhart? The search for John junior?

When the view pulls up and out of the water desert, a distant coastline appears, and the shock is near electric. The human brain gains some traction and begins processing data. At first, it is the data of absence, a quick analysis of what is not in evidence. No metropolitan city looms, no sea-port with blue-gray aircraft carriers or fleets of tall-ships. Only a beautiful coast of red and adobe-colored rock and green hills along the horizon. All of it, dominated by an enormous rock headland jutting out into the sea.

Inland, the rock flows into the green hills of farmland like a neck into a shoulder, and the enormous head rises one thousand feet into the air. At this point, the only dwellings exist on top of the rock; the remains of a castle wall, four or five smaller building, all of it left over from the Romans, and all of it abandoned and in decay. The Rock itself has many mythological interpretations, but at this point, it is the petrified head of an ancient beast, an octopus, said to have been turned to stone by Perseus who was using Medusa's head as a weapon in the time before he decides to give it to Athena to put on her shield.

None of this matters nearly as much as the jagged rock tentacles which are said to stretch far out underwater where they wait for the unsuspecting sailing vessel.

Finally, some sound rises up from the ocean like fog. The occasional slap of the water asserts itself above the gentle rush, the slosh of tranquility.

A ship enters into view. Thankfully there is nothing modern about this boat, nothing smacking of Disney or computer animation. Too small for Noah, too unspectacular for general audiences. This wooden ship does not fly the black skull and crossbones flag, but a brightly colored, though not altogether rectangular, red flag featuring two yellow, blurry creatures. Familiar, but not finished, either a first draft or else the results of a younger brother, trying hard to appear official and legitimate and part of the bigger picture.

This sudden ship appearance relieves the rest of the tension that develops inside the sensory deprived human mind. If the mind is an information gathering machine, hardware meant to process data, then the movement of the boat, and of the figures on the boat, provides an anchor, a fixed (though moving) point of reference; somewhere for the viewer to place their squirming attention and escape the discomforts that gather like vapors inside the mind.

The sudden close-up of the ship's deck begins to inform the viewer, begins to provide details and substance around which the limitless threads of conscious and unconscious babble begin to spin. Water-stained sails and pink-faced Scandinavian men working on the rough dark-wood stage. They carry buckets or climb rope ladders or repair the floor. Some wear tight fabric swatches on their heads, and their exposed arm and back muscles assert themselves as the men labor through the scene. The shine on their taught skin flashes under the sun and creates brief peripheral movements that mimic the occasional rodent in the shadows.

The sky darkens. One man stands tall at the helm and stares ahead, his blond hair tied in a pony-tail, his face as defined as sculpture. His icy-blue eyes seem at once to scour the immediate landscape and stare it down. A sinister expression rests comfortably on his face.

This is Count Roger, commander of this ship, and the younger brother of King Edmond the Norman. His aggressive stance makes clear his displeasure with his inferior younger brother status; Count versus King. His internal rage causes his thick fingers to twitch on the hilt of his sword and boiling jealousy occasionally clouds over his eyes.

A short and bald older man stands a good distance behind Count Roger and his lips move. His face appears wise and good, a trustworthy face and he wears a vest over his white pirate's shirt. Although this advisor speaks to Roger, the captain does not acknowledge the man behind him, he does not even make the effort to toss an insult over his shoulder. And it would have been an insult, to be sure, because the old man was asking Count Roger to be careful in these waters. Count Roger would have insulted the man in the presence of the crew lest they would deem him a weak and ineffectual leader. An emotion that, if not destroyed at once, could seduce a crew into mutiny.

It will never be learned (because Jeremy the advisor to the Count will soon sink to the bottom of the ocean like a rock) that this was the moment when the wise old man, Jeremy of Norkington, warned Count Roger about the mythic monster that dwelt beneath the surface of the Mediterranean water. La Monstrum was an octopus of rock that rose from the depths, it was said, and crushed ships beneath its powerful granite tentacles.

The sound of shouting foreign voices does not distract Roger, but instead leads the focus away from the handsome angry count and through a large grate on the deck floor, allowing a clear view into the dimness of the holding cells below. Arab slaves look up out of the grate and the whites of their eyes appear almost comically bright in the cavern. Their mouths move and they hold up their cupped hands as if giving praise or releasing invisible butterflies into the air.

A sailor drags a wooden bucket across the deck and pours water onto the men below. Behind the blur of water cascading over their dark and unshaven faces they drink and swallow with the fury of thirsty beasts.

In a few moments, more water will rush in on the group of men. From all sides, they will feel the pressure of the ocean surrounding them, tugging them down, further away from the gray sky which they only barely glimpse now as they drink. Their collective deaths will represent a moderate loss of revenue that King Edmond, when he finally arrives with a rescue party at the spot on the beach where his brother (the only suspected survivor) kneels in torn clothing and prays, his blond hair the image of a tempest itself, will deem a small sacrifice to pay for the life of his only brother. Instead of mounting the horse that King Edmond had brought, Count Roger will insist that they remain and send for more soldiers and slaves who will help build a cathedral to the spirit who descended from the heavens at the last moment and plucked him from certain death. A spirit in the form of a nude woman and as Roger insisted on the nude aspect, as he described (in detail) the curve of the spirit's breast and her hips, it seemed unlikely to Edmond that they would be able to dedicate the cathedral to the Holy Virgin Mother Mary, who had, in the past, saved a royal Norman sailor here and there. No, it would not be appropriate to reveal the nudity of such a holy woman; Rome would not hear of it.

The same water-delivering sailor spends the last moments of his life, walking down a flight of wooden stairs into another part of the ship. He carries a large mug covered with a hunk of disfigured bread. He arrives in a small room, illuminated from the grate in the ceiling, and a single young Arab woman sits tied to a chair in the center of the room. She wears ornate robes made from red and gold thread and her long black hair hangs behind her, almost touching the floor. Surrounding the woman, stacked in coffin length wooden crates along the walls are Count Roger's treasures, his rewards from the most recent battle. The crates, with tufts of straw sticking out through the slats in places, are stacked along the walls. They contain statues and golden relics, seized from the barbarians.

There is a marble sarcophagus at the base of one stack; it is precisely the same length and width as the other crates, and elaborate decoration has been carved along the visible side. Strings of beads and letters the size of a fingernail cover the roman coffin from corner to corner.

As Count Roger recalled, each side of the sarcophagus had displayed the same amount of quality detailed carving. He remembered thinking that it would probably take a man at least half of his life to carve a sarcophagus as intricate and detailed as this. The dull color of the crates and carved stone make the woman, Princess Hatucha, appear beyond alive with flaming color and energetic movement even though she is as inert as the dead men inside the stone box.

Before the mass drowning and complete destruction of the ship, it was to have been a love story, a symbolic tale about the love of two people from drastically different parts of the world. Count Roger and Princess Hatucha from Arabia would have been brought together in a holy marriage ceremony at the King's Court in Palermo and in this one moment Sicily would live and breathe as the first multicultural success in all of known history. She would have come to love the brute Count Roger whose tenderness would have been brought to the surface by her touch and mythic beauty. She would have given birth to eleven children, mixed breeds, who would nonetheless occupy important posts throughout the Norman Empire signaling to the world that those people considered slaves were not so simply because of their inferior race, but only by virtue of the successful oppression of rulers. An awareness that all could be made slaves, under the right circumstances, would creep like mold through the known world. Sicily, with the Arabic Puppet shows and distinctly European Christian religion would have become the true 'island of the sun,' as Plato named it, a slave-less place of paradise and harmony.

When the sailor breaks off a piece of food and approaches the young woman's mouth with it, she spits directly into his face. The sailor angrily attempts to shove the piece of food into the woman's clenched mouth, her neck twisting and struggling from side to side.

Enough, Count Roger says. He stands in the doorway to the small room and the sailor makes one last, childish push at the young woman's closed mouth before dropping the bread onto the floor and leaving.

Count Roger enters the room, picks up the bread and places it on the woman's lap. She turns away and he studies her neck.

My own cave of wonders, Count Roger says. He walks around the small room, surveying the crates, letting his hand pass against the straw that sticks out in places. He kicks one of the sarcophagi and stares down. The princess and the stone box, he says, both sealed tight, silent, and mysterious. Both concealing a discovery beyond imagination.

This stone box, he continues, could be the final resting place of a Roman mystic, a brilliant observer of the natural world who carried into death the very meaning of life on earth. The knowledge and power by which this man who was said to have perished at the foot of Mount Vesuvius, could have escaped that certain death and arrived in your country to live another twenty years. Buried with his secret at long last in the rarest of coffins, signifying the influence and power he continued to wield even in a foreign land. Count Roger crouches and runs a finger along the rim of the lid. A secret that has fused stone to stone over the years, turning this box into a single rock that has defied any man's attempt to remove the lid.

Count Roger stands erect and walks to Princess Hatucha; he places his hand on her chin and she does not struggle. And you, are you fused closed as well, he asks. The princess turns her eyes up and stares at Count Roger.

What do you want from me, the princess asks.

A good question. The princess does not have information, nor does the count suspect that she does. He wants something different from the princess; one of these sarcophagi will reveal the power he seeks to become king. The dead man will provide instructions, explanations, and evidence to help the count pursue his destiny: the secret of cheating death or else the mystical power required to return from the dead. But what then does he wants from the princess? Is she not part of the destiny that the count feels throbbing in his chest?

The sarcophagus will eventually yield to the strength of men; even if the count has to smash the box and remove all the fragments one by one, the information will be obtained. The count suspects that what he wants from the princess cannot be taken by force; I will break into you, he wants to say, but he does not yet speak. The question of why remains. Perhaps he is on the verge of an epiphany, a moment when he understands that anything of value contained inside the princess, inside any human being must be given willingly, must be offered in order to retain its value. As soon as it is extracted by force it turns to dust, becomes worthless and crude.

Count Roger teeters on the verge of this monumental comprehension, but his moment is cut short by the sudden jarring of their present reality and the squawking sounds of human confusion that seem for a moment to join together as the sounds of trumpets might at a Royal ceremony: an announcement or introduction of the granite that punctures through the bottom of the ship, tossing the bound princess to the floor, and seems to lift them all before gripping them (stone bursting through floors that have become ceilings, walls that have become floors) and plunging them deep into the ocean with bone-crushing force.

Unfortunately, Count Roger is never again able to approach a moment of comprehension as profound as the one that was about to occur just before his ship cracked apart and sunk.

The statue of the black Madonna with child and the unconscious body of Count Roger and are the only two remnants of the disaster that wash up on Maladu's beach. The one, carved from black cedar and sealed with African tree sap, manages to survive and intercede on behalf of the other, who will know that a miracle has taken place almost immediately upon opening his eyes.

The Path Made Ready

"Human beings can hardly move without models for their behavior, and from the beginning of time, in all probability, we have known no greater purveyor of models than story-telling." John Gardner <u>The Art of Fiction</u>

Dama walked through another rainy night. Dressed in his black slicker and black boots he splashed through the puddles without hesitation. A black bag bumped against his hip with each step.

His hair stuck to his head and rain-water streamed down his cheeks. Follow the bird; he glanced up. The enormous black form sat on top of a lamppost half a block away, as still as a gargoyle, one of its unmoving eyes shining. Warm rain pelted his face. He lowered his head; the shattered concrete passed under him.

The bird lifted off when Dama approached the lamppost, and the wings sent a burst of wind and rain against his face. A weak fog developed around his ankles and rose up around him, lifting the aroma of diesel fuel and eggs.

Dama turned a corner and saw the façade of a stone cathedral. The bird had settled on the furthest corner; the huge black eyes stared at Dama through the fog and drizzle. Warm water continued to stream down his face. Dama felt a weight in his left jacket pocket. His wet fingers touched a large smooth metal ball.

Just around the church corner, cement stairs descended to a large wooden door. Dama looked up, but the bird had not flown away. The door was a light maple color. He stared at the bright blond wood; he smelled cut tree and polyurethane. Someone tapped his shoulder. An old woman with white hair smiled at Dama. He relaxed his grip on the metal ball. She held a small purple purse clutched in her blue-veined hand, and she wore a white sweater and dress embroidered with pink and blue flowers.

"Excuse me," she said. She passed by Dama, pushed open the door and walked inside. The door closed with a loud click.

The woman, soaking wet, wearing jeans and a white tee-shirt appeared on the staircase. She smiled and lifted both of her hands to gather her wet hair into a pony tail. Rain-water moved down the inside of her arm and disappeared passed her shaved armpit. She was not wearing a bra.

"You made it," she said. She reached out and squeezed Dama's arm. "Good for you." She smiled at him. She was probably in her early forties. "Almost there now," the woman said. She brushed passed Dama. He saw water droplets on the back of her smooth white neck. He smelled fake green apple. She opened the door and paused to look over her shoulder at Dama, "Coming?"

Dama followed her through the door and into the church basement. Everything in the room, including the people sitting in folding chairs, looked used and worn out.

"I've got to change," the woman said, leaning into Dama.

Dama stood in the doorway and watched the woman greet a few people as she made her way into a bathroom along the back wall. The rows of chairs faced a single wooden podium with a black microphone and Dama scanned the people's faces.

"I see you-hoo," a woman called out. A short wide woman smiled and waved at Dama. "The Lord does not turn His back on anyone," she added in a high-pitched singsong voice.

Dama didn't move.

"Don't be shy," the woman said. "I'm Cheryl," she called out, pressing a hand to her chest. She had thin brown hair on an eggshell colored scalp.

Dama nodded and walked behind the last row of chairs toward a silver coffee urn and a plate of cookies. He filled a styrofoam cup halfway and took a few broken cookies to an empty seat near the podium.

Dama dumped the large cookie-bits into his mouth, licked his palm and then wiped it on the side of his pants.

"Thank you all for coming," Cheryl said into the microphone. "Let us greet one another, and I expect the old timers to give a warm welcome to some of the new faces."

When Dama turned, a man wearing an obviously fake black mustache and a green hat extended his hand to Dama.

"Alan," the man said and Dama lifted his moist palm and shook the man's hand.

The woman was moving toward Dama to sit in the seat next to him. Her wet tee-shirt had been replaced by a red blouse, buttoned up to her neck. She wore red boots with heels and when she moved her legs to face Dama squarely he saw that the torn crotch of her jeans was fastened with a safety pin.

She smiled at him and touched him briefly on his thigh. She leaned forward and whispered into his ear.

"Don't you worry about a thing," she said. "These people are great." She left moisture on Dama's ear lobe.

"Patrice," Alan said. The man pushed Dama aside with his elbow and affectionately grasped Patrice's shoulder.

"Alan, it's so good to see you," Patrice said with a broad smile. "How have you been, nice costume you got there." When she leaned to kiss Alan's cheek, she looked at Dama and rolled her eyes. Dama smelled strawberry shampoo and cigarette smoke from Patrice's hair, and he felt the heat return to his face.

"I find that a little pretend helps keep me off the path," Alan said.

"Have you found a job?" Patrice asked.

"Something temporary," he said. "It's still hard."

Patrice smiled sympathetically and said, "Keep of the path."

Alan nodded and responded, "Keep off the path." Alan sat back in his chair, and Dama felt the man glaring at the back of his head.

Patrice turned to Dama and asked, "How long have you been off the path?"

Dama looked straight into Patrice's green eyes.

"Three days, for me," Patrice said. Then she looked at the red watch on her wrist and said, "Well almost three days."

"Let's begin," Cheryl said into the microphone and Patrice reached out and squeezed Dama's hand. She winked and gave him a nod of support. "You'll be okay," she whispered. "You're with me."

The chatter in the room faded as Cheryl said, "For those who don't know, I am Cheryl, the coordinator, and it has been twelve hours since I last walked on the path."

"Hi Cheryl," the crowd responded.

"And I have one question for you," Cheryl paused and took a deep breath. "Who are we?!" Cheryl shouted.

"Real People!" the crowd responded.

"And what do we have?"

"Self-Respect!"

An uproar of applause and catcalls and whistles filled the basement. A few people stood and clapped with their arms raised.

Cheryl extended both hands to quiet the crowd. The noise subsided and everyone sat down.

"Let us pray," Cheryl said.

She stepped back from the podium and bowed her head. The congregation fell silent. People bowed their heads and closed their eyes. Dama mimicked their gestures.

"Dear higher power, give us the strength to resist the path that has been set before us. Praise be."

"Praise be."

"Stay off the path," someone shouted and a few people yelped in agreement.

"The floor is open," Cheryl said. "Who'll share their story?"

Patrice stood up. A few people clapped and shouted encouragement. She squeezed in front of Dama, and he felt her body heat press against his legs. She steadied herself, placing one hand on his shoulder and squeezing. She gave him a quick, shy smile before stepping into the side aisle and walking to the podium.

"My story," Patrice said leaning forward to speak into the microphone. "It's not unlike many of yours. At one time I was just a regular woman, a wife, a mother to two wonderful teenagers, a 14 year-old son and a 17 year-old daughter. I worked in the garden, read novels, nothing out of the ordinary. That all changed on the day that I began to read my trigger-book." There were a few sympathetic sounds and nods.

"There were many similarities between the book and life. For example, the narrator in the book was married and had two children and she worked in her garden. The narrator was living a normal life, but secretly, she felt alone and desperate. To find some relief, the narrator started to smoke pot during the day while her kids were at school. And, in the story, the smoking became selling and moved on to crack, and so on, until this woman basically turned into a prostitute, turning tricks for money to buy heroin. When it became clear that her children would need enormous sums of money to pay for college, the mother begins to allow her daughter to earn money, one man at a time. As I read, I was shocked and appalled by the woman's behavior. I kept thinking, how could a seemingly normal suburban wife and mother change into a drugged out sex worker who exploited her children and hid her stash inside stuffed animals?"

There was a reverent silence, a few sympathetic shakes of the head. Patrice composed herself and finished her story. "I spent a week thinking about the woman and her sense of loneliness and bit by bit her situation didn't seem so shocking at all."

"We've all been there," someone yelled.

"It felt like the story was really about my own crushing loneliness and desperate need for escape. I fell into a depression and well, the next thing I knew, I was loading groceries into the minivan and waiting for a friend of mine to show up. I bought my first plastic baggie of marijuana, but I kept it hidden in my sock drawer for a week before I tried it. My friend insisted that it was like Zoloft or Prozac, but it was more natural with no side effects. That's how I started on the path. I re-read parts of the book and then took the next step. After each step, I would shake myself out of it and promise to give up the story for good. But I couldn't stop.

"Once I found out about this group, it was easier for a while to get back to my usual, gardening, casserole-making self. But even with the meetings, I'd only last a day or two, and then BAM, I'd be back on the path. My husband took my son and moved away. By the time my trigger-book hit its sixth week on the bestseller list, I was cutting bricks of cocaine for my daughter to sell at school. You all know how easy it is, just to start right up again, like the path is just waiting there for you, calling to you." She paused and took a deep and unsteady breath.

"Last week, for the first time, I paired up my daughter, Allie, with a handsome, disease-free, and kindly businessman. Before they went at it in Allie's own bedroom; I took down posters of the shirtless male musicians and movie-star men tacked to her walls. Can you believe it? My daughter was about to sleep with a businessman in her childhood bedroom, and all I could worry about was whether he would be offended by the images of much sexier men. God, I'm a monster."

Earnest shouts of, "No Patrice," and "No, you're not," and "We're here for you Patrice," bounced around the room.

"And I know some of you are struggling with your third or fourth book, and I want to believe that it gets easier, but I don't think it ever will. I am thankful for all of the support, thankful that you all take me back no matter how many times I fall off the wagon, but down deep, I think we all know that our situation is hopeless."

The room was silent. Cheryl looked around from her seat, unsure what to do.

"By now I should probably be crying. I should be dabbing a crushed tissue to my face and struggling to compose myself. But I'm not, and I'll tell you why. Because today, my friends, is the day that we are all set free."

While looking directly at Dama, Patrice said, "I need everyone to give me their undivided attention. I know we're not supposed to mention this, but I know that each of us, deep down, is waiting for the Maker to arrive."

Cheryl stood, an expression of disapproval on her face, and said, "Okay Patrice, I don't want you starting anything. Why don't you sit down and give someone else a chance? Who'll go next?"

Patrice didn't move. "It's useless to pretend," she said. "All of us are aching for the Maker to arrive and while we'll roll our eyes and assure each other that we don't believe in such nonsense, I know that deep down, we are counting on it. We probably spend hours and hours researching the maker, learning little details, too afraid to share our information with each other. But we are all waiting for the Maker to pull us aside one day and—"

All at once, people started to talk rapidly and loudly to one another.

"That's enough, Patrice," Cheryl said sharply, and she approached the podium. Without a microphone it was almost impossible to hear Cheryl. "I'm surprised at you Patrice, you should know better."

Patrice grasped the microphone. "The Maker is real," she said. "I have brought him here tonight."

Everyone stopped talking and in the sudden silence, they stared at Dama. He looked back at them and then stood up. One hand pressed his black bag against his thigh and the other hand slipped into his pocket and tightened around the metal ball.

"He'll wear all black," someone shouted out.

"He will sit among you in an attitude of serenity," someone else said.

"He will carry with him the key to your new life," a different person said. They moved toward Dama.

"Why don't you tell us where you came from?" Patrice asked. She looked at Dama with an expression of encouragement.

"I don't know."

"Of course you don't," Patrice said. "Because you have been sent here for us, today. I promise you Dama, there is no reason to be afraid. Just take a few moments and think. Then simply tell us what we have to do."

A few people had started to cry and a few were on their knees in a posture of prayer.

Patrice still stood behind the podium. "Let me try to help you," she said. "Go ahead and tell us if anything has felt different for you since you've walked through the door. And I don't mean anything you've heard us say; I mean the way you feel, anything that you might have noticed."

"Color," Dama said. "I've never seen bright colors like this."

Patrice smiled and nodded. "What's in the bag?" Patrice asked.

Dama hesitated. Shaking his head, he slipped off the bag and held it out to Patrice.

Patrice took the bag, unfastened a strap and flipped open the top. Her slender hand pulled out a large manila envelope and then a box of ballpoint pens. She handed the empty bag back to Dama.

Patrice tore open the envelope and pulled out a large booklet. "We are saved," she shouted. Printed on the front of the booklet in large black letters were the words **Character Profile**.

The group began to push and strain toward Patrice. Dama took the packet out of Patrice's hand and put up his palm. "Quiet," he shouted, and the room fell silent. "Everyone take a seat. I will hand out the profiles. There are plenty for everyone."

Everyone returned to their seats and a few people hugged each other before they sat down. Dama looked around the room and then at Patrice. Slowly he walked up to the podium and bent the microphone closer to his lips. He pulled all of the booklets out of the envelope, held them in the air, and spoke. "I have something to say, before I hand these out." The excited murmurs and conversations dies quickly.

"Right now we, you and I, exist on a boundary of sorts; in between two possible forms of existence. This temporary relaxation of my own confinement, give me a chance to warn you. What I'm going to say now, is off the record," Dama said. "I have the official instruction sheet to read, but what I'm about to say is from me alone." Dama cleared his throat. "I know what you want," he said. "I know about the desire that pulls you time and time again back onto the path. Some of you have been in jail or prison because of what you've done. Most of you have been married at least three times. I know all of this because I was once just like you. And just like you, I believed that being made into a full character was the only way to break the cycle. You must understand that once you commit, once you fill out one of these, your fate will be determined.

"Characters have no power to alter the path set before them; you'll exist only as a function of something else, some plan that you cannot know until it ends. It's possible that you will never know what your role was in the larger story. So I am trying to warn you; the torment you feel each time you slip back onto the path, the pain you endure when you step off the path and attempt to proceed as a real person, these are nothing compared with the despair you can feel as you slog from one episode to the next, obeying without choice, blocked from having any thought or any idea that does not suit your higher purpose. If there is anyone who doubts their conviction, I am here to tell you to leave before you decide to enter into this slavery."

Silence. People stared up at Dama from their seats.

"Some of you want this. You want to be controlled and used and made to act in a certain way, made to think pre-designed thoughts. You imagine that by surrendering yourself, you will find relief from the agony of personal choice and failure. So this is what you must weigh before you continue; do you want to give up the last threads of your freedom in exchange for the security of your limited and pre-determined fate. Understand that once you have been Made, the chances of coming into contact with the real world, ever again, is beyond remote. The Makers are the only exception and even this, I've learned, only deepens the despair, because we are able to see all that we have lost. I assure you, if it was offered, there is not a single individual who would not immediately return to your real existence. Who now, would like to fill out the profile?"

Dama stood back from the microphone. After a few moments of quiet, someone near the back raised their hand. One by one, hands appeared in the air and Dama walked around and distributed the profiles. He paused in front of Patrice and her raised hand. He shook his head and walked passed her without giving her a profile.

Patrice leaned back in her seat and crossed her legs. She kept her hand held high.

Everyone in the room requested a profile form and Dama stood in front of Patrice, holding the last form in his hand. He looked at her and shook his head again.

Patrice nodded vigorously, lunged forward and yanked the form from Dama's hand. Dama stared at her for a long time. Then he picked up the box of pens and sent them around. Dama picked up the sheet of paper that he'd left on the podium. Printed at the top were the words, **Read Aloud Before Beginning:**

Dama read: "By filling out the information in the character profile, you are committing yourself to the transformation process. You certify that your answers are true and detailed to the best of your ability. Some of the questions are extremely personal and intimate, and these details are essential in developing a character that will suit everyone involved. By submitting this profile you agree to participate in the process. Thank you for your attention to detail, and for your cooperation."

Dama looked up. Heads were bent over their profiles, pens moving. He sat down in the chair and stared at Patrice, who was bent over her paper, the tip of her tongue pressed against one corner of her mouth as she wrote.

After slipping the forms into his black bag, people returned to their seats. A few of them closed their eyes and let their heads tilt back or to the side. When Patrice was finished she walked over and knelt to slip her paper into the bag. She leaned forward, pressed one hand on Dama's thigh and gently kissed his lips. When she turned to walk back to her seat, Dama picked up the bag and set it on his lap. He put his hand inside the bag, took Patrice's form in his hand, and folded it once and then again. While he folded, he moved his lips as if he were counting. He folding it over until it fit inside his clenched fist. He pulled his fist out of the bag and pushed the folded paper into his jacket pocket.

Once all profiles and pens had been turned in, Dama zipped up the bag and read from his instruction sheet. "Once all profiles have been completed, the Maker will deliver the profiles for authentication. This process will take no longer than thirty minutes. As we will need to match your voice and speech patterns with your record, the Maker will leave the necessary communication device in the room. When you hear your name called, please speak loudly and clearly; you may answer the questions from your seat. All others are asked to maintain complete silence. Thank you for your cooperation.

"Please move your chairs into a tight circle," Dama said. He placed an empty chair in the center of the circle, took the metal sphere from his pocket and placed it on the seat. He looked at Patrice and said, "Regulations require that someone accompany me on the delivery. Would you be so kind?"

Patrice smiled and blushed. She stood and bounced a little on her knees. "It would be my pleasure," she said.

Dama looked at Alan and then at the metal ball. "Will you take care of that?"

Alan smiled broadly and nodded. "I would be honored."

"After we leave, wait five minutes and then press the button," Dama said. "That will connect you with headquarters. After a few minutes, you should hear a voice testing the connection." Patrice was hugging some of the people in the room and laughing with others. With the bag over his shoulder Dama gripped Patrice's arm and led her out the door and up the cement stairs. The rain had stopped and he scanned the night sky until he saw, a few blocks away, the black bird perched on top of a missile-like stone monument. Dama pulled Patrice and started to jog.

"What are you doing?" she asked, still smiling, her words bouncing.

"Saving you," Dama said.

The explosion happened when they were only a few blocks away from the church. The ground vibrated.

Patrice stopped, "What happened? What's wrong?" She stared at the smoke pouring out from under the church.

"Nothing's wrong," Dama said. "We've got to keep going."

The black bag had vanished from around Dama's shoulder. He felt Patrice's folded profile safe in his jacket pocket, and he grabbed her wrist and pulled her along.

"Should we go back? Maybe they need help," Patrice said, looking over her shoulder as she ran.

Dama yanked Patrice into an alley. He stepped into one of the several doorways and pressed himself flat against the door. "Keep quiet," Dama said.

"What are you doing?" Patrice asked in a whisper.

Dama turned to look at Patrice; he smiled. He leaned forward and kissed her. After a moment, she kissed him back. "I'm escaping," Dama said. "And I'm saving you from making the biggest mistake of your life."

They waited, standing, in complete stillness, occasionally whispering to one another until the night sky began to lighten. When sunbeams shot pink across the sky, Dama reached out and took Patrice's hand in his. "We need to get as far away from here as we can," he said.

"Is it safe?" Patrice asked.

"Stay close," Dama said. He led Patrice out of the doorway. They crept, slightly hunched, down the alley toward the main street. Dama stepped onto the sidewalk and looked down one side of the street and then down the other.

A deafening animal shriek blasted through the sky.

Patrice screamed.

Dama looked up and saw the bird dive toward them. The head grew larger and the beak opened. The blackness of the throat expanded as the bird approached, eclipsing the sky into night. Dama closed his eyes; Patrice pushed her head into his chest.

Dama felt a slight breeze before the darkness swallowed them whole.

The Story of My Success by Carl Diffenrocket,
(Automotive and household appliance swallower of the year '07)

Rest assured I'm cranking out the insights even as you read this; I've put together a contraption using an old bathtub, a broken lawn mower, and several pieces of rotted two by fours. Turn the crank on one end and a somewhat nicely wrapped tin foil package falls out the front. Insight. And of course, like a good aspiring writer, my job is to tape it onto my stories. If I can figure out a way to add calcium, I'm sure my work would sell.

This story has visited slush piles all around the world.

My baby boy falls asleep in a peculiar way, he tosses his head from side to side, really whacks his cheek against my leg, or else his crib mattress. Trying to latch onto sleep. And it strikes me how much like life this really is, how true an action my child is performing. I pick him up and push him into the machine. Bing, insight anyone?

Some people nod at me and they say, yes, yes this is precisely how it is, trying to latch onto sleep, trying to connect with that super darkness, that blackness of gravity that pulls our consciousness down until we drool. These people say that I must be an insightful writer, which is good, because stories in magazines are supposed to contain insight; I should be in good shape.

In the beginning I calculated how many stories I would need to write per month in order to make a living, and then I set off. Multiple rejection syndrome followed with all of the usual results. If you're like me then you've heard it a million times. The writer saves rejections in shoebox, moves forward, and struggles with all the delusional energy of an actual idiot. If only I'd had the machine back then.

I walked down Main Street one afternoon dressed like a bum. Details like torn flannel shirt, scraggly brown beard, curly brown hair (unkempt), cigarette in my mouth. I squinted into my palm and wrote in a small notepad.

A tuxedoed fat man with a gray goatee and a top hat strolled to a stop; a buxom young woman hung on his arm. He gripped the hook of a polished mahogany cane and looked me over. The woman could have been, but clearly was not, his daughter. A diamond tiara glittered on her ocean of blond hair. An emerald choker necklace attached her head to her body. She wore an ivory Cinderella ball gown, fringed with lace.

"I say," the man said. "What have we here? My, my, a real struggling writer—a live one indeed." He lifted his cane and prodded my side with the fat rubber tip.

The woman stiffened, smiled, and pulled herself closer to her father-like date.

The man reached into his breast pocket and withdrew a wad of cash; he peeled away a single dollar bill and held it pinched in between his fat thumb and forefinger. "You there," he called to me. "I say, my good man—do me a favor and struggle a little for the lady."

"Honestly, Harold," the woman said.

He looked at her and stroked her hand. He stared at her, a little too long, and said, "Isn't she precious?" He turned and aimed his shiny black stare at me. "What do you say to a little struggle on this fine day?" He waved the dollar bill. I could have lunged forward and grabbed it with my teeth.

His date watched me intently; her eyes widened, her red lips parted, her choker bobbed once when she swallowed. "Do you think he's drunk?" she asked in a false whisper.

"Come now my good man, that's the way," the man said and he bent a little at the knee, dangling the money off to the side, showing me, persuading me.

I collapsed onto the ground. I rolled on the sidewalk with my tongue out of my mouth. I groaned and gagged and spit onto my chin. I flailed onto the street and my legs slammed against a parked car. I growled at the air and pretended to weep. It actually felt good, this writhing, this fake crying: a physical performance of my inner turmoil. Real pain, instead of blurry anxiety. I scraped my chin squirming back onto the cement.

I barely heard them laughing as they walked away.

But the struggle didn't end; after a while, I rolled over and picked up the money. My first writing-related dollar. I sat for a long time against a building with the dollar crushed in my hand. My body shuddered while I watched the people pass by.

I saw my notepad under a parked car. It must have slid out during my fit. I decided to retrieve it after I'd composed myself, after I'd regained control.

While I waited, the crying went on and on.

Nice writing here, some clarity would probably help this get published.

Though I haven't the tactile sensation, I have snuggled up with hundreds of other writers in editor's piles all across the country. Coffee stains, dog drool, hours of mindless babble, all co-habitating for a while in the pile being readied to be shipped back home.

I thought at first that I had been called by God, and so having been thusly chosen my effort would simply require to allow the Great One access to my puny mind, the skills of my opposable thumbs. And so I did, I streamed out a bunch of words, lumped into stories and then sent them off. I ended up working in a restaurant. My wife said I should be patient, that it could take years. And I remember thinking tenderly, how the hell would she know?

The more I learn about words, the more they fail. In the car I drive and speak to my wife, sitting beside me. We drive in a bathtub it seems, a shower scene because when we stop at a light and I turn to the car next to me, the gentleman looks at me like, *hey man I'm a little busy in my shower here.* So I look ahead. All of this intimacy and so I say certain words in order to communicate my good will toward my wife, remind her of my affection.

She responds in accordance, also making familiar sounds, forming words that have lost meaning. As if to say, right back at you. Love.

And we drive on.

To avoid disappointment I begin to look instead for secret signals, gestures that I hope can communicate something true, not warped or distorted by hollow words that can no longer be filled up. When we were young I wanted to make up a new word for love, a way to break with the past, since we'd both already used it enough. God knows. And then I thought, why not a new language altogether, our own secret code. But after one usage the words fell like cellophane smeared with mayonnaise.

Let us say that my wife had a peculiar look, an arrangement of her facial muscles, completely involuntary, unconscious and so not tainted by plans and intent. A look of adoration, holy and beatific, that I orchestrate into existence, not unlike a conductor. A secret recipe that I could not write down, which means of course that it is real, that it signifies. I maneuver based on intuition, based on direction provided by impulse and the gods. As if I stood over a caldron on the correct day of the year and stirred with a broken broom handle and happened to look into the pot at precisely the right moment and there it would be, her look, the facial muscles stretching the skin in order to show this connection that we have. It is a numb mastery over the workings of her blood, an invisible control over her hormonal release. I could not detail it, who could? But I know it and I have seen it appear over the table as I cracked a lobster claw and she held a glass of wine in her hand.

Of course I must often use generic words in the dance of elicitation, fabricated gestures, planned revelation of sentiment. I dance on the court, boxing out potential distraction, dodging and spinning and then pulling and there it is, coaxed into existence, my reward, my certification. I dwell in her, how else can it be?

And so it appears, the look, slowly coming over her face, not unlike a weather pattern, but I have done no work at all. We sit side by side, and as I watch her I consider the idea that perhaps I've grown so expert at the process that I can make the look appear just by the pulsing of my blood, through the invisible transmissions of my body heat.

But I see that she watches television as she sits next to my and horror excites my blood. She does not look at me, but at the images, the millions of electrical impulses that make up pictures and fabricate drama. And her look is aimed there, at the screen, at the appliance and I do not move for fear of dissolution. A television drama has pulled the look from her, that same look; of this I am more certain that I care to be.

The next night at dinner she says, "We never talk anymore." And the sounds of the words, the way in which she holds her fork, they are like lightning flashes and I cannot look, I must close my ears to the thunder.

"I love you," I retaliate. And already I can see through my hand, my arm. I rise out of my seat like a helium balloon. I think, *I am connected to nothing.*

"I love you too," she says and then she displays what used to be the look, she puts it on her face like make-up. Obviously I must be a television show; I must be a fabricated bit of drama—put together with blocks of meaning, sewn together with proven ways to elicit emotion. No anchors at all now and my head bangs on the ceiling but she does not notice or does not comment. What could she say after all? *Where's the story? No plot here.*

By now this story has been sent back to me 23 times.

Books about writing are like chocolate cakes. Sometimes you've just got to have one, and after you eat the entire thing you may want to vomit into the trash bin, but find that you cannot. The magic assimilating chocolate cake. I look past the writing. I develop my wild mind. I set up a writing schedule, I read good books and bad books, I alternately care and don't care about the type of pen I'm using. I try to entertain and then shun entertainment in favor of depth and confusion. I learn about art and serious fiction and then I read a serious published story in a serious magazine. It is chock full of insight, and I find that I can vomit. Hurrah for insight.

Here's a cohesive narrative structure.

I read, "*...the editors regret to inform you......*" and then I think, "I have been rejected by places ten times better than you buddy." And so they do not get put into the shoebox labeled *TRY AGAIN I*. Oh no, it is straight into the shoebox labeled *TRY AGAIN II* for those pompous bastards.

I read stories about impossibly famous writers and their disastrous beginnings. I count my rejection slips, and until it got out of hand I used to organize them from best to worst. Somehow now, it is all the same. But the cohesive narrative point is that I begin to believe that despite my continual failure, I am one of those up and coming famous authors. Rejection only solidifies my status. Even as I write in my journals, which have become numerous, I write as though someone will be reading my words in years to come. I look at posterity and try to get it right for them, so that when they go through my journals and sell each one for thousands of dollars I will have accurately detailed my tortuous journey.

Even now as this story sits in a slush pile, I must wonder who I am writing to. But it is to You, of course, the ever emerging You who waits for me though you do not know it. Just then another associate editor slipped this story in the return envelope and went on with the day's business. Listen up—

My grandfather said: "For dinner you must eat as many fresh clams as possible. You must have scrubbed them thoroughly and left them in salted water overnight, maybe two nights. You must wipe them down so that they appear as polished gray stones, perfectly symmetrical, and containing what you need. Steam them in some white wine, some stock, in a giant pot. Pick through them, burning the tips of your fingers and removing the solid ones, the heavy ones feel loaded down with sand, they are dead. You work on this for two days maybe into a third and you make pasta on Christmas Eve for the calms to lie upon. You pluck out the still warm flesh and toss them with olive oil, sprinkle with chopped parsley.

"You must do this so when, with the spaghetti wound tight and with the clam resting like an infant between the folds, fleeting, you will see the grain of sand. But only as your mouth closes down on the fork, lips tight as you pull away leaving the warm food in your mouth, only then does it register what you saw and when you chew, and when your tooth comes down on that rock granule that the ocean has not completely dissolved over the past few centuries, then you are ready to grow up and grow old. All of your preparation can not stop the forces beyond your control, all of your intense concentration on how things ought to be, on what you want, erased in a flash, by the gritty sand scratching your tooth and sending a shudder down your back. You have learned not to expect satisfaction, and so you are closer to your grandfather during that bowl of pasta than ever before in your life. Finish eating and drinking, you have also learned that there are more moments to come."

I promised myself at one point that at the very least I would never write about being a writer. How absolutely dull and banal would that be? Bing!

Guy goes to writing program and meets beautiful woman who works at a restaurant. Her name is Beth. She does not talk about point of view or character development and he sort of wants to eat her because of it. But this guy is already married. Do you see the tension? Could it be any more obvious? Well he sneaks around on his wife in the interests of art, of course, in the interests of pursuing emotion over reason. His wife finds out, and does she forgive him? Hell no, she's outta there like a flash of light. The man is sad and poetically wonders what it could all mean, and the story ends with a barely enigmatic line like, "Then he took off his shoes for the last time."

Like he went barefoot from then on, became Jesus of Nazareth. Something.

A year later, Ike calls me one day, eating.

He says, "Hey man you got any stories for me?"

At first I think he's tearing into a bag of chips. And then I think he's pulling off strips of fruit roll-up. "How's it going?"

"Shitty," he says. "I'm stuck in this cabin supposed to be making masterpieces and everything turns into masturbation. You?"

"Good." I hear the sound of fabric tearing and his mouth sounds full. "What the hell are you eating, a pillow?"

The words, "my chair," barely audible beneath the muffled sounds. His chewing continues and he finally swallows which makes me want a drink. "Yeah, it's one of those office ones with a padded butt and back. Blue fabric, white fluffy stuffing." Another rip and another mouthful. "Got stories?"

I'm trying to understand Ike. Trying to decide if he's called who he thinks he's called because I haven't written anything in almost a year. I'm not convinced that he knows who I am. "How's the art going?"

"Shhhuty." Then he either swallows or else shoves the fabric into his cheek like a ball player and talks. "It's hell up here Jake. Fire all summer, snow all winter. You should see the black trees all over the goddamn place. The animals were smart to get the hell out. It's like a time warp, a fast forward version of evolution." He continues to chew. "I've already swallowed eleven screws, the easy ones."

I feel like I should somehow already know, but I ask, "Why are you eating your chair? Do you need money?"

"I don't need money Jake," he says and then begins to cough. I wait until he's cleared his throat. "I need stories Jake, some goddamn honest to goodness art. I also need a new chair."

"I haven't done anything for a while Ike."

"Did you burn everything like every good genius does?"

"No. It's sitting right here." He probably didn't even know that I had a job and a life, of sorts. I was a software tester for a computer company, and I wasn't sure if I would tell him this or not. No one wants to say they've failed.

I heard more fabric tear and then a loud thump. "Fell over," he said and I assumed he meant the chair. "Send what you got," he said. "Need story," he said as if he were drowning.

"How's Beth," I ask. Maybe she would arrive in time to stop him from eating the metal ball bearings.

"Good," he says and I hear him hitting something. "Well, not so good. I'm training to eat a car, of course, and she doesn't think it's the greatest idea. She's still a waitress up here in god forsaken land. This plastic is a mother to swallow."

"Well, I could send you the charging ram story. If you want."

"I sit in this cabin Jake and I stare out the one window and I can't figure out what the hell I'm doing. Then I look down at the plywood and paint in front of me and remember, I'm not doing a goddamn thing. Oh yeah, you ever sleep with Beth?"

He chews now in a different way, like he's got a large piece of gum in his cheek. He makes sucking sounds, trying to keep saliva in his mouth. I look at my own office chair and try to picture it in fragments, inside a stomach. I have the idea that a sharp edge could puncture the whole scenario without much trouble.

"Sure I slept with her," I said. "But that was before you guys were going out. What's my story going to do for you anyway? You going to eat it?"

But Ike didn't laugh, instead I heard the sounds of a small saw working through plastic and in went another piece. "Sometimes I think she might've been happier with you, you know? She comes home now, all distant and depressed. Of course I wonder if it's because I suck. I mean I haven't sculpted a goddamn thing in months, and nothing salable in my life. So I take up eating things. I tell her I'm going to make it into the Guinness book of world records. There's endorsement money in that. Eating a car has been done of course, that's just part of the training. You have to build up to it. I'm looking at a semi or maybe an old space shuttle. Or maybe a fleet of cars, like all brands of Ford or something like that."

"And the story?"

"Jesus do I have to spell it out. It's for inspiration Jake, it's so I can surround myself with creative shit, remind myself that what I'm doing is making art and not just fucking around. I need more relationship in my life."

Beth was a beautiful girl. Young, maybe immature, but smart and tough. She wasn't the type of girl who wanted to be cuddled and who hoped to settle down. She wanted adventure. Motorcycle rides at night without headlights, tattoos, piercings, cliff diving. Together, we were adventure for a while, but not because we did any of those things. Mainly because I was legally unavailable, my love spoken for, and I think she liked the feeling of stealing it. It was a game for her, even when the flashlight came through the car windshield and Beth hoped it was the cops and I already knew that it was Emily. Beth saw everything as a challenge, an adventure. I remember when she kissed me on the cheek and told me good luck behind the restaurant one night. It was such an excellent movie scene, her expression like take care kid, be good, it was real.

"These wheels are a bitch, man I'll have to smash them to bits just to get them to go down."

And so I began to think that I obviously never knew Ike at all, and apparently he never really knew me either. I mean I couldn't have been further away from writing when he called. I guess it's what happens when you don't keep in touch.

"You should tell Beth to pay me a visit," I say. "You know I'm a lonely bachelor now." I was being funny, sort of.

Ike stopped chewing. "I thought you had a kid."

"A kid and a divorce in the space of three years," I say. "Talk about the Guinness book. Anyway, what do you want a relationship with a story for, when you've got her."

Ike sighed which sounded more like a gurgle. "You don't have relationships with people Jake. Look, I have a relationship with this tee-shirt I'm wearing. You know why? Because I wash it in a tub with my own two hands, then I wring the hell out of it, and then I hang it over a lampshade to dry. You get to know things that way, and I mean actual things. They don't go and turn into a brick overnight, or a mountain lion. But you don't ever wring out a person. You don't know what's in there."

"Seems like I wrung the hell out of my marriage."

"And that's what you're left with, a whole lotta nothing. Animating the inanimate, that's the way to go. You said you're not writing anymore?"

"I test software."

"For what, herpes?"

"To see if it works, how easy it is to use, the usual. Did Beth ever get that tattoo of an apple around her belly button? I told her to go for it, but I wonder if she did. It was supposed to be the top of an apple, you know, with her belly button being the stem. Only it would be an emerald ring instead. I've thought about that."

"That's' exactly what I mean. She's a character to you, hell she's a character to me. We're all a bunch of characters, walking around making guesses about everyone else. Now when you wash dishes, it's the same thing. You see the familiar blue plate, you touch the chip, wonder if it's getting bigger, wonder where the hell you got the plate in the first place. This is life experience, Jake, not touching people." He stopped to insert another piece of something in his mouth. "Do you see your kid?"

"Sometimes. I mean it's not a regular deal at all, no weekends or every other Wednesday, nothing like that. Just once in a while. Is Beth there, why don't you put her on while you go smash those wheels?"

"No, she's out."

"You've been watching television," I said. I knew this because the story had made the rounds about a guy eating his Ford explorer. He was doing commercials for Ford now, about how he would never have eaten any other brand of car. They show various x-rays of his stomach. I really want to talk to Beth.

"Of course I've been watching television, how else do you think I got in this mess? I'll tell you about TV." I couldn't stop thinking about her, and hoped that she would take the phone and start talking to me, but instead Ike drank some liquid, maybe Pennzoil and kept talking. "We all grew up watching this crap and so we developed this little part of our brain, this little filter. When we were kids and we saw some guy fall off a building and land on the cement the filter kicked in and whispered, 'Don't worry little guy, it's all pretend.' And so we grow up with this little voice and soon I'm watching bodies being pulled out of a crumbled building and my filter keeps on saying, 'Don't worry.' Nothing is real now and even when I try to convince myself, I'm no match for that practiced voice. Even when I say to myself, 'Dude this *is* real' I get nowhere, feel nothing."

Then he made the sounds like he was gagging and choking, and I heard a loud thunk which I guessed was the phone falling on the floor. And I thought that most people probably underrate the danger of eating furniture and cars and all that. Especially people like Ike. They probably don't even think about the possibility of choking to death. And I'd bet that Ike hadn't even given it any thought at all.

And while I waited for him to pick up the receiver, I secretly hoped that Beth would come back to me if things went bad with Ike. We would be perfect together, and I began to fantasize about how I'd cook her dinner, and how great it would be to be free with her. To spend time without the sensation that I had to keep looking over my shoulder. She would get comfortable on the couch with a glass of wine, her legs crossed beneath her black skirt and I'd sit next to her, brush her cheek with my hand. Maybe I'd talk about fate. Maybe I'd even propose marriage. That would be exciting. And by the time I had taken her glass of wine and made love to her on the couch, swirling my tongue around her belly button, pretending to eat the apple, I realized that the line had gone dead.

Eventually I hung up the phone and went to bed hoping that I would have some sort of erotic dream about Beth and her soft skin.

If you're like me, you probably thought that everyone in the world knows the Heimlich Maneuver, or at least they know to punch a choker in the gut. That's what I thought, anyway. Which is why I'm done with stories, have been done with the whole writing thing, and unlike my boy Ike, may he dress the beef, I start with chainsaws.

The body needs time to adjust to the new diet, and reorient the bodily functions to take in an excrete the new materials without doing damage to the organs or soft tissues. I'm in training and so I don't do much but sleep and eat and…excrete. Some have asked me how I do it, others wonder just how badly a person needs to fail at regular life to end up like me. My answer to both is the same, "Until you feel a four-inch iron bolt move through the inside of your body, towing a chainsaw rip-cord behind it, you have not experienced what it means to be alive.

Crushed Blue Corn

"Julio appeared one morning at the back door of the restaurant, dressed in white jeans and a white shirt studded with purple gems. As if he had descended in the palm of God. He carried a forged social security card and slipped an apron over his beautiful clothes. Before he began on the pile of dishes, he handed me a picture of his sister that he'd torn out of a magazine. She is lovely beyond description, a haunting beauty."

"Undoubtedly. Let me guess; she has long brown legs, black hair to the middle of her perfect back and dark eyebrows. Curled eyelashes frame her eyes, two pools of oil. A professional model, what luck. Are you officially engaged?"

"She wears blue and yellow flowers woven in a band across her head and tucked behind her ears. Her beautiful voice rises in the Mexican air with the evaporation of the morning dew and her song joins hundreds of others. All of the girls throughout the land sing while they milk the cows or throws seed to the chickens. The whole region wakes to this beautifully woven chorus of voices. Like maidens from the gods, their sweet song rouses the brothers and uncles and fathers. The sound renews the men's faith in life, weaves a cloth of harmony to wrap around them as they head into the fields, kneel down, and thrust their confident hands into the soil."

"His ranch is probably little more than several consecutive plots of dry dirt. Cows sunken into walking ribcages, malnourished pigs that squeal from the pieces of black rubber they cannot digest, and mangy chickens that cannot lay eggs. Probably some other starving animals that he can't name in English."

"Llamas and buffalo and peacocks that brighten the ranch with their glorious colors. The white-haired grandmother weaves traditional clothing from the feathers, and from the animal's skins. The white and brown coats shine like expensive pelts, soft and plush from the nurturing

Mexican sun, the secret family mixture of grain. The white-haired grandmother is a witch, the town sorceress, and the keeper of the family secrets, the ancient potions. Pure cold water shoots up from a spring near her cave and douses the naked and squealing children in the summertime, cools the men's sweaty heads at the end of the day."

"And your poor homesick dishwasher, dying to get back to the fruitful bounty of his imagined homeland. He thinks you should go with him and marry his sister. Then you'll be like a brother to him, part of the enormous loving family. The real world will fade like an ancient map, become a theory, an illusion. A bad dream. You think you will finally be finished with your missing child James, and that the story will finally end, the way it has almost ended many times before. With a crack of your knuckles you'll be back in action, Mexican-style, a brand new man. Your final escape into fantasy with your homesick dishwasher."

"Crazy homesick. Julio's eyes fill with tears the moment he mentions his grandmother. He can taste the homemade tortillas, smell the roasted chilies. When the sun sets on the ranch it casts the world in rich orange light. The children's faces beam, as glossy as oil paint, and they play soccer, shine with sweat."

"What specifically, may I ask, did he promise you?"

"A festive celebration for our arrival. Mexican wine from wooden barrels, traditional dancing in the main square. The girls will arrive in embroidered dresses, black and red lace, the boys in black cowboy boots and black leather pants, vests. They form a circle around me, and then Julio's sister arrives, twirling her way into the circle, her leg muscles tight, her toes pointed. She leaps around me as if she were a nymph, trailing her red silk scarf behind, letting it caress along my shoulders, hide my face. She smells like roses, and her body moves around mine like a serpent. She whispers Spanish in my ear."

"Brothers?"

"Seven older brothers. The three oldest live in the States, the younger three remain in the bosom of Mexico, building their back muscles as they work the land with their young hands. Their biceps and forearms already of men. They protect the ranch, keep the mother and the grandmother healthy, and surround the land with love, comfort, security. These brothers prepare the land and the house for the eventual reunion, when all members of the family will return and live together again."

"How rich. Your dishwasher is the baby, the last one to make up his mind. The oldest brothers live in big American cities, carry wads of cash, drive sports cars, and get laid every night. Your dishwasher thinks that they might visit Mexico more often, but they can't return to America so easily anymore. An army of border guards shoot bullets into the night backed by good American citizens who shine headlights into the dark. The dishwasher has not yet experienced American life, so he still misses the desolate ranch with decaying cows and horses that bleed from the eyes."

"Buffalo and llamas and goats. The Garden of Eden, with all of the beasts roaming around under the hot Mexican sun. The oxen meander through the orchards, nuzzle the ripe fruit that bends the branches with sweet promise. Black mustangs stand next to one another, their cropped hair falling across their eyes as they bend down and drink from the clear ponds crowded with fish. Harmony. A life of balance, of proportion, of sense."

"And you're serious. You actually believe that if you take the bus, marry his sister, and work side by side with the brothers on the ranch, you'll be able to enjoy life once again. You'll start a new life with the long legged sister. A life that won't shatter like the one you're running away from."

"Long smooth legs and dark brown, appetizing in every way. She poses for underwear ads in Mexico. Real breasts and dark nipples. As gorgeous as Eve herself, with straight black hair to the middle of her shapely back, pure eyes, dark eyes that mean seduction, as deep as forever."

"Eyes like escape hatches. Eyes that you can fall into, sink away from yourself, from your memory. You think this is possible. You believe that you will slip away from yourself by leaping blindly into Mexico. Your chance to finally quit hating yourself, blaming yourself. This plan, you believe, will drown your hope once and for all."

"Fresh corn tamales, fish tacos with spiced onion and jalapeno."

"I've got about a quarter tank of oxygen left James, and I want you to stop and think for a moment, I want you to remember. When I first became your sponsor, after we'd met at the national convention, after we'd eaten roast beef and lobster tails and lost thirty dollars at blackjack, what did I tell you James? When I turned to face you and I put my hands over yours, what did I say? Do you remember?"

"You said you will always be there for me. And I want you to come with me Maria. His brothers would adore you; they would treat you like a queen, and serve you beer with pieces of lime, grilled trout with lemon and fresh tomato salsa. We could dance together and laugh and talk long after the sun has gone down, when the cool wind blows off the desert and the sounds of Mexican crickets fill the air with a version of quiet."

"............"

"Come Maria, where peace reigns and your mind can empty into the night sky."

"On the day you've replayed in your head James, that day you walked out of the liquor store and looked into the backseat of your car, dropped the glass bottle from under your arm, lost your breath—you saw a car pulling away and your heart began to race. You instinctively ran after the car, waving your hands, but it did not stop. In shock, you watched it recede in the distance, remembering only the Nevada license plates. A vague and useless detail as far as the police were concerned. Maybe six months after the conference, you called me and told me about your revelation. You had accepted the fact that your boy must have been killed, and now you only sought to lay him to rest, to give him over to heaven so that you might continue trudging through the world. So that you could stop wondering and looking and believing in miracles. You were exhausted and you had planned a trip to Nevada. You believed in the trip because the signs pointed to it, your intuition, the license plate. Even the fact that the conference had been in Las Vegas added to your evidence. All arrows pointed to the same place and the pieces fit together in your mind, as if fate had whispered in your ear. I drove for 12 hours to meet you in Las Vegas and we set out. Do you remember that James? How was Nevada?"

"So very hot. Unbearable. We drive into the desert and I know where to go. I've made calculations and now I follow my instinct. We pull off to the side of the empty highway and park. We walk across the burning sand. The heat burns through the bottom of my shoes. I carry the shovels and my shirt soaks with sweat before we arrive at the proper spot. Nothing grows around us and this convinces me, proves my hypothesis. We stand on the surface of death. You set up the umbrella and we dig in the sand. We talk at first and then become silent. Sand continually slides down into our hole, making it twice as much work."

"That's exactly right James. For two days we dug, moving locations every few hours. Before we left for good, before I let you lean on me as we walked back to the car what did we find?"

"Bones. Like ivory splinters from a prehistoric time. I sink to my knees and the setting sun casts my long shadow out over the spot. I pull out the bones and dust them off with my handkerchief. I stack them next to me like firewood."

"You stopped and looked at me, James. You looked crestfallen, destroyed. What was the problem then? Why did you stop?"

"They are adult bones, not dinosaur bones. Not a child's bones. A rupture happens inside my chest; I feel my heart collapse and shrivel even as the cool desert winds begin, drying the tears on my face."

"You fell to your knees and screamed, James. You looked up at the first star of the night and you screamed. Then you punched at the sand until your knuckles bled, racked by sobbing you threw down your fists, and I let you. I stood back and watched you, until you slowed, until you pawed at the ground like a doe, rocked back and forth. I thought it was part of the process, the healing. I still believed in the process back then. I believed in recovery."

"The signs vanish, my instinct becomes as quiet and stoic as the pile of bones. The puzzle I had pieced together, the theory I had derived, the maps I had analyzed, the calculations I had made—all of it, disappears like dust from the desert. Twirling away like a tornado and dissolving into air, into nothing."

"Mexico is that very same desert, James. It's hot as hell for one thing. And it will suck you in with a promise, until you're too deep to crawl out. Until you're buried alive, and I won't be the one to come down and dig up your bones. I won't even know what has happened to you. You will have disappeared from here, yes, from this country, but not everyone who vanishes from here arrives at the same place, James. There is no secret waiting room, no cabin in the woods with tables of refreshments and magazines for those who have disappeared to gather together."

"The family has a cabin in the mountains, where orange and lemon trees grow and it's so cool that you need a sweater or a sweatshirt in the evenings. They gather to celebrate the children's birthdays, their first communions. Everyone meets on the concrete patio outside the house, and steaming food is brought from the kitchen in red and blue and yellow ceramic bowls and placed on a table draped with a festive red tablecloth. Marinated venison speared with zucchini and squash and tomatoes. Bowls of rice and red beans spiced with cumin and cinnamon. People hold beers and the children run back and forth and ride bicycles around the house. They are dressed in miniature suits with blue clip-on ties, or expensive party dresses, fringed with white lace, embroidered with gold. The music comes from the house, vibrates through the walls and uncles dance arm in arm as the sun sets on the cabin. The women stand in circles and talk. They hug one another and laugh, they pet one another, groom each other's hair. And everywhere you go, you smell the citrus from the groves and the smoke from the small fire that keeps away the mosquitoes."

"Everyone carries guns in Mexico, James, but maybe you would like that. You could turn the corner and gun someone down, anyone, anywhere you want. Or you could shoot animals and kill them if you feel like it, and nobody will try to stop you. The three brothers on the ranch always carry guns, even when they go to the cabin. They carry them because they have looked down into the valley from that very same cabin and seen men shot like animals, one after the other, in the back of the head."

"We honeymoon at the cabin, lie out on the roof, peer into the night sky. Billions of stars reveal themselves to Mexico, more than anywhere else in the world. The saints and the gods regard the Mexicans as their own people, their children, and they favor them with plenty of moisture, the fragrance of fresh flowers. My wife and I sweat together on the roof, our bodies exchanging, adapting to one another, mapping the geography of each other's skin. Her flesh moves like silk against my chest, her hands delicate and strong, determined."

"Let me guess; she's unlike a normal woman. She craves constant sex and she wants it more than you, but you manage to keep up. She's only content when you're inside of her, rocking her world. Am I close?"

"The women love men, the feel of the man's rough warm skin, the smell of his sweat. To be enveloped by a man's body is like being in a cocoon. The women bloom inside and the heat draws forth their startling beauty. They unfold their wings. His virgin sister blossoms within herself like a hundred roses, containing all of the energy and fragrance of a woman. Swollen with desire, the need to connect, to grow into another human being. The union of souls, like butterflies attached to one another behind the red fall leaves. An explosion of spirits, a watershed of emotion. Love that you can taste and hold in your arms.

"I'm scraping the bottom of my oxygen tank, James; don't make me laugh with your exotic nymphet. I'm sure she revs with sexual energy beyond the capacity of the universe, James, drips with it. A gift from the gods, an insatiable beauty. Your dream woman. A woman in your dreams."

"For three days after the wedding, the new couple remains in the cabin, to merge into one being. They explore one another, touch the emotions, and meld together like a sculpture. Physical paths lead to spiritual glory. Relatives stop by to say a prayer outside; they leave food in baskets, wrapped in cloths of cornhusks. Jugs of wine sit next to buckets of cool spring water. Each mother in the family leaves a lock of hair which will be woven into the first baby blanket. The grandmother arrives from her cave and she carries with her an ear of dried blue corn. She peels away the brittle husk and the kernels shine like rows of purple gems, each one symbolizing the soul of a child. The stiff ear a symbol of fertility, the union of the male and the female, the infinite potential of procreation. The grandmother may hear us behind the cabin door, perhaps we argue or else we scream out in the process of draining into one another, immersing and submerging, but she will not interrupt."

" . . . . "

"Glass breaks, ecstasy rattles the windows and the grandmother genuflects, hangs the blue corn on the door, and walks away. She knows all we do and it is beautiful to her, sacred, and holy."

"You're ignoring the whole picture, James. The brothers in Mexico are in serious trouble with the law. One of them dies in the field, crumpled under the green plants. A soccer ball kisses against his forehead and he does not move. He feels smoke and heat rising from his wounds. He feels his soul struggling to be free."

"When the white-haired grandmother communicates with spirits, she wears a white robe and a necklace made with locks of hair around her neck. Hair from her children and grandchildren who have passed away. Green trees hide the entrance to a cave at the base of a red sandstone mesa. Collections of animal bones, poisonous red leaves, and ancient herbs are stored in hand-carved wooden boxes. She draws the future with her finger in the dirt, and paints the past on the cave wall with ox blood and blueberry juice. The dead visit the grandmother when she summons them. She delivers messages. The grandmother is the family's translator for the spirit world."

"You've heard whispers from the spirit world and the gods yourself, haven't you James? They've tipped you off, told you secrets. After the car with the Nevada license plate disappeared you ran back to your own car, scouring the parking lot pavement for clues, for something to spark your mind, tell you what to do. You tried to tell yourself a story about what had just happened. This was the moment that would be resurrected many times inside your mind and you absorbed each detail. The back door of your car was slightly ajar and the seatbelt dangled above the pavement, the silver buckle twisting and reflecting the glare of the sunlight. You did not touch anything because at that moment you believed in a full scale investigation, armies of police and citizens combing the country, leaving no stone unturned. Truth and justice and the inherent good in every human being. You believed in this so you tried to preserve the scene. A green beer bottle lay against the curb, and you saw the word "Boulder" on the label. The blue Rocky Mountains briefly accompanied the word, the vague sense of a rich town in a shadowed valley. A detail that remained asleep until you saw the news story, two years later, after you began to seriously drink again. After the official search that never materialized, officially fizzled out."

"The grandmother absorbs clues about the past from the natural world. She has learned ancient Indian ceremonies and made potions from poison, purple berries, and petrified bark. She cures the ill, calms the disturbed. She has cast out demons and brought peace to the tormented. Julio has seen her float in the air and wrestle with evil."

"After Catherine finalized the divorce she refused your phone calls. She was the only other person who could help prop you up and she turned away to grieve with her family. Vodka diluted your blood and you watched a news report about the black market baby industry. Well-to-do communities with older couples wanted babies and they were buying them on the black market. The reporter stood on the campus of the University of Colorado, Boulder. The evidence suddenly fell into place again, as if the gods had whispered in your ear, and you rose from the couch infused with hope, radiating the very joy you sought to capture. You called me on the telephone. You now knew that your boy was alive, and you knew where he was. You'd developed a different ending to the story, but an ending nonetheless. A finality. Single father launches into the world to save his child, warm his bone-chilling sorrow."

"Parents do not separate in Julio's village because everyone raises the child. Uncles, aunts, and cousins give the child a sense of belonging, a feeling of security. Everyone takes responsibility because there is a sense of pride. Support exists like two giant arms around the family, so the parents do not buckle under the stress of tragedy, they do not experience the alienation, the sensation of being lost. Even when the parents fight, the burden remains shared and light, and the couple does not dissolve. They do not shatter like a leg bone and drift in space like dead stars, space junk."

"You began with the calculations again, James, scouring maps and reviewing your profiles of the phantom kidnappers. I flew into Denver at night and took a bus to Boulder, where you sat on a wooden bench in the station with an old leather briefcase in your lap. You held a bottle in your hand. You looked at me with the saddest eyes and said 'They shouldn't have done it. He was my baby.'"

"Babies are not taken for granted in a traditional society, one that is not medically advanced, because babies are delivered at home and sometimes they can't fit through the mother's hips, or else they become tangled in the umbilical cord, blocked from the exit by the placenta. Babies die and it is not unheard of, it is not beyond the scope of imagination. Even after a few months, babies can develop a flesh eating virus and expire in their sleep. Grief is allowed, expected, and a ceremonial dance is performed. The grandmother moves inside the circle of family members, bowing and turning away from the pile of burning corn husks. She holds the mother's ear of dried blue corn and raises it over her head. Then she plucks a single blue kernel of corn from the ear. With a mortar and pestle, the sorceress grinds the kernel into a fine blue dust and makes the sign of the cross on the mother's head. The ritual purifies the mother. The mother does not despair, does not give up, because she sees infinity on the blue ear of corn she holds in her hand. The rows and rows of purple gems signify her endless potential and she moves forward, gives birth many more times. Only one small kernel has been taken from the mother."

"By the time we found the warehouse at the north end of the city it was nearly midnight. We stood in front of a green metal door with rusted hinges; the silver garage shutters along the side of the building had been pulled down and locked. Your calculations had led us into the pot-holed parking lot, onto the oil stained driveway. The headquarters. You looked up at that door and I held your hand. As your sponsor, I was supposed to help you through the process. I had already begun to question the process, the possibility of recovery, but being there in the cool night air, smelling the faint odor of diesel, I watched you stare at that door. Recovery or not, I knew that I served some purpose. We walked hand in hand, like husband and wife, straight up to the unmarked door. Your body shook and your breath vibrated. You thought you'd find him on the other side of the door. Like a movie miracle, there he'd be, sitting in his car seat and kicking his legs, looking at you like nothing had happened. Tilting his small blond head in question, wondering at your distress, at the lines of panic carved into your forehead, the sadness under your eyes. The door opened and we stood in an empty warehouse, abandoned, barely lit by starlight and without even a trace of what it had once housed. You did not scream or strike out. Instead, you fell to your knees with your face in your hands, and I knelt behind you and held you together with my arms. I squeezed tight so that you might not rattle into pieces and roll along the concrete floor, into the darkest shadows. You vibrated through my chest and into my heart. It was the last time I would even think about the process. Recovery would never happen for you, or me, or any of the people we met at that conference. It was not possible."

"The Mexican brother's look out for one another. They protect each other. If a bandit injures one in the group, the rest grab their guns and baseball bats and set things right. If something so dear and so precious is stolen from one member, the reaction is quick and severe. The bandit's head is bashed into rotten peach pulp. The brother's dance in ceremony on his twitching torso."

"You want to be part of that group, a member of their gang. Don't you see that they want you to run special errands to the United States? They expect you to dodge bullets and deliver packages to the oldest brother

"Once in a while I would be sent to America to deliver presents from Mexico to Julio's brothers in the cities. They cannot find fresh tortillas or exotic hot peppers and so I'll have to keep these hidden from the guards. Food is not allowed across the border, but I'll smuggle in pints of rich venison chili as well, maybe some fried cinnamon dough, still warm. It's a way to keep the family unit together, maintain the intimate relationship. The brothers would kiss me on the cheek and embrace me after my journey. They would give me cold beer as they opened their packages, and pat me on the back, impressed by my accomplishment. Small wooden Mexican dolls and brightly colored slippers. Bits of their homeland to keep them connected, keep them alive. I would do it as a favor for my new family, for my wife, my children. My honor. Just to prove that I was in solidarity with them, that I wasn't some wishy washy gringo."

"You still don't see it. Before they shoot the one brother, all three brothers are kicking a soccer ball back and forth in a giant field of marijuana. Their faces are partially covered by the field of tall pot plants and they duck and hide and tackle one another. Their rifles sit on the ground at the edge of the field. They roll around and laugh so loud that they do not hear the garbled announcement over the bullhorn. The message that informs them that the U.S. drug agents are raiding their field. They wrestle and laugh until they hear the first gunshot, like a rocket into the sky. They roll to the side of the field and pick up their guns. They crouch low and hold their breath. One brother puts his knee on the soccer ball and waits."

"It's a passion, soccer. The endurance that it requires, the sculpted muscle tone it develops. The development of the foot skills is tantamount to practicing magic, and so their soccer heroes are not merely men, but wizards. The people worship the supernatural physical skill and they understand the high degree of intelligence and physical fitness involved in a team's success. They live for this game."

"Since the brothers miss the announcement in Spanish that tells them to put down their weapons and raise their hands high above their head, the brothers think they are under attack by bandits looking to loot their crop. They hear voices approach and another gun shot into the clouds. Without looking at one another, the three brothers aim their guns and fire into the field."

"It's true that fights break out all the time in Mexico, but they are not filled with homicidal rage. They understand the ebb and flow of emotion. At one moment, two brothers scream at each other as if the world has come to an end. They threaten to tear the other's head off, beat him to death with his own arm. And then slowly, the anger subsides, and the two brothers toast one another with a fresh beer. They put their arms around each other and laugh. All is forgotten, understood, forgiven. They know what it means to be human, to struggle with the complexity of our emotions."

"It's as if the marijuana plants fire back. Bullets fly through the air and one brother takes three bullets in the chest. The soccer ball slips out from under his knee and he falls to the side, crumples onto the ground. The ball rests against his forehead and air makes no inroads into his lungs. Gunshots explode like strings of firecrackers and another brother is hit in the shoulder. Then abrupt silence, smoke rises, and the U.S. agents emerge from the green plants with guns drawn. Two agents have been killed and the surviving brothers are kicked repeatedly in the stomach and in the face. Blood pours from their mouths and the agents kneel on their backs, tighten handcuffs that feel like razor wire. They are punched in the stomach when they stand and the brother that vomits is slapped across the face. One agent says the boys shouldn't have been kicking a soccer ball in a field of pot. The brothers are dragged into a van and taken to a Mexican jail."

"They can kick the ball wherever they like because there are no ridiculous rules. On the road, in the fields, wherever. No regulations, no forms to fill out. There aren't even any stoplights in the small town, Maria, or painted lines on the roads. These people live in freedom. They are not bound by imaginary rules like we are. They make common sense decisions, based on what's best for them. No adherence to arbitrary laws set down by some rich politician. Real freedom to live as they see fit."

"And you're not feeling very free right now, is that it? You're feeling more trapped than ever? I'm basically out of oxygen, James, so I'm going to talk softly. The other day when you got that piece of junk mail, the one with the photograph of your boy on it, the one put out by the foundation asking if you've seen these children, you didn't sink to your knees. What did you do?"

"I stared at the picture and my heart stopped. The one second I hadn't been thinking about him and there he suddenly was, staring me in the face, reminding me that there was no escape. Rage soared inside my chest. I smashed the mailbox off of its post with my fist. I walked into my house and climbed the walls, tearing at everything like an animal. I unloaded the dishwasher by pitching glasses through the kitchen window. Plates flew like discs into the opposite wall. I went crazy, I let myself go. I fell down at one point and lay on the ceramic dust, the glittering pieces of glass. I rolled from side to side with my baby's picture in my hand and I groaned."

"............"

"After a couple of days, the restaurant manager sent Julio to check on me and I was still on the floor, weeping without tears."

"And Julio couldn't get you to move, he couldn't get you to respond to him, so he sat down on the floor next to you and told you stories. After a while you began to hear the stories and then you eventually sat up, accepted a glass of water. Then it came to you, another way to finally end this goddamn story, to put your baby to rest."

"I want to have children, babies I can hold on my lap, lift up to my nose. They love big families, so maybe I'll have ten or twelve kids, all running around, patting me with their tiny hands, kissing me on the cheek. Like swimming in a pond of young bodies, my children's limbs caressing my soul, running their small hands through my hair. They will grow and marry and return to kneel around my bedside as I die, praying for my eternal rest."

"The family makes their money from the weed, James, can't you see that? Not by selling dying pigs or starving cows or molting chickens. Now you see why they are wealthy. They send Julio to work on their next American outlet, a drug port that his family can service."

"Sometimes they sell livestock at the market on Saturday. Wicker baskets full of the least bruised tomatoes, ears of pale blue corn, and stunted and deformed chili peppers. Americans smoke tons of pot, Maria, the country is like vacuum. Maybe the brothers just grow a little on the side, throw it up in the air, and watch it disappear. They sew the wads of cash into their mattresses to pay for weddings and first communions. The Mexicans are intelligent because they never touch the stuff. Julio says it makes a person crazy."

"The U.S. gets into the act and demands that the brothers be sent to Texas where they will pay for killing those two agents. Right now they sit in some dingy Mexican jail cell eating sticky rice and cold chicken. They have only one chance. The brothers might accidentally escape, if you reach deep into you pockets James, and pays the police well."

"The brothers have had fistfights before. Boxing matches that took place while they screamed at one another, threw curses and punches. I watch two of them dance like prizefighters in the dust, and I wait for the moment when their energy dissolves and they finally smile at one another with blood on their teeth. Maybe I'm standing too close to the fight."

"Listen to me James, you have to believe it. They take your money and then load you up like a donkey with saddlebags of pot and whip your ass until you scamper across the border. You die alone James, no children at your side, no adults saying prayers by your bed."

"Without warning the brothers swallow me in their flurry of fists and shouts, and I try to duck, but knuckles connect into my stomach. My chin bounces off a knee as I fall and a forearm delivers a chop to the back of my neck. I land in the dust and turn on my side, spitting dirt and blood from my mouth. How can this be? When I look up, they are not fighting one another and suddenly they never were. They fall on me with open, salivating mouths. Sharp teeth. I close my eyes and do not wake up. I cross the final border, alone."

"The guards shoot you as you run across the border with your backpack full of weed. This is only a couple hours after you've paid the cops and freed the brothers. They shoot you before you ever get to see the sexy sister."

"It's simply life, Maria. The women's chapped hands make tortillas, mixing drops of blood and tears and sweat into the dough. They try to sing traditional songs, but lose the words among the cackle of vultures that descend on a cow. The women wear wilted yellow and blue flowers in their hair, and they smell like acrid sweat, like discarded lilacs in a sweet moldy heap. They must create a sense of pride."

"You could be stabbed as you walk on the streets of Chicago to make a delivery to one of Julio's brothers. A knife in and out of your gut and you sink to your knees. Your backpack is stripped from your body. A foot kicks you in the head, knocks you over, and your blood forms a puddle, but you don't die. You lose the package, but escape with your life. Do you think your new family rejoices and embraces you because you have cheated death? They condemn you as a fool and a traitor because you have brought a fate onto them that cannot compare to the U.S. agent invasion. They blame you for destroying their lives; they curse you as they die."

"The red bell peppers burn black Maria, in an old stone fireplace. Drunken men stumble and cannot link arms to dance during the hazy dry sunset. They drink beer and vomit in the bushes, wipe their mouths and pretend to kiss the young girls. Women gather in separate circles and spread gossip about the others, raise questions about which boy is gay, which girl is a whore. A little girl with black hair wears a lace white dress and sneers at the drunk who lunges for her bare legs. She twirls away, a frayed pink ribbon in her hair."

"My oxygen tank is empty James and I'm having a little trouble, but now you're beginning to see, aren't you? Now it's coming clear. A drug lord owns your family's operation as well as a hundred others around the region. The drug lord comes down hard on drug runners who lose packages and live. He thinks you've betrayed him, sold the goods out from under him. Lessons must be learned, examples set. He and his men visit your beloved ranch on horseback. He lines up the fathers and brothers and uncles behind the main house and shoots them like animals, one by one, in the back of the head. He laughs and orders his men to drag away the sisters, the aunts, the mothers. Other ranchers eventually find the women's' naked bodies on the side of the road, ravaged and covered in layers of dust. The drug lord loses nothing, gains respect, and instills fear."

"What have I done, Maria? The white-haired grandmother who once blessed me, who brought me into the family's embrace now sits alone in the dark of her cave. The smoke inside grows thick and although it leaks out of the entrance, fresh air cannot make inroads. The bonfire consumes dozens of ears of dried blue corn, and the spirits of the slaughtered family fill the old woman's lungs. She suffocates on the souls of the dead. Too many crowd together in the hot smoke and seek refuge inside the grandmother's heart and blood, even as her organs shrivel and hiss in the crackle of the fire.

"..........."

"It's too terrible Maria, I'm done. I'd better hang up now. I'm done."

"I give you permission to give up hope James, to give up on your calculations, your theories and false clues. To cease believing in miracles, in goodness, in recovery. Know that he is lost forever and that even if you disappear from this country James, you will not have slipped away from yourself. It is not possible. But now you can see that you still have your ear of dried blue corn James. Your infinite potential. Crush the single kernel, make the sign of the cross on your forehead, and begin again. Don't toss infinity into the fire, James. You must try to release yourself. Now I must change my oxygen tank."

"Goodbye Maria."

"Goodbye James. Call me tonight."

"........."

19739909R00264

Made in the USA
Middletown, DE
02 May 2015